Deception

Deception

DONNA HILL

Recycling programs
for this product may
not exist in your area.

DECEPTION

ISBN-13: 978-0-373-53452-4

Previously published by BET Books' Courageous Hearts collection
in 2005

www.kimanipress.com

Printed in U.S.A.

This novel is dedicated in loving memory of my grandmothers: Clotilda Braithwaite and Mary Hill. You both are always with me.

Prologue

Oh what a tangled web we weave,
when first we practice to deceive.
　　　　　　—Sir Walter Scott, *Marmion*
　　　　　　　　　　(1808) stanza 17

"Just stay calm. Getting all worked up isn't going to solve anything," Terri muttered to her reflection as she partially wrapped her shoulder-length dreadlocks atop her head. Cool brown eyes stared back at her, revealing none of the turmoil that had precipitated her three-month leave of absence from her self-named corporation.

To look at thirty-year-old Terri Powers, no one would imagine what the past two years had done to her. Her New York–based public relations and advertising company had skyrocketed since its inception five years ago. With a minimal staff she had almost carried the company single-handedly. Because of that, she would always blame herself for the miscarriage of her baby. That trauma was compounded by the disintegration of her four-year marriage to photographer Alan Martin.

She took a breath and slipped long silver earrings into her lobes. The reality was, her marriage to the flamboyant Alan Martin was over long before the divorce. She'd just been unwilling to see it. She and Alan were a disaster waiting to happen. Even now she questioned her attraction to him. She'd been young, eager for love and eager to have someone love her back. She had been captivated by his charm, his vision and exuberance. His looks and his blatant sexuality only added to the total facade. So much so that she overlooked and made excuses for his flaws—which, she finally had to admit, were too numerous to mention. Her collapsed marriage she'd begun to deal with. The loss of her baby was something else entirely. A topic which she did not discuss with anyone. Losing her baby had resurrected too many painful memories, and her hopes for a family of her own had died with her child. Although her losses were more than a year behind her, the aftereffects had finally taken their toll and drained her spirit over the months. Pretending that everything was wonderful and right with the world took all that she had left, she thought sardonically.

It was to that end that she'd hired her vice president, Mark Andrews, at a time when her world seemed to be slipping beneath her feet. His résumé was outstanding. He was charming, had a razor-sharp mind, was exceedingly good-looking and had brilliant ideas for company growth. The fact that he vaguely struck some familiar chord within her only endeared him all the more to her.

Over time, she'd given Mark more and more responsibility as the events of her life and the pressures of the job slowly overwhelmed her. Terri finally realized that for her own good and the good of the company, she needed to take a break. Now it was time to go back and reclaim the reins.

Terri frowned as she lightly coated her bow-shaped lips

with a soft orange lipstick. Mark had crossed the line and deliberately ignored her instructions. If it hadn't been for her director of promotions, Stacy Williams, informing her of Mark's activities, the whole deal would have gone down without her knowledge or consent.

As things stood now, her company was in the midst of negotiations with a man that she wouldn't give the time of day. *Clinton Steele*. Everything that she'd ever read about the man set her teeth on edge. He was in the business of buying small African-American companies on the verge of collapse and turning them around for his own profit. From everything that she'd read, he paid the owners nothing near what the companies were worth. He called himself a businessman. Humph! She considered him nothing more than a predator— one whom she would have nothing to do with. To think that he wanted her company to run an ad campaign for him had her head spinning.

Terri strutted down the short foyer and slipped into her heels. Wouldn't they be surprised to see her returning to work three weeks earlier than scheduled. She smiled. If Mark Andrews and Clinton Steele thought that they would be dealing with the Terri who was haunted by her past, they were wrong. This was Terri Powers—new and improved, rested and rejuvenated. And someone had a lot of answering to do.

Chapter 1

"Good afternoon, gentlemen."

Sultry was the only word that stroked all of Clint's senses when the distinctly feminine voice, coated with just a hint of a Caribbean accent, pervaded the low rumble of male conversation.

"Terri." Her vice president, Mark Andrews, looked up and rose in greeting, as did his client Clinton Steele. "We were just going over Mr. Steele's proposal," Mark added, slipping back into his discarded charcoal-gray suit jacket, in an effort to camouflage his surprise at her unannounced return.

Terri stood in the doorway, taking the moment to assess the man who towered head and shoulders above the six-foot-tall Mark, and was in sharp contrast to Mark's light cocoa complexion.

Clinton Steele's reputation preceded him, and from all appearances he confirmed Terri's image—from the expensive tailor-made suit to the formidable persona. But maybe it was those eyes. They seemed to have a way of mesmerizing you, she thought, feeling herself pulled into the bottomless inky pools that seemed to dance with dangerous lights. But then a flicker of something deeper flashed through those coal-black orbs. An involuntary shudder ran up her spine. Then just as quickly the look was gone and replaced with what Terri believed to be condescension.

She'd seen that look before. Most men were either intimidated or mystified by her ethnic appearance, as though she either withheld or could unlock some great ancestral secret. Her shoulders straightened as she walked into the room.

Clint was immediately taken aback by the quiet power Terri exuded. Her shoulder-length, glistening ebony dreadlocks were not what he perceived to be the coiffure of the cosmopolitan woman. Rather hers was the image of a woman awakened to their nubian ancestry and determined to flaunt it in the most exotic of displays. Her obvious sense of cultural pride intrigued, yet put him off, his own sense of roots having been buried beneath years of equal-opportunity rhetoric, stirring only periodically into the light.

The instant observation, combined with her cool appraisal of him, rubbed him the wrong way and nudged him off balance. His thick lashes lowered to shield his eyes, and his jaw involuntarily tightened.

Mark moved from around the table and stood between Terri and Clint, breaking through the tension-filled silence.

"Terri Powers, this is Clinton Steele, CEO of Hightower Enterprises."

Clint stretched out his large hand and enveloped Terri's petite one.

"Mr. Steele," Terri responded with a slight incline of her head, observing his perfectly clipped nails.

For one crazy moment Clint wanted to say, "Your Majesty," and he knew that if he opened his mouth, he'd say something equally ridiculous.

As a result he held her hand a moment longer than necessary, and Terri felt the tingling warmth spread through her fingers and glide up her arm. The sensation nearly caused her to snatch her hand away, but her inherent good manners interceded. Slowly she removed her hand, letting it fall casually to her side.

Terri raised her eyes to meet Clint's, and he quickly discovered that they were a fascinating shade of brown that seemed to darken or brighten with the play of light from the window.

"I'll leave the two of you to get acquainted," Mark interjected into the torrid air. "I'll be back shortly, and we can go over the details." He quickly exited the office, leaving Terri and Clint to face each other.

"I understand that we have business to discuss," Terri said, her low melodic voice again caressing him.

He watched her graceful movements as she moved to a leather chair at the head of the long oak conference table. Her sheath of golden linen barely shadowed the curves beneath, Clint realized with a twinge in his loins. He took a seat to Terri's right.

"Mark has informed me that you're interested in using our advertising services to promote your…new cable stations, Mr. Steele." She folded her hands in front of her.

Did he detect a note of sarcasm in her voice or was it just his imagination? "That's right." He rubbed a hand across his bearded chin. "Your agency comes highly recommended from everyone here in New York. And from all that Mark has told me so far, I believe Powers Incorporated will do an excellent job."

Clint leaned back in his seat and boldly surveyed her sculpted mahogany features, letting his eyes drift down her long neck to the tempting V in the front of her dress.

Terri felt a hot flush spread throughout her body from the intensity of Clint's appraisal. But she would not let his daring looks distract her.

"I'm sure that Mark also told you that I've been out—" she swallowed back the memories "—away for the past three months?" She raised a naturally arched eyebrow in question.

Yes, and what happened to cause that haunted look in your eyes? "He mentioned it."

Why did his voice seem to pump through her like an overactive pulse? "I'm sure what he didn't tell you, Mr. Steele, is that I have very firm beliefs about who I do business with."

The hairs on the back of Clint's neck began to tingle. "Don't we all?"

"In other words, Mr. Steele, I would appreciate it if you took your business elsewhere."

Clint's eyes creased into two dark slits. He leaned dangerously forward and the scent of his cologne raced to Terri's brain, quickening her heartbeat.

His voice lowered to a deep rumble. "Let me get this straight. I've been working my butt off in negotiations with *your* partner—" he pointed an accusing finger at Terri "—and now you're gonna tell me you don't want my business?"

Pure unadulterated anger flared in his black eyes and hardened the velvet voice. "What in the hell is going on around here? Is this some kind of game?"

"Had I been here, Mr. Steele," Terri answered calmly, not intimidated by the vehemence in his voice, "these talks would not have gone beyond the first phone call. Mr. Andrews is well aware of my policies. I'm sure that his…oversight was not intentional. However, *my* decision stands."

Terri rose regally from her seat, and Clint had the overwhelming sensation of being dismissed like a common errand boy by this very self-centered, arrogant—

"I'm sorry," Terri said gently, the soft sincerity of those two simple words mysteriously calming his fury. "I'm sure that this inexcusable situation has cost you a great deal of time and energy. I only wish that I could offer more than an apology."

Why did even her refusal sound so pleasant to his ear? "Have you at least looked over the proposal?" Clint found himself inexplicably yearning for her approval. The revelation pissed him off, but he couldn't seem to stop himself. "I'm certain that it will be a great campaign."

"I have looked it over. However, there's—"

"Is it money? You don't think it's adequate?"

Now she *was* annoyed. Why did they all think that money was the answer to everything? What about integrity?

"This has nothing to do with money," Terri answered, forcing a steady calm into her voice. "It wouldn't matter if your offer were ten times the amount. It's you, Mr. Steele, that I have the problem with. You and your business practices. I cannot in good conscience allow this company to be associated with Hightower Enterprises."

Clint felt as if all the wind had been kicked out of him. All of his work, his sacrifices, his dreams and accomplishments, came to a grinding halt with just those few callous words. Did she have any idea what he'd been through…did she…? Slowly he shook his head. Of course she didn't. No one did. That was the way he'd wanted things. Now, for the first time, he was paying for that choice.

Clint rose from his seat, looking at her with a mixture of regret—that she'd fallen prey to the things that had been said about him—and disappointment. He'd begun to look forward to working with this tempting woman against all of his reservations.

Terri held her breath as Clint's powerful body rose and spread before her. His dark blue suit fit the massive shoulders and long, muscular legs to exquisite perfection. She dared to steal a glance at the short wavy black hair that capped his proud head. For one dizzying moment she wondered what it would feel like to run her hands across it.

Had this been any other time...other circumstances... maybe... But she still had wounds to heal, emotions to mend, and unfortunately the darkly handsome Clinton Steele represented everything that she had grown to resent.

Terri extended her hand and the warmth of his grip shot through her again. Steadily her eyes held his.

"Perhaps my director of promotions, Stacy Williams, can give you some referrals, Mr. Steele. I could—"

"Believe me, you've done enough already." He shook his head, looked at her from beneath silken lashes, a sheepish grin tipping his lips. "I mean, I'm sure that I can find another agency."

Terri nodded her head and made a move to turn away. Clint's intentionally intimate tone stopped her.

"Regardless of what you may think of me, Ms. Powers, I still feel that you're the...that your agency is the best one for the job. If we can't be business associates, at least let's be friends. You *can* call me Clint."

The radiance of his smile washed over her like morning sunshine. Her heart thumped.

"Thank you for the compliment. However, in reference to your last statement, I must apologize again. Our association ends here, Mr. Steele. Good day."

She turned and walked from the office, leaving a fuming Clint and the heady scent of her *kush* body oil lingering behind.

Stepping out into the corridor, she forced her breathing to slow down to normal. What had happened to her in there? Taking a deep breath, she continued down the hallway, just as Mark left his office, to the conference room. Terri stopped short.

A feeling of disaster spread through Mark. "How did it go? I think this is one great deal, Terri," he said a bit too enthusiastically.

Terri glared at him. "We'll talk later. Right now I think

you'd better soothe Mr. Steele's ruffled feathers. There's no deal, Mark. Understood? When you're through, I'll see you in my office."

She turned on her heel, leaving Mark to throw daggers at her back. She'd screwed him. Dammit!

Quickly Mark made his way down the hallway and rushed into the room just as Clint was putting the last of his notes in his briefcase.

"Clint," Mark began apologetically, spreading his hands in a plea. "I had no idea that she was going to react this way. I can assure you that everything was set," he lied. Actually, he had no idea that she would return to work three weeks early. He'd planned to have this deal signed and sealed before she returned.

Clint threw him a glowering look over his shoulder.

"I just need some time to talk with her," Mark added. "I'm sure I can get her to—"

Clint turned to Mark. "I don't beg for anything, Andrews. Boss lady has her reasons—fine. The hell with her. You should have known better than to waste my time."

"Listen, Clint," Mark implored, grasping at straws, "Terri's just being difficult. She's probably on a hate-all-men campaign. She's recently divorced, and she lost her baby. Today's her first day…"

Mark's voice droned on as Clint absorbed the implications of what was being said. My God, what she'd been through was enough to floor anyone. Yet she'd stood there resolute and determined, only once letting emotion seep through that picture-perfect demeanor. His defenses weakened. How could you not admire a woman like that? He felt that he understood her. He knew all too well about pain and loss. That part of him wanted to soothe away the hurt that still lingered behind those mysterious brown eyes.

The snap of Clint's voice cut off Mark's litany.

"Try to see if you can get Ms. Powers to change her mind, and keep me posted."

Mark hid his surprise behind a wall of conversation. "I won't disappoint you, Clint. This deal is important to me, too." *You just don't know how much.*

Mark's calculating mind went into overdrive. He'd have to pull this off and soon, or... No. He refused to think about the possibilities.

"Will you be attending the reception tonight at Tavern on the Green for the producers?" Mark asked.

Clint picked up his briefcase. "I hadn't planned to. Why?"

"Well, I'll talk to Terri again. I'll be escorting her tonight. Maybe she'll be in a more receptive frame of mind," he concluded, giving Clint a sly grin.

Clint pursed his lips, considering what Mark had said. He generally shied away from formal affairs, believing them to be frivolous. But if it gave him the chance to see Terri again, he'd make an exception.

"I never confirmed my invitation," Clint said slowly, "but I don't think it should be a problem."

"Great. So I'll see you tonight."

Clint reluctantly shook Mark's hand and strode purposefully from the conference room.

There was one thing that bugged Clint more than anything else—a *brownnose*. And Mark Andrews fit the bill, he thought, as he waited for the elevator. But there was something else about Mark that disturbed him. He just couldn't put his finger on it. At least not yet. But he would. Maybe he'd just let Steve check him out.

Terri plopped down onto the overstuffed, cream-colored couch that stood against the far wall of her office. Waves of apprehension swept through her. She wasn't sure if what she was feeling was the stress of first-day jitters or the eruption of buried feelings that Clinton Steele had inadvertently dug up.

Adrenaline pumped through her limbs, forcing her body into action. She sprang up from her seat and paced the floor, crossing and recrossing the earth-toned-print area rug covering the parquet floor. Absently she stroked the polished wooden artwork and the array of greenery that adorned strategic locations throughout the tropiclike office.

Clinton Steel *disturbed* her. There was no other word for it. Without effort, he'd made her think and feel things that she'd promised herself she'd never fall prey to again. Her husband, Alan, had been enough.

Terri shut her eyes and wrapped her slender arms around her waist as if to ward off some unseen attacker, momentarily reliving the months of agony. The knocking on her office door jarred her back to the present.

She spun toward the door, blinking back the visions to focus on Mark standing in the doorway.

She cleared her throat. "Mark. Come in." She took a seat behind her desk.

"I think you're making a big mistake here, Terri," Mark began as he crossed the room and sat down, handing her a stack of documents to be signed.

She gave them a cursory glance and turned her attention back to Mark. "You know perfectly well how I feel about Hightower Enterprises."

"Your opinion is archaic!" he snapped. "You left me in charge, and I've been doing a damn good job of running things around here. At least give me the courtesy of believing that I know what I'm doing. Do you honestly think that you can get anywhere in this world being a Goody Two-shoes? Be for real, Terri."

Slowly she rose from her seat, her anger shielded behind her veil of serenity.

"You seem to have forgotten that this company is where it

is today because we have values—whether you believe them to be legitimate or not." Her eyes locked onto him.

Mark heaved a sigh and ran a finger around his shirt collar. Alienating her was not the answer. "Listen," he said, forcing calm into his voice, "at least think about it. Three million dollars is nothing to sneeze at. Maybe this one time we could make an exception."

"I doubt it. But I will give the proposal the benefit of another look."

Mark's hopes lifted. "That's all I ask." He headed for the door, then paused. "Do you still want me to pick you up this evening?"

"What? Oh, I'd almost forgotten. Yes, thanks. Is eight o'clock good?"

"I'll be there," he said, opening the door.

Watching his hasty departure, Terri realized that something was very wrong.

The swish of Terri's black satin-and-chiffon gown blended delicately with the soft music and laughter that wafted from the ballroom.

Mark, clad in an elegant-fitting tuxedo, dutifully took Terri's elbow and escorted her down the carpeted corridor of Tavern on the Green. Stopping briefly to check Terri's stole, there were many who gave them a second look as the two made their way down the hall.

Bowing his close-cropped curly head, Mark whispered in Terri's diamond-studded ear, "Are you ready for your grand entrance?"

"No way," she whispered back as they neared the open ballroom. "And don't you dare leave me, Mark Andrews," she threatened. "You know how self-conscious I get in crowds. You're going to take your share of wet kisses and damp handshakes like a man," she teased.

"Thanks, I can't wait," he answered drolly, rubbing his index finger across his mustache.

At the entrance Terri was awestruck and took a moment to absorb the magnificence of the glittering room. Crystal chandeliers, lit by hundreds of candles, gave the room a dramatic, effervescent shimmer. The round dinner tables were covered with gold linen tablecloths, and crystal goblets stood as the centerpieces. The enormous buffet table was laden with every delicacy imaginable, the aromas taunting the senses.

The main ballroom opened out onto two huge rooms that led to enclosed balconies, giving a sweeping view of New York City. Complementing it all was the array of designer gowns and tuxedos that moved with the wearers like a second skin.

Mark felt Terri momentarily stiffen as the patrons turned to look at them as they stood in the archway. He gave the hand that held his arm an encouraging pat.

"Are you ready?"

Terri gave a tiny nod. Taking deep breaths and putting on their best smiles, they made their entrance.

Within moments Terri was separated from Mark and swept up in a flurry of greetings. Between hugs, handshakes and rapid-fire conversation, Terri tried to peer over the sea of heads to locate Mark.

Finally she spotted him on the far side of the crowded ballroom, apparently in deep conversation with a striking-looking woman.

With her hopes of imminent rescue dashed, she continued to make conversation and field questions about her next endeavor.

"So, what's next, Ms. Powers?" asked Gordon Burke of Columbia Studios.

"This current project with the McPhearson Group and the networks will take up a great deal of time and energy," Terri confessed. "But I do have some proposals that have been submitted for our consideration."

"Would you care to elaborate?" asked a reporter from the *Times*.

"I don't think that would be fair to my prospective clients," she said, flashing an indulgent smile. She knew when she was being put on the spot, and her standard response was always a sure out.

Then, out of the corner of her eye, she saw that Mark was finally standing alone. Seeing a way out from the probing questions, she made her excuses.

"If you all will excuse me—" she lifted her chin in the direction of Mark "—I see my partner over there." She made her getaway, breathing a sigh of relief.

Shaking a few hands and giving smiles of acknowledgment along the way, she eventually made it across the packed room, only to be greeted by a look of pure enjoyment from Mark.

"You think this is all very funny, don't you?" Terri asked, twisting her full lips.

Mark smiled broadly. "Why, of course. Where else could a single man have the opportunity to be entertained by so many fabulous single women?"

"You are behaving yourself, aren't you, Mark Andrews?" she warned with a sparkle in her nut-brown eyes.

"That all depends on what you mean by behaving." He grinned and took a sip from his wineglass and wondered where Clint was.

Terri tapped Mark playfully on the arm while walking around him to the buffet table.

On the far side of the room, Clint made his entrance, accompanied by his vice president, Melissa Taylor. His six-foot-plus height cut an exquisite figure, bedecked in a black Armani tuxedo.

His arrival instantly caught Terri's attention, and an inexplicable heat rushed through her body. Her eyes were drawn to him like a magnet, totally oblivious to the shimmering female form that stood at his side. Terri quickly looked away. When she furtively looked back in his direction, she was shocked, yet thrilled, to find that his eyes were locked on her, openly assessing her, even as his stunning companion clung possessively to his arm.

He gave an almost unnoticeable nod of acknowledgment in her direction.

Flustered by the intensity of his stare, she nodded back and silently prayed that she wouldn't humiliate herself by dropping her food all over the thick carpet.

Holding on tightly to her plate, and with as much grace as she could summon, she walked across the room to her table, not daring to look back. Yet somehow she felt those warm eyes burning through her exposed back.

Clint had zeroed in on Terri almost immediately, and he couldn't help but admire the way the black gown seemed to float over her slender body. Or how her deep brown skin glowed radiantly, tantalizing the viewer with teasing peeks of bare flesh as the dress flowed with her movements.

He had an almost uncontrollable desire to run his fingers through the locks of ebony hair that she'd wrapped magnificently on top of her head. Unconsciously he squeezed his companion's arm to stifle the urge to touch her. There was no way that he could deny the instantaneous attraction he felt toward Terri. The powerful sensation unnerved him. She wasn't like any woman he'd ever known. He'd always been attracted to women like his wife, Desiree. Women who were needy, women who... Desiree was dead, he reminded himself. And it was his fault.

"Is something wrong?" Melissa asked, sensing the change in Clint's mood.

"No. Nothing's wrong," he answered offhandedly, as they moved into the center of the room.

Melissa cut her eyes across the room to where Clint's gaze rested, then back to him in time to catch the look of longing in his eyes. "Why don't we find a table and get something to eat? I'm starved," Melissa said, a bit put off.

"You go ahead. I'll catch up with you later. There are a few old friends that I want to speak with first."

He gently eased her arm from his and crossed the floor, quickly engaging himself in a group discussion before she had a chance to protest.

For several moments Melissa stood alone, disappointed. Her hope of spending an elegant evening with Clint dissolved. But it was rare that she allowed her true feelings to show. And right now she needed something to soothe her injured ego. Putting on a practiced smile, she straightened her bare shoulders and began to do what was second nature—making men's heads turn.

Terri made a valiant effort to focus on the food in front of her while keeping up with the conversations of the movie executives that flowed abundantly. But her mind kept wandering back to Clint. What was he doing here? She dared not ask her dining companions, knowing that her true interests would be obvious. Perhaps she would have a chance to find out before—

"Would you care to dance?"

The rich rumble of the voice seemed to shimmer down her spine and arrest her heart. Instinctively she knew it was him and was almost afraid to look up. But the large warm hand gently held her shoulder, and a surge of heat swam to her head, clouding her judgment.

She turned to look up at him and the most devastating smile assaulted her, causing her breath to catch in her throat.

Terri felt hypnotized by the intensity of his dark, heated gaze. She didn't know whether or not she had even answered him before she was gently eased onto the dance floor. In a matter of seconds her body was pressed next to his as he artfully moved with the slow, pulsing music of the band.

The scent of his cologne enveloped her senses, and she felt an overwhelming urge to snuggle closer to the hard lines of his broad frame. Their bodies seemed to fit perfectly together, like pieces of a puzzle, each dip and curve matching the other, she mused. How long had it been since she'd been held in a man's arms?

Why did she have to feel so good? Clint wondered, his mind running in circles as he held her slender waist in one hand. He wanted to pull her fully against him, but dared not. He was sure that his untimely arousal would be evident.

The music drew to a conclusion, but he continued to hold her, searching for something to say, not yet ready to let her go.

She looked inquisitively up at him, a tentative smile lighting her face.

Finally he found his voice. "Can I get you something from the bar?"

"A glass of tonic water with lime would be perfect."

The melodic cadence of her voice floated to his ears. It almost didn't matter what she said as long as she would continue talking.

He placed his hand on the small of her back and ushered her toward the bar. "Two tonic waters with lime," he instructed the bartender, his eyes never leaving Terri's face.

Clint handed her the glass. "So we meet again," he stated, his eyes boring into hers.

"I wasn't aware that you would be attending."

"It was a last-minute decision." He took a sip of his drink, and his voice dipped intimately. "You look fabulous."

Terri lowered her eyes at the unabashed compliment.

"I hope there won't be any acceptance speeches tonight," he added, rescuing her from her apparent uneasiness.

"No," she breathed, thankful for the change in topic, "not tonight. This is more of a who's-who gathering than anything else, Mr. Steele."

He looked at her for a long moment. "My friends call me Clint. I wish you would."

"You seem to have a lot of those," she commented.

He grinned slyly, his eyebrow lifting. "I didn't think you noticed."

A hot flush of embarrassment seared her cheeks.

"Don't be uncomfortable," he said smoothly, as though reading her mind. "I've been watching you, too." His eyes trailed over her curvaceous form, and she felt her heart begin to race.

"So where is your escort—boyfriend…husband?" he probed in the hope that she would reveal or confirm what Mark had said.

Terri smiled, melting Clint's heart. "Sorry, none of the above. I came with Mark, who seems to have vanished. What about you? I thought I saw you with someone earlier."

He knew good and well that she saw him, but he was more than happy to play along. At least there were no stray boyfriends or husbands to contend with. "That was *my* business associate, Melissa Taylor, who seems to have made quite an impression on Mark."

Terri followed Clint's gaze across the room to see Mark and Melissa laughing intimately.

"Mark does have a way with women," she stated, a wry smile tilting her lips.

"Let's dance," Clint suggested in a low, urgent voice, taking her hand before she could deny him.

"I catch a faint accent in your voice," Clint whispered in her ear as they moved easily across the dance floor. "It's absolutely delicious."

Terri's pulse fluttered. "Barbados," she answered softly.

"Hmm," he hummed into her hair. "Don't ever lose it."

The hours seemed to float away as Terri and Clint became enamored of each other's company. They talked of the places that they had traveled, the current economy and its effects on business. But whenever Terri directed questions to Clint about his line of work, he was subtly evasive.

"Let's not talk about work." He looked deep into her eyes. "Not tonight. I'd rather hear about you."

"There's really not that much to tell," she breathed as they walked side by side out to the balcony. "I came to the States when I was eight. I went to New York University and studied advertising and public relations. My business has been in existence for five years. That's basically all there is."

"I find that hard to believe. There has to be some life behind all of those facts and figures." He smiled encouragingly at her.

Terri stiffened. "I suppose there is," she said softly, "but I don't care to discuss it." She turned her head toward the skyline, wishing that the pain would somehow go away.

He raised a hand to touch her, wanting her to know that he'd be willing to listen, but he knew that she wouldn't give in. At least not yet.

"I know we got off to a bad start this afternoon," he began, pacing his words and her reaction. "I'd like the opportunity to change that."

Terri turned to him, the haunted look in her eyes stunning him with its intensity. She absently ran her hands down the sides of her gown, and Clint's insides went haywire with the motion. He forced himself to look at her eyes instead of those delicious hips.

"I have no idea what you mean."

"I mean," he said, taking a step closer, "I want you to see the real me."

"Why would that be important?"

"Because it's important to me," he stated simply.

Terri swallowed and placed her hand on the balcony railing.

She looked at him from the corner of her eye. "What is it that you think I need to know?"

"That I'm not such a bad guy—and that I'm sure you've heard and read a lot of things about me that aren't true." He leaned against the railing, inching closer to her. "I'd like to correct that."

"Is this account that important to you?"

"It has nothing to do with the account."

"Your ego, perhaps?"

The implications riled him, but he remained unruffled, realizing the truth of her words. He chuckled and ran a hand across his beard in a sensuous motion that rushed through Terri in waves.

"You do have a lovely way of stepping on a person's ego," he answered lightly.

Terri lowered her long, sooty lashes and gave in to a grin that Clint wanted to kiss away. "Believe me, it's not my intention."

"That's good to know." He leaned closer. "Can we just forget about business for a minute?"

Terri nodded.

"I'd like to get to know you—outside of the office." His steady gaze held her, and she felt her pulse begin to pick up its pace.

"I've always been a man who speaks his mind," he continued, his voice dropping to a soothing beat. "And you interest me."

"In other words, you want to satisfy some curiosity?" she tossed back.

"Maybe."

Terri jutted her chin forward. "I'm not a curiosity piece, Mr. Steele," she said, emphasizing the word *piece*.

Clint took the barb in stride. "You also have a way of twisting my words around."

Terri sighed. "What's your point, Mr. Steele?"

"I'd like to take you to…lunch."

Her heart thumped. "I don't think…"

"Dinner?" He flashed her a taunting grin. "I'd love to prove you wrong," he challenged.

Terri knew her fragile emotional state was not yet equipped to handle a relationship, especially not one with a man who effortlessly made her senses go crazy. Yet she couldn't deny that she was just as interested. Maybe a night out was the medicine she needed after so many months of loneliness. And she was never one to back down from a challenge.

She looked boldly up at him. "How about tomorrow? I finish about seven."

His voice stroked her. "I'll meet you out front."

"I'll see you then. Good night, Mr. Steele." She made a move to leave in search of Mark, when Clint's captivating voice stopped her.

"It's Clint," he said, throwing her a heated look that turned her center into liquid fire.

Her voice wrapped around him in invitation. "I'll try to remember that."

Chapter 2

The following morning was filled with chaos. There were press releases to go out, writers to interview and an assortment of trivial things that taxed the brain.

Yet even in the midst of the confusion and harried schedule, Terri could not shake Clinton Steele from her thoughts.

How could a man whose unsavory reputation preceded him evoke in her such warm feelings of desire? Terri had found herself lying awake the previous night reliving his touch, the depth of his voice, the scent of him that had clung to her hours after she'd left the reception.

She just found it difficult to believe that a man who could be so warm, so charming, so sensual would have done the unethical things that had been associated with him. Could she have been wrong?

The ringing of the phone intruded on her thoughts. She snatched up the receiver from its cradle.

"Terri Powers," she said, her mind snapping back to business.

"I thought I'd wait at least twenty-four hours before I called."

She swore that her heart stopped beating. A rush of heat flooded her body.

"Who is this?" Her fingers gripped the receiver— knowing.

His tone was lightly teasing. "I guess I shouldn't have been so presumptuous to think that you'd remember me." He paused a heartbeat of a second. "It's Mr. Ego."

She leaned back in her seat, took a silent deep breath and smiled. "Mr. Steele. What can I do for you?"

"Ah, so you do remember."

Terri laughed outright. "You're not an easy man to forget."

"Then I guess that means we're still on for dinner."

His voice gently caressed her, and she trembled as if she'd been stroked by fire and ice.

"Yes. Of course. Did you have anyplace special in mind?"

"Why don't I surprise you?"

"All right. Just as long as it's not a late night. I have a very heavy schedule on Saturday."

"What might that be? If you don't mind my asking."

"Well, if you must know—" she pretended to sound annoyed but she was proud of her work, and it came through in her voice "—I teach African dance to a group of kids in my building on Saturday morning."

Clint was impressed. "You're full of surprises, aren't you? Are your students any good?"

Laughter bubbled in her voice. "Let's just say they have potential."

"In that case, I promise to get you home early."

"Then I'll see you at seven."

Terri gently hung up the phone and tried to suppress the exhilaration that had taken control of her body. Then reality struggled for the upper hand. What in the world was she doing? She'd been divorced for only a year, although her marriage had been over before then—and now she was considering another man. A man who she had serious concerns with regarding his principles. Was it too soon? Well, maybe tonight she could put her unsettling feelings to rest.

The cheerful greeting from her friend and employee wrestled her away from her musings.

"Girl, it's good to have you back," Stacy declared as she hurried over and gave Terri a warm hug. "You have definitely been missed," she added in her North Carolinian drawl.

"Thanks." Terri chuckled, returning the embrace. "I feel as though I've been away forever instead of three months."

"It felt like forever." Stacy groaned as she took a seat on the sofa and slid her shoulder-length blond hair behind her ear with the tip of her finger. "With mad Mark Andrews in charge, I thought I'd go stark ravin' outta my mind."

Terri smiled knowingly. "He can be a bit much at times, but he's one of the best advertising men in the business. Unfortunately we don't always see eye to eye." A slight frown creased her otherwise smooth mahogany brow.

"I can tell by that look that you're not too pleased with that deal he's been working on with Hightower Enterprises," Stacy said. "I just got wind of it myself when I got back from vacation. I knew you'd want to know, and I was pretty sure that Mark hadn't breathed a word to you about it." Her green eyes, fringed with long black lashes, widened in question. "Am I right?"

Terri slowly crossed the airy office and took a seat behind her desk, twirling one of her ebony locks between her slender fingers.

"That's an understatement. Mark knew perfectly well how I felt about Hightower Enterprises and its head honcho, Clinton Steele, in particular."

"So what are you going to do?"

"We met yesterday, and I initially told Steele to find another agency. However, I'm considering taking another look at the proposal. But there's some investigating I want to do on my own about Mr. Steele before I make my final decision." She paused a moment. "We're having dinner tonight."

Stacy looked at her quizzically. "Really? That's not usually your style."

Her eyes held a faraway look as she spoke. "Mr. Steele is a very unusual man."

"Do you want me to tag along?"

"No. I'm sure I can handle it. I suppose I could use the stimulation of a good debate to get my thoughts back in focus."

Stacy heard the emptiness that filled the usually rich voice that she had come to know so well. She spoke softly. "Terri...I know that the divorce and then losing the baby right on top of it has been hell. But, well, if you want to talk, you know I'm always here."

Terri forced a weak smile. "I know. But it will be a while before I can talk about it." She lowered her thick lashes. "I really just want to put it out of my mind, Stacy. At least I won't have to run into my ex anytime soon," she added cynically.

"I heard through the grapevine that Alan is in L.A."

Terri nodded, the acute pain of betrayal seizing her. "I can only hope that he finds what he thinks I couldn't give him."

Her turbulent four-year marriage to Alan Martin ran through her brain in a kaleidoscope of images. Everyone said that they made such a beautiful-looking couple, but that opposites must certainly attract. Terri, with her exotic natural beauty, had a sense of purpose rooted in the age-old philosophy of family and work for the common good. While Alan, with his playboy good looks, lived for the fast life, the quick money and personal gratification.

It was a marriage almost doomed to fail, but Terri had loved Alan unselfishly almost to the point of losing a part of herself in the process. But after the first blush of passion began to fizzle, Terri saw how unalike they truly were.

Involuntarily her hand stroked across her empty stomach—a place that not long ago had been filled with budding life. Terri blamed herself for the breakup with Alan, feeling that she could not be the kind of woman that he wanted. She'd *never* allow herself to be that vulnerable to anyone again.

"Terri," Stacy called softly.

Terri shook her head, dispelling the visions, and focused on Stacy.

"Are you all right?"

"Sure," Terri answered absently. "I'm fine." She took a shaky breath and put on her best smile. "Now, if I'm ever going to get back in gear, I'd better get busy with the contracts for McPhearson. We're scheduled to meet in a few days."

"I have the promotional campaign almost all mapped out. I'd like you to take a look at it before I put on the final touches," Stacy said.

"You've done a great job on it so far. I can't see how they won't love it. If you're not busy this evening, maybe you can drop it off at my apartment. I'll go over it during the weekend."

"I'll try. If not, it'll be ready for you on Monday. But do you think you'll be up to it after a night on the town with Mr. Steele?" she teased.

Terri shook her head in amusement. "Very funny." She pushed herself up from her seat and walked Stacy to the door.

"Thanks for caring, Stacy." She gave her a warm look. "It means a lot."

Stacy patted Terri's shoulder. "Don't worry about it. Anytime."

Terri flashed a fleeting smile as Stacy left the office.

"Mark," Terri called.

He stopped and waited for her near the elevator.

"I'm going out to lunch. I was expecting a call from McPhearson's secretary. She hasn't called yet. If she calls while I'm out, I've told Andrea to pass the call to you."

She slipped into her lightweight, copper-colored trench coat.

"Do you want me to set up the meeting time?"

"Yes. Just check my calendar. I think any day next week will be fine."

"No problem. I'll take care of it. Oh, by the way, these need your signature." He angled his head to the pile of folders under his arm. "I'll leave them in your office."

"Have you reviewed them?"

"With a fine-tooth comb."

"I'll take your word for it. I really don't have the time to go through all of them. I'm swamped."

"I figured as much."

"I don't know what I'd do without you, Mark." She started to walk away.

Mark gave a derisive laugh that stopped her. "You'd do just fine. You have so far, haven't you?" he challenged, his tone heavy with sarcasm.

Terri frowned. The cynicism of the remark grated on her. "What is that supposed to mean?"

"All it means is what I said. You'd…do…just…fine." His jaw clenched.

"Is everything all right, Mark? You seem…"

"Listen." He sighed. "I apologize." He fingered the collar of his shirt and looked away. "I'm just a little tired—the pressure. That's all."

Terri noticed his nervous gesture. "Pressure never seemed to bother you before."

"Well there's a first time for everything," he snapped, his expression growing hard. "Have you had a chance to go over the Hightower proposal again?" he asked, quickly shifting the direction of the conversation.

"I'll get to them sometime next week," Terri answered warily.

"Then I'll check back by the middle of next week." He turned to walk away.

"Mark."

He turned to face her, his eyes widening in question.

"We need to make some time to talk."

"Really? About what?"

"About us."

"Us?" He tossed his head back and laughed. "You flatter me. I didn't know there was an us."

Terri cocked her head to the side and placed her hand on her rounded hip. "You know perfectly well what I mean. You've been on edge ever since I've been back."

"I think you're overexaggerating, Terri." He laughed mirthlessly. "I have work to do, and you have to do lunch." He turned and strode down the corridor, leaving her completely bewildered by his behavior.

Mark returned to his office, his agitation barely held in check. He reached for the phone, tapping his fingers impatiently on the desktop as he waited. Finally the line was answered.

"Melissa Taylor," said the low, controlled voice.

"Hi. This is Mark. I promised to call."

"How are you, Mark?"

"Fine. But I'd be even better if you'd have dinner with me."

Exiting the building, Terri turned left onto Lexington Avenue, ignoring the rush of lunch-goers as she strolled aimlessly down the busy street. Thoughts of her conversation with Mark unbalanced her usually light nature.

Something wasn't right. If she didn't know better, she'd think that Mark was jealous. Immediately she discarded the notion. She and Mark had worked side by side for nearly a year. She trusted him. She just couldn't imagine—

"You look lost."

She stopped short, a breath away from running into hard, muscular chest. Her heart thumped when she looked up into those eyes and down to the smile that spilled sunshine across her face.

"Clint…I mean…"

"You got it right the first time." His eyes roamed slowly over her. "Now that wasn't so hard, was it?"

Her eyes briefly focused on her beige suede shoes, and her only wish at that moment was that the tiny crack in the sidewalk would open and swallow her.

"I was on my way to grab a bite and decided to take a stroll," he said. "Are you out to lunch or just doing the window-shopping thing?"

Her eyes flashed at the last comment until she saw the laughter in his eyes. She couldn't stop the smile that matched his.

"That's better," he said, his voice enveloping her like a cocoon. "I'm not into the shopping part, but could I interest you in something from—" he quickly scanned the busy avenue "—Original Ray's?"

Her eyes followed his to the famous pizzeria across the street and her stomach gave a hungry twist at the mention of her favorite treat.

"Now don't tell me you don't eat pizza. That's almost un-African-American."

This time she laughed outright, and he memorized the way her eyes crinkled when she laughed and the high sculpted cheekbones that gave credence to her Caribbean heritage.

Hesitating a moment, she sucked in her bottom lip, looking at him then across at the pizzeria.

"Okay." She held up a slender manicured finger tipped

with soft orange. "But just one slice. I have to get back to the office."

"And," he said intimately, "I wouldn't want you to ruin your appetite for dinner." Then, like a conjurer, he took her proffered hand and it magically disappeared in his. Before she had the presence of mind to react, he was walking her across the street. As much as she hated to admit it, her hand felt fantastic in his.

"I guess you've heard all of the ugly rumors about me?" he asked, tearing off a piece of the steamy pizza and looking at her questioningly.

Terri took a deep breath. "Maybe. The question is, are they true?"

He smiled without humor. "That all depends. If you've heard that I'm a tough businessman, then it's true. If you've heard that I make it my business to take what I want in life, then that's also true." He shot her a penetrating look that made her avert her gaze.

"Beyond that—" he shrugged his broad shoulders "—I'm just your regular guy." He took a napkin and wiped his full lips, waiting for her response.

"You make it sound so matter-of-fact."

"I have nothing to be ashamed of."

Terri noticed the momentary flash of pain that hovered behind those dark eyes. Then it was gone. Briefly she wondered who or what had pierced the impenetrable armor.

"You're a very complex man, Clint."

He laughed a deep soul-stirring rumble. "I've been called worse. Coming from you, however, I take it as a compliment."

She took a nibble at her pizza and returned it to the paper plate.

"So have you changed your mind about me? My offer still stands." Hope filled his dark eyes.

Instead of a direct answer, she toyed with him. "I very rarely change my mind once it's made up. But I'm always open for discussion. *If* I have reason to listen."

His voice lowered to a deep whisper, his response rattling her feigned poise. "Then we have a lot more than business to talk about."

For several breathtaking seconds, their eyes held. "I've got to be getting back to the office," she said, smoothly disguising her shredded composure. "I'll see you later."

Without another word, he rose from his seat, rounded the table and helped her on with her coat. The nearness of him set her heart racing and she knew she had to get away—fast.

"Thank you." She looked up at him one last time. "I've got to go," she breathed.

With that she made a hasty exit, darting in and out of the flow of traffic, the sensation of Clint nipping at her heels as eagerly as the fall breeze.

Terri massaged her temples. The figures just didn't seem to make sense. She shook her head. Maybe she was just tired. It was past six-thirty and she had been going over the books and comparing dates for hours. *Clint would be downstairs waiting.* Her pulse quickened at the thought.

Closing the huge ledger, she reached into her desk drawer for her purse just as Andrea, her secretary, tapped on the door and entered.

"Present for the boss," Andrea said, her face hidden behind long-stemmed flowers.

Terri eyed her secretary with skepticism. Andrea's arm was laden with what looked to be more than two dozen Casablanca lilies. Quickly she got up from her desk to help with the burden.

"Where on earth did these come from?" Terri asked.

"They just arrived."

Terri gently searched through the huge bouquet.

"There's no card, if that's what you're looking for."

Terri frowned. "Are you sure? How did they get here?" She placed the flowers on the desk and selected a vase from the credenza large enough to accommodate them.

"A messenger just brought them up. All I did was sign for them. They were addressed to you."

Terri was puzzled. "I don't understand. These are my favorite flowers," she said in a wispy voice. She pressed her face against the bouquet and inhaled the heady aroma. "But who knows that?"

"Obviously someone does." Andrea smiled. "I'll put these in water and bring them right back." She picked up the lilies and the vase and left the office.

"Thanks," Terri answered absently.

For several moments she paced the room, trying to figure out who could have sent the flowers. The only people who knew of her passion for lilies were her adoptive parents, and she was sure that they hadn't sent them. They were hundreds of miles away and weren't the type of people who sent gifts just to be thoughtful. If it wasn't an act that would get them a blurb in the society column, they didn't bother. She'd probably mentioned it to several people, but to no one who would have gone to this extravagance. *Clint?*

She shook her head and smiled. "Don't look a gift horse in the mouth," she whispered, remembering her nana's favorite line. Then she chuckled to herself, wondering for the zillionth time what in the world was a gift horse anyway?

Moments later, Andrea returned with the lilies safely deposited in the crystal vase.

"Where should I put these, Ms. Powers?"

"On the small table by the window. That should give them just enough light."

"I'm all finished out front. If you don't need anything else, I'm going to go home."

"Of course, Andrea. I didn't mean to keep you here so late. I'll see you on Monday."

"Good night, Ms. Powers."

"Good night."

Left alone in the room Terri took one last look at her beautiful bouquet. It had been a long time since someone had sent her flowers. And she was going to enjoy every minute of it. She closed the door gently behind her.

Terri exited the building and was greeted by a cold burst of wind. October was a mysterious month. There was no telling what Mother Nature would send. The temperature had already dropped considerably since the afternoon, and she was thankful that she had decided to wear her trench coat. Her only wish was that she'd put in the lining.

Pulling the trench tightly around her trim body, she took a quick look up at the cloud-filled sky and wondered how far off was the first snowfall.

She checked her watch, noting that it was seven on the dot, and approached the curb to wait for Clint. Just as she neared the curb, a black Mercedes-Benz pulled up in front of her. Annoyed that the car had stopped and blocked her view of traffic, she started to walk to the corner just as the driver got out.

Leaning over the hood of the car, a look of pure mischief on his face, Clint held out one Casablanca lily between his fingers. "Can I take a few dozen lilies off your hands in exchange for dinner?"

Chapter 3

Terri tried to keep the conversation light and impersonal throughout dinner, but the mellow atmosphere and soft music at B. Smith's Restaurant lent itself to intimacy. Within a short space of time she found herself laughing at Clint's wry sense of humor and actually forgetting all of the things she'd heard and read about him.

He was animatedly recounting an incident that had occurred in the health club. "My friend Steve really had me just where he wanted me," he laughed. "There I was, spread-eagled on the bench with a hundred-pound weight hanging over my head."

"What did you do?"

"Cried uncle, what else?"

Terri shook her head in laughter, visualizing Clint's precarious plight.

"What do you do in your spare time?" he asked, loving the way her crimson dress hugged her curves.

"Read mostly. I play tennis in the summer, dance all year

long and I love riding through the park. But it's gotten so dangerous lately, I've cut back."

His voice lowered and raked over her. "I'd be more than happy to be your protector."

She looked at him coyly. "Maybe." *Now why did I say that?*

"That's the best answer you've given me to date. My faith in humanity is restored."

She lowered her thick lashes, her heart beating wildly. Then she looked up. "How did you know about the lilies?" she asked softly.

"I always make it my business to find out all I can about anything or anyone that interests me. In other words, I ask questions. I had my secretary dig up an article that was written about you in *Black Enterprise.* You mentioned your passion for the lilies in the article."

Her stomach lurched at the pointed look that he threw her way, but she kept her expression unreadable, which enticed Clint all the more.

"I believe I'll have to follow that philosophy," she replied.

"So, you've found something that has piqued your curiosity," he tossed back, enjoying the game.

"Perhaps. If there's anything of interest, I'll be sure to let you know." Her smile was a taunt, and Clint's insides tightened.

"Would you like anything else?" His voice was thick with the emotions that he struggled to control. Terri unwittingly brought out the passion in him that he hadn't felt for anyone in years. Every time he heard her voice or saw her face, he thought of what it would be like to unleash that cool control that she displayed so well.

"No. I'm stuffed. The red snapper was delicious." She finished the last of her spring water, secretly enjoying the heat that blazed in Clint's eyes and shook his voice.

"I'm glad you liked it. I haven't been here in a while, but the food is still the way I remember it."

"Do you come here often?"

"From time to time. Usually on business meetings."

The mention of business brought her back to reality.

"From the look on your face, you'd think I said a bad word." He stared at her.

"It just makes me wonder what you want with me. After all, you're in a very nasty business."

"Let me set the record straight." He took a deep breath. "I involve myself in businesses that are on the brink of folding, or businesses that I feel can be better managed by me. Where is the crime in that?"

"That's putting it delicately." She crumpled the linen napkin into a ball, her temper flaring.

"Delicate but true."

"You make what you do sound like a humanitarian gesture. How can you sleep at night knowing what you've done to so many people?"

He clenched his jaw. "I don't do anything that I'm not allowed to do within the law." Exasperation filled his voice. "If I make an offer to a company and they accept, what's the harm?"

"The harm is that they give you everything they've worked for, and you reap the benefits. You've built your fortune on the backs of other people. Our people!" Her voice rose in anger. "What gives you that right?"

Their eyes locked in a battle of wills.

Clint glared at her. How dare she make him feel guilty? He was never one to blow his own horn, and he'd be damned if he'd start now. If she really wanted to know about him, let her do her own homework.

Clint was the first to break the icy contact. "If you're ready, I'll drive you home," he said in a tight voice.

"I can catch a cab, thank you," she answered, annoyed with herself for letting her emotions get out of control.

Clint signaled for the waiter and paid the check. Terri rose to slip on her coat, but not before Clint rounded the table and took it from her.

Slowly, deliberately, he helped her into her coat, the nearness of him sending her pulse on a wild gallop. He pressed his lips close to her ear, inhaling her scent, his warm breath tingling her neck.

"I don't want the evening to end like this, Terri. I'm not interested in the campaign with your company. I can get another agency to do it. I want you and I to be friends—more than friends."

The suggestiveness of his words forced her to look up at him.

Was it sincerity that she saw brimming in those pools of midnight or was it something else?

"I—I don't know how that could be possible. We come from two different worlds."

"Not two different worlds, Terri. Two different points of view. But that's what makes a relationship interesting."

She stepped out of his grasp, her body on fire. She reached for her purse. Her voice shuddered. "I've got to be going."

"I'll get you a cab."

A cold wind blew viciously around them, and a shiver ran up Terri's spine. Clint instinctively put his arm around her shoulder, easing her next to his body.

Before she could protest, a yellow cab pulled up to the corner and she thankfully stepped out of his embrace.

Clint reached around her and opened the car door. With her nerves strung to near popping, she threw out her address in a gush.

"Get the lady home safely," Clint instructed the driver. He looked down at Terri's upturned face. "Until we meet again," he said softly, "and we will." He smiled and closed the car door.

It seemed an eternity before she finally reached her apartment on Twenty-eighth Street. Her head was pounding, and she massaged her temples hoping to relieve the nervous pressure.

Taking the short elevator ride up to the third floor, she put her key in the door and stepped into the cozy comfort of her apartment.

Mechanically she hung her coat on the brass coatrack and deposited her shoes in the foyer. Then she headed straight for the fireplace, and within moments the finely decorated rooms were filled with the warmth from the crackling flames.

Crossing the gleaming wood floors, she sank down into the cottony soft comfort of her bronze-colored couch, closing her eyes against the events of the evening. Instantly a vision of Clint bloomed before her, and she involuntarily trembled, remembering all too well the feel of him, the richness of his scent, the timbre of his voice.

She jumped back up from the couch, afraid of where her feelings were taking her, and turned on the stereo, hoping to muffle the rapid beating of her heart, just as the doorbell rang.

She frowned, wondering who could be ringing her bell. Then she remembered that Stacy had said she might stop by.

Without thinking further, she padded across the room and flung open the door, a small smile of expectation lighting her face.

Clint's lips swept down on hers. His arms enfolded her in a powerful grip. Terri's heart slammed against her breasts as she was helplessly carried away by the sensation of his lips.

Her mind commanded her to pull away, but her body succumbed to the temptation of his tongue toying with her lips, separating them as he entered her mouth. He tasted of wine and a touch of mint. How good the two were together, she thought dizzily.

How long had it been since she'd been held, been kissed, been made to feel like a woman by just a look? Suddenly the emptiness began to slowly fill and like one ravaged by thirst, she drank of the waters.

He never knew a simple kiss could be like this. He stroked her back, delving into her mouth, wanting to seek out all of the hidden places. She was soft and strong all at once, a candy sweetness that demanded that he take more and more. He moaned against her mouth as arousal overtook him, hardening him to near bursting. His body demanded release, but his mind took control.

He released her, and she was sure that if it wasn't for the hand that still gripped the doorknob, she would have crumpled.

"I knew I'd forgotten something," he stated in a ragged voice, his eyes stripping her bare. With that he turned and strode down the corridor, leaving her trembling.

As she drifted off to sleep that night, her last conscious thought was that she'd have to do some serious checking on the devastating Mr. Steele.

Chapter 4

Rising early Monday morning, Terri completed her half hour of meditation, prepared her usual glass of carrot juice and took a quick shower.

Searching through her closet she selected a brilliant green silk dress with fiery splashes of red and bold gold throughout. As an added accessory, she chose an oblong gold silk scarf that draped dramatically across her right shoulder. A small gold pin in the shape of Queen Nefertiti held the scarf in place. To take away from her girlish looks, she twisted her shoulder-length locks into an intricate twist on the top of her head, accentuating her sculpted features.

Satisfied with her look, she completed her outfit by selecting a pair of green suede pumps. With shoes and purse in hand, she padded to the door in stockinged feet before slipping into her shoes.

She checked her watch. It was almost ten o'clock. She wasn't due in the office until after twelve. That would give her at least an hour of research time in the business library.

She was going to dig up every article, news item and gossip clipping that she could find on Clinton Steele and Hightower Enterprises.

Nearly two hours later, armed with a dossier full of information, Terri left the library, hailed a cab and headed for her office. She was stunned to discover the volumes of information that had been written about Clint over the past ten years. It would take days, maybe even weeks, to sort through it all. But she would—of that she was sure.

She leaned back in the cab and considered her next step. As soon as she arrived at work, she'd give her friend Lisa Barrett a call. Lisa had worked as the head of proposals for the Gateway Foundation for fifteen years. Gateway solicited help from all of the major corporations in the United States to support charitable causes and community services. Any company worth its salt had contributed at some point. Powers, Inc., had made sizable contributions over the years, and Terri was sure that if anyone knew about the inner workings of the businesses in New York it would be Lisa.

Arriving at her office, Terri quickly placed a call to Lisa.

"Lis, hi, it's Terri."

"Hey, hon, how are you? I haven't heard from you in days. Are you back at work?"

"In answer to your first question, I'm okay. And yes, I'm back at work, but I need a favor."

"Doesn't everybody," Lisa commented drolly. "What might yours be?"

"I need you to check out Clinton Steele. He owns—"

"Believe me, I know what he owns." Her voice was filled with amazement. "You're really moving into the big time. What do you want to know?"

"Anything that you can find. He made a bid for us to do an ad campaign, but I don't like what I've heard about him. Still, I'd like to give the man the benefit of the doubt."

"I'd like to give the man a lot of things, but doubt isn't one of them," Lisa quipped wistfully.

"Lisa," Terri moaned, "come on, this is serious."

"All right—all right. I'll see what I can find out."

"Thanks, Lis. Call me when you do."

With that out of the way, Terri diligently tried to focus on the meeting with McPhearson ahead of her. She'd prepared her notes, gone over Stacy's campaign strategy and had dressed the part of the executive to the hilt.

Yet even with all of her preparation, she could not shake thoughts of Clint from her mind. Every free second for the past two days, visions of him assaulted her. She couldn't count how many times she'd relived his kiss. Just the thought of it sent jolts of electricity whistling through her veins. Damn you, Clinton Steele! she thought. Why now, when my whole life is in a tailspin? And why you?

Sighing deeply, she got up from her desk and smoothed her dress. She hadn't heard from him since that night, and maybe it was just as well. Things were getting too complicated too fast.

She checked the antique grandfather clock that stood against the wall. The representatives from McPhearson were due in her office any minute.

Where was Mark? she wondered, her agitation building. He should have been here an hour ago. She crossed the room in long-legged strides and pressed the intercom.

"Andrea?"

"Yes, Ms. Powers?"

"Has Mark arrived yet?"

"He just walked in."

"As soon as he's ready, would the two of you come in? You'll need to bring your Dictaphone, Andrea. I want every word recorded. And buzz Stacy also."

"Yes, Ms. Powers."

Terri returned to her desk just as her private line rang. "Terri Powers," she answered.

"Ms. Powers, this is Mr. McPhearson's secretary."

"Oh, yes. I wasn't expecting a call. Is there a delay in the meeting time?" She immediately flipped open her plan book, hugging the phone between her shoulder and her ear, pen poised and waiting.

"Uh, Ms. Powers—Mr. McPhearson wants me to inform you that he's changed his mind about the campaign."

"What?" She dropped the pen between the ivory pages. "I don't understand. Everything was set."

"That's all the information I have, Ms. Powers."

"Let me speak with Mr. McPhearson." Her pulse pounded in her ears.

"He's in a meeting."

Terri would have laughed at the practiced line if she wasn't so furious. "Would you have him call me as soon as he's through?"

"He's leaving directly for the airport when the meeting concludes."

"I see." Terri swallowed, her back stiffening. "Thank you."

Blindly she hung up the phone, a sinking feeling taking over. This deal was critical. She couldn't believe that McPhearson would pull out, just like that. There had to be some explanation, and she was damn sure going to find out what it was.

She paced the floor, her teeth biting her bottom lip, trying to contemplate a course of action.

There was a light tap at the door.

"Come in," Terri said offhandedly.

Stacy stepped in.

"All ready for the big boys?" Stacy asked. She took a seat at the round conference table on the far side of the office.

Terri blew out an exasperated breath. "McPhearson's secretary called."

"About what?" Stacy took a sip of black coffee and tossed her blond hair behind her ears.

"It wasn't what I wanted to hear. They reneged."

"What?"

"You heard right. They pulled out," Terri said.

"But why? They couldn't have gotten a better deal if they'd whipped it up themselves."

"Apparently they did."

"I don't believe it." She ran a hand through her hair.

"Neither do I."

"So now what?"

Terri raised her eyebrows. "I'll have to think it through and explore some other options. We'll really have to push for a confirmation with Viatek Studios. I want you to work on that right away."

Stacy nodded and jotted down some hasty notes. "Does Mark know about McPhearson?"

"I haven't seen Mark yet."

"This was his advertising deal originally, wasn't it?"

"Yes." Then almost as an afterthought, she added, "And so was the account that fell through with Conners, the independent producer," in a voice filled with awakening.

She turned to Stacy, her eyes burning with purpose. "As soon as I inform Mark that the deal has been canceled, I want you and I to go over Mark's files with a fine-tooth comb, as he puts it. I went over the books last week, and there are things that don't make sense. I thought it was because I was tired but now I wonder…"

Stacy nodded, her sea-green eyes reflecting Terri's concern. "I'll see what else I can dig up from the logs," Stacy added just as Andrea peeked her head in the door.

"Mark is here, Ms. Powers."

"Tell him to come in, Andrea."

Mark strolled in moments later, his light brown eyes shifting from one woman to the other. "Why the long faces?" He walked over to the water cooler and filled a paper cup.

"McPhearson canceled the deal," Terri stated. She watched for his reaction.

"You're kidding? I worked weeks on that deal." He ran his index finger around the collar of his shirt.

She registered the move. "I'm sure you did."

"What the hell is that supposed to mean?"

"It means we'll have to do some rearranging of our finances."

"Well, if you'd accept Steele's proposal we'd—"

She cut him off. "What time is your flight to Detroit?"

"I have to be at the airport in an hour."

Terri turned away, unable to look at him another minute. "Tell your folks I said hello. We'll talk when you get back."

"Fine!" Mark snatched up his notes and his briefcase and slammed out of the office.

Terri turned to Stacy. "As soon as he's out of the building, I want you to pull his files. Everything."

Hours later, exhausted and wanting to disbelieve what was in front of her, Terri closed the folders that Stacy had given her. The evidence was clear, and she had no alternative.

Slowly she got up from her desk, her heart heavy with regret, wondering what she could have done differently. She didn't know. All she could do now was prepare for Mark's return.

Stretching, her body aching with fatigue, she envisioned sinking into a steamy bubble bath, when a picture of Clint intruded on her thoughts. Her pulse raced at an alarming speed as she remembered the feel of his lips against hers... The part of her that wanted more wondered what it would be like to make love with him.

This was getting crazy, she thought, angry at herself for

fantasizing about a man who definitely was not for her. She hadn't heard from him since their dinner date, and the thought that he was playing games with her renewed her frustration and misgivings.

Gathering her purse and briefcase, she took her coat from the rack and began to leave the office just as the phone rang.

She started to let the answering service pick up the call but decided against it, thinking that it might be important.

"Terri Powers," she answered by rote.

"Terri, it's Clint."

Her heart skipped a beat. *Does he read my mind, or what?* "Yes?"

"I haven't been able to get you off of my mind."

Me, either. Silence.

"How are you?"

If you only knew. "I've been better."

"You don't sound like yourself. Is something wrong?"

"I couldn't begin to explain." But she desperately wanted to. She wanted to feel his arms around her again, to hear his laughter, to taste his lips. But she couldn't.

"Listen, uh, I'm really tired, Clint. You wouldn't believe the day I've had."

"Maybe you should talk about it. That helps, you know."

"Not this time."

He wouldn't be dismissed. "Why don't I meet you? We could go for dinner or something. Maybe a drive." He drummed his fingers on the desk, waiting for her response.

"Clint, I really…"

"I'll be downstairs in ten minutes. Wait for me, Terri."

The next sound she heard was the dial tone.

Terri waited in quiet agitation for the elevator to reach her floor. Why was he doing this to her? A better question was, why was she doing this to herself? She knew perfectly well that Clint was not the kind of man to be taken lightly. What was more disturbing, he was the kind of man that fascinated her against her better judgment. That reality frightened her.

Finally the elevator arrived, and her heart raced as the metal box made its painstakingly slow descent.

She pulled her white cashmere coat tightly around her as a shiver jetted up her spine at the thought of seeing him. Maybe he wouldn't be there, and she could just escape to the sanctuary of her apartment. Just like she'd been doing for months, hiding from the possibility of life as she once knew it—too frightened to take any more chances. But there was another part of her that longed to be fulfilled again, the part that hoped he'd be waiting.

The doors of the elevator opened on the lobby level. Terri stepped out, her head held high. Casually she looked toward the revolving doors. Her spirits sank when she realized that Clint was nowhere in sight. Fine!

She strode purposefully forward, anticipation replaced with annoyance. Why did it matter? she chastised herself, pushing through the revolving doors. This was probably just another game to Clint.

Her temper rolled to the surface as she stood on the windy corner to hail a taxi. She waved her hand at an oncoming cab. As it approached, the cab's dome light flashed the off-duty sign.

Terri went livid, wanting to scream and cry all at the same time. That was the final insult of the day. She really didn't know how much more she could—

"You weren't going to wait?"

Clint's voice seemed to massage her spine and unlock the tension that had gripped her. She turned toward the sound of his voice and looked up at him, the anxiety and frustration of the day brimming in her brown eyes. How easy it would be to just walk into his arms and let him soothe the aches away.

She remained immobile.

Something in the way she looked at him touched a hidden corner of his heart. He reached out and placed his large hands on her shoulders. "Terri, what's wrong?" Concern softened his voice. "You look like you've been crying."

Terri blinked and swallowed back the lump in her throat. "It's just the wind," she answered with a calmness that surprised her.

"I got stuck in traffic," he said by way of apology.

"Oh."

Why did he suddenly feel like a little boy having to explain his misbehavior? The awkward feeling left him unnerved. He shoved his hands into his coat pockets. "Can I at least give you a lift?"

She gave him a half smile and shrugged her right shoulder. "You could drop me off at my apartment. If you don't mind."

"No problem. My car is over—" He looked across the busy intersection to see a traffic cop sticking a ticket on his windshield.

"Hey!" he yelled as he immediately darted through traffic to the other side of the street. He snatched the ticket from the window, intent on making the offender eat it.

Clint strode over to the "brownie," as they were dubbed by New Yorkers for their brown uniforms, and shook the ticket in his face.

"Listen, buddy," Clint hissed, interrupting the officer from writing another ticket. "I was there for only a minute. What's the deal with this ticket?" He checked his watch. "It's five after seven. I can legally park here."

"Not by my watch," the brownie said, dismissing Clint.

"Your watch is wrong!" Clint stalked the officer as he moved to the next car.

"If you think so, then take it to court."

The officer walked away, leaving Clint to throw daggers at his back.

Terri gingerly eased alongside of an irate Clint, fighting hard to stifle the giggles that bubbled in her throat. This was the first time that she had truly seen the cool, controlled Clint totally bent out of shape. Her only regret was that she didn't have a camera.

"How much is it?" she asked in a tiny voice.

"Fifty damn dollars!" he spat, slamming his palm against the hood of the Benz. He looked at the ticket in disbelief, then across at Terri, whose face was contorting in silent hilarity.

"Go ahead—laugh," he said, his own anger giving way to the ridiculousness of it all. A reluctant grin lifted one side of his mouth.

Finally, through tears and giggles, she pointed a finger at him, the laughter still bubbling over. "You should have seen the look on your face," she said.

"You think this is all very amusing, don't you?" he said, trying to sound threatening.

Terri wiped her eyes and took several deep breaths. "Actually I do. I mean, let's face it, you can afford it."

"Now that makes me feel a helluva lot better."

"Well," Terri offered, pulling herself together, "I guess the least I could do is treat you to dinner. After all, if you hadn't come to see me, none of this—" she covered her budding smile with a gloved hand "—would have happened."

"You know what?" He looked at her hard and braced her shoulders. "I'm gonna take you up on your offer."

After a delicious meal in Chinatown, punctuated by congenial conversation, Clint drove Terri to her apartment building. The plush luxury of the Benz was like a soothing balm to her tense body. Slowly she began to relax, her voice a mere whisper when she spoke.

"I've always wanted to learn to drive a stick shift," she said dreamily, "but it's such a hassle with the stop-and-go Manhattan traffic."

"I know what you mean." He switched into Second gear.

"But after living in England and driving on the open road, it became second nature to me. I love the feel of power," he added, tossing her a searing look as he held on to the stick.

"I didn't know you lived in England."

"Yeah, for a while," he said, wishing that he'd never mentioned that part of his life. Just the idea of her saying she wanted to learn to drive a standard drove the knife of guilt through his gut, painfully reminding him of his daughter, whom he'd left behind in the care of his sister-in-law, because he'd caused her mother's—his wife's—death.

"You'll have to tell me about it sometime."

"Hmm."

Terri looked at him from the corner of her eye, in time to see the hard, dark expression that passed across his face. She decided not to probe and leaned back against the leather cushion of the headrest. Maybe some other time.

Where had all of the tension gone? As much as she was reluctant to admit it, she enjoyed being in Clint's company. He made her laugh, he lightened her spirit. He was intelligent and witty, and he was undeniably sexy. Clint made her feel things that she hadn't felt in so long. Only this time it was more powerful, more compelling. And she wanted it.

"What are you thinking about?" he asked, breaking into her thoughts as he made the turn onto her street.

If she could have turned red, she would have been crimson. She felt certain that he could read her thoughts, and she felt suddenly exposed.

"Oh, just about some things at the office."

"You never did tell me what was bothering you." He pulled up in front of her door.

She looked at him, her voice softening. "It doesn't really matter now."

"If it affects you, Terri, then it matters."

She fumbled with her purse. "It's getting late. I—"

He reached for her, turning her to face him. "You keep running from me."

His voice wrapped around her.

"Every time we get close, you run from me like a scared little girl."

He gently stroked her face.

She held her breath.

"You're a woman, Terri." His eyes roamed over her, igniting her. "A desirable, sensual woman who I want in my life. But you have to give me a chance."

Could he possibly mean what he was telling her? Or was this just a ploy? Maybe he was right. How would she ever know, if she never gave him the chance? Curiosity won out.

"Would you like to come up for a nightcap?" She smiled a tentative smile. "I think I have some fruit juice and chips."

"Sounds perfect."

Terri opened her apartment door and immediately stepped out of her shoes, instructing Clint to do the same. She grinned at his perplexed look.

"When you leave your shoes at the door," she explained, "you leave all of the bad vibes behind you and just bring peace into your home."

"Hmm…" Clint nodded, handing her his shoes "…sounds good to me."

"Well, come on in and make yourself comfortable. You can hang your coat on the rack." She pointed to the brass coatrack and headed for the living room. She turned on the CD player, and seconds later the music of Miles Davis blew a soulful tune in the background. Terri left Clint and went to prepare a platter of chips with a cheese dip and a bowl of pretzels.

"You have a great place, Terri," Clint commented, admiring the ethnic artwork and handcrafted sculpture. Huge earthen urns sat majestically in corners, overflowing with fresh-cut flowers in some and arrangements of silk in others.

"Thanks," she called from the kitchen, quietly pleased that he liked her taste. "Would you light a fire, please?"

"Sure." He walked to the fireplace and got the fire going. Finished, he roamed over to her bookcase and saw that she had volumes of poetry as well as what appeared to be every espionage and crime story ever written. What a strange combination, he thought, more fascinated than ever.

Terri entered the living room and placed the tray of snacks on the smoked-glass table.

"I see you've found out my secret," she said, walking up behind him. "I'm a closet poet with a murderous streak."

"The poet part I don't mind," he answered jovially, "it's the other half that scares me. Actually, as quiet as it's kept, I read a lot of poetry. It relaxes me. Especially after a rough day."

Terri's eyes widened in disbelief. "Really?"

"Let that be our little secret." He lowered his voice to a pseudo-whisper. "I don't want to ruin my dubious reputation."

Terri replied in kind. "Your secret is safe with me. Just don't cross me," she teased. "Come on and sit down. After I've been slaving over a hot stove for hours, I want you to eat every drop."

Clint chuckled as he followed her to the couch.

"...So when I discovered that the books didn't jibe, it made me do some additional checking. To make a long story short, I don't like what I found." She was still reluctant to tell him too much. The last thing she needed was his sympathy or for him to think that she was totally incompetent. "I've worked hard to get to where I am, Clint. This company means everything to me. I've sacrificed a lot and I've given a lot. All I expect in return is honesty and a good day's work."

Could he dare tell her that he'd embarked on his own investigation? Good sense told him to hold off revealing his suspicions. He had to be absolutely positive, first. His years in business had honed his instincts. He was certain that something was amiss at her agency. Tentatively he put his arm around her. "What are you going to do now?"

"I have a few things in mind," she said, enjoying the weight of his arm around her shoulders. But she wasn't sure she should divulge her plan.

Clint moved a stray lock from her face and tucked it behind her ear, pleased with the silky quality of her hair.

She looked at him and felt her heart lurch.

With painful slowness, he lowered his head, his eyes holding hers. The flames from the fireplace appeared to dance in her eyes.

She knew her heart was going to explode into a million little pieces as his mouth slowly descended to meet her own.

The contact was incendiary, and Terri was certain that she heard fireworks erupt in the background.

The velvet warmth of his lips gently brushed over hers, taunting, tempting her with what was to come.

And it came.

The fire of his tongue played across her mouth as he spread his fingers through her twisted mane, pulling her completely against his hungry mouth.

Instinctively her lips parted and the tip of his tongue played teasing games, exploring her mouth, sending jolts of current surging through her.

He moaned against her lips, a deep carnal sound that vibrated to her center. Terri felt the heat race through her limbs as his fingers traced the pulse that pounded in her throat.

She wanted to scream when he pulled his mouth away from her lips, only to plant wet, hot kisses across her face, down her neck. Then he let his tongue play havoc in her ear, and every fiber of her body ignited.

"Clint…" She trembled against him.

A tingle of excitement ran through her as his hand trailed

down the curve of her back, pulling her closer, caressing her, causing her body to arch, her rounded breasts to press against his chest, and he knew he would go out of his mind.

"I want you, Terri," he groaned in her ear.

His mouth covered hers again, his tongue slashing against hers, demanding, urgent.

Her arms tightened around his hard muscular frame. She stroked the strong tendons of his neck, the outline of his chest. She felt as if she was falling, spinning weightless through space, and she never wanted the feeling to end. But she knew it had to stop. The door to her past was still ajar, and until she could empty it fully, no one else could enter.

His mind spun in a maelstrom of confusion. What was he doing? This was not part of the plan for his life. He wasn't supposed to feel this way, to want her from the depth of his being. His body ached to be a part of hers. But he couldn't do this to her. She was sure to think that he was just trying to romance her in order to get her to agree to the deal. He wanted her to want him for the right reasons, or not at all.

As if reading each other's minds, slowly they pulled away—each trying to control the shudders that ripped through them.

"I…I'm sorry." He stroked her cheek. "I didn't—"

"It's okay, Clint," Terri stuttered, breathless and in awe of what had almost taken place.

He gently pulled her into his embrace, fighting back the desires that wrestled to engulf him.

"I won't rush you, Terri," he whispered in a ragged breath. "As much as I may want to," he added with a soft smile.

She touched his lips with her own. "Thank you," she whispered.

Reluctantly he rose from the couch. "I'd better go." He smiled mischievously down at her, mimicking an old Western movie. "I cain't guarantee your honor, m'am, if'n I stay."

Terri released a shaky laugh and stood up in front of

him. She slipped her arms around his waist, looking up into his eyes.

"Then I'd say you'd better mosey on outta here, mister," she teased, matching his parody.

He held her for a long moment, burying his face in her hair, his confusion complete. Then he released her.

"I'll get your coat," she offered.

At the doorway Terri felt ridiculously like a teenager on her first date. Her nerves rattled, and her heart was pounding so loud she just knew Clint could hear every beat.

"I'll call you tomorrow," he said.

"I'd like that."

Clint leaned down and brushed her lips. The contact was too brief and he wanted more. Pulling her into his arms he kissed her fully, her own desire matching his every rhythm.

He eased away. "I've got to go," he said, his voice thick with desire. He started to leave, then turned back. "You'll be happy to know that I've found another advertising agency to do the work. So now there's no more business to interfere." His dark eyes bored into hers. "This is purely personal. The rest is up to you." He turned away, never looking back to see the expression of astonished relief spread across her face.

As if on a cloud, Terri glided back into the living room, a smile of contentment lighting her face as she replayed his final words. *This is purely personal.*

She changed the CD, replacing Miles Davis with Kenny G. Crossing the living room, she walked down the narrow hallway to the bathroom. Mechanically she turned on the tub water, adding her favorite bubble bath. Soon the herbal aroma filled the room, and her weary body nearly screamed for relief. Piece by piece she stripped out of her clothes and stepped into the steamy water.

Terri sank into the tub, the bubbles coming up to her chin.

She closed her eyes, letting the steam envelop her, and a picture of Clint sprang to life before her eyes—and she trembled.

His mouth seemed to caress every part of her body, kneading all of the aches away. A soft moan of remembrance filtered through her lips, and she silently wished that he was there with her.

She felt the slow, steady warming that spread through her body and knew that it had nothing to do with the steaming water. And she wondered what it would have been like making love with Clint. How soon, if ever, would she know?

After a fantasy-filled half hour, Terri finally curled up into bed, sinking into the comfort of the freshly washed sheets. She reached for the book of poetry she kept by her nightstand, determined to ease away the last vestiges of tension and images of Clint.

Just as she was about to drift off to sleep, the ringing of the phone jarred her back to consciousness.

Annoyance replaced curiosity as she drowsily reached for the intrusive instrument.

"Hello?" she mumbled.

"Terri, it's me, Lisa."

"Lisa," she groaned. "It's late."

"I know. But I got the info you wanted. I thought you'd be interested."

Terri sat straight up in her bed. *Please let it be good.*

"Your Mr. Steele is, anonymously, one of the biggest individual benefactors that the Gateway Foundation has."

Chapter 5

The morning sun was barely up in the sky when Clint rose from his bed. He'd spent a torturous night, reliving what almost was. More times than he cared to count he'd reached for the phone to dial Terri's number. Each time, halfway through dialing, he'd hung up. The next move was Terri's. He'd put his cards on the table.

Pulling on a terry-cloth robe he padded across the bedroom and opened his dresser drawer. Rifling through his possessions, he pulled out a cutoff T-shirt and an old pair of shorts. Crossing to the closet, he selected a navy blue sweat suit and a pair of sneakers. Usually a brisk run around the park revitalized him and cleared his head.

An hour later he lay sprawled across his king-size bed, drenched in perspiration from his morning jog. His frustration was still alive and well.

Staring up at the stucco ceiling, his hands clasped behind his head, a slow smile of acceptance spread across his face. Terri was under his skin to stay, and no amount of jogging was going to change it.

* * *

Terri strode down the office corridor, looking neither left nor right. How could she have been so narrow-minded and gullible to be taken in by rumors and speculation? She should have gone along with her instincts in the first place. She smiled ruefully. There was no way that her senses could have been that far off base if they went into crisis every time she thought of Clint.

She closed her office door with a thud, tossing her briefcase on the desk, her coat shortly behind.

Her head ached from the hours of reading she had done after Lisa's call. She'd forced herself to go through as many of the reports that she'd gotten from the library as she could before she'd fallen asleep. That, compounded with the company ledgers, was enough to keep her head spinning for weeks. But she had work to do, and it would begin with a process of elimination.

She reached for the phone and dialed Stacy's extension.

Stacy picked up on the second ring.

"Stacy Williams, here."

"Stacy, I need you in my office in an hour. In the meantime I want you to pull the accounting records for the past six months and compare them to the figures we came up with last night."

"Sure. Anything else?"

"The sooner the better. I want to get that SOB out of here as soon as possible."

"I'll get right on it."

"Thanks."

Terri hung up the phone, then proceeded to unlock the file cabinet, retrieving the files that she had examined the previous night. The pages in front of her seemed to laugh at her naïveté.

She shook her head in disbelief. Powers, Inc., was on the brink of deep financial trouble, and she had let it happen. Her trusting nature had overruled her business judgment, and it had cost her dearly. For the past year she'd felt like a failure as a wife and then as a mother. All she had left was her business, and now even that was threatened.

No more.

She quickly crossed the office and went out into the small reception area. Andrea was just taking her seat.

"Good morning, Ms. Powers," she greeted cheerfully, then changed her tone when she saw the thunderclouds raging in Terri's dark eyes. "Is something wrong?"

"Not for long," she responded. "I need you to get Al Pierce, the accountant, on the phone. Tell him to stop whatever he's doing. I want him here within the hour, along with all of the records that have anything to do with Powers, Inc. Make sure that he understands that this is not a request. This is a command performance. If he gives you the slightest bit of a problem, put me on the line and I'll handle him."

"Yes, Ms. Powers," she said meekly.

"Thank you. Oh, and as soon as Mr. Andrews arrives, send him into my office."

Terri turned back toward her office before Andrea had a chance to respond.

Andrea couldn't remember ever seeing Terri this angry before. This must be serious, she thought, thankful that the boss's rage was not directed at her. She flipped through her Rolodex and found the accountant's number.

Clint stared pensively at the folders in front of him. He'd wrestled with what he had to do for several days. His decision was made. His friend Steve's investigation of Mark had come up with some very damning information, and he felt compelled to tell Terri, whether she accepted his help or not.

The tapping on his office door snapped him to attention. Melissa strolled in.

"You wanted to see me, Clint?" she asked, beaming a brilliant smile.

"Yes. Have a seat."

Melissa took a seat opposite Clint, seductively crossing her long legs. She regarded him thoughtfully, gaining a joyous satisfaction in studying his profile. Her strong admiration and loyalty for Clint bordered on the romantic, but she was always careful never to cross that line. She sighed silently, wishing that one day he'd see past her brains to the woman who could rock his world.

"You've been seeing Mark Andrews." His question was more of a statement, and Melissa wasn't sure if she should be angry or flattered by his interest.

"I won't even begin to ask you how you know," she stated candidly, the years of working together being enough of an answer. "Is there a problem that I should know about?"

Clint slowly crossed the room, sliding his hands into his pants pockets. He turned to face her.

"There could be. I got some bad vibes from him when the deal with Powers, Inc., fell through. Some things didn't sit right with me. I've had someone do some investigating on our Mr. Andrews, and I don't like what I've found out."

Melissa's heart tripped. The only man that had truly interested her in years had been Clint. There'd been others to fill the gaps, even Clint's buddy Steve. When she met Mark, she thought that she had finally found someone to take her mind off of Clint—permanently. Or at least until Clint woke up and truly saw her. Now she had a bad feeling that she wasn't going to like what she was going to hear.

Melissa returned to her office, slamming the door behind her, the vehemence of her tirade toward Clint reverberating in her head. Her hurt and anger were so intense that she shook with its force. She swung back toward the closed door, wanting desperately to throw something. Then feeling totally impotent, tears of frustration and defeat filled her hazel eyes.

Terri and Stacy sat in Terri's office awaiting Mark and the accountant's arrival.

Stacy took a sip of her coffee. "I just can't believe that all of this was going on right under our noses."

"Neither can I," Terri replied, the soft lilt of her voice laden with regret.

Stacy shook her head just as Andrea peeked in the door.

"Ms. Powers, Mr. Pierce is here, and Mark just arrived. Should I buzz him?"

"Yes. But tell him to wait about ten minutes. Send Al in now."

"Who gave you authorization to allocate all of this money, Al?" Terri demanded, tossing the stack of check releases across the conference table.

Al Pierce swallowed and adjusted his glasses. He made a small showing of reviewing the documents in front of him. "Why, you did," he replied after several moments.

"In all of the years that we've been dealing with each other, when have I ever given you verbal instructions? Every transaction has been clearly written by me. Is that correct?"

"Yes. However, Mr. Andrews said that they were your instructions." He fidgeted in his seat, uncomfortable under her steady gaze.

"How much was he paying you to maintain two sets of books, Mr. Pierce?" she quizzed, throwing him totally off guard.

"I...I don't know what you mean," he mumbled, raking a nervous hand through his thick gray hair. "Certainly you don't think that—"

"Think what—that you and Mark were behind-the-scenes,

undermining me for personal gain?" Her voice rose. "Is that what you think is on my mind?"

"Ms. Powers," he stood abruptly. "I resent the implication."

"Resent whatever you want, Al. You're through! And if I have anything to do with it, the only things you're ever going to add up again are cash-register receipts," she spat. "Now get out of my sight and out of my office."

Al Pierce gathered up his belongings. "If you think that I'm your only problem, then you have more of a problem than you can imagine." He threw a cursory glance in Stacy's direction and stalked out the door.

"What was that supposed to mean?" Stacy asked.

"I really don't know. More than likely it was an idle comment." But silently she wondered if it were that simple. She inhaled deeply. "Now for round two," she said, her tone morose. "I think it would be best if I handled this one alone." She crossed her arms with resolve.

"Are you sure?"

Terri nodded gloomily. "If I need you for anything, I'll send Andrea for you."

Stacy rose reluctantly and slowly approached Terri, who stood as if cast in stone. "Listen," she began softly, "it all looks real bleak right now. But everything is going to work out."

"Sure," she whispered. "On your way out tell Andrea she can buzz Mark now."

They stood facing each other like two gladiators waiting for the signal to attack.

"I've had the misfortune of going over your records," Terri began, pacing her words evenly. "It's amazing how yours are so different from mine," she added with sarcasm. "You've tried to destroy me," she said, her voice edged in granite. "No wonder you were so hell-bent on sealing the contract with

Hightower. You needed the money to cover up what you'd done before I found out."

"You brought it on yourself," he tossed back in a malevolent tone that chilled her.

"What? You—with the help of Al Pierce—systematically set out to ruin this company. A company that I put together." She counted off his misdeeds on her fingers. "You sabotaged contracts, made us lose potential deals, lined your own pockets and God knows what else. Then you have the gall to stand there and tell me that I brought it on myself! Do you hate me so much that you'd risk ruining this company and me as well as your own name in this industry?"

"Yes!" he shouted. "You'll never know how much. You with your holier-than-thou attitude. The woman who could do no wrong. This is no more than what you deserve. I was the one left with the crumbs of your success."

"Crumbs!" Her indignation came full circle. "You've always been a part of the success, Mark."

He chuckled. "But it was always Terri this and Terri that," he mimicked in a singsong voice. His face twisted into an ugly mask. "Terri Powers received the accolades, her name in the papers—not me." He jabbed a finger at his chest, glowering at her.

"So that's what it all boils down to, does it? You can't stomach working with a woman who has made it."

He looked away, clenching his jaw. "You're not a woman. If you were, you could've kept your husband and your baby!"

His personal attack stabbed her. She fought for control as nausea threatened to overtake her. "Not the kind of woman you expected me to be," she said smoothly, camouflaging her hurt. "I want you out of here within the hour. Security will oversee your departure." She turned her back to him, her spine rigid.

Mark tossed her a hate-filled stare. "You've had your time to shine. I'll guarantee you that I'll have mine, as well." He turned toward the door then stopped. "I was willing to risk anything to make you know how it feels to be forgotten. Now that you know everything," he paused, "you won't ever forget me again." He stormed out of the office, leaving the door swinging on its hinges.

For several moments Terri stood in the tension-filled silence that permeated the air. Finally she let out a breath that she didn't realize she'd held, and a tremor raced through her. She lowered her head, feeling weak and beaten.

She'd always prided herself on being fair to everyone. Or at least she'd thought so. How could she have not seen what was happening to Mark? She'd been so wrapped up in her own personal problems over the past months that she'd been blind to what was going on, allowing Mark free rein with the company. He'd used that trust against her.

His painful words rushed back at her, and her resentment and hurt resurfaced. No one could ever begin to imagine the pain and worthlessness that she'd felt. She'd shared her private hell with no one, and she wasn't sure if she ever could.

But she could not let it immobilize her. She forced her body to move, her mind to work. She still had work to do. It was time that she reclaimed control of her life, for better or worse.

Snatching her coat from the rack and putting her purse under her arm, she walked purposefully out of the office, stopping briefly at Andrea's desk.

"I'll be away from the office for the balance of the day. Any problems, call Stacy. She'll know what to do. Oh, and security will be escorting Mr. Andrews out of the building."

"Yes, Ms. Powers."

Terri stood in front of the elevator, her face resolute, her spirit determined. Her next stop was the offices of Hightower Enterprises.

Chapter 6

Clint had just hung up the phone when his secretary buzzed him on the intercom.

"Yes, Pat?"

"Mr. Steele, there's a Ms. Powers here to see you."

Clint's heart stirred with excitement. "Send her right in."

Quickly he stood up and put on his navy blue blazer and straightened his blue paisley tie. He approached the door just as Terri entered.

His full lips curved into an unconscious smile and widened in silent approval as he took in her regal, dark beauty. Her hair was swept away from her face, held in place by a wide headband, highlighting those large earthy brown eyes. The winter-white cashmere coat was flung open, revealing the flowing dress that gently brushed her curves.

He ached to take her in his arms, but his smile slowly dissolved when he saw the shadow of despair hovering in her eyes.

Immediately he crossed the room to where she stood, ready to do battle with whoever had crossed her.

"Terri, what is it?"

She took a deep breath. "May I sit down?"

"Sure." He pulled up a high-back chair for her, one for himself and sat down in front of her, his arms braced on his muscled thighs as he leaned forward.

She looked across at him, hesitant at first, but then decided to plunge right in. "I fired Mark today, along with the accountant," she said in a monotone.

Briefly Clint lowered his head, nodding in a way that let her know he understood. He looked up, his gaze holding hers. "I've had to fire my share of employees over the years, and it's never easy, especially under these circumstances. You not only feel guilt, you feel betrayed," he added softly.

Terri felt the weight slowly ease from her chest. She didn't realize until that moment how much she needed him to understand and not see her as weak and ineffectual.

"I take it Mark was the man behind-the-scenes all along?"

Terri nodded, a feeling of humiliation whipping through her, but her face remained resolute.

Clint easily saw through the facade of control. Once again he felt the overpowering need to take her in his arms, to protect her. But he sensed that wasn't what she needed or would accept. At least not now. That was one thing he was gradually learning about her—she did things in her own way, in her own time, without fanfare.

"Is there anything that I can do?"

She looked across at him, a weak smile tugging at her polished lips. "You could accept my apology."

His thick brows knitted. "Apology? For what?"

"For misjudging you. For doubting your sincerity. It's not like me to doubt people."

"Don't lose that part of yourself, Terri," he said, his voice full of warmth. "That's what makes you the wonderful woman that you are."

She looked away as though searching for words, then chuckled mirthlessly. "*That's* part of my problem. Being too trusting at the wrong times." She sighed deeply and Clint waited, knowing that she needed this time to come to a decision. One that would change the direction of their relationship. Then, as if a dam had sprung a leak, she slowly began to reveal bits and pieces of her failed marriage, her retreat from relationships as a result of Alan's infidelities and her recent revelations about Clint.

The one thing that she left out was the loss of her baby, Clint noticed, a subject that must still be too painful to discuss. In time, he thought. In time. For now, he would treasure this small gift of trust that she'd given him.

"...I was so wrong about so many things, Clint. And I always believed myself to be a fair-minded person. I let my own personal prejudices overshadow practical good sense." Her eyes leveled with his. "That was unfair to you. And when I did trust someone, it was the wrong person."

Warily Clint reached over and placed his hand on top of hers, and Terri swore that if he said anything sweet she would burst into tears.

"Thank you for that," he said, his voice a silken caress. "Thanks for trusting me enough to tell me. Just don't blame yourself. You had every reason to believe the things you did about Mark and about me."

"That doesn't excuse my behavior." She looked away, then turned to face him. "Why didn't you tell me?"

"What?" He knew what she was fishing for but refused to rise to the bait.

"About what you really do? Why do you allow the papers to print such trash about you? They have you portrayed as this vulture that would walk over anyone to get what he wants. They never print the positive results of your business endeavors and the good that you do for struggling black businesses. It's despicable."

Clint lowered his head, then looked across at her. He shrugged his shoulders. "I suppose I want to keep that part of my life private. My reputation as a hard-nosed businessman has allowed me the financial flexibility to make those contributions. Let the public think what they want about me. Inside—" he pointed a finger at his chest "—I know what I'm about. That's what's important."

Terri nodded in understanding, pressed her lips together and slowly rose. She felt totally vulnerable now, having shared some of her darkest moments and being witness to a side of Clint that she'd believed could not exist. The combination of new emotions crumbled her fragile sensibilities. She began to question her sudden spontaneity with him, realizing that it was brought on in a moment of weakness. Instinctively her defenses locked into place and she turned the subject to neutral ground. "My main concern right now is getting the company back on solid financial footing. I owe that to my staff."

Clint stood in front of her, catching a delicious whiff of her scent. He looked down into her upturned face. "How bad are things?"

Her smile was empty. "Bad enough."

"Listen, I could loan the company enough funds to get you over the hump."

Terri vehemently shook her ebony head, her locks swinging behind her. "No way. I got myself into this mess. I'll get myself out." Her voice softened, and her fingers splayed and stroked his arm. "But thank you. I appreciate the gesture."

He nodded and his admiration for her grew.

Terri pulled her coat around her and picked up her purse. "We're pretty close to clinching a deal with Viatek Studios. I feel very confident about it."

"I'm sure it will work out." His smile embraced her as he

took a cautious step closer. "With you behind it, Viatek should consider themselves lucky."

She didn't trust herself to speak, feeling the heat of his nearness engulfing her. Instead, she eased away and moved toward the door.

Clint checked his watch. "Can I take you to lunch?"

"I'm sorry. I've got some things to take care of and I'm meeting a friend in about an hour. Maybe another time?" Her question was hopeful.

"I'll call you—soon."

She smiled. "All right. Goodbye, Clint." She turned to leave.

Clint's voice held her in place. "Terri." She looked up at him, expectantly. "I'm glad that everything is out in the open. I hope that we can move on from here."

She nodded in silent agreement.

But even as he said the words, the ache of his own hidden pain and buried truths burned his guilty conscience. He needed so desperately to open the doors to the feelings that raged within him. It had been so long since he'd shared the deepest part of himself with anyone. He wasn't sure if he still knew how. For now, all he could do was watch her walk away.

Terri picked up her glass of sparkling cider and took a sip.

"So what are your plans for the company?" Lisa asked over lunch. In all of the ten years that she'd known Terri, she'd never seen her so distraught. Terri was one of the most decent people that Lisa knew and the best friend she'd ever had. Terri was the last person who deserved the things that happened to her.

Terri took a deep breath, twirling the delicate glass between her fingers. "Well, the first thing is a total review of all of the files and a revamping of the staff. Stacy will take over

Mark's responsibilities as of tomorrow. I plan to make an announcement in the morning. And of course I'll have to hire a new accountant." She gave a halfhearted grin.

Lisa nodded as she took a forkful of sautéed shrimp. "About Mark," she began slowly, "do you plan to press charges?"

Terri tossed the salad in her plate. "I thought about it, Lisa." She sighed. "But what's the point? Mark has dug his own ditch. Word travels fast in our circles. He'll never be trusted again. He's finished. That's enough punishment."

Lisa was unconvinced. "If you want my opinion, I'd say to press charges against the crummy bastard. Cutting him out of the *club* isn't enough," she added vehemently.

"I'll keep that in mind."

Lisa doubted that Terri would have a change of heart. Terri may not have been good in displaying her feelings, but she never wanted to see anyone hurt, no matter what they may have done to her. Terri kept her feelings bottled up inside, and Lisa didn't know what, or who, would ever make her change.

"So what's the progress with the advertising campaign for Viatek Studios—moving on to a more pleasant topic?"

"I'm positive we'll pull this off. If we do get it, I'll have to go to L.A."

"You don't sound too enthusiastic about the possibility." Lisa took another mouthful of her shrimp, her gaze full of question.

Terri hesitated a moment. "I was informed that Alan is being considered as the photographer." She had painstakingly tried to keep Alan in the recesses of her mind. She and Lisa had agreed after the divorce that any mention of Alan was taboo, and she regretted that the door was pried open once again.

The fork stopped midway between Lisa's mouth and the plate. "You're kidding."

"I wish I were."

"Can't Stacy handle this one?"

Terri shook her head. "No. Not really. Something this big I'd be required to deal with. There are contracts involved, and Stacy is not experienced enough in that area yet."

"So how does Alan fit in? He's not part of your package. You have your own photographer."

"I know. But Viatek has him as a subcontractor. He's worked with them before. And it seems that he's made quite a name for himself in L.A."

When was this woman gonna get a break? Lisa swore under her breath but gauged her words carefully.

"I know this may not be much of a consolation, but you've moved on with your life, Tee, and I'm sure that Alan's moved on with his."

"I'm sure he has," Terri said, her voice dripping with sarcasm. "Alan was always good for taking a situation and working it to his advantage...with someone."

Lisa took a deep breath. "Terri, what happened between you and Alan is a part of the past. There's no point in beating yourself to death about it because it didn't work out." Lisa cringed, remembering the countless warnings she had given Terri before she married Alan. He was a womanizer and as selfish as they came. But Lisa would never add salt to Terri's still-open wounds by saying, "I told you so." She had enough heartache to deal with.

"It didn't work out because of me," Terri said sadly. "Maybe if I'd been able to see past my own life and open up to accepting Alan completely in it, we'd be together today. And he wouldn't have had to go searching for what I couldn't give him."

"Don't be absurd! Alan was the consummate playboy, before and after you married him."

Lisa's temper rose as she fought to control the irritation that lifted her voice. She'd never told Terri that Alan had tried to make a play for her, too. That would have been too devastating for Terri to handle. She'd dealt with Alan herself, in no uncertain terms. She had the connections to cut the cords of his success with just one phone call. And she made sure that he knew it. It was months before he would even stay in the same room with her for more than a minute.

"My God, Terri, he had a part in it, too. A big part."

Lisa saw the veil of hurt descend over Terri's eyes.

"Listen, I'm sorry if I sound callous, but you can't keep doing this to yourself. I'm your friend, and I'd do anything in the world for you. I can't sit quietly by and see you tear yourself apart—especially over an SOB like Alan Martin."

Lisa reached across the table and took Terri's hand. Her voice lowered to a soothing whisper. "You're a wonderful person and when the time is right, that special someone is going to see it. Believe me."

Terri tried to absorb the veracity of Lisa's words. She knew Lisa was right. Alan was a bastard. But she'd loved and trusted him. She'd almost had his child. That wasn't something that you could just forget because someone told you so. Over time it had gotten easier, she had to admit. And maybe a special someone would be there to help her forget completely. A secret place in her heart hoped that the someone would be Clint.

Moments of silence passed with both women absorbed in their own private thoughts. Lisa desperately wanted to share the news of her recently discovered pregnancy with Terri, but deep inside she felt that the news would only add to Terri's misery rather than make her happy for her friend. She'd discussed it with her husband, Brian, and he'd advised against telling Terri, at least right away. Reluctantly Lisa had agreed. This was the first time in the ten years that she and Terri had been friends that she kept something this special from her. The feeling left her empty and a little melancholy. She searched for something to say to ease the tension-filled silence.

"Were you able to use the information I gave you on Clinton

Steele?" Lisa asked finally. She instantly noticed the faraway look that passed across Terri's face and the faint smile that tugged at her lips. *Interesting.*

"Yes. Thanks," Terri said softly.

Lisa's brown eyes creased into a taunt as she leaned forward and ran a hand through her mop of auburn curls. "Come on, tell…tell."

"There's nothing to tell."

"Don't give me that. I'd know that little smirk of yours any day. So?"

"All right, all right. Just don't beg," Terri teased, itching to tell her friend about Clint.

She paused for a moment to collect her thoughts. She began slowly. "Well, at first, I had real misgivings about him. Everything that I had ever heard or read was negative. Hightower Enterprises was notorious for buying up smaller companies, and that's how he built his fortune—along with very wise investments in the stock market and profits from the companies." She laughed a self-deprecating laugh. "Little did I know that Mr. Steele never took control of the companies, but helped to rebuild them for the owners. And when they were back on solid ground, Clint turned the reins back to the original owners if they decided that they wanted them. A lot of them didn't, of course, preferring to put that part of their lives behind them—"

"It's a shame," Lisa interjected, "that the media never tells that part of the story. They only publicize the buyouts, but not the positive end results. If you hadn't asked me to investigate him, I wouldn't have known myself. He actually started out as a runner on Wall Street. He's a remarkable man, Terri. Huge amounts of his profits go to the black colleges, universities and community organizations."

"I know. The worst part is that I fell right into step with the bad press, eating up every word. And he never said a thing to me. He just let me believe those things about him, too proud to tell me anything different. He said he preferred to keep that side of his life private." Terri sucked on her bottom lip, disappointed in herself.

"So—where do things stand between the two of you now?"

A slow smile lifted Terri's lips. "Well, I never thought I'd be interested in anyone again, Lisa." Her eyes roamed off into the distance. "But there's just something about Clint that reeks of stability, honesty and a magnetism that I can't shake." She wrapped her arms around herself as if to gather the warm feelings closer to her body. "He's very intense and I know very protective of his private life. He presents this rough, macho exterior to the world, but I've seen the vulnerability in his eyes. I've heard the gentleness in his voice. I think he's just afraid to show anyone that he has any weaknesses, as if it could be used against him somehow. In that way we're a lot alike." She turned to look Lisa fully in the face, a radiant glow illuminating her features.

"It sounds as if it may be a lot more than that," Lisa gently probed.

Terri's gaze drifted away. "There are still so many things I have to work out, Lis, before I could even consider a real relationship again." She took a breath. "In the meantime, I still have my company and my career. That's what's important now."

Lisa heard the hollow lack of conviction that permeated Terri's voice. Her painful marriage to Alan had changed her. And Lisa slowly realized that the company and a career were no longer enough to fill Terri's life.

The only sounds that could be heard were the grunts and groans of the two men and the crack of the ball as it hit the racket.

Clint slammed the tiny black sphere against the wall with all of the force of a speeding train, whizzing it past Steve on its return. Steve lunged for the ball with his racket and slapped it back with equal force.

The game had been going on for nearly an hour, and the two men were drenched in sweat. Clint's rock-hard thighs bulged and tensed as he jetted back and forth across the marble court, playing like a man possessed. With each swing he tried to annihilate his frustration and rid his mind and body of Terri.

Terri.

That's all he could think about nonstop since she'd left his office a week ago, he realized grimly as he darted after the spinning ball. She seemed to creep into his subconscious when he least expected it. Like now. And he couldn't stand it. He hadn't called her or tried seeing her to maybe give her some space, and she'd made no attempt to contact him. The stalemate bruised his male ego and frustrated the hell out of him.

The ball spun past him on a return volley from Steve, and the game ended.

"Whew! How did you let that one get away from you, man?" Steve gasped, trotting over to Clint and patting him on the shoulder.

"I don't know," Clint grumbled, snatching a towel from on top of his bag. He roughly wiped his face, his breathing barely noticeable.

Steve reached for his own towel and draped it around his neck. He faced Clint, puffing hard. "You want to tell me what's buggin' you?"

Clint grabbed his gym bag and strode across the court toward the exit, ignoring Steve's question. "I'm going to the steam room," he threw over his shoulder. He stomped away, pushing through the swinging doors.

The two friends sat shoulder to shoulder in the steam-filled room, watching the ghostly images of the health club's patrons sitting in various positions. Steve knew Clint well enough to know not to push him. He'd open up in his own time. He always did. And Steve would be ready to listen.

Clint lowered his head, trying to form the words that were causing chaos in his life. Steve was the one person that he had confided in about his growing feelings for Terri. Periodically he grudgingly had to admit that he respected Steve's opinion. It was several long moments before Clint began to talk.

"It's hard to let go again, Steve," Clint began, his voice heavy with old guilt. He lowered his head. "Ever since Desiree, I just—"

Steve cut him off. "There's no way that you could have prevented what happened to Desiree. It wasn't your fault."

"It was my fault." He shook his head, pressing his palms against his eyes as the old wounds seeped open. "It was because of me."

"You don't know that."

Clint shot up from his perch. "Of course I know. Desiree took those pills because of me." He slapped his hand against his bare chest. "She got behind the wheel because of me!"

Steve looked up at his friend and saw the marks of guilt sear a path across Clint's face. "So your answer is to block out everything and wallow in a life of martyrdom? Is that supposed to make it right?"

Clint sliced hardened eyes toward Steve. "It's the only way I know how to be."

"It's the way you want to be. Haven't you learned anything?"

The question tore at Clint's gut. He visibly flinched but said nothing.

Steve continued to speak, but with a patience and wisdom that astounded Clint. "You've lived with this self-imposed guilt for three years, and I've watched it turn you into someone I hardly know. You've let it affect your relationship with your own daughter, man!" Steve's usual mild manner shifted to anger.

"Ashley doesn't understand that it hurts you to be around because she reminds you of Desiree. She's just four years old. A baby. Your baby! And Jillianne is no substitute for you, even if she is Desi's sister."

Steve took a long calming breath, searching for the words to shake some sense into his lifelong friend.

"For the first time in those three years I've finally seen you really care about someone again." He let out a breath. "Not many of us get a second chance. Don't blow it. If Terri is the one you want, you have to let her know, and stop playing these macho power games with her. The only person you're fooling is yourself. And by the looks of you, you haven't done too good of a job at that, either."

Slowly Steve rose from the bench and clasped Clint on the shoulder, leaving him in the steam-filled room to sort out his turbulent thoughts.

Chapter 7

Terri and Stacy sat huddled over the round work desk in Mark's vacated office, putting together the final touches on the Viatek deal.

"I think that we should push the youth angle on this one," Stacy advised. "Since the director is in his early twenties, I'm sure that would be a great selling point."

Terri nodded, nibbling on the tip of her pen as she spoke. "We'll outline a thorough media saturation pushing that idea."

"I'll place some feelers out to the wire services, magazines and morning talk shows," Stacy added, "and see who bites."

"That will definitely be a factor for the Viatek Board to consider if we can drum up a large interest from the media beforehand. You get on it, and let me know something definite by the end of the week. I want to tie the knot with them as soon as possible."

Stacy rose, tossing her sheet of golden hair behind her

shoulder. "I never got a chance to say thanks." She slipped off her designer glasses, her green eyes sparkling.

Terri looked up, perplexed. "Thanks?"

"For giving me the promotion and for having the confidence in me to handle the job."

"Stacy, there's no question in my mind that you're the best person for the job. You have both the talent and the experience. You deserve it."

Stacy lowered her eyes, the depth of sincerity in Terri's words filling her with pride. Terri had given her a break when she needed it. Stacy had pounded the pavement for months before she'd landed the job with Powers, Inc. At every ad agency that she'd interviewed with, the first thing the male owners thought was that she'd be quick and easy—and some weren't very subtle in their comments. They never took into consideration that behind her cover-girl looks there was a brain and talent.

Disgusted and disillusioned, she'd been ready to pack her bags and return to North Carolina when she spotted the help-wanted notice placed by Powers, Inc. The ad said that they were looking for a public-relations specialist—Stacy had leaped at the chance. But after talking with Terri, who was so impressed with her qualifications and educational background, Terri designed a position specifically for her: director of promotions. Now, less than three years later, she was vice president at one of the fastest-growing and most innovative advertising agencies in the city.

Stacy looked across at Terri, a mischievous light dancing in her green eyes. "In that case…" Stacy smiled brightly, looking around her new office with a sense of really belonging "…can I do some redecorating?"

Both women tossed their heads back and laughed.

"Go for it," Terri answered, delighted. "Give Tempest Dailey a call. I'm sure she'd love to make your visions a reality."

* * *

Terri headed back to her own office, for the first time in quite a while feeling positive about the future. A confident smile lit her face as she passed Andrea's desk.

"Oh, Ms. Powers."

Terri halted. "Yes, Andrea?"

Andrea flipped through her message pad and tore off a message. "This call just came in for you." She handed Terri the green-and-white slip of paper.

Terri looked down at the neat scrawl, and Clint's name leaped out at her. She forced her hand not to shake.

"Thank you," she said, never revealing the exhilaration she was feeling.

Terri walked into her office, gently closing the door behind her. Please Call was checked off. Her heart thudded as she stared at the phone.

She reached for the phone, then stopped midway. Did she really want to pursue a relationship with Clint? She'd forced herself not to call him, much as she'd wanted to. She knew that she needed time to sort out her feelings about him and where their relationship was going. And she hadn't heard a word from him since that day in his office, even though he'd promised that he'd call her. She'd felt inexplicably abandoned at first, but then decided it was just as well. But now—

Abruptly she paced the office. She tugged on her bottom lip with her teeth, her arms wrapped around her waist. What was the harm in a phone call? At least she wouldn't have to look into those eyes that seemed to read her very soul.

Briefly she shut her eyes, and she heard the low rumble of his voice vibrate through her, and the air seemed to fill with his manly scent.

This was ridiculous, she thought, opening her eyes and turning toward the phone. It was only a phone call, she concluded, listening to that part of her that eagerly wanted to hear his voice again.

She reached for the phone just as the intercom buzzed.

"Yes, Andrea?"

"Mr. Steele is on line two."

She swallowed. "Thank you."

Terri took a deep breath and pressed the flashing red light.

"Clint," she breathed, "I was just getting ready to return your call."

"I thought I'd save you the trouble. How are you, Terri?"

The question was so simple, his voice so gentle, yet it aroused the complexity of how she was truly feeling. She couldn't begin to explain.

"I'm just fine. And yourself?"

"I wanted to know if your offer was still open," he said, his voice gently teasing.

"My offer? What on earth are you talking about?"

His voice dropped to a low throb. "Showing your appreciation for my offer to bail you out."

Terri felt her body go rigid with indignation. Clint heard the quick intake of breath and the unsaid, "How dare you?" in the brief silence that followed. He chuckled.

Terri opened her mouth to lash out a retort, but Clint cut her off. "I only wanted to know if you'd care to accompany me to City Center tomorrow night."

Terri felt her body slowly relax, and she envisioned the smile that must surely be brimming on his devilishly handsome face.

"Very funny." She tried to sound admonishing but failed miserably.

Clint's burst of hearty laughter was infectious, and she found herself laughing in answer.

By degrees the merriment ceased, and Clint's pulsing voice filtered through the lines. "How about it? The Dance Theater of Harlem is appearing."

Terri's eyes lit up. "Really! Oh, I love them. I studied

with Arthur Mitchell for a while. They're fabulous," she enthused.

Clint grinned, enjoying her elation. "So I can take that as a no?"

"Don't be a wise guy. I'd love to go," she agreed happily.

"Should I pick you up at home or at the office? The show starts at eight, but I thought we could go to dinner first."

"That sounds wonderful. Why don't you meet me at the office. It'll save time. Is six good?"

"Perfect. I'll see you then, Terri."

Terri spent a fitful night anticipating the next evening with Clint. Every time she thought of him, her heart raced at breakneck speed and her eyes flew back open.

Finally, unable to rest, she rose from her bed, sat in the center of her bedroom floor with her legs crossed.

She closed her eyes and inhaled deeply until her breathing became slow and regular. She forced her mind to cleanse itself of troubling thoughts and began to visualize the lapping waves of the ocean, which always had a soothing effect on her.

Inch by inch she tightened then relaxed each muscle of her body, beginning with her toes all the way up to her head, which she slowly rotated.

After twenty minutes of meditation, she crawled into bed and was asleep within moments, to awaken the following morning feeling refreshed and invigorated.

The day sped by and before she realized it, six o'clock was rapidly approaching.

Quickly she straightened up her desk and collected her belongings, wondering all the while if Clint would like the outfit she had selected.

Slipping into her cream-colored wool cape, she picked up her purse and headed for the elevator. With each footfall, she commanded her heart to be still.

She walked across the lobby toward the exit. Clint was

there waiting, looking for all the world as if he'd just stepped off the cover of *Ebony Man Magazine*. All of her preparation to quiet her jangling nerves was a complete fiasco when his heart-stopping smile embraced her.

"You look fabulous," Clint crooned, planting a smoldering kiss on her cheek. His eyes swept admiringly over her magenta palazzo pants of wool crepe with a matching trapeze jacket. He took her arm and guided her toward the revolving doors.

"Your chariot awaits, madam." He gave a mock bow and Terri smiled up at him, fully realizing that she had never felt happier.

They spent a glorious evening together with Terri intermittently telling Clint tales of her dance-school days and relaying hilarious stories of her budding dance students. Clint animatedly recounted the days of his youth as a stock clerk in the local supermarket and the eccentric customers that frequented the central Harlem store.

That evening signaled a major turning point in their relationship, and they both sensed a new level of awareness in each other. Even the simple things that they shared took on new meaning. A mere brush of fingers was electrifying. A look spoke volumes. From that night they tried to spend all of their free time together, from racquetball, which Clint taught Terri with relish, to bike riding.

"Race you around the park," Terri challenged as they walked their bikes up to the entrance to Central Park's bike trail the following morning.

"You're on," he retorted with a wicked grin and suddenly zoomed out ahead of her.

Terri threw her leg over the seat and took off after him, yelling, "Cheater! Cheater!"

Clint threw his head back and roared with laughter even as she gained on him with startling speed. He enjoyed her competitive nature and her willingness to try new things. He even sat in on some of her dance classes and was amazed at her talent and her gentleness with her young students. As he witnessed her patience with them and the love and admiration that each of them had for her, he longed for his own daughter, and realized that he wanted Terri as a permanent fixture in his life. He'd have to find a way to tell her about his past and about Ashley, soon.

The more time that Terri spent with Clint, the more she realized all that they had in common. And Clint understood day by day that the budding feelings he had for Terri were in full bloom and pulsing with life. Their relationship steadily tread on new tempting territory, and the thrill of the unknown lent an intensity to their being together that was almost too much to withstand. Even so, Terri was completely thrown off by Clint's pointed invitation.

"I have a small cabin in the Poconos," Clint stated one evening over dinner. His voice took on a smooth storytelling tone. "It's a great place—wood-burning fireplace, snowcapped mounts in the background, good food, dancing and plenty of indoor activities for nonskiers."

"It sounds great," Terri said, leaning back in the kitchen chair and eyeing him speculatively.

"I was planning on spending Thanksgiving weekend up there."

Her spirits instantly sank. She had hoped that they would spend the holidays together. She'd become used to Clint being a euphoric fixture in her life. The prospect of spending the holiday alone wilted her spirit. But she kept her disappointment well hidden.

She slowly rose from her seat and took the dishes into the kitchen, carefully avoiding Clint's all-seeing eyes.

"You'll be joining me," he said, as though it were an already moot point.

Terri nearly dropped the dishes in the sink. She turned cool, confident eyes on him, totally in contrast to the wave of apprehension that flooded her. "Go away with you?" she asked, with a calmness that stunned her. "For the weekend?"

"I know you heard me," Clint said, rising from his seat and closing the distance between them in three fluid strides. He stood a breath away, and Terri felt the blood rush to her head and cloud her vision when she looked up at him. He lifted her chin with his index finger and held her eyes with his own. "So stop trying to stall for time."

She eased back until she was pressed against the sink. Her thoughts raced. The implication of any answer from her, one way or the other, would assuredly change the direction of their relationship—permanently. Was she ready? Yes, an inner voice whispered. Yes.

She straightened her shoulders, tilting her head to the side, her eyes taking on a smoky hue. Her voice dropped to a titillating whisper. "What day did you want to leave?"

Clint lowered his head by inches, his ebony eyes boring into her own. His powerful arms slipped around her, pulling her slender body fully against the hard lines of his. Slowly his mouth opened to cover hers.

"How about right now?" he groaned into her mouth as her silken tongue stroked hungrily across his lips.

Chapter 8

In silent amusement, Lisa sat on the chaise lounge with her long legs crossed at the ankle, watching Terri scurry around her bedroom.

"What should I take?" Terri moaned, after having already deposited half of her wardrobe on her bed.

"Why don't you just take everything?" Lisa advised. "Then you'll be sure to have the right outfit."

Terri halted, swung around and saw the taunting smile. She turned dark eyes on Lisa, her hands planted firmly on her hips. "I thought you were here to help me. Not torment me with lousy jokes."

Lisa cracked up laughing, seeing the pained expression on Terri's dark face.

"You look like you have it together to me, girlfriend. You just need a bigger suitcase."

Terri rolled her eyes and sucked her teeth, a trait she'd inherited from her grandmother and doled out to those who really rubbed her the wrong way.

"You really vex me, ya know," Terri said, easily slipping into dialect, something she hadn't forgotten even after more than twenty years in the States. "Ya good fer nuttin' except to give me a hard way to go." Terri spun around in a huff and collapsed faceup across her bed, her mound of clothes fanning out around her.

"What am I going to do, Lis?" Terri whined.

Lisa sighed and pulled herself up from her resting spot with some difficulty, intending to put some order to the mess that Terri had created.

Terri eyed her curiously. "Are you putting on weight, or is it my imagination?"

Lisa knew she couldn't duck the inevitable forever. She was already having trouble fitting into her clothes, and Terri would have to know sooner or later.

Lisa pressed her lips together before she spoke and ran her fingers through her hair.

"You're not imagining things," she said softly. "I'm pregnant."

Terri felt a tightness in her chest and a momentary flicker of jealousy. Her own loss rekindled with painful intensity. But just as quickly as it had taken hold, it was released. Terri popped up from the bed and ran over to where Lisa stood and heartily embraced her.

"Oh, Lis, I'm so happy for you." She pressed a kiss to her friend's cheek. "I know this is something that you and Brian have wanted for so long."

Terri took a step back and peered down at Lisa's rounding stomach. "How many weeks?"

Lisa swallowed. "Two and a half months."

Terri frowned in confusion. "Two and a half months? You just found out?"

Slowly Lisa shook her head. "I knew a few weeks ago."

Hurt and disappointment filled her voice. "Then—why didn't you tell me?"

Lisa reached for Terri and braced her arms. Her eyes pleaded with her to understand. "I didn't want to upset you. After everything that you'd been through with Alan and then the baby... I just thought..."

Terri's voice shook. "Lis, I would never begrudge you your big moment." She shook her head in amazement. "Even at the happiest time in your life, you thought about my feelings." Tears filled her eyes, but Terri blinked them away and sniffed. "You're some friend."

"You're not mad at me?" Lisa asked with caution.

"Of course not, silly. So long as I can be godmother."

Lisa beamed with relief. "Absolutely! Who else?"

"When's the big day?"

"The fifteenth of June."

"Time will go by so fast, you won't even realize it." Even as she spoke, the loss of her own baby loomed before her, and the emptiness threatened to engulf her once again. Swallowing the knot of pain, she steered her thoughts onto a happier trail.

"Well, since you're not going to be much use to me, before you know it, I'd better get all I can out of you while the going is good. Help me sort through these clothes!"

On the surface everything appeared to be the same between them. They chatted merrily, and Lisa teased Terri mercilessly as they selected Terri's wardrobe for her long-weekend rendezvous. But deep inside they both realized that they had moved into different worlds. A place they could no longer share, and the silent understanding of that reality left a hollow emptiness that echoed soundlessly in the room.

After Lisa left Terri's apartment to return home, Terri prepared a basket of food for the two-hour drive.

She filled a thermos with herbal tea, arranged a platter of fruit, chips, whole-wheat crackers and assorted dips, and placed it all in a wicker basket.

She checked her watch. Clint wanted them to be on their

way by three o'clock in order to arrive before the rush, and give themselves time to get settled. He would be arriving in moments. She smiled. Clint had become such a familiar face over the preceding weeks that he was like a member of the family in the small six-tenant building.

Her pulse raced as she imagined the next five days—alone—with Clint.

She inhaled deeply, willing herself to be calm. Since the evening he'd asked her to go away with him, she'd been in a constant state of flux—exhilarated one minute and terrified the next. She couldn't count how many times she'd almost called him to back out. But desire and a deep-seated yearning for fulfillment would take over.

As a result she had made an appointment with her doctor and had a thorough exam. Dr. Walters said that Terri was in excellent health and that the miscarriage had not caused any lasting effects. Although Dr. Walters had advised Terri to take it slow, she'd assured Terri that she was just fine.

They discussed birth control and Terri was given a prescription, but the doctor strongly cautioned Terri to use additional protection for at least the first two weeks.

Even as she thought about it, her stomach fluttered. Her life was rapidly changing, moving in a completely new and hopefully positive direction. She had to put her past behind her and start fresh, she resolved. She could only dare to hope that Clint would remain a part of that future.

Terri took a quick look around her bedroom and spotted the stacks of notes and articles she'd gotten from the library. She made a mental note to get rid of them when she returned. Satisfied that she hadn't forgotten anything, she picked up her suitcase, walked into the living room and placed the bag in the foyer just as the doorbell rang.

For several unbelievably long seconds, she stood there staring at the door, wondering what in the world she was getting herself into. The second ring jolted her into action. She pulled open the door and when she looked up at Clint's smiling face, all of the anxiety seemed to melt away, replaced by a burning longing that she knew would be totally satisfied.

"I know you like jazz," Clint commented, giving Terri a sidelong glance as he shifted into Third gear, "but I guarantee you'll love this." He leaned over and popped a CD into the player.

Seconds later the symphonic rhythms of Harry Connick Jr. filled the Benz. Terri closed her eyes. The quality was so crystal clear she could imagine herself in the concert hall with the young impresario in command of the orchestra.

Clint took a quick glance in her direction, satisfied by the grin that had spread across her face.

"Like?"

"Like," she said happily. "I've heard some of his work, but I haven't had time to pick up the CD. It's fabulous."

Clint's low voice reached out and stroked her. "There's more fabulous things where that came from."

Terri instantly felt a rush of heat sweep through her as she thought wickedly to herself, *You don't know how right you are.*

Clint only hoped that he could keep the demons of his past safely locked away.

Terri was beyond impressed as Clint gallantly bowed when he opened the door to his hideaway. The cabin was more fantastic than Clint described.

The first thing that caught the eye was the breathtaking view of the mountains seen through the enormous window that swept across one entire side of the cabin. Adding to the ambience were the redwood rafters that majestically complemented the natural atmosphere, while giving the inhabitants a sense of home and comfort.

The polished wood floors gleamed, covered in areas with

fluffy throw rugs, huge floor pillows and a large fur rug that sat directly in front of the fireplace.

Terri stepped into the front room and looked around in wonder, taking in the wood and Italian leather furniture. Slowly she strolled into the inviting space and felt instantly at home.

The entire layout was a combination of rustic and ultra-modern. The kitchen, which was directly to the right of the living area, was something straight out of *Architectural Digest*. Every electronic gadget known to man must have been installed. And it was spacious enough to have a helping hand in there without regretting it.

"Let me show you the upstairs," Clint offered.

Terri followed Clint up the wooden spiral staircase. The entire second floor was embraced by a balcony. From any room you could step out and look down onto the ground floor. It was magnificent.

"The bathroom is down the hall." Clint walked in the direction of the guest bathroom, opened the door and flicked on the light.

The perfect-looking room was done all in light green and white, with matching towels, rugs and curtains, and recessed lighting that gave the cool-green tiles a warm glow.

"Very nice," Terri commented softly.

Clint turned to his left and opened the next door. "This is the guest bedroom."

The room was warm and cozy, seeming to beg the visitor to step inside and stay awhile. The huge four-poster bed was covered with a multicolored quilt that looked as if it had been hand sewn with love, with overstuffed pillows that you could sink into. The hardwood floors were covered with a thick ecru-colored carpet. Two large windows draped in sheer white chiffon, with an overlay of crushed velvet that matched the carpet, opened onto a small balcony overlooking the ski village. There was a dresser topped with all of the basic toiletries, a nightstand, a large television and a small fireplace, which added the finishing touch.

"I love it. Who did the decorating?"

The question momentarily threw him off. He and Desiree had purchased the cabin the year before their marriage and had tirelessly decorated every inch of it themselves. After her death, Clint had slowly begun to replace items, change color schemes, and eventually gave the place a new look. He knew that he would not have been able to continue to come here if the memories remained.

"I did."

Terri's eyebrows rose in question and in appreciation. "And you say I'm talented." She pointed a playful finger at his chest. "I think you may be in the wrong profession. Well, now that I'm suitably shocked, show me the rest of this *cabin*."

Clint chuckled at the barb. "Right this way." Several feet away was the master bedroom. Clint swung open the door and stepped to the side to give Terri a full view.

The master suite was sprawling. In this room the hardwood floors were covered in a plush midnight-blue carpet. Sitting in the center of the room was a lavish, king-size, four-poster bed made of solid oak. The coverings were in the same midnight-blue with gold-and-white throw pillows. All of the furnishings appeared to be hand carved from the same polished oak. The large bay window was draped in a sheer blue chiffon, trimmed in a brilliant gold that was repeated throughout the room. One wall contained a built-in bookcase that overflowed with volumes of work, next to which sat an elaborate state-of-the-art computer system.

Stepping into the room, Terri saw that it had its own private bath, with a built-in Jacuzzi. Once again, Terri came face-to-face with Clint's unrestrained tastes. He demanded the best from himself and everyone that came in contact with him, and that ideology transferred itself into his living space. Everything was just perfect, almost larger, better, than real life.

The realization suddenly frightened her, and she wondered if he would expect the extraordinary from her, as well.

Clint eased up behind her and slid his arms around her waist, dispelling the disturbing thoughts. He lowered his head and planted tiny, tempting kisses along her neck. A shiver of delight raced up Terri's spine as she arched her neck, inviting the sensation of his taunting mouth.

"Which room would you prefer?" he asked in a throaty whisper.

Her heart raced. She wasn't going to make it that easy on him. She turned into his embrace and looked up into his ebony eyes. A slow, seductive smile curved her lips, her lids lowered.

Clint's pulse quickened.

"The guest room is just perfect," she said softly. She waited for his reaction and was mildly disappointed. If there was any degree of surprise by her response, Clint hid it well.

He smiled. "Of course." Slowly he released her and stepped back. "I thought we could drive into town about seven. There's a great club that serves excellent seafood." He turned to leave, then said over his shoulder, "Dress casual."

While Terri adjusted to her new surroundings, the soft trill of music seemed to mysteriously float into her room. She looked around to all of the obvious locations in search of speakers. Her eyes trailed across the room and then upward to discover four hidden speakers tucked neatly into the wall above the oak molding.

Slowly she shook head in amusement. Clint certainly knew how to live, and she wondered what other secrets lay hidden within the enchanting hideaway.

Clint returned to the lower level of the rambling abode. He lit the fire in the hearth, adjusted the volume of the music that flowed throughout the house, then began going through the cabinets and refrigerator to see if they were stocked to his satisfaction. He had left specific instructions with the middle-aged woman who came in weekly to check on things and straighten up. He was pleased to see that his instructions had been followed to the letter.

Satisfied that everything was in order, he decided to fix himself a light drink before changing for dinner.

He crossed the spacious living area to stand in front of the window, leaning casually against the wide beam, sipping a glass of white wine.

He stared unseeing at the swell of the hills and mountains that jutted erotically upward toward the heavens as one eager for a loving caress. He watched the maneuvers of a lone car as it threaded its way around the winding turns, which had been known to be treacherous, and down into the village below. Without warning, images of Desiree loomed before him, as real as if she'd stood by his side.

Swiftly the visions took hold, and his mind sped on a whirlwind of events that he had tried so desperately to forget.

It was four months after Ashley was born, and he and Desiree had decided to get away for the weekend. Their marriage was in trouble. Clint knew it, and Desiree demanded that they do something about it.

They'd been at the cabin for less than an hour when Desiree started in on him. She'd been doing that a lot, and it was driving him crazy. The doctor had assured him that it was postpartum depression and she'd get over it. Clint was seriously beginning to doubt it. The more she complained about his not being home, the more he stayed away, which compounded their already growing problem.

It was his fault, she'd accused over and again, her silken mane of chestnut hair swinging around her shoulders as she paced restlessly across the floor. Her hazel eyes blazed. He didn't have time for her or their infant daughter, she'd cried. Things were just so consuming at work, he'd argued. Why couldn't she understand? He loved her. Didn't she realize that? He didn't know how to love anyone other than himself and his work, she'd railed. There wasn't room in his life for anything else.

She'd stormed off to their bedroom, locking the door, refusing to let him in. After an hour of banging and begging her to listen, he'd finally given up and gone downstairs.

He'd tossed his weary body on the leather couch. He was so tired. Tired of the arguments, tired of the way things were between them. Maybe even tired of what he'd become.

He hadn't known how long he lay there, thinking of the things Desiree had said. He'd thrown his arm across his eyes and tried to convince himself that he was right. But even to him, his explanations began to sound weak. Suddenly nothing was clear. Where had he gone wrong? He'd worked hard to get to where he was, and he lavished his wealth on his beautiful wife and daughter. He'd married his college sweetheart, and he'd made a solemn vow that she'd never again have to suffer the ravages of poverty. Her mother had worked two jobs to raise Desiree and her older sister, Jillianne. She never knew her father. They grew up in the tenements of Harlem, but the hard life never toughened up Desiree. Instead it made her insecure, needy, always seeking assurances and comfort. Clint was her knight in shining armor. She needed him and Clint needed just that.

His goal—to make the best life possible for his beloved Desiree—was all consuming. As a result, she had everything anyone could ever ask for. A beautiful home, clothes, cars, bank accounts, luxury trips. So why was she so unhappy? She had everything.

And just as exhaustion had threatened to consume him, he'd heard the soft whisper of reality struggle to the surface. *Everything except you.*

The next thing he'd remembered was waking up to absolute stillness. His head snapped up from the couch when he'd realized that he'd dozed off. He tried to collect his fuzzy thoughts, knowing that he had to talk with Desiree. She was right.

Slowly over the years he had built a world and a life that he no longer shared with her. That wasn't part of their plan, their dream. Desiree needed him, more than the furs, the jewelry, the money. How many times had she said that and he had not heard her? It was just so hard for him to express his feelings. He'd never been shown tenderness in his youth. His father had instilled in him that real men didn't show their feelings. Women needed men to be strong and take care of the family. Words and acts of affection were for women. He didn't want to lose his wife and he knew he would if he didn't change.

He pulled himself up, swinging his long legs onto the floor. A sense of peace had filled him, and he'd believed that everything was going to be different. He could make it different. Hadn't he always been the master of his fate and ultimately Desiree's, as well?

Quickly he'd bounded up the spiral stairs, a sense of purpose putting a lightness in his step.

He'd halted abruptly at the top of the staircase, a haunting sensation of foreboding rooting him to the ground.

The bedroom door was open. The room was dark, and he knew deep in his gut that Desiree was gone.

His body had jerked with dread when the shrill ringing of the phone reverberated throughout the cabin, and his world as he knew it came to a complete end.

"Clint..."

Clint spun around, dark raging clouds swimming in his eyes. Her breath caught and for the barest instant, Terri was frightened.

"Terri." His voice sounded strangled, almost as though he hadn't expected to see her standing there.

"Are you all right?" She took a cautious step closer.

Clint fought back the urge to sweep her into his arms and

exorcise his pain. Instead, the facade that he'd mastered so well slipped easily back in place.

"Yeah, sure. I'm fine. Just thinking…about…work."

"Oh." She nodded, somewhat mollified but not totally convinced. She took a step closer and reached out to touch him. His insides twisted.

The gentleness of her touch almost did him in. He couldn't let her see him break down or be weak. He had to be strong—always. Wasn't that what his father had always said? "You'll never get anywhere in this world, boy, being no weaklin'." The words still haunted him. But Terri was changing him in subtle ways, day by day, and he was afraid of the weakness, the vulnerability, that was sure to follow.

He brushed a light kiss across her lips. "Your outfit is perfect," he complimented smoothly, skillfully camouflaging his confusion. "Can I fix you anything before I change?"

"No. Thanks. I'm saving my appetite." She flashed him a smile that made the rhythm of his heart pick up a beat.

"Is that a threat?" he teased.

Instantly he held up his hands to ward off the onslaught of miniature blows that Terri rained upon his muscled body. He collapsed on the couch in a hysterical heap, pulling Terri solidly down on top of him.

But the frivolity slowly dissolved, and the deep rumble of his laughter softened into a provocative smile. His eyes darkened with dangerous lights, racing across her exquisite face. "I'm falling in love with you, Terri," he whispered roughly. "It seems that I've waited all of my life for you—for this moment to show you how much."

Elation surged through her veins as she trembled from the awesomeness of his confession. "Clint, I—"

"Shh. No words. Not now. Not yet." Terri held her breath when his hand clasped her head, pulling her slowly toward his waiting mouth.

She'd come to know these lips, the velvet feel of his tongue as it traced the cavern of her mouth. She'd savored the taste of him, felt the sensation of his kisses that thrilled her to her toes. She'd felt it all before.

This was different. There was an urgency, a yearning, a fire between them that was burning out of control—something that neither of them had permitted before, until now. And she felt the power of it in every fiber of her being. She shivered when the balls of his fingers played a concerto up and down her spine, compelling her to press deeper against the hard contours of his body—only to feel his undeniable arousal pulse steadily against her thigh.

Clint moaned almost painfully against her mouth, his fingers pressing into her back as he seductively ground his hips against her.

Terri's thoughts ran in chaotic disarray when Clint's hand slipped beneath her blouse. Her body shuddered when he pulled his lips away from hers, only to trail heated kisses along her neck, causing her to gasp with pleasure.

Her spontaneous reaction stirred him further, and he intensified his ministrations, caressing her full breasts in his palms. Her heartrending moan filled the music-soaked air, then floated away in a sensual melody.

Terri closed her eyes against the tumult of powerful sensations that ripped through her at his touch. The tips of her breasts hardened above his fingertips, sending ripples of raw electricity shooting through him. He locked her snugly in his arms, rising with her as he stood and carried her across the floor in front of the fireplace.

Gently he lowered them both to the thick fur rug, partially covering her body with his weight.

He unbuttoned her silk blouse one tiny button at a time, while he basked in the flame of desire that danced in her eyes. With each button that came open, Clint placed a searing kiss on the exposed skin that beckoned to him. The prolonged anticipation was almost unbearable, but Terri knew that Clint was determined to take his time. Even if it took all night.

And it seemed that's exactly what was happening as the tip of Clint's tongue mercilessly sought out the hollow of her ear, and he whispered erotic, soothing, unintelligible sounds that flooded through her in waves.

Practiced hands freed her of the silk top and expertly removed the matching shirt and all beneath. Within moments, she lay bare and breathtaking before him, and he realized with awe that he had never seen such exquisite beauty.

She was an artist's treasure, with full high breasts that reached toward him longingly. Her flat stomach tapered to an hourglass waist, flaring outward to rounded hips and down to endlessly long dancer's legs.

Clint groaned, an almost physical agony gripping him as he lowered his head to suckle the sugar-tipped breasts and temper his thirst for her.

Terri's breathing escalated into short, stilted breaths as Clint lovingly stroked every inch of her body with his hungry mouth.

She pulled him to her, teasing his back with long sensuous strokes from slender fingers. Terri whispered his name over and again as wave upon wave of pleasure shot through her.

Slowly Clint rose above her and piece by piece shed his clothing, to hover naked above her.

Her breath caught as the firelight danced off his well-honed physique. The raw power of his body was almost terrifying. Hard, rippling muscle defined every inch of his massive frame. Gingerly she caressed the bulging biceps of his arms, causing him to shudder with pleasure.

Deliberately her hands traveled downward over his taut belly, seeking out the core of his arousal.

Clint's eyes slammed shut as he reared back in ecstasy. "Oh, God," he groaned. The butter-soft fingers boldly enveloped him, nearly throwing him over the edge.

Hungrily his mouth covered hers, cutting off her cry as he joined them as one.

Millions of tiny lights seemed to explode at once, igniting every nerve in her body, as Clint found refuge within the honey-soaked walls.

She clung to him, wrapping her long legs around his waist while reality collided with fantasy. How long had it been since she'd felt such intense wanting—such a need to be connected and thoroughly loved? She gave herself to him—totally, willingly, irrevocably—welcoming the multitude of sensations that rocked her. "Clint," she whispered over and again, dizzy from the power of his thrusts into her welcoming body. "Love me some more," she moaned.

Together they found their own perfect rhythm, beating, moving steadily toward the pinnacle of complete satisfaction.

The flames from the hearth danced and sparked in a frenzy as though enchanted by the vision of loving before them. The overburdened heavens filled with moisture while the clouds rolled in competing formation, spilling onto the waiting hills and valleys, saturating the starving earth with a blanket of pure milky white, only to be swallowed up by the heat of their passion.

Terri's climactic cries of release were met by Clint's carnal response, taking them soaring upward to the mountaintop and over into the valley of total, unsurpassed bliss.

They clung together as one, nestled in the cushiony warmth of spent lovers, dinner all but forgotten. Terri had never felt so complete, so secure as she felt Clint's heart beat steadily against hers. This was what it was all about, she thought, pure happiness filling her. "I love you, Clinton Steele," she whispered, seconds before she drifted off into a satisfied sleep.

Chapter 9

"I'm starved," Clint mumbled wickedly in Terri's ear, stirring her out of a magnificent sleep. He pulled her closer, nuzzling her neck. "And I know just what'll satisfy my craving."

Tiny giggles bubbled up from her throat, while Clint ran his hands down her bare hips and nipped at her flesh.

"Clint!" she squealed, trying unsuccessfully to wiggle away from temptation.

Too late.

His velvet tongue and probing mouth sought out and captured her downy center. The explosion of sensations that followed tore through her like a volcanic eruption. Her body trembled, writhing beneath him as he delved deeper, stroking, teasing, caressing.

Her nails dug into his shoulders as she felt the shock wave of release make its steady climb—pulsing—stronger than a heartbeat.

She opened her mouth to cry out, but all sound and air

seemed to catch in her throat as she was hurtled across the threshold of simple pleasure to the surreal world of absolute ecstasy.

Clint stood over the kitchen sink wearing only a pair of silk boxer shorts, running cold water over the pounds of shrimp. He turned a lecherous eye in Terri's direction. "You look great in my shirt," he commented, taking a long, slow look at her bare legs. He reached up and began rifling through the cabinets, then the refrigerator, pulling out an assortment of spices, spinach, mushrooms, a box of wild rice and other goodies.

Languidly she curled up in the kitchen chair, tucking her long legs neatly beneath her.

She smiled, the glow of satisfaction illuminating her face. "Since you seemed to have discarded my clothing, I didn't have much of a choice."

He turned to her, his dark eyes raking across her face. He reached out and touched the top button on her shirt with his index finger. "This little number will be even easier to get you out of."

Terri clasped his hand in a grip that surprised him. She glared at him hard, but he saw the flickers of laughter dancing in her eyes. "Don't even think about it," she warned.

"Whoa!" Clint threw up his hands in feigned surrender. "Okay—just remember you said that." He gave her a quick peck on the lips and rubbed his hands together as one who'd come up with a master plan.

Clint surveyed the spread that spanned the long countertop. "Well, let's get this show on the road."

Clint tossed out instructions like a commando, sending Terri scurrying in one direction and then the other—mix this, get that. If she weren't so hungry, she would have laughed.

Finally, all of the effort paid off. Together they placed

a small table in front of the fireplace and sat down to an exquisite meal.

"So...you are good for something," Terri commented drolly, sending Clint an appreciative look across the table.

Clint wiped his mouth with a linen napkin and chuckled. "Don't you dare tell anyone, either. Between cooking and poetry, I'd be finished."

Terri nearly choked on her wine as ripples of laughter edged up her throat.

"Trust me," she said, taking in small gulps of air, "no one would believe me."

He gazed at her, deep sincerity replacing the laughter in his eyes. "It doesn't matter about anyone else, Terri." He leaned closer. "Not anymore." He stroked her cheek. She tipped her head to the side, holding his hand in place with the gentle pressure of her shoulder. "Only you matter to me." Terri held her breath as their gazes locked in a heartrending embrace. "I want you to keep that with you. Always," he said, his voice a velvet whisper.

"I will," she whispered.

And he meant it, even as his other life tapped impatiently against the glass wall he'd constructed around himself.

Mark turned over on his side, noting the sleeping form with a mixture of pleasure and disdain. She was good. There was no doubt about that, he thought. He cupped his head in his palm and leaned on his elbow. Good enough to make a man forget his troubles. He absently stroked her sheeted hip.

Yes, Melissa Taylor was a man's dream come true in more ways than one. And he was determined to use her to his benefit. She was the key that would unlock the doors to a very solid future for him. He'd become a very patient man over the years. He'd learned long ago what it meant to wait. Only now, his waiting would no longer be without its rewards.

The voluptuous figure turned over. Long silken lashes fluttered open, and a slow smile crossed the chiseled face.

It was true, she thought dreamily, happiness spilling through her as she looked up at Mark. One of the most incredible nights of her life was no fantasy.

She'd had so many doubts about getting involved with Mark after the things that Clint had said. She'd been furious with Clint for spoiling her happiness. How dare he try to steal it from her when he'd never offered any of his own? He couldn't tell her what to do, or who to see. The things he'd said about Mark couldn't be true. Mark was a loving, gentle person. Maybe a little ambitious. But she liked that in a man. The quest for power was intoxicating. That's what had drawn her to Clint.

Clint. Just thinking about him in those terms turned her insides to fire. Without thinking she reached for Mark, hoping to put out the flame.

"Hmm." Mark leaned down and kissed her full, parted lips. She snuggled closer, shutting her eyes. Imagining.

They were partners now, she thought, as Mark expertly caressed her warming body. They were joined, body and soul. Hadn't Clint—Mark—said that?

"What are you thinking about?" Mark asked.

"Just how happy I am." She sighed, shaking off her illusion. She adjusted the sheet over her body and sat up.

Mark kissed her neck. "Did you get the information I asked for?"

She swallowed as a pang of guilt struck her. She was getting confused as the two men momentarily merged into one, until Mark caressed the twin swells beneath the sheet.

"Yes," she said on a sigh, breathless, her thoughts slowly beginning to clear.

"That's my girl." He lowered his head, kissing her full on the lips. He pulled away. "Get it for me."

Melissa slipped out of the bed and padded across the floor

to her briefcase. She'd been so angry with Clint these past few weeks, she thought. Angry and hurt. She'd barely said two words to him since their blowup about Mark. That only made it easier for her to turn a blind eye and do what Mark asked her. She'd gathered the information almost with a sense of glee. As though this one act would compensate for Clint's betrayal. Then why was she having these twinges of doubt?

"Are you coming or what?" Mark snapped, shaking her out of her swirling thoughts.

She returned with a sealed manila folder. Hesitating, she held the folder against her breasts. The confusion hovered, then it fled.

"What's wrong?"

"Why—why do you need all of this information?" Her voice sounded childlike, perplexed.

Mark's face hardened. "I thought we had an understanding, Mel. You don't ask questions. I do all the work, and you and I live happily ever after."

He held out one hand for the folder and rubbed her bare leg with the other. "Right?"

Reluctantly she handed over the folder, her pulse beating wildly. Mark smiled as he ripped open the seal, absorbing every written detail.

Patiently Steve sat in the dark automobile, far enough away from the lamplight to go unnoticed, but close enough to the entrance of Melissa's apartment building to monitor the comings and goings. He checked his watch and yawned. Mark had arrived nearly three hours earlier and had yet to emerge. Steve noted that fact on his pad, then leaned back against the leather headrest.

The life of a private investigator was often a lonely one, he mused, suppressing the urge to light a cigarette. His chosen field made it difficult to maintain relationships. The women who had filtered in and out of his life could not appreciate the type of work he did or deal with his often bizarre hours. More often than not, when he met women he told them he was an investor. That generally went over well and for the most part he kept his line of work a secret. There were very few people who would ever suspect that the dashing, sweet-talking Steve Coleman was a P.I.

He chuckled without humor, wishing that Melissa had never found out. He truly believed that something hot could have happened between them. Something permanent. From the moment he'd laid eyes on her in Clint's office three years earlier, he'd known she was the one for him. She'd just started working for Clint, and it took Steve nearly six months to get up the nerve to ask her out. Melissa's interest peaked, simmered, then dried up when she found out what he did for a living. Steve had fallen hard for Melissa, and her rejection of him had thrown him for a loop for a while.

Now, as fate would have it, here he was sitting outside of the bedroom window that he had hoped to have continued access to. He shook his head. Life was a bitch. 'Cause if it wasn't, he wouldn't be sitting there.

He twisted the cover off of the red-checked thermos and filled a cup with black coffee. He certainly hoped that Clint appreciated the personal sacrifice he was making. He took a swallow of coffee and waited.

Terri and Clint spent a glorious four days together. Clint taught Terri how to ski and tried valiantly to teach her to drive a stick shift. She taught him how to dance the latest dance steps at the clubs that they frequented and to use meditation as a means of relaxation.

Terri had never felt so happy, so fulfilled. Her days sparkled with fun and laughter, and her nights were heady with unbridled passion. Clint was a master at all that he did. He had irrevocably won her heart, and she was falling deeper in love with him day by day.

The hurt and disappointment of her marriage to Alan steadily faded under Clint's loving attention. He made her feel secure, worthwhile and thoroughly adored. But she knew that their idyllic interlude was rapidly drawing to a close. The prospect of being without him left her feeling empty. And her upcoming trip to L.A. had suddenly lost its luster.

"I'll have to go to California when we get back," Terri said as they watched the snow fall silently outside their bedroom window.

"Really? The deal came through with Viatek?"

"Mmm-hmm."

Clint turned on the stereo, then sat next to Terri on the window seat beneath the bay window. He put an arm around her shoulders and kissed her heartily on the cheek.

"Congratulations, babe. I knew you would pull it off. How long will you be gone?"

"Probably about two weeks," she answered in a thin voice.

He nuzzled against her neck, and she closed her eyes, enjoying the sensation.

"How about if I meet you out there? Where will you be staying?"

"I'll be at the Hilton in L.A. But I don't know how much free time I'll have." She sighed as he nibbled at her ear.

"Your day has to end at some point. Besides, I don't think I can stand being away from you for two whole weeks." His voice lowered. "Not after the last four days."

Terri felt a hot flush seep through her at the mention of their intimate times together. She had never been so free with anyone before. Not even her husband. And the things they did with and to each other still left her shaky with need. Then the thought of Alan and his unmistakable presence in L.A. flung her back to reality.

She'd have to tell Clint eventually, and she could certainly use his emotional support. Now was as good a time as any.

She took a fortifying breath. "My ex-husband, Alan, is working on the project also," she expelled in a rush. She looked at Clint, her heart racing, her eyes searching, waiting for his reaction.

"I see." Slowly he got up from the window seat, and crossed the floor to the other side of the room, keeping his back to her. "Would you prefer if I stayed in New York?"

"It's not that. It's just—" she fumbled through her thoughts for a reasonable response.

"Are you sure you're over him?" he tossed out, the look of brewing accusation simmering in his eyes. It infuriated him immeasurably to think that she had a life before him, as unrealistic as he knew that to be. His own sudden insecurity translated into irrational fear. What if Alan won her back?

"How can you ask me something like that?" she snapped. "After what I *thought* you and I meant to each other—after everything that I've told you about Alan and I—how could you? Do you think that I can just turn off and on at will? Be with you one minute and with my ex-husband the next?" She sucked her teeth in disgust.

Clint's eyes clouded over and he felt his heart constrict, seeing the pained look on Terri's face. His stubborn streak set in with a vengeance, and he held his ground. He'd come too far with her, letting his feelings become totally exposed. He couldn't risk being hurt—losing again. He just couldn't. She was going to have to prove herself to him before he crossed that final threshold. How could he even contemplate telling her about Ashley if he wasn't sure of the woman he loved?

He slung his hands in his pants pockets and looked away. He inhaled deeply.

"Let's be realistic, Terri," he blew out in frustration. "Regardless of anything else, you were married to him. That counts for something. A husband isn't someone you can just erase from your mind." Or a wife, he thought, guilt stabbing him in the gut.

Terri witnessed the confusion and insecurity whip across his face and wrestle for position. Her heart went out to him.

Slowly she crossed the room until she stood directly in front of him. He clenched his jaw, refusing to look at her. Terri almost grinned as the image of a stubborn little boy took hold of her thoughts.

She took a deep breath. "Clint, it's over between Alan and me," she said softly. Warily she stroked his arm as she continued to speak. "He decided a long time ago that I wasn't enough woman for him." A hollow sound came from her throat. "I just had to find out the hard way."

Terri bit back the knot of regret. "There's no way that there could ever be anything between Alan and me again." She desperately wanted to tell him how abandoned she'd felt, how empty after she lost the baby. But the words wouldn't come. It was still so painful. Maybe one day...

Clint lowered his head, then looked at her. His eyes flickered, then settled. "I can't stand the thought of you and him, of you and anyone," he grumbled, pulling her into his arms. He buried his face in her hair, inhaling her scent.

She listened to his heart slam against her ear as she snuggled near. "There's nothing for you to worry about," she assured in a soft whisper. "Nothing."

Chapter 10

They stood facing each other in front of Terri's apartment door.

"I'll call you tomorrow," Clint said. His eyes softened as he held her waist in both hands. "I don't know how I'm gonna make it through the night without you." He lowered his head and kissed her gently on the lips, then with more urgency as desire sent up its warning cries.

Terri quickly felt the steady beat of yearning seep through her as she surrendered to the tempting kiss.

Reluctantly Clint eased away. "I'd better go," he said in a ragged breath.

Terri reached up and caressed his cheek. "I feel the same way." Her eyes glided lovingly over his face. "I had a beautiful time, Clint."

He pulled her closer while fighting the urge to pick her up and take her to bed. "I'd say *beautiful* was putting it mildly." Abruptly he stepped back, reclaiming his composure. "Get some rest." He gave her one last long look, then turned and walked away.

Terri floated into her apartment, the euphoric aftereffects of her long weekend hovering around her like a halo. A smile of complete contentment stayed on her face as she glided into her bedroom and plopped down on her bed.

She took a brief look at the stack of news clippings and photocopies of information piled at the foot of her bed.

With a sigh she pushed herself up, intent on discarding the remains of a less happy time once and for all. She gathered up the stack and headed for the kitchen, when the ringing of the phone stopped her midway. She turned toward the phone, momentarily undecided which way to go, until the phone rang again. She looked at the stack under her arm, then at the phone, and decided to answer it first.

"Hello?"

"Terri! Hi. It's Lisa."

"Hey, Lis. I just walked in the door a few minutes ago," she said, placing the stack precariously on the edge of the nightstand, and trying unsuccessfully to hold it in place. While Lisa chattered, Terri watched the papers flutter to the floor.

"I was just calling to be nosey, girl. So...how was it?"

"Which part?" Terri teased, fighting to stifle a giggle as she gathered up the fallen papers.

"The best parts of course, smarty."

"Well, my dear, to put it in two words, *absolutely incredible!*"

"Now didn't I tell you your day was coming?"

"Yeah, girlfriend, and it just came and came."

"Whew, child!"

Both women erupted into a fit of laughter at the play on words.

"Listen," Terri said, trying to catch her breath between giggles, "let me get myself settled and I'll call you later."

"No. That's okay. You go ahead and get yourself together.

Brian and I were going to a movie. Why don't we try to get together tomorrow?"

"Sounds good. I'll give you a call. If I don't forget," she added, frowning.

"Oh yeah, this is the big week, right?"

"Uh-huh. I'll be leaving Wednesday morning."

"Don't you dare skip town and leave me in suspense!"

"I won't—I promise." Terri giggled. "Give my love to your handsome husband."

"I will. Talk to you tomorrow."

"'Bye, Lis." Terri hung up the phone with the same whimsical smile still on her face. Taking a long breath, she marched to the kitchen and dumped the pile of papers into the trash.

That part of my life is behind me, she thought. No more looking to the past. She'd done enough of that for too long. She'd buried herself in her old misery, and now that she finally saw daylight, there was no turning back. Especially with Clint waiting at the end of that tunnel.

Resolved to her newfound philosophy, Terri sauntered to the bathroom and ran a steamy tub of water.

A half hour later, relaxed, happy and drowsy, Terri slid under the sheets determined to get a full night's sleep. She'd fought hard for the past several hours to keep thoughts of Clint at bay, knowing that if she didn't she'd reach for the phone and sleep would be a total impossibility. She smiled when she thought of him and how things had changed, and before she realized it her mind and body were buzzing with visions and needs.

She tried closing her eyes, but a steady shudder of wanting tripped through her, warming her body. This was crazy! She'd be one wreck if she couldn't learn to spend a night without him.

Restless, she turned on her side, easily falling prey to the recollections of the nights of passion that flared between her and Clint. He was everything that she could want in a man:

handsome, loving, secure, successful—and the most incredible lover.

Her body heated at the thought as if an inner dial had been switched to slow cook. Yet there was still something nipping at her. Something vague and unsettling. There was still that fine line that neither of them had dared to cross. So often during their weekend together, she'd wanted to tell him about the baby she'd miscarried, how it had affected her life and how it had made her feel so inadequate about herself.

In the night when they had lain together, whispering to each other, she'd wanted to share with him the lonely childhood she'd lived, always the outcast, and how important a family of her own was to her. But something always held her back. That disturbed her. If they were ever to have a meaningful and trusting relationship, they were going to have to be honest with each other.

She turned over on her back and stared up at the ceiling, folding her hands across her stomach.

Children were important to her. She wanted a child of her own more than anything. Alan could never understand that, so her loss never affected him in the least. He never understood her desire to want to shower her affections on anyone other than him. But it was a deep obsession with her, as though a child would somehow eradicate her parents' lack of love for her during her youth. Everyone would always tell her that she was "special" because her parents had "chosen" her, as if that would make up for the loss of her real family. Funny, she never felt special, just different and alone.

Terri let out a long troubling sigh and slowly pulled herself upright. She looked at the clock: 11.30 p.m. At this rate she'd never get any rest. Tossing off the sheet and quilt, she swung her long legs over the side of the bed and got up, crossing to the center of the bedroom.

Several moments later, inhaling deeply, she let her mind and body sink into the relaxing tranquility of meditation.

When she finally felt her mind and body going limp and free of tension, she expertly uncrossed her legs and rose in one graceful motion.

Trancelike, she crossed the room to her bed, but stopped short of sinking in when her bare foot was tickled by the sensation of paper.

She bent down and picked up what appeared to be one of the countless newspaper articles she'd acquired on Clint.

Without thinking further, she started to put the article on her nightstand when the small foreign date and headline caught her attention.

Her breathing quickened, and suddenly it felt as though all of the air had been sucked out of the room.

API London 20 February—Businessman Clinton Steele's Wife Killed in Car Accident.

Her eyes raced across the tiny black print, trying to absorb the information before she read the words. *Desiree...his wife of three years...found dead...Porsche turned over...leaving behind an infant daughter, Ashley...drugs may have been involved...husband questioned...*

Ashley, Desiree, the names began to blur. Clint had a daughter. A daughter! The startling reality slowly seeped through the fog that had blanketed her brain, then plunged her repeatedly with the blade of irrational jealousy.

The small slip of paper floated from her nerveless fingers. She felt light-headed and strangely empty, the conflicting combination leaving her bereft of any tangible emotion. It took several more moments for her to completely absorb what she'd read, and she replayed it in her mind.

Why had Clint never mentioned his wife? She shook her head in confusion. Her brow creased. Perhaps she could accept his reluctance to speak of his wife's death, but never to mention the fact that he had a child?

"A child. Clint has a child." The softly whispered words floated through the silent room, then echoed in her head like a school-yard taunt.

Images of her painful childhood, the loneliness, the revelation of her beginnings as an accidental birth, being told casually over dinner that her brother, her reason for going on, was dead, and that she would no longer be spending any more summers with her beloved grandmother in the Caribbean—who, too, had passed away. All of it swept through her in a wave of remorse.

Slowly she sat down on the edge of her bed. Clint never once said anything about his daughter. Why? Where was she? Who took care of her?

Her blood thickened, then turned to ice in her veins. Something deep inside switched off. The light of hope dimmed, and the door to her heart slammed shut.

"This changes everything, Clint," she whispered into the night. And the realization of her own hypocrisy left her trembling.

"I could handle anything, Clint—anything." She lowered her head, her heart constricting with the weight of her selfishness. "But not someone else's child. I know what it's like to always be someone else's child. But how will I ever be able to make you understand so that you won't hate me?"

A broken sob struggled upward from her throat as the tears slowly spilled over her closed lids.

Chapter 11

"Ms. Powers, good morning. How was your holiday?" Andrea asked, with more enthusiasm than Terri could handle.

"It was fine, Andrea. Thank you." Terri adjusted the dark glasses on the bridge of her nose in an attempt to shield her swollen eyes. "Is Stacy in yet?"

"No. Not yet. She called and said she should be in around ten-thirty."

Terri nodded absently. "I need you to reschedule my flight reservations. I want to leave this morning instead of Wednesday."

Andrea looked quizzically at her boss but didn't question her. "Will you still be staying at the Hilton?"

"Yes. As soon as you confirm my flight, give them a call, as well. Then contact the studio and advise them that I'll be arriving today. Perhaps they would care to get the initial meeting over earlier than scheduled. Let me know."

"Certainly," Andrea answered. "Ms. Powers, is something wrong? You don't look well."

"Everything's fine, Andrea. I guess I just did too much this weekend." She gave Andrea a weak smile and walked toward her office. Just as she reached the door, she stopped and turned toward Andrea. "Hold all of my calls today, will you?"

"Of course."

"And I'm not accepting any calls from Mr. Steele. Understood?"

"Yes, Ms. Powers." *So that was it.*

Terri walked into her office and closed the door softly behind her.

"The developers want you to come to Nassau in two weeks to take a look at how the work is going," Melissa advised, taking a seat on the couch and purposely avoiding his gaze.

Clint nodded. "Have our lawyers finished going over the contracts?"

"I'm expecting a call from Elliot Landau this afternoon," she answered in her most practiced professional voice.

Clint recognized the tone and knew that it stemmed from their argument, weeks ago, over Mark Andrews. She was still upset. But that was her problem. As long as she did her job, that was all he could expect. Although he reluctantly had to admit that he missed the lighthearted camaraderie that had always been a part of their relationship.

"I'm considering giving the Nassau account to Powers, Inc. What do you think?"

Inwardly she cringed. "Haven't you had enough problems from that woman? After all the work that was put into the cable-television proposal and she just—" Melissa caught herself when she saw the dark look pass across Clint's features. She briefly looked away. "I mean, they're not the only agency in town."

Clint's jaw clenched. "Maybe we should discuss this later."

Melissa stiffened, drawing herself up to her full height. "Will that be all?" she asked in a clipped voice.

Clint stood and walked toward the window. "Yeah." He turned and looked over his shoulder as Melissa sauntered toward the door. "There is one thing."

Melissa halted and turned toward him. "Yes?"

"If you hear from the *real* Melissa Taylor, tell her I'm looking for her." He turned back toward the window while Melissa strutted out, a half grin lifting her lips.

Clint slammed down the phone, total disgust creasing his face. There were few things that really got on his nerves, but one of them was a secretary that ran interference.

He pushed himself up from his chair with such force, he sent the wheeled leather armchair sailing across the room.

What in the hell could be wrong? When he dropped Terri off last night, everything was fine. He'd made three phone calls to her office, only to be told she was unavailable.

"Unavailable!" His voice boomed around the room. "Why are you so suddenly unavailable, Terri?"

He loosened his tie, clenching his jaw. He sure as hell wasn't going to give up that easily. That secretary was going to tell him where Terri was whether she realized it or not!

He smiled devilishly. Next time charm would be the key.

The six-hour flight to Los Angeles International Airport had been delayed for nearly an hour. Terri impatiently tapped her foot as the cab sat in the midmorning traffic.

Annoyed, she checked her watch. So much for stopping off at the hotel. She was scheduled to be at the studio in less than twenty minutes. After her request that the meeting time be moved up, it wouldn't sit very well for her to show up late.

Thank heavens she'd had the presence of mind to wear her

pink cotton suit beneath her winter coat. It would just have to do, she thought, amazed at the seventy-degree weather near the end of November.

"Driver, I've changed my mind about the hotel. I won't have time. I need to go straight to Viatek Studios on the Boulevard."

Resigned to the fact that there was nothing she could do about her present situation, she settled back in the cab and popped open her briefcase. Absently she stroked the smooth burgundy leather surface, remembering all too well where the case had come from. It had been a congratulatory gift from Alan for her first major contract.

As much as she'd tried to prepare herself, she just couldn't shake the butterflies that had claimed a stake in her stomach. She knew that Lisa was right. It was over. Or was it?

She forced herself to push aside the unsettling thoughts and sifted through the proposals that she and Stacy had worked out. Her full lips tugged with pride, feeling assured that the movie executives would be pleased with the promotional campaign.

Finally the cab halted in front of the imposing studio. Terri reached into her purse and quickly paid the driver. She had five minutes to spare.

Hours later, tired but satisfied, Terri crossed the threshold of her hotel room. Her one consolation was that Alan had not been present at the meeting. However, he was expected the following day. She would just have to deal with the situation when it arose.

"Thank you very much," she said to the young bellhop who carried her bags. She slipped out of her shoes, stepped into the suite and paid him.

"Thank *you,* Ms. Powers!" The young man beamed, eyeing the ten-dollar bill in his hand. He backed out toward the door, smiling all the way.

Terri grinned wistfully, recalling her own college days waiting tables, cleaning hotel rooms, whatever it took to pay her tuition. She knew how much those tips meant when you were earning only minimum wage.

As if pulled by an unseen magnet, she crossed the sun-bleached wooden floor to the terrace. Swinging open the French doors, she was greeted by a whiff of salty sea air. She inhaled deeply of the scent and closed her eyes as images of her childhood blossomed before her.

How often had she and her brother, Malcolm, raced across the white, sandy beaches of Barbados with Nana always yelling for them not to stray too far? Nana had raised them since Terri was a two-year-old toddler, and when Malcolm came along she raised him, as well. After the death of their mother in a boating accident and the disappearance of their respective fathers, Nana was the only relative that she and Malcolm had.

Malcolm.

The old knot tightened in her belly. His face was vague now. She'd tried to always keep his image engraved in her memory, but the years had slowly worn it away like water beating relentlessly against a rock. All that remained was a hazy figure with laughing eyes and an easy smile, which at times were so similar to Mark's. The thought brought on a shudder.

A deep sigh lifted her breasts, then drifted across the pale blue sky. What she did remember, all too clearly, were her baby brother's anguished pleas when the social workers separated them. Nana had gotten too ill to care for them. They had no one else. The last time she'd seen Malcolm was a week before his fifth birthday. She was only seven years old, and she promised him that she'd return.

Terri shook her head vehemently, trying desperately to dispel the painful memory. Her guilt, at times, was almost more than she could bear. She'd been Malcolm's only hope, and she'd abandoned him. Then he was gone—forever.

Moments later she slowly looked away, knowing that the solace she sought would not be found in the ocean depths.

Turning, she reentered the main room, picked up her two suitcases and walked into the bedroom—oblivious to the white wicker decor. She urged her body to go through the ritual of unpacking and sorting through the stack of notes and documents she'd brought along, afraid to be alone with her thoughts. "An idle mind is the devil's workplace," she could hear her Nana say.

She tossed her lingerie into the dresser drawer, and without warning, her thoughts shifted erotically to Clint. She hugged her negligee to her face. How long could she put off thinking, feeling, wanting Clint?

The weakness that she felt for him left her vulnerable, a sensation she was unable to handle. Even Alan had never been able to evoke such profound feelings of longing in her. She'd kept the key to her heart safely tucked away, out of reach. Clint had been able to unlock it as smoothly as a cat burglar slid into the family safe. The only difference was that his tools were charm and an irresistible sexuality that left her reeling. But feelings had been her downfall from the beginning. She could no longer allow them to misguide her.

With that determination made, she reached for the phone and dialed her office in New York. She had yet to let them know that she'd arrived or to pick up any important messages. It was already six o'clock New York time, and she knew that jet lag was right behind her.

She listened patiently as the phone hummed to life.

"Powers, Incorporated," the familiar voice answered.

"Hi, Andrea. It's me."

"Ms. Powers! How was the trip?"

"Long. Is everything all right?"

"Fine. Stacy has everything under control."

"Do I have any messages?"

"You sure do." Andrea flipped through her message pad and reeled off the messages, but dared not tell her that she had revealed her whereabouts to Mr. Steele. If she ever found out...

Terri took hasty notes and fired out instructions on who to call back.

Andrea swallowed hard. "The last three messages are from Mr. Steele."

Terri felt her stomach shoot up to her throat.

"Really?" Her calm voice surprised her. "What did he say?"

"He asked to speak with you. And he wanted to know where you were."

"And...?" She eased her stomach back into place with a silent gulp.

"And—" Andrea hesitated "—I told him you were unavailable." She knew her boss was adamant about giving out personal information. But he was just so nice and seemed to really care about Terri. And somehow, Andrea believed that she'd done the right thing.

"Is there anything else?"

"No. Everything is fine."

"Good. Well, tell Stacy that I'll call her in the morning and bring her up to date. I won't have time this evening. I was invited to a studio party."

"Wow. A real Hollywood party!"

Terri chuckled. "I'll fill you in on all the juicy details when I get back."

Andrea's eyes lit up. "Just bring me back an autograph of someone famous and gorgeous. Of the male gender, preferably." She sighed.

Terri shook her head in amusement. "I'll try. Talk to you tomorrow."

Slowly Terri replaced the phone in its cradle. She picked it up again and punched in the numbers to Clint's office. Then halfway to completion, she hung up.

She closed her eyes and hugged the receiver to her breasts. She wasn't ready to confront him. Not yet.

"Like I said, man, this thing with Melissa and Andrews is hot and heavy. I sat outside her window for a full night, and believe me, he never left." Steve tossed his notes across the desk toward Clint.

Clint's eyes narrowed. "With everything that we know about Andrews, I have to have some serious concerns about my own vulnerability with Melissa being the one on the inside."

Steve nodded. "It's possible," he began reluctantly, "that she may be feeding him info, but I find it hard to believe that Mel would stab you in the back. Her loyalty runs pretty deep."

"I know." Clint sighed, rubbing his hand across his bearded chin. "I guess on top of everything else, I don't want her to get hurt, either. That Andrews is a slime." He rolled his eyes in disgust.

"Listen, Mel's a big girl. She can take care of herself. I really think that the last thing you have to worry about is Mel, or her giving away company secrets."

The corner of Clint's lip lifted slyly. "Are you sure that the ole fires aren't still lit for Mel, and that's why you can't see the real deal?"

Steve cut his eyes in Clint's direction. "Very funny. You really know how to twist the knife."

Clint popped up from his reclining position. "Just kiddin', man. Just kiddin'." He thumped Steve on the back.

Steve looked at Clint through thick lashes. His smooth eyebrows raised in question. "Speaking of fires, what's the latest with you and Ms. T?"

"That's a damn good question. I *thought* everything was

great. After this past weekend I didn't think anything in life could ever be wrong."

"But?"

"But now she's pulling some kind of game on me. I called her office, and her secretary gave me the runaround, only to find out, after numerous attempts and considerable charm, that Terri left for L.A. early—without saying a word to me!"

"You're kidding."

Clint began to pace. "Do I sound like I'm kidding?"

"Maybe something came up...suddenly."

"Too suddenly for her to call me?" Clint shook his head. "I find that hard to believe."

Steve smiled. "That sounds like your ego talkin'."

Clint flashed him a dangerous look, which Steve openly ignored.

"Do you think you're so damn irresistible that a woman like Terri is just going to up and change her whole agenda because she spent the weekend with you?" Steve laughed outright when he saw Clint practically swell up and explode before his eyes. He fought back the laughter. "But seriously. You know women, they run on emotion. Maybe she's trying to sort things out."

"What things?"

"How should I know? Whatever things they always have to figure out. Why don't you call her and find out for yourself instead of being pissed off."

"She's the one who took off without a word."

"And you're just going to leave it like that, I suppose?"

"I *suppose* you're right," Clint snapped sarcastically.

"Yeah, and look what happened the last time you were playing Mr. Toughguy. You nearly blew it. Maybe she needs you to call her. For whatever the reason. From everything that you've told me about her, she doesn't seem like the kind of woman who'd play games."

Clint blew out an exasperated breath. "Damn, I hate it when you're right!" He grinned reluctantly at Steve.

Steve patted Clint on the shoulder. "Don't take it too hard." He chuckled. He looked up at the clock. "Hey, I've got to go. I have to meet a client in fifteen minutes. I'll check with you later."

Clint walked Steve to the door. "Thanks. For the info and the advice."

"Anytime." He began to leave, then turned back. "Women love surprises," he said in a stage whisper. He gave Clint a conspiratorial wink and strolled down the corridor.

Clint chuckled silently. "Surprises, huh?" He walked around his desk, sat down and ran his hand across his beard, the beginnings of a very tempting idea brightening his darkly handsome face.

He reached for the phone and dialed the international operator. If he was going to make changes in his life, it would have to be on all fronts, beginning with his daughter. And there was no time like the present.

Patiently he listened to the lines hum and click, then finally ring countless miles across the ocean.

"Hello?" answered the polished English voice.

"Hi, Jill, it's me, Clint."

Jillianne tried to control the excitement that flooded her at the sound of her brother-in-law's voice.

"Clint, I was wondering when you were going to call." Her soft English accent drifted across the lines. "It's been weeks. When are you coming home?"

Her favorite question. "Soon." *My standard response.* "I'll definitely be home for the Christmas holidays."

Her spirits sank. "That long?"

"I know. I'm sorry. But I don't think I can get away any sooner. How's my girl?"

"Ashley's just fine and as busy as ever. She misses you."

Clint heard the silent reproach. "Is she awake? I'd like to talk with her."

"I just put her down for a nap."

"Oh." Disappointment filled him. He rubbed his hand across the beard that braced his jaw. "Please tell her that I called, Jill."

"Of course I will."

Seconds of silence ticked away. Jillianne gripped the phone until her knuckles locked, hoping that she could hold on to his voice just a little longer.

"How have you been, Jillianne?" Clint finally asked. "Have you been getting out?"

"I've been doing well. But you know I don't go out much."

The soft tinkle in her laughter filled his ears. So much like Desiree, he thought.

"Ashley keeps me suitably busy," she added.

He smiled as an image of his precocious daughter sprang to life. "You need more in your life than Ashley. What about a man? You're a beautiful woman, Jill. There must be countless available men waiting in the wings." He worried about his sister-in-law's solitary life. Ever since Desiree's death, Jillianne had devoted her entire life to him and Ashley. She deserved more than that.

"There are a few men, but none who really interest me."

If only she could tell him that the only man she'd ever wanted was him. Every time she thought about her love for Clint, guilt pummeled her. He had been married to her sister, and it didn't seem right that she should feel the way she did about him. Yet she couldn't help it. She'd been in love with Clint almost from the moment she saw him. She'd envied Clint's love for her sister. And God help her, she'd almost been relieved when her sister died, even as much as she'd loved Desiree.

"I'm sure that the right man is out there waiting for you, sweetheart. You deserve it."

Sweetheart. She hugged the endearment to her breasts. "But what would become of you and Ashley?"

"You let me worry about that," he said, his thoughts immediately turning to Terri. She'd make a wonderful wife and mother. He just knew it, although he had yet to tell Terri about Ashley. But he was certain that she would love Ashley just as much as he did.

A light tapping at his office door drew his attention.

"Hold on a moment, Jill."

He looked up and saw Melissa standing in the threshold. Clint crooked his finger, signaling Melissa to come in. He covered the mouthpiece. "I'll be right with you. I'm talking long distance."

He turned his attention back to his phone call. "Listen, hon, I've got to go. I'll call you in a few days. All right? And give Ashley a hug and kiss from me."

Jillianne shut her eyes. "Of course. We'll be waiting to hear from you."

"Take care of yourself."

"You, too, Clint," she said softly. Reluctantly Jill hung up the phone as she mentally ticked away the days until Clint would return. He had never so much as shown more than a brotherly interest in her. So she kept her secret, silently hoping that one day his eyes would open. To only her.

Clint replaced the receiver. "What are you doing here so late, Melissa? It's close to seven o'clock."

Melissa took a seat on the long leather couch that spanned one wall of the office. Her short black skirt crept seductively upward as she crossed her shapely legs.

Clint self-consciously tore his eyes away, but not before Melissa caught the look of appreciation that lit the ebony orbs.

"I had a few things I wanted to finish up," she said. She

laced her long fingers together. "Was that our procurement office in Ghana?" She shrugged her shoulder. "I mean—you mentioned long distance."

Clint shook his head. "No, that was my sister-in-law in England. I was just checking in."

"Oh." The momentary grip of jealousy released her.

Clint looked at her for several long seconds. "Is something wrong?"

Melissa lowered her eyes, then looked up at him, framing the words in her mind. "Can we talk?"

Clint leaned forward, giving her his full attention. "Anytime."

Melissa swallowed. "I know I've been a real bitch lately."

Clint chuckled. "I wouldn't go that far." He smiled at her. "But pretty close."

"And—well—I thought I'd make it up to you."

"That's not necessary, Mel. I understand that you were upset, and sometimes we just say things."

"That's no excuse for the way I spoke to you. I realize that you were trying to look out for me." She ran an expertly manicured hand up and down her skirt. "I guess what I'm trying to say is that I'm sorry."

Clint rose from his seat and walked over to Melissa. He crouched down beside her, briefly catching the scent of her White Linen perfume. "No apology necessary," he said gently, his words tripping her heart.

She wanted to reach out and touch the slender silver threads that ran through his hair, but she knew better.

Her large hazel eyes held his, and what Clint saw in them took him aback. But just as quickly as that look had appeared, it vanished. Maybe he was just imagining the longing in her eyes. He really must be losing it, he thought. Melissa was the most controlled woman he had ever met—logical, dependable, sensible. That was Melissa.

Her voice drew him out of his reverie.

"I, uh, was wondering if I could take you to dinner?" She tilted her professionally coiffed head to the side and slightly lifted her shoulder. "Sort of a peace offering. My treat," she added in a hurry.

Maybe an evening with Melissa was just the distraction he needed to get his mind off Terri. Even if it was only temporary.

"Now that you mention it, I'm starved. And guess what? I think my calendar is free," he teased, chucking her playfully under the chin. He rose from his crouched position. "If you could wait about ten minutes, I'll be ready."

She nearly sighed aloud with relief. "I'll get my things and meet you in the lobby," she said, trying to control the breathless elation that gripped her voice.

Maybe tonight, she thought, as she hurried down the carpeted hallway to her office. Maybe tonight.

Chapter 12

The brilliant whitewashed walls of Alan Martin's beachfront duplex apartment were covered with the stark images of his profession.

Huge black-and-white photos of lush, naked models, the human eye magnified hundreds of times, breathtaking shots of storms at sea, not to mention the countless photos of the Hollywood elite, adorned every available wall space.

Alan took pride in his work and what his innate talent—to spot the perfect picture—had afforded him. He lived well as a result.

Prior to leaving New York, Alan had solidly established himself as one of the most sought-after photographers in the business. His work was impeccable, appearing in ads and magazines across the country and in Europe. Arriving in Hollywood only enhanced his marketability. His morals, however, remained a hot topic of the social set. He wholeheartedly did everything he could to live up to his "bad boy" reputation.

Alan stepped out of the steamy bathroom, covered from the waist down in a printed towel.

Padding across the carpeted hallway, he entered his bedroom only to find his latest conquest sound asleep.

Indifferently he shook her until her bleary eyes opened and slowly focused.

"Hey, baby," she mumbled, flashing him a seductive smile.

"It's time to go, sweetheart. I have plans for the evening." He slid open his closet door and scanned his vast array of tailor-made suits.

"Can't I go with you?" she whined.

He threw her an exasperated look from soft brown eyes. "Listen, doll, I thought we understood each other. I don't mix business with pleasure."

The young woman pulled up the sheet to cover her exposed breasts. "But I thought I meant something to you, Al," she pouted, running a hand through her tousled hair.

"Of course you do, baby," he crooned by rote, not even remembering her name. A night of booze and drugs had dulled his memory. "But I have business to take care of, and it doesn't include you." He patted her hip. "So hurry it up."

He pulled out a lightweight, mustard-colored suit and collarless shirt. Secure in his prowess, he dropped the towel from his waist and meticulously began to dress.

Christy silently fumed. She'd been sure that her womanly charms would win her an invitation to the biggest bash this season. She'd expected Alan to take her along—in gratitude. This could have been her opportunity to be discovered. *Who could she connect with in a hurry to get herself invited?*

She stormed off to the bathroom, shutting the door solidly behind her.

Alan breathed a sigh of relief. He wasn't in the mood for a scene. He stepped into his pants and slipped into soft Gucci loafers. Crossing the room to his dresser, he selected his favorite cologne, dabbing it generously across his face. He picked up a diamond-stud earring and inserted it into his left earlobe.

He turned toward the full-length mirror, admiring what he saw, and wondered if Terri would feel the same way.

Clint leaned back against the red velvet chair. The intimate dining room was filled with late-dinner patrons who frequented the Russian Tea Room after Broadway performances. The hushed voices, soft music, and tinkling of crystal and silver blended in perfect harmony.

"Dinner was delicious," he commented, briefly shutting his eyes in satisfaction. "I didn't realize how much I needed to get out."

He looked across the table at Melissa. "Thanks for asking me."

"It was my pleasure," she purred.

Clint rubbed his full belly. "It'll take hours of jogging to get this off," he joked.

Melissa's eyes sparkled. She leaned forward. "I didn't know you jogged. I love jogging." The lie dripped from her lips like honey.

"Really?" He was clearly surprised. Melissa didn't look like the kind of woman who ever broke a sweat. "Maybe we could get together sometime."

"Whenever you're ready." She quickly thought of all the gear she'd have to charge on her gold card.

Clint took a swallow from his fourth glass of wine. "I guess there are a lot of things we don't know about each other."

Melissa lowered her long lashes.

"I stay so busy with business, I've never taken the time to really get to know you," he added.

Her heart raced, searching for an opening. "That's to be expected. I mean—we haven't had time for more than a professional relationship." She looked at him suggestively.

He felt himself treading on dangerous ground, but the good food, easy music and the wine, which he rarely drank, were all going to his head.

He smiled. "Perhaps that will change. Why don't you tell me about Melissa—the woman." His eyes held her captive as he languidly leaned back in his seat.

"Well," she began slowly, "I grew up in Chicago, attended Northwestern University and graduated with honors."

He grinned indulgently. "Tell me something that I haven't read on your resume."

Melissa laughed softly. "What do you want to know?"

"What about your family? I'd love to know what kind of people raised such a remarkable woman."

She reached for a lie that would fulfill the image she thought he had of her. But before she spoke, she opted for the truth.

"I didn't really know my parents," she said in a near whisper, fiddling with her glass. "My mother was a nightclub singer. She traveled a lot. And my father—" she shrugged and her voice trailed off "—I spent most of my life living with my aunt and uncle. My mother visited occasionally, but she never stayed very long."

"Melissa—I'm sorry. I had no idea."

"It's all right." She gave him a pained smile. "I've learned to live with it."

"And very well, I might add."

His warm words wrapped around her like a down quilt. She knew he'd understand, and her desire for him intensified like white heat.

Clint and Melissa pulled up in front of her apartment building on Ninety-sixth Street and Central Park West.

"I had a great time, Clint." She looked across at him. "And—I'm glad we had the time to talk."

She dug in her purse for her keys. "Uh, would you like to come in for a minute?"

The reality of his situation finally took root. What was he doing here—with Melissa—when it was Terri he wanted?

"No, thanks, Mel. It's late, and we have a full day tomorrow." His skull was beginning to pound. He touched his head self-consciously. "And I think I need to sleep off all that wine." He offered her a crooked grin.

"Tomorrow then," she said softly.

She looked at him for a brief moment, imagining the feel of those luscious lips against hers. She knew she had to find out.

Without warning, she leaned toward him and pressed her moist lips against his, both startling and stimulating Clint with the fiery contact.

Instinctively he returned her kiss, until he felt Melissa's arms slip seductively around his neck, pulling him closer.

He eased away. "Mel—" he breathed, holding her at arm's length. He shook his head. "This isn't right. I'm sorry. I shouldn't have let it get this far."

She swallowed. "Clint, please. You don't have to apologize." She tore her gaze away from him. "It was my fault."

He took a deep breath. "Let's put it this way." He tilted up her chin with the tip of his index finger. "We got caught up in the moment." His smile was warm. "Still friends?"

She nodded.

"Good." He lightly kissed her forehead. "I'll see you in the office."

She turned and, with as much dignity as she could summon, opened the car door and walked toward the building entrance.

Briefly Clint shut his eyes and took a breath of relief, thankful of what he'd gotten himself out of. What had he been thinking about? Without looking back, he sped off down the darkened street.

* * *

Melissa inserted her key in the lock, flicked on the hallway light and tossed her purse and coat on the Queen Anne settee in the foyer.

Kicking off her shoes, she plopped down on the rich damask couch—a smile of total contentment outlining her full lips—committing to memory every detail of her evening with Clint.

The aroma of grilling steaks cooking on the huge open pit filled the late-night air. Lighthearted laughter, pulsing music and loud splashes in the Olympic-size pool added to the opulence.

Everywhere that Terri turned, a familiar face was spotted. It was rumored that Spike Lee and John Singleton were expected. But in the meantime, she was tickled to see her favorite late-night talk-show host being doused in the pool.

Slowly she threaded her way through the richly dressed crowd of revelers and headed toward the buffet table. Her mouth watered at the display of exotic delicacies. The studio obviously spared no expense, she observed.

Terri picked up a plate and made her selections. Taking her spoils, she strolled across the grounds and found an empty lounge chair near the pool, between two bikini-clad beauties.

Terri nibbled away while watching the comings and goings of the guests, when a waiter in formal attire stopped by her chair and offered a glass of champagne.

"No, thank you." She smiled, looking up at the waiter—then, over his shoulder, she caught sight of that familiar swagger coming in her direction.

Her whole being became infused with an unspeakable heat. She willed herself to get up and run, but her mind seemed to have lost all control of her limbs. Her body remained immobile, but her heart raced at breakneck speed.

Within moments he stood above her.

"Hi, Terri." His silky voice embraced her.

He was still so gorgeous. His café-au-lait complexion held a healthy glow and those eyes, the color of ginger, still held the old magnetism. She inclined her head in acknowledgment. "Alan."

Slowly she urged her breathing to return to normal and forced herself to smile. "You're looking well."

He crouched down next to her and stroked her bare arm. "You're as beautiful as ever," he said in a husky whisper.

He expertly scanned her flawless mahogany features, the layers of jet-black locks that were wrapped stylishly atop a brilliant headdress of black and gold. His eyes quickly traveled downward. Momentarily he stared at the rise and fall of her full, round breasts, peeking teasingly out from her low-cut black-and-gold satin top. Then down to those legs that he remembered so well, covered in gold satin pants.

His hand trailed up her left arm.

With her right hand she lifted the wayward fingers and placed them solidly on the arm of the chair.

"Still have hand problems, I see," she stated in a flat voice.

He tossed back his head and let out a deep robust laugh, his diamond earring twinkling in the moonlight. Then he focused those cool browns on her.

"You haven't changed a bit either—*I* see."

The woman sitting next to Terri got up and strutted toward the pool. Alan's eyes followed the shapely form as she dived gracefully into the pool.

Terri's mind flashed backward to the countless stream of women who'd interrupted their life together. If she'd witnessed his behavior a year ago, her ego would have been crushed. But things were different now. She was different. Suddenly it didn't matter anymore. She finally realized, in that brief instant, that Alan was just Alan, and he'd be the same way if he was with her or any other woman. That long-awaited realization set her free.

She smiled an easy smile of acceptance and forgiveness, just as Alan returned his gaze to her, which he characteristically interpreted as being directed at him.

He grinned. "Why don't we get away from here, talk about—things? I could show you around. We could—"

Her voice was cool, controlled as she cut him off. "Forget it, Al. That was then, this is now. It's strictly business between us."

The smug smile slowly dissolved. "Business? Come on, baby, we had something." He eased closer, his warm breath fanning her face. "You know that as well as I do."

"Had, Al. Had." She made a move to get up. "And whatever it *was,* is a matter of perspective."

He put a restraining hand on her arm. "I was wrong. You have changed, Terri," he said, secretly pleased. He never could tolerate a woman who was too easy. That had been part of his and Terri's problem from the beginning. She gave too much, was always too willing to please, too trusting—just *too* everything. If you looked up the definition of a "good woman" in the dictionary, you'd see Terri's picture. She made it easy for him to live the kind of life he lived. It seemed as though the worse he behaved, the kinder and more giving she became. His stomach lurched with a mild pang of guilt.

She eased her arm away. "You're right about that, Alan. I have. In ways you'll never know." She rose from the chair. "If you'll excuse me, I think I'll find our host. See you later."

Alan pursed his lips in perturbance as he watched her move gracefully away and wondered why he had dumped what's-her-name for this. Well, what was life without a challenge? Terri would be in L.A. for two weeks. He was sure that he'd have her back in his bed long before then.

* * *

The evening wore on as the multitude of guests continued to ebb and flow throughout the magnificent expanse of property.

Although being in crowds usually unraveled her, Terri was thankful that she wasn't the focal point, and she was able to relax. She had to admit that she was truly enjoying herself as she raptly listened to tales of Hollywood scandals from a reporter from the *Globe*.

"...They never knew that his wife had hired a photographer to sit outside of his window," said the young reporter, chuckling. "That is, until the photographer fell out of the tree and crashed into the bed of roses."

The small group laughed uproariously at the vision.

"How were they able to keep it out of the papers?" Terri wanted to know.

"Believe me, honey," commented Gail Holloway, the newest big-screen sex symbol, "when you have the kind of money and clout that Paul Arkin has, you can cover up anything."

Terri lifted her eyebrows. "I guess you're right."

Gail extended her hand. "I'm Gail."

"Terri."

"So what brings you out here? I can tell by your New York accent that you're not a native."

Terri grinned. "I'm working on the ad campaign for Jonathan Montgomery's newest film, *Outburst*."

"You're kidding! I tested for the lead in that film. They said I was too—well, you know." She thought for a moment, putting a tapered finger to her famous lips. "So you must know Alan Martin? He's the public-relations photographer."

"Oh, yes. I *know* Alan."

Gail caught the disapproving tone in Terri's voice. "Maybe more than just professionally?" she asked, her interest sparked.

"We worked together on a few projects in New York," she answered noncommittally.

"Hmm. Well, he's definitely an interesting specimen," Gail said, taking a sip from her glass of champagne.

She remembered all too well the long nights with Alan Martin when she'd first arrived in Hollywood. He might be a real dog, but his photos gave her that first big break. For that she would always be grateful.

The two striking women—one a rich mahogany, the other a golden saffron—caught the attention of every male eye as they passed. Neither of them took notice.

"When did you know you wanted to be an actress?" Terri asked, totally at ease in Gail's company.

"For as long as I can remember," she answered wistfully, flashing Terri the smile that made men want to reach out and touch her—among other things. "A lot of directors say that I have natural talent." Her voice lifted in pride. "I've never even been to acting school."

"That's fantastic. You must be very proud of your accomplishments."

"Oh, I am."

The two women stopped in front of the enormous buffet table and loaded their plates.

"Well, well, well. If it isn't the two most gorgeous women in this joint."

Terri and Gail turned simultaneously to find Alan standing behind them, a look of pure appreciation brewing in his eyes.

"Gail, sweetheart." He bowed his head and kissed her full lips. He slid a possessive hand around her tiny waist. "I didn't know you were acquainted with my ex-wife. She's pretty hot stuff back in New York."

Gail's picture-perfect face seemed to crumple, and Terri instantly knew that she, too, had been to bed with her roving ex-husband.

Gail swallowed. "Really?" She looked from one to the other, and it all sank in. This was *the* Terri Powers, of Powers, Inc. Damn! Al only briefly mentioned his marriage. He'd never gone into detail with her. Who would have thought that she would wind up chatting with his ex? To think that she'd been on the verge of telling Terri about some of the unforgettable nights she'd spent with Alan Martin. A brief chill scooted up her spine. But Gail quickly regained her composure. "How's everything with you, Al?"

"Couldn't be better." He grinned broadly. "I suppose Terri's already told you that she and I'll be working together." He gave Terri a pointed look. "Just like old times, eh, Terri?"

"Not quite." Her words were velvety smooth, but her meaning was coated in granite. She turned to Gail. "Listen, I'm going to leave. I have an early morning." She dipped into her purse, pulled out her business card and handed it to Gail with a smile of understanding. "If you're ever in New York, look me up. And if you ever get tired of your PR people, give me a call. We're always looking for new clients."

Gail looked at the card and then at Terri, finding a new level of admiration for her.

Terri nodded curtly to Alan. "Good night."

"See you on the set," he replied smoothly.

"Whew, what's with you two?" Gail asked, shaking off the tension that had chilled the balmy air. "Nasty divorce?"

"Let's just say—unfinished business." He smiled that roguish smile. "But you and I don't have that problem." He leaned down and breathed in her ear, "We never leave things unfinished."

Out of the corner of his eye he caught a glance of what's-her-name on the arm of a studio executive. Alan smiled in her direction, silently admiring her for her ingenuity.

"Touché," he mouthed as she turned up her cosmetically corrected nose and sashayed away.

* * *

Clint lay sprawled across his king-size bed, wearing nothing but a pair of silk boxer shorts. He stared up at the ceiling.

Thank heavens he hadn't let things get out of hand with Melissa, he thought. Never before had he allowed his professional relationships to cross the thin personal line. And certainly never within his own office. He wouldn't start now. What was worse, he'd never be able to explain that one to Terri.

Terri. How badly he wanted her. His loins ached with unfulfilled need.

She would be gone for two weeks. He wouldn't wait that long to see and talk with her again. That was too much time for things to go wrong between them. And she had some serious explaining to do.

He was going to do something about it—and soon. In the meantime, he got up from bed, determined to withstand a cold shower.

Chapter 13

Clint arrived at his office the following morning with a new sense of purpose. He stopped in front of his secretary's desk, his darkly handsome face beaming with excitement.

"Good morning, Mr. Steele. Don't you look happy this morning."

"I feel great, Pat." There was a slight tinge of wonder in his voice as though he, too, was realizing his joy for the first time. "I need you to do something for me right away."

"Of course." Pat automatically pulled out her notebook.

"Call the airline and book me on the next flight to L.A.—first class. Once you have confirmation, reserve a suite for me at the Beverly Hilton. And pull together all of the data on the resort project in the Caribbean. I'll be taking it with me." He tapped the desk with his palm and jauntily strolled off to his office. "Oh, and Pat," he tossed over his shoulder, "don't forget to rent a car for me also."

Pat reached for her Rolodex just as Melissa approached.

Pat looked up. "Good morning, Ms. Taylor. I didn't know
you were—"

"Did I hear Mr. Steele say that he was going to L.A.?"

"Yes. It was a surprise to me, too. I guess I'll have to cancel
his appointment for—"

But before she could finish, Melissa turned on her heel and
stormed off down the corridor.

Pat shrugged her narrow shoulders at everyone's peculiar
behavior and proceeded to dial the airline.

Terri'd spent a night full of endless, erotic dreams of Clint.
She awoke with every nerve ending on fire, her emotions
strung to near breaking, but through sheer willpower she'd
been able to push him to the back of her thoughts, if only
temporarily, as she plowed through her day.

Her first day at the studio had been exhilarating. Even the
time spent under Alan's watchful eye and provocative remarks
hadn't been as painful as she'd anticipated.

Since she'd come to terms about Alan and concluded that
the dissolution of their marriage was in no way her fault,
she'd allowed herself to relax in his company—knowing that
they could never be more than friends. So—she'd accepted
his invitation to dinner. What could be the harm? She was
confident that she could handle Alan Martin. She was no
longer the young, love-struck girl who craved his love and
attention. That hot little news flash would certainly raise Lisa's
eyebrows a notch, she thought merrily.

He'd said he wanted to take her someplace elegant. She
sucked on her bottom lip and searched her wardrobe for the
appropriate ensemble.

Terri chose a sleeveless top in peach silk, with a white
chiffon jacket and matching palazzo pants that had a peach
satin lining.

She had to admit, however, as she lay the outfit on her
bed, that it was because of Alan that she'd started her own

business. His ambition and his vision were contagious. But while she was struggling to get her business off the ground, Alan was keeping himself busy by photographing and bedding every beautiful woman who crossed his path. She tossed the disturbing thoughts off and looked at her selection. Perfect, she decided, and wondered what tricks good ole Al had up his sleeve for tonight. Whatever it was, she decided with conviction, she was up to the challenge. But first a long, relaxing bath.

Alan slid behind the wheel of his red Audi convertible and pointed the nose in the direction of Terri's hotel.

His plan was simple. First dinner, dancing, a few drinks, a drive across the beach and then he'd invite her up to his apartment to see his etchings. *His etchings.* He cracked up, laughing at his own cleverness.

Thirty minutes later he pulled up in front of the Beverly Hilton Hotel. He tossed the valet his car keys and pushed through the revolving doors into the lobby.

He sauntered over to the front desk and asked for Terri.

"I'll ring her room. Just a moment, sir."

Alan turned sideways and leaned on the smooth oak desk, quietly observing the elegant women as they passed. He gave several a wink and was pleased to see that many winked back. *I haven't lost my touch.*

Several times he considered approaching a few and giving them his number but decided against it. It would be just his luck that Terri would come down and catch him in the act. That wouldn't do well for the night that he had planned.

Casually he turned his head toward the elevators just as Terri emerged.

His breath caught as he watched her seemingly float across the lobby floor. She had to be the most sensational-looking woman in the place. Now this—was a lady. *A lady.* Was this the first time he had attached that description to her?

His conscience nudged him in the ribs.

"Hi," she greeted. A radiant smile accompanied her salute. "I don't have to be led to the car blindfolded, do I?" she teased.

He looked at her as though seeing her for the very first time.

Her brow furrowed. "Is something wrong? Do I have lipstick on my teeth or something?"

Alan shoved his thoughts back into place. "No. Just a revelation."

"Well, I'm certainly not going to touch that one," she said, completely at a loss.

"Trust me." He took her arm and placed it in the crook of his. "If I told you, you wouldn't believe it."

She looked at him curiously. "I'm sure I wouldn't."

Dinner finished, Alan contemplated the veracity of his plan. Being in Terri's company had shaken him. She was nothing like the woman he once knew. And she never would be again. She was the kind of woman that you settled down with, not for one night, but forever. Without thinking further, he made the turn back onto the highway, away from the beach. So much for the best-laid plans.

Terri never noticed the detour as she commented on the lush scenery and chatted about dinner.

"That restaurant was fabulous," she said emphatically.

"Angelo's is one of my favorites. I'm glad you liked it." He turned briefly and caught her profile.

"If I stay around here much longer, it'll be mine, too." She chuckled. Terri took a long searching look at Alan as he maneuvered around the turns, passing rows of swaying palm trees and picture-perfect homes. "Alan, you've really surprised me. You were actually a gentleman tonight."

Alan tossed his head back and laughed. "That's the first time anyone has ever used my name and *gentleman* all in the same sentence." He eased the car alongside the road and stopped.

He turned to face her, all humor absent from his demeanor. "That's because you bring out the best in me." He leaned toward her.

"Whoa! Now just hold on a minute. I thought we had an understanding." She subtly slid farther over in her seat.

"I really screwed things up between us, Terri. You deserved better than what I had to offer. I hurt you, and I know I can never make up to you for the loss of our baby, but…I want to try. I know I can." His voice was tender, almost a plea.

Terri sighed deeply before she spoke, measuring her words. "Alan, what's past is gone, buried. We can't go back. You don't want me, now, any more than you're going to want the next woman who catches your eye." She focused on her hands in her lap and continued without rancor. "I always thought it was me—something I was lacking." She looked across at him. "But it's just the way you are, Alan." She smiled and stroked his cheek. "I've tried to stop holding it against you and against me.

"The good thing is—" her voice held a gentle softness "—I don't have to deal with it. Let some other poor, unsuspecting soul fall for the 'Martin magic.'"

He was momentarily speechless, absorbing the simple truth of her words, and he didn't know whether to be relieved by her dismissal of him or pissed off. He generally didn't take too well to being turned down. No matter who it was.

"You're sure that's the way you want it?" he asked.

She nodded.

He lifted his eyebrows and exhaled. "Then I guess I'd better get you home." He turned the car in the direction of the hotel.

The balance of the ride was completed in silence, each having to come to grips with this newest crossroad of their turbulent relationship.

* * *

Terri leisurely stripped out of her clothing and put on a hand-printed, floor-length silk robe. She searched through her suitcase and pulled out a volume of poetry by Nikki Giovanni, one of her favorite poets.

Taking the book, she opened the French doors leading to the terrace and relaxed on the chaise lounge, intent on getting through several selections before turning in for the night.

But the warm sea breeze was like a balm to her bare skin. The air blew caressingly beneath her robe, teasing her, taunting her, stimulating her.

She leaned back and shut her eyes, absorbing this secret moment of uninhibitedness. Languidly she ran her hand down her leg, then up across her smooth belly, heightening the electricity that charged unchecked through her veins.

Her imagination flew as she envisioned Clint's large strong hands caressing the places that she had touched. An unheeded sigh rose from deep within her as the liquid fire erupted, warming her center.

She wanted to shake off these tempting erotic feelings of longing, but she couldn't. Every fiber of her being screamed for Clint.

Shaken, she rose from her haven and walked aimlessly back into the suite, her thoughts a kaleidoscope of confusion.

She stopped at her bedroom door but was afraid to enter, sure that her unfulfilled desires would assault her once again. Maybe a cup of herbal tea would help to soothe her. She walked toward the phone, dialed room service and placed her order.

She hung up and turned away just as the phone rang, startling her. Shaking her head to clear it, she took a calming breath and picked up the receiver.

"Hello?"

"Terri. It's me, Alan."

"Alan? Is something wrong?"

He hesitated a moment as a long-legged beauty walking her dog caught his eye.

"Alan?"

"Oh, sorry. Must be some interference. You know how these car phones are."

"No, I don't." She sighed, her sarcasm blatantly clear. "Is there a problem?"

"In a manner of speaking."

"Alan, don't be cryptic. I really don't have the energy."

He chuckled. "I need to see you."

"Excuse me?"

"You heard me. I need to see you. I'm five minutes away. I know I won't sleep tonight until I get this off my mind."

"Sorry to disappoint you, but forget it, with a capital *F*. Now good—"

"Terri—wait."

She blew an exasperated breath into the mouthpiece. "You have five seconds."

"Terri, I still love you. I didn't realize it until tonight. If you'd let me come up, I'd show you just how much. Like old times, baby."

"Alan—the next sound you hear will be the dial tone."

She promptly dropped the phone onto the cradle and gave in to the tremors that had taken hold of her.

Alan grinned as he heard the low hum buzz in his ear. He replaced the phone.

So his meek ex-wife had truly developed some backbone. But if she thought that was going to turn him off, she was sadly mistaken. If anything, it was a turn-on. No one turned him down. Not even ex-wives. His eyes narrowed. The hunt had only just begun. Automatically he shifted into gear and jetted down the freeway.

Stark, blinding outrage boiled and rose to the surface, exploding in a string of expletives.

How dare he? That self-centered SOB. Still in love with me! He wants to show me. He must think I'm crazy!

She paced the floor, her silk robe fanning outward and behind her. Rage flamed in her dark eyes. She balled her hands into small fists, wishing that she could land them where they would do some good. Right between Alan's big eyes.

After everything that he had done to her, put her through, and then left when she was at the lowest point in her life, he really thought that just seeing him again could erase her memory? He was an egomaniac.

She'd been a fool to be taken in by his charm once again. She'd let down her guard. No more. She was through. She'd have as little to do with Alan Martin as possible, and just try to get through the next week and a half the best she could. Without killing him!

She had to get her life on track. She wanted that life to be with Clint. But now... She shook her head in frustration and confusion, running her fingers through her locks. When would she ever have any happiness? Was it just not meant to be? When—

The knocking on the door halted her pacing in midstep.

Her heart raced as adrenaline pumped through her. Alan!

Well, they would have it out once and for all, she fumed. It was long overdue.

Terri stormed toward the door and nearly snatched it off its hinges. Her pulse was pounding so violently in her ears she wasn't sure what she said to the uniformed man who stood on the other side of the door.

Chapter 14

Melissa lay in bed, staring sightlessly up at the ceiling, unable to sleep. She felt Mark's muscular form adjust itself next to her.

He rolled over to face her. "Can't sleep?" he mumbled. He craned his neck to check the bedside clock. "It's nearly three a.m." He rolled on his back. "What's bugging you?"

"Clint is in L.A."

"And?"

"He's there with Terri. I just know it."

Mark sat straight up in the bed, sleep forgotten. "Why are you just telling me this? Your job is to tell me Clint's every move. Especially if Terri is anywhere in the vicinity. How in the hell do you expect our plans to materialize if you can't hold up your end?"

He threw off the blanket and sheet and stomped out of the bedroom into the kitchen. Melissa hurried behind him.

Gingerly she reached out and touched his back. He flinched

as if touched by something unmentionable. "Mark, I—I'm sorry. I just had so many things on my mind. I—"

He spun to face her, his face a mask of anger. "Let this be the last time," he warned through clenched teeth. "We can't afford any slipups. How long will he be gone?"

"I think for the next week, at least."

Mark nodded. "That will give you plenty of time to get our plans in motion for that resort deal."

Melissa swallowed.

"It all hinges on you. Remember that. If you love me like you say you do, you'll do as I ask." His hand slowly rose and stroked her chin, then trailed down to the opening in her nightgown.

Then he abruptly turned away. "I need some time to think. Alone." He walked off into the living room, leaving Melissa to deal with her twisted thoughts and misplaced loyalties.

Mark opened a small desk drawer and pulled out the thin photo album that contained only one picture. He stared at the small, weather-beaten photograph, and his hatred was renewed.

The first thing Clint did when he arrived at the Hilton was place a call to the front desk to check and see if Terri was in her room.

"I'm sorry, sir. There doesn't seem to be any answer," the desk clerk had said.

"Thank you." He hung up the phone.

He'd tried several more times. All without success, until fatigue and jet lag won the battle.

When he next opened his eyes, it was the following morning, 10:30 Pacific time. Rubbing his eyes and stretching his stiff body, he made his way into the shower.

By the time he'd finished scrubbing the fatigue away and checking in with the front desk, he was informed that Terri had already left for the morning.

In that case, he decided, he'd pay her a surprise visit at the studio, take her to lunch and find out what was going on between them. There was no way that he was going to let any more time slip away.

Once again he reached for the phone. This time he dialed the hotel florist and ordered a huge bouquet of Casablanca lilies.

Terri sat in the third row of the screening room, avidly watching the dailies from the previous day's shooting. She found that reviewing clips helped immensely in preparing a surefire ad campaign. Today, especially, they helped to take her mind off what a fool she'd made of herself when she'd flung open the door the previous night, only to find that room service had delivered her order. It was almost funny the way the young man looked at her, as though he expected her to leap at him with a knife—or something worse. He must have thought she had completely lost her mind.

She shook her head in silent amusement, clipped her notes together and rubbed her eyes when the film came to an abrupt end. Checking her watch, she was surprised to see that it was nearly one o'clock. Stretching, then smoothing her salmon-colored skirt, she rose from her seat and inched her way out from the dark viewing room into the bright lights of the studio corridor. The drastic change in lighting made her want to slip on her sunglasses. But then she thought with wry amusement, she would truly look *Hollywoodish.* The image made her giggle out loud, causing several curious heads to turn in her direction. Flashing a "you know how it is" smile, she continued down the corridor.

Her stomach growled with hunger. But she wanted to make some last-minute recommendations to her original proposal based on the scenes that she'd just viewed. She smiled as the ideas began to formulate in her head. She was sure that the studio executives would love it.

Instead of running an ad campaign solely on clips from the movie, she wanted to do it more like a commercial. A takeoff of the Calvin Klein commercial for Obsession and Eternity, with a variation of course to avoid any lawsuits. But it would be perfect. The male and female leads of *Outburst* oozed sexuality and would explode on the television screen with a clip like that. The audience wouldn't be able to get to the theaters fast enough.

Quickly she made her way down the busy corridor, side-stepping the multitude of studio employees, and turned left, heading for the small but efficient office that had been designated for her.

She stopped short when she opened the door and found Alan sitting behind the long wooden desk going over what appeared to be hundreds of photos. The conversation of the following evening came rushing back, infuriating her again.

His curly head snapped up when she entered. Automatically his smile slipped into place.

"Sorry to barge in on you like this, but they had some last-minute meeting or something and decided to utilize my space down the hall." His grin widened. "Hope you don't mind."

Terri inhaled, then blew out a deep breath. She spoke through her teeth. "And what if I do?"

Alan shrugged. "I guess we'll have to compromise. You get half of the room, and I'll get half. How's that?"

Terri's shoulders slumped. This was the last thing she needed today. And Alan didn't seem to have any memory of his last words to her. Just the thought that he could be so blasé fueled her temper to the boiling point.

Momentarily, she considered her other options in terms of work space. But before her thoughts had completely materialized, she knew that space at the studio was at a premium. She exhaled an annoyed breath and straightened her shoulders. She had work to do. There was no getting around it. She just would not let Alan interfere. Hopefully he'd have the good sense to act like the professional he claimed to be.

She stepped into the room, intentionally leaving the door cracked. Just in case.

She took a deep breath. "What are you working on?" she asked, more out of curiosity than civility. She stepped closer to the table.

Alan was in his element. His eyes lit up just like she remembered whenever Alan talked about his work. It was the only time that he seemed genuinely interested in anything.

He stood up and propped one hand on his hip; the other pointed out the various shots as he spoke.

"These were all done yesterday. I wanted to catch the lead characters unaware. I think the candid shots are going to go over well."

Terri nodded in agreement. "These are fabulous, Alan. I know the studio is going to love them." She picked several up for closer inspection.

Within moments they were engrossed in their individual projects—exchanging ideas, laughing, giving criticism as well as advice. For one frightening moment, it was almost like old times, Terri thought. Alan seemed to feel the same way when their eyes caught and held.

"Terri, I—"

"Alan, don't." She instinctively moved away, inching away from the table to the other side of the small room. Her heart raced.

"Just listen to me for a minute."

"There's nothing to say, Alan."

He quickly crossed the short distance between them and backed her against the wall. Her scent raced to his head, fanning his desire.

He reached out and grabbed her arms before she had the chance to move. Her eyes rounded with apprehension and a morbid sense of anticipation.

"Let go—"

But before she had a chance to finish, his mouth covered hers. He pushed his hard body solidly against hers, pinning her to the wall as he ground his hips against her unyielding body.

She tried to struggle, to break free, but that only aroused him all the more.

To Clint, who stood in disbelief in the open doorway, listening to Terri moan, it appeared that she was thoroughly enjoying every minute of her ex-husband's kisses.

Chapter 15

Anger, hurt, and humiliation fought for control of his emotions, blurring his vision. He didn't pay any attention to which direction he headed. All he knew was that he had to get out of there. Get some air. And he'd never give the two lovers the satisfaction of breaking up their little tryst by announcing his presence.

Terri reared back and slammed her knee deep in Alan's crotch. An agonizing cry erupted from his gut. Blinding pain shot through his body, so intense that his cry hung in his throat. He doubled over as nausea swept through him, and he began a descent to the floor. Terri gave him a little added incentive when her open palm connected with his face, sending him sprawling to the floor.

Somehow Clint found his way to the main entrance. He looked down at the bouquet of lilies in his hand and his stomach turned over with revulsion. Without thinking, he tossed them onto the receptionist's desk, pushed through the glass doors and out into the blazing California sunlight.

Terri's breathing filled the torrid office air in rapid, panting breaths. "If you ever—come near—me—or touch me—again, you'll wish you were dead."

She snatched her notes from the desk, causing the piles of photos to spiral to the floor as she swept past, leaving Alan in a heap on the floor, groaning for all he was worth. She threw him one last scathing look of disgust and slammed out of the door.

The first thing she did was rush to the ladies' room, praying as she hurried down the hallway that she would have a moment of privacy.

It was no less a miracle that she found herself alone when she arrived. She went straight to the sink, immediately splashing cold water on her face. Her eyes stung with the tears that she refused to shed. And she swore that the water actually sizzled on her skin.

Bracing her hands on the sink, she lowered her head and tried to calm herself down long enough to think clearly. Her head pounded with the effort.

How could he? How could she have left herself so vulnerable to Alan? She'd given him credit where he didn't deserve any. A better question was, what was she going to do now? How in the world was she ever going to continue her work, knowing that he was always a heartbeat away? This was a nightmare, worse than any she could have imagined. And she had stepped right in it.

She shook her head. She needed time to think. She needed to get away from there as soon as possible.

She took one last look in the mirror, wiped off the last traces of her smudged lipstick, picked up her belongings and headed for the exit.

* * *

"Oh, Ms. Powers!" The young receptionist popped up from her seat as Terri sped by her desk.

Terri kept heading for the door, totally oblivious to anyone or anything.

"Ms. Powers!" The young woman ran up behind her and stopped her just as she reached the door.

Terri turned around with a start—a look the receptionist would always remember, that reflected true terror.

The woman stammered. "I, uh, didn't mean—to startle you." She pushed the bouquet toward Terri. "Some man dropped these on my desk. When I checked the card, it had your name on it."

Terri's heart began to race mercilessly. Clint! Oh, God. With trembling fingers she took the bouquet of lilies.

"How long ago did he leave?"

"Not more than ten minutes. He tore out of here like there was a fire."

Terri swallowed back her greatest fear. "Did you know where he was coming from?"

"Of course. I'd directed him to your office when he came in. He asked me not to announce him. He said he—"

Terri didn't hear anything else but the buzzing noise that swept through her head. She spun away, clutching the bouquet to her breasts, and raced through the door. She had to find him. To explain. But where? She looked up and down the wide expanse of the studio lot. Clint was nowhere to be seen. She ran toward the parking lot.

When she finally found her car, her hands were shaking so badly she didn't think she would ever get the key in the ignition. She wanted to scream at this final act of frustration, until mercifully she was finally able to insert the key and start the car.

She tore off down the scenic freeway, the rented Mustang convertible leaving a halo of dust in her wake.

* * *

Terri arrived back at the Hilton in record time. She was heading directly for the elevator when the desk clerk called out to her.

"Ms. Powers." He came from behind the enormous oak desk. "Ms. Powers," he said as he approached, his sunburned face a mask of humility. "Please excuse our oversight. These messages came in for you last night." He handed the small slips of paper to Terri.

She barely looked at them—knowing.

"Please excuse the error. I suppose during the shift change last night—" he shrugged his shoulders "—there was some mix-up." He handed her one more message. "This was left for you this morning. But you had already departed."

Terri looked down at the neatly scrawled message. *I'm in suite 1701. Call me. Clint.*

She fought to keep the tremor out of her voice. "You mean, he's here in the hotel?"

The clerk looked exceedingly uncomfortable. "Well, uh, m'am, the gentleman checked out about fifteen minutes ago."

Terri felt weak, bordering on being ill. She struggled for calm. "Did he say where he was going by any chance?"

"I'm sorry. No, m'am." He cleared his throat. "If this mix-up has caused you any inconvenience, I assure you I will bring it to the attention—"

But Terri didn't want to hear any more. Slowly she walked toward the elevator, still clutching the lilies. Whatever it was this ridiculous man was saying, it didn't matter. It was too late.

Chapter 16

Clint drove mindlessly, heedless of the picturesque homes and manicured lawns. *Faster.* The swaying palms blurred before his eyes as he whipped around the winding turns and mountainous roads.

He was a fool. He shifted into Fifth gear, ignoring the roadway warning signs. *Faster.* The tires squealed, barely holding on to the tarred highway. He'd allowed himself to feel again and he'd been used, like a welcome mat in a snowstorm. He gripped the wheel. She was good. There was no denying that. He almost laughed, a malevolent smirk spreading across his lips. He'd begun to believe her whispered adorations, soft caresses and moans of pleasure. *Idiot.* It was all a lie. But he loved her.

This time his heart constricted into a tight, twisted, anguished knot, then eased up to his throat in a ball of fire. An agonized groan of pain rose from his throat. Quickly, he swallowed it back as the entryway to Los Angeles International Airport loomed ahead.

* * *

Terri entered her suite just as the phone began to ring. She tossed the messages and bouquet of flowers on the foyer table and ran for the phone. Let it be Clint, she prayed.

"Hello." Her first word poured out in a gush.

"Terri, hi, it's Lisa."

Terri's high hopes fizzled away like a deflated balloon.

"Oh." She sat down on the wicker lounge chair, expelling a deep sigh.

"Well, if I'd known I was gonna get that kind of greeting, girlfriend, I would have saved my call. What's wrong?"

Terri shook her head. "You name it. Listen, I'm sorry to take it out on you," she added.

"I've got the time if you feel like talking. Is it Alan?"

Terri shut her eyes at the memory. "Among other things. And...oh, Lis," her voice broke. "Everything is wrong."

Through silent tears she explained, as best she could, what had transpired.

"Damn!" Lisa said, her own anger searing through the lines. "Talk about bad timing. I always knew that Alan was a real bastard. Now there's not even a name in the dictionary to describe him. So what are you going to do?"

"That's the fifty-thousand-dollar question." She blew out a shaky breath. "You know, Lis, I've really begun to second-guess myself. I'm beginning to wonder if I'm too naive or just plain stupid."

"Terri, come on, you—"

"No. Seriously. It seems that every man that I trust kicks me right where it hurts. Look at what happened with Mark. I treated him like my own brother. And Alan...I was silly enough to give him the benefit of the doubt. Which he didn't deserve. Now Clint. I'm sure he believes everything he saw."

Terri massaged her eyes with her free hand. "Maybe it's just as well." She sighed. "Now I won't have to face him."

"Face him? About what?"

"I was going to break things off with him when I returned to New York."

"What? Why in the world would you do that? I thought you were in love with him."

Terri swallowed. "Just before I left for L.A., I came across a news clipping…"

Lisa listened, her own heart breaking for her friend as Terri spilled out the long-buried memories and how they'd been forced to the surface with the information about Clint's daughter.

Lisa waited several long moments after Terri finished before she spoke. "Terri, hon, I know that someone else's child would be hard for you to deal with. Maybe you think you'd never be able to handle it. But I know you. I know the side of you that couldn't help but love a child. Any child. And if you love Clint, you'll love his daughter. In time. Don't let your fears destroy a chance at happiness."

Lisa waited, measuring the silence as her words sank in. "And what about Clint?" she asked gently. "If you're still intent on breaking off the relationship, don't you think he deserves to know the truth and not go on believing that you betrayed him with your ex-husband?"

Terri strolled off toward the terrace, hoping to find the strength and the words she would need to confront Clint. It would be another week before she would return to New York. A whole week to let the damage settle in.

She shut her eyes. Lisa was right. Clint did deserve to know the truth. Even if they didn't pursue their relationship, she couldn't let him continue to think so little of her.

Chapter 17

Everything was happening too fast. Melissa felt as if she were sinking into a pit of quicksand, and Mark was the anchor that weighted her body downward. He seemed to have cast some kind of bizarre spell over her, and she didn't have the willpower to break free. He'd convinced her, during their nights of unleashed passion, that what they were doing was justified—that Terri deserved to be brought down a notch for what she'd done to Mark over the past year. Most of all because she'd taken Clint away from her. And when Mark made her body sing with each stroke of his, she'd agreed over and again.

Melissa sprang up from her seat and began pacing her carpeted office, her svelte silhouette cutting a stunning figure against the plate-glass background.

Absently she chewed on a red-lacquered nail, contemplating what she should do, when the phone rang, halting her in midstep.

She took a long breath, then picked up the receiver.

"Melissa Taylor."

"Mel, it's me, Mark."

Automatically her pulse began to escalate, and she felt suddenly breathless. "Mark," she answered, forcing a lightness into her voice, "where are you?"

"At my apartment. Did you get a chance to check the files?"

She swallowed while her mind ran through a million reasons why she shouldn't give Mark the information.

"Yes, I did." She looked down at the stack of files on her desk. "I—I have them here."

"Great." He checked his watch. "I'll pick them up on my way out to the airport. See you in a few."

"Mark. Wait."

"What is it, Mel? I'm really pressed for time."

She ignored the annoyance in his voice and let the words pour out. "I don't know if I can go through with this."

"What do you mean, 'you don't know'? You'd better know! This is no time for you to start acting shaky. This is just the beginning." His voice grew hard. "I expect you to hold up your end. I don't like screwups." He slammed down the phone before she could respond.

Melissa shut her eyes as Mark's words tugged on the anchor.

Clint pushed open the glass doors of Avis Car Rental, his suitcase in one hand, his garment bag slung over his shoulder, and headed across the airport terminal. As he drew closer to the airline ticket agent, he knew he was making a decision that he would not allow himself to reverse once it was done.

Terri.

He hesitated as the huge flashing board announcing arrivals and departures seemed to beckon to him.

He moved forward.

* * *

"So far the project is developing smoothly. I even came up with some new ideas," Terri said into the phone, trying to sound enthusiastic.

"Then why don't you sound as excited as you should be?" Stacy probed, slipping her glasses off her nose.

Terri sighed. "I really don't feel up to talking about it Stacy. But," she added quickly, "it has nothing to do with the job. Believe me, everything is fine."

"If you say so. Is there anything you need on this end?"

Terri frowned while she thought. "No. I don't think so. I'm sure you have everything under control."

"If you need me to come out there, just let me know. My new assistant is very capable of handling things in my absence Just say the word."

"No. Honestly, everything is fine. It's just—never mind." She inhaled deeply. "Do I have any messages?" She continued to hold her breath while she waited for Stacy's response.

"Nothing urgent." Stacy flipped through her notes. "There's nothing here that can't wait until you get back. The one big bit of news is that we may have a new contract opportunity with Anita. Her agent called yesterday after he heard how well things were going with Viatek Studios. He suggested that we're being considered to handle the PR for her next album."

"Wow, that *is* big news." But not the news she really wanted to hear. "Listen, I've got to run. And you need to get home. It's nearly eight o'clock out there."

"I know. And I'm exhausted. I'll give you a call at the end of the week if there are any new developments."

"Good. Take care."

"You, too, and keep up the good work, boss!"

Terri chuckled. "Thanks."

Slowly she replaced the receiver. So Clint hadn't called. She didn't really expect that he would. Now she had no way

f finding him. He wasn't in the hotel, and more than likely
e was on his way back to New York.

Her already sunken spirits sank deeper. She hadn't remem-
ered feeling quite this miserable for some time. She'd begun
o believe that her days of heartache were behind her. Maybe
he just wasn't meant to be happy.

At least her career was on stronger footing, she thought
ardonically. At this pace she would be able to live very com-
ortably in a very short space of time. That would have to be
er consolation.

Terri retraced her steps, and picked up her briefcase from
he table in the foyer, mentally convincing herself that she
vould push the myriad of unhappy thoughts to the back of
er mind and try to concentrate on the final details of the ad
campaign. Things were going too well for her to lose her edge
ow.

Curling up on the sofa, she pulled out her notes, pain-
takingly forcing herself to concentrate on the pages in front
of her.

Just as she was finally beginning to absorb the words, the
phone rang. This time annoyance replaced hope as she reached
or the phone that sat on the white wicker end table.

"Hello?"

"Terri, don't hang up. Just listen to me. I know—"

Her hand began to shake, but her voice remained calm,
controlled, steely. "If you ever come near me again, I'll
have you arrested, Alan. Do you understand me? There is
nothing—absolutely nothing—that you have to say to me."

"Terri, if you'd just let me come up and explain. Please,
Terri, I'm sorry. I—"

Terri slammed the receiver into the cradle and tried to
fight off the tremors that rocked her from head to foot. Her
breathing rose into rapid, panting breaths as if she'd been
chased by an assailant.

Dear Lord, this was a nightmare, she thought, a twinge of

fear whipping through her, tempering her anger. Was Alan
intent on stalking her during her entire stay, or was he trying
to push her over the edge? Whatever his motivation, he seemed
to be succeeding on the latter.

She buried her face in her hands, willing herself not to cry
when the doorbell rang, nearly jolting her out of her seat.

Terri sat wide-eyed, staring blindly at the door. She
couldn't—wouldn't—move.

It rang again, sending a chilling numbness up her spine. If
she stayed quiet, she thought, Alan would just go away. Heaven
only knew what would happen if she opened the door to him.
Once he was inside, she was fair game. She shuddered. The
worst part would be that no one would believe her story. She
felt sure of that.

The bell rang again.

This time instead of fear she felt a sweeping sense of outrage. She could not allow him to reduce her to a quivering
nonfunctional mass of fear. She was better than that. If she
submitted to this torment now, what else might he do to
her?

Resistance welled up inside of her, renewing her. If she
didn't face him down now, she'd never be able to live with
herself.

Calling on all of her willpower, she urged her body to rise
and compelled her feet to move, one foot after another.

She took a long calming breath, determination etched across
her face. She reached the door, ready to face the inevitable,
and snatched it open.

A sudden heat infused her. Her heart seemed to shimmy
up to her throat and thump wildly as she watched the elevator
doors slowly open to admit its lone passenger.

Chapter 18

"Clint." She only whispered his name when what she wanted to do was scream. Was it an apparition, or could the improbable be real? "Clint!"

This time sound found its way out of her throat, reaching him, wrapping around him, and he stopped, with one foot in the elevator and one foot out.

He turned toward the sound of the voice he'd come to know so well. Only moments ago he'd thought that he'd made a fool of himself for having come back. But just one look into her eyes and he knew that he hadn't made a mistake at all.

Terri was suddenly weak with joy as she watched that all-too-familiar stride move steadily toward her. A smile of total happiness lifted her full lips, making her face glow with radiance.

I love him, she thought with an intensity that shook her. And I'm going to make it right, she told herself as he drew nearer. I'm going to make it right.

Seconds later, without words, she was in his arms, burying

herself in his embrace. She lifted her mouth to his, unable to still the desire to taste him once again.

She felt his heart slam against her breasts as his own longing for her mounted.

"I'm so sorry," she mumbled against his mouth. "It wasn't—"

"Shh," he crooned, welding her to the contours of his hardening frame. "I didn't give you a chance." His tongue lashed against hers. "I should've known better."

Unwillingly she eased back and looked into his eyes. "We have so much to talk about," she breathlessly whispered.

Her arms slid from around his neck, down his arms, and her hand found his.

"Come in. Let's talk."

Clint's coal-black eyes flashed with rage as he listened to Terri recount the events that led up to the scene he'd witnessed at the studio.

Slowly he rose from his seat on the couch as Terri drew her story to conclusion.

He turned in her direction, and the look she saw blazing in his eyes sent shards of fear ripping through her. Immediately she stood up, placing her hands against his chest.

"Clint, don't. It's over."

"It's not over!" he bellowed. "He needs to be taught a lesson. I'm just the one to teach it to him."

"Clint, I'm asking you to leave it alone. I can handle Alan."

He looked down into her eyes. "So you think a swift kick is enough to hold off a slime like him." He let out a mirthless chuckle. "You're wrong, Terri. He'll be back. I can guarantee you."

She took a deep breath. "I have less than a week left to go. Then I'll be back in New York, a millions miles away from

Alan. He's out of my life, Clint." Her voice pleaded with him to relent.

Clint lowered his head, his mouth pursed in contemplation. Then he looked at her again. "If that's the way you want to handle it."

She nodded. "It is. I think it's the best thing to do. This may sound feministic to you, but the last thing I want Alan to think is that I have to have a man come to my rescue. He'll never respect me."

Clint shrugged, still unconvinced. He raised his palms in submission. "All right," he said grudgingly. "All right." But even as he said the words, he knew he couldn't let it rest. He would pay Mr. Martin a visit before he returned to New York.

"Thank you." Gingerly she raised up on tiptoe and brushed his lips with hers. "There's more."

Clint briefly shut his eyes and braced himself.

"I was planning on leaving you," she began slowly. She lowered her eyes when she saw the look of disbelief in his. "Just before I came out here, I came across a news clipping—about you, your wife and your daughter." She paused and cleared her throat. "I guess I missed it when I looked at the articles weeks ago." She waited for what seemed to be interminable moments, gauging his reaction before she continued.

Clint stood rooted to the spot. He didn't dare interject. He wanted to hear her true feelings without any interference from him.

"I couldn't understand why you didn't tell me something that important. I was hurt and angry and disappointed in you—in us. I convinced myself that if you hid something like that, what else weren't you telling me? Then I realized I hadn't been completely honest with you, either, and just like I had my reasons for hiding from a part of my life, you did, too.

"When I found out that you had a daughter, hundreds of

disturbing, buried and painful thoughts resurfaced. I remembered what it was like always being someone else's child. I didn't believe that I could love a child that wasn't mine. And if I couldn't, how could you and I continue?" She sniffed back her tears, took a breath and continued. "I was adopted, you see, after my brother and I were separated. He was five and I was seven. After our nana died, all we had was each other. All I ever wanted, all of my life, was to have a real family to belong to, to have a family of my own. After I was so callously told by my adopted parents that my younger brother, Malcolm, had died, something inside of me died, too. I felt that if we had natural parents, we would have had a chance at life. Not the kind of loneliness and ostracism that I always felt. I believed that we would have been treated differently if we could have had our own parents—and that Malcolm wouldn't have died."

Slowly she crossed the room to stand by the terrace, her misty eyes scanning the lapping waves. Her voice trembled when she next spoke. "I lost my baby about a year ago. I blamed myself and looked at it as another failure in my life."

"I have to believe that there was nothing you could have done, sweetheart. You have to know that, too."

"A part of me does know. It's just so hard to get beyond the hurt sometimes. I had so desperately wanted my own family. Because of my experiences I didn't believe that a child that wasn't your natural child could ever truly be loved. I was sure it would be that way for me, too." Her eyes shimmered with unshed tears as Clint crossed the short space that separated them and gently gathered her in his arms.

He stroked her locks. "And now?" he asked softly.

She looked deeply into his eyes, her own pain and indecision reflected in the obsidian orbs. "I want to try to change those feelings, Clint."

His smile seemed to light up the room. "That's all I need

o hear." He ushered her toward the couch and wrapped his arm around her shoulders, his warm breath brushing against her hair. "We will work through this—together. I never meant to keep all this from you, sweetheart. I just never knew how or when to explain. It's been hell on me, too. Since Desiree's death—" he shook his head in shame and regret "—I haven't been able to be a father to Ashley."

"Who takes care of her? Where is she?" She sniffed.

"Ashley lives in England with my sister-in-law, Jillianne. Jill has lived there since her college days. After Desi died and with no family in the States, she stayed. I felt it was the best place for Ashley—to give her some stability."

"But she should be here with you, Clint. You're missing the best parts of her growing up."

"It sounds so simple. I've tried, but every time I look into Ashley's face, I see Desiree, and the guilt is too much for me to handle."

"Guilt? Why guilt? The paper said that it was an accident."

"It's a matter of opinion." Abruptly he got up and began to pace the floor as he spoke. "It was my fault that Desiree died."

Terri's brows grew together in confusion and fear. Her heart began to race. Was this the secret that he withheld?

"We'd had a fight. The same fight we'd been having for months…"

Terri listened as the words poured out, unknown to Clint, exorcising him, relieving him of his self-condemnation.

"Desiree sounded like she was on a path to self-destruction. That wasn't your fault. You couldn't have known that she would take all of those sleeping pills," she added gently as his story drew to conclusion. "You said the doctor was prescribing all kinds of medication, diet pills, antidepressants, stimulants. He's the guilty party."

"I've told myself that hundreds of times. It's never seemed true—" he looked at her "—until now."

Terri stood up, raised her hand and stroked his cheek. "You have to put it behind you. For your daughter's sake. No one, no one, understands better than I what it feels like to be raised by someone other than your parents. Your daughter was cheated out of her mother. Don't let her be cheated out of her father too."

He was silent for a long moment. "Will you help me, Terri? Will you stand by me?"

"Clint, I—"

"Come to England with me for Christmas."

Her soft brown eyes widened in trepidation. "Christmas? But Clint, what about—?"

"Forget about business. Forget about bills. Forget everything and say that you'll come with me." His voice deepened to a throb. "I need you, Terri. It's as simple as that. I need you, love you, and I want you with me. Period."

Terri swallowed the knot of joy that lodged in her throat and blinked away the tears that clouded her vision of his beautiful face.

His eyes glided over her face. He caressed her cheek in his hand. "I love you, woman, more than I ever thought I could love anyone. More than I can put into words," he said in a voice so low, so full of awe, it sounded like a prayer.

"And I love you, Clinton Steele." She wound her arms around him, pressing her head against his chest. She listened to the rapid beat of his heart, and hers soared to the heavens. "I'd go with you anywhere," she admitted, "even to England," she added, the excitement of the unknown and the exhilaration of being loved stirring her. "But on one condition," she said, taking a step back so she could look at him.

"Anything, baby. You name it."

Her eyes darkened with desire. "The condition is that we seal it with a kiss." She flashed him a seductive smile.

He stepped closer, his steady gaze warming her by degrees. "Now those are the kind of terms I can agree to without—" his lips teased hers "—question."

He pulled her solidly into his embrace, his arms locking around her, molding her to his body.

Involuntarily he sighed as the sweet nectar of her tongue glided seductively across his lips, seeking the warm caverns of his mouth.

When had a simple kiss touched her to the very core of her being, she wondered, as she willingly succumbed to the tempting, taunting sensation of Clint's lips. His mouth covered hers, his hot, moist tongue playing tantalizing games in her mouth. She shuddered with pent-up longing, unfulfilled passion.

"I missed you, baby," he groaned against her mouth, his large hands stroking her slender waist, gliding down to her hips, cupping her against his rigidity.

She couldn't suppress the sigh of yearning that rose from her throat when she felt his fingers subtly unbutton her skirt and release the zipper, allowing the thin cotton skirt to skim down her bare legs.

Terri's heart quickened with uncertainty. She rarely wore panties when the weather grew warm. It was a secret pleasure that she had. How would Clint respond to her seemingly wanton behavior? But the look of smoldering desire that welled in Clint's eyes instantly quelled all of her fears as his hand glided over the silken, bare flesh, leaving him powerless to resist her a moment longer.

His shuddering groan was intoxicating, and she willingly submitted to his maddening caresses.

Without effort, he swept her up into his arms and carried her through the open bedroom door, gently placing her on the floral quilts. Clint eased alongside of her, his agile fingers stroking and unbuttoning her blouse simultaneously.

Terri's pulse quickened as she watched the fires of arousal

dance in Clint's eyes. Her sharp intake of breath was all tha
could be heard in the torrid air when Clint's eager lips taunted
her sizzling exposed skin.

She reached for him with eager, slender fingers that had
the ability to make him weak—humble—submissive, like no
other hands he had ever known. He gave himself to her as
she opened herself to him. They abandoned themselves to th
whirl of shuddering ecstasy that they knew would be their
to share in utter completeness.

"I love you, Clinton Steele," she whispered as their world
collided.

Chapter 19

She felt the warm, steady breathing tickle the wisps of hair on the back of her neck. Terri snuggled closer, contouring her body to mold with Clint's.

He stirred, moaning softly as he slowly rose from the depths of sleep, unwilling to relinquish the magnificent dream of being with Terri again.

She angled closer, commanding his body to stiffen with wanting with each scintillating gyration of her hips, her own desire mounting in intensity as his arousal grew.

Reluctantly Clint's dark, sleep-filled eyes struggled open, only to ignite with yearning realizing that his dream was real—supple flesh and blood—tempting him in the most erotic of ways.

"Mmm," he groaned in her ear, caressing her heated body with long sensuous strokes. "Rule number one, you shouldn't rouse a man out of his sleep like that."

Terri turned over on her side to lie face-to-face with him. "Why is that?" she whispered against his full lips.

Clint turned her on her back, pinning her body down with his. "Because you never know what he may do to you."

She opened her mouth for a quick retort, but the only sound that was heard was Terri's shuddering moan as Clint made his dream a reality once again.

"Since we're going back to New York together," Clint said, stretching his muscular form and rising from the bed, "it doesn't make sense to use two cars." He reached for his discarded clothing and began to get dressed.

Terri turned on her side and looked up at him through dreamy eyes. "Hmm," she mumbled.

"I'll take my car back to the rental agency and we'll use yours."

"How will you get back?"

"Take a cab." He bent down and pressed his lips to hers. Languidly she raised her arms and wrapped them around his neck.

"I'll hold your place." She flashed him a wicked grin.

Clint slid his hand beneath the sheets and slowly stroked the silky skin. "Oh, you'll do more than that," he taunted. "I promise you."

The evening sun hung low on the horizon, casting a brilliant orange glow across the intimate pastel-and-white bedroom.

Terri eased out of Clint's embrace and headed for the shower. Turning on the jets full blast, she stepped in, refreshing herself under the pulsing water.

"And rule number two..."

Terri jumped at the sound of Clint's voice. He pulled back the curtain and stepped under the water. "You shouldn't leave me alone in bed." He gave her a quick peck on her shoulder and began lathering her body.

Moments later they emerged, covered in thick terry-cloth robes, courtesy of the hotel.

"I'm starved," Terri stated, entering the living room with Clint only paces behind her. "Do you want to go out and get something, or order room service?"

"Either is fine with me. You decide." He rubbed a towel across his damp hair. "So long as we have a chance to talk."

Her heart beat just a bit faster. He's changed his mind about us, she thought frantically. After the pitiful tale of my childhood, he's changed his mind. She stopped in her tracks and turned, causing Clint to collide with her.

"Whoa," he sputtered, catching her by the shoulders before she lost her balance. "You look as if I said a nasty word, or something—worse." A mischievous grin eased across his face.

"No, uh, I mean, you said you wanted to talk. About what?"

"Nothing that has to be discussed in the middle of the hallway. And definitely nothing so horrible to cause that look on your face." He rubbed his hair again. "Actually it's a business proposition."

"Business?" Her anxiety slowly diminished.

"Yeah," he grinned, "how unromantic."

"Well, are you going to tell me?" Her curiosity level was at full throttle. She took a seat on the couch. Clint elected to stand.

"I have the opportunity to open a string of bed-and-breakfast inns, actually resorts, on several of the Caribbean islands. There's a developer, Nathanial Carpenter of Mega Development, who's very interested, and I'm going down to Nassau next week to finalize things." He paused.

"And?"

"If all goes well, which I'm sure it will—" he stopped pacing and looked at her "—I'd like you to do the PR work. If you agree, I'll need you to go with me to Nassau to get an idea of what I want and to pitch a campaign to the owners of the land I intend to buy."

Terri remained speechless.

"I know it's short notice, and it's a pretty big job—"

"Pretty big?"

"Well, huge, but I know you can do it. In fact—" he looked at her sheepishly "—I sort of told them that you were part of the deal." His lips rose on one side in a crooked smile.

"Clinton Steele!"

"Don't answer just yet. Think about it. I know it'll be fabulous. It's a dream I've had…"

She felt the excitement in his voice and the caged energy that charged the room as he spoke. Her own creative juices began to flow as ideas flashed through her mind. The Caribbean! The possibilities were endless, and she'd get the chance to visit her homeland—Barbados, which she hadn't returned to since she arrived in the States at the age of eight.

"…With the right campaign, design team and location, there's no way that it won't be sensational. All I—"

"I'm sold!" Terri sprang up from the couch, delighting in the look of relief that lit Clint's face. "There are just a few things I have to tie up in New York, and then I'm all yours."

He stepped up to her, his grin warm and inviting. "I hope you mean that in more ways than one."

"Definitely."

He wrapped his arms around her and lifted her off the floor, spinning her around in a circle.

"We're gonna make a winning team, baby. Just you wait and see." He kissed her solidly on the lips. "Oh, and I guess I'm your new roommate until you check out of the hotel. They're all booked up."

Terri giggled and her pulse beat with anticipation.

"Mr. Brathwaite, your offer and your ideas are fantastic," Nathanial Carpenter conceded. He took a sip from his glass of wine. "I must advise you, however, that we have also received very substantial offer from Hightower Enterprises. His proposal came as a complete package."

Mr. Brathwaite nodded. "I understand that, and I'm sure Hightower would do a wonderful job, but—" he reached into his attaché case and pulled out a black leather portfolio "—can Hightower offer you this?" Expansively he opened the pages and watched with smug satisfaction as Nat Carpenter, one of the world's leading developers, reviewed the pages with awe.

Mr. Brathwaite smiled. This was only the beginning. With a bit more luck and timing the deal was his. They'd never know what hit them.

"These ideas are... I can't find the words to describe them," Nat said. He sighed heavily. "However, I must be fair. I'm scheduled to meet with Mr. Steele next week. I feel obliged to at least look at what he has to offer before I make a commitment one way or the other."

"Of course." He reached across the table and slid the portfolio toward him. "I'll be returning to the States tomorrow." He pulled out his business card and handed it to Nat. "Call me." He rose from the table and shook Nat's hand.

"I'll be in touch once the meeting is concluded next week, Mr. Brathwaite."

"I'll be looking forward to hearing from you. And, please, call me Malcolm. I have the feeling we're going to become very good friends. I'm sure that you will also keep in mind our agreement that our meetings are strictly confidential."

"Of course. Don't concern yourself that it would be otherwise."

Malcolm Brathwaite smiled.

Chapter 20

"Welcome home, boss lady," Stacy greeted as Terri stepped off the elevator.

Terri eagerly walked into Stacy's warm embrace. "How is everything?" She took Stacy's arm and ushered her toward her office, smiling and waving at her staff as she passed. "Catch me up on all the goings-on—and I have some great news. I'll need your help," she rushed on.

"I see your old enthusiasm is back." Stacy gave Terri a pointed look as they entered Terri's office.

"Believe me, I have every reason to be enthusiastic."

Stacy took her favorite seat by the window. "Don't keep me in suspense. What's the great news?"

Terri turned and faced Stacy, her face illuminated with a grin. "How does a few weeks in the Caribbean sound to you?"

A slow smile of disbelief lifted Stacy's lips and infected her green eyes with astonishment. "What? The Caribbean?"

she squealed. "Don't tease me, Terri," she warned, holding one hand to her heart.

Terri's peals of laughter tinkled throughout the room. "Believe me, this is for real!"

"Yes!" Stacy whooped, balling her fingers into a fist and shooting a blow through the air. "Tell me, tell me, when do I get my bikini out of mothballs?"

"I figure just after the holidays. But I'm going down to Nassau in a couple of days to get a better feel for things."

"Lucky you. Are you going to tell me who our benefactor is, or what?"

"Clinton Steele."

"You're kidding?" She looked at Terri with wry suspicion. "You're not kidding. Well, well, Miss Thing, still waters do run deep." She gave Terri one of her naughty-girl looks.

"Don't start, Stacy," Terri warned. "This is business." But even as she said the words, she couldn't keep the grin off her face.

"Yeah, okay, whatever you say. So, what do you need? What's the project?"

Terri sat down behind her desk and pulled out her preliminary notes from her briefcase. Within moments the two women began mapping out a tentative campaign for the resorts.

"This is going to be fabulous, Terri. I can feel it."

"I think so, too. This could be our biggest project to date. If all goes well, Clint is planning on opening connecting bed-and-breakfast inns in England. In other words, a trip would be all-inclusive—you stay in one of the Steele resorts in the Caribbean with the second leg of the trip being England, and your accommodations are automatic."

"Does that mean we get to go to merry old England, too?"

"You bet."

"This is getting better by the minute." Stacy checked her

watch. "Wow, we've been at it for almost four hours. It's one o'clock already."

Terri got up and stretched. "And I'm starved. Let's take a break."

"Sounds good."

"Oh, Stacy." Terri briefly shut her eyes and pressed her palm to her head in embarrassment. "I didn't mean to overshadow your news about Anita. What's the latest?"

"Right now it looks good. But it's not definite yet. I'm expecting a call with the go-ahead sometime this week."

"Well—Powers, Inc., is moving right along. Wouldn't you say?"

"I'd say more than that. We're flying high."

"To think that just a short time ago, we were on the brink of possibly going under." She shuddered slightly, remembering, then shook her head to get rid of the images of Mark. "But," she added quickly, "we should be seeing the fruits of our labor with Viatek Studios before Christmas. They loved everything."

"I knew they would. You may have to think about expanding, Terri, if this pace keeps up. I mean, we're good, you and I, but it may get to a point where we can't handle the load. You especially. You pour your heart and soul into every project."

Terri fingered a stray lock behind her ear and smoothed the red-and-gold headband that held her hair in place. "I've thought about expanding, Stacy, but to be honest, I like the personal touch we give our clients. I think that's what sets us apart from the other agencies."

"Hmm, you're probably right. Anyway—" she shrugged her shoulders and grinned "—whatever works." Stacy gathered her notes. "I'll get on this right after lunch. I should have some preliminaries by morning."

"I'll work on the scheduling and put some feelers out for sponsors."

"Some celebrity faces would be perfect."

"Absolutely." Terri paused for a moment. "I just had a flash."

"What?"

"Check through all of our previous clients and look through their bios. I think the perfect touch would be some celebrities with a Caribbean background. What do you think?"

"I think you're a genius! I'll have my assistant, Celeste, take care of it."

"I have to get a moment to meet her. I only hope she's half as good as you, Stacy."

"What scares me is that I think she may be better." Stacy's eyes widened in a mock look of fright. "I'll see you later." She walked toward the door, stopped and turned, her face aglow. "Congratulations." She gave Terri the thumbs-up sign and walked out.

"You've been as jittery and edgy as a cat in heat since I walked in this morning, Mel. Is something wrong?" Clint took a stab at his crabmeat salad. He gave Melissa a long questioning look.

Melissa fidgeted with her napkin and shifted in her seat. Her lashes shielded her hazel eyes. "No, I'm, uh, just a little tired I guess." She smiled. "It's been a rough few weeks." Her smile weakened. She cleared her throat. "So, I guess you got Ms. Powers to agree to run the campaign?" She took a sip of her spring water.

"I most certainly did. That's what I wanted to talk with you about." Clint motioned for the waiter to refill their water glasses.

Melissa raised her eyebrow. "Really? The decision and agreement have already been made, haven't they? What is there to talk about?" She put her glass down a bit too hard, spilling some of the contents.

"What do you have against Terri Powers, Mel? What has the woman ever done to you?"

The on-target questions seemed to slap her, catching her off guard. Melissa stiffened, jutting out her chin defiantly. "You're too blind to see what's really going on. All she wants is a piece of the Hightower pie!"

Clint was stunned by her vehemence. "Mel! Don't be absurd. Terri is the president of her own company. One that is doing very well. She doesn't need my money. And she's not the kind of woman who would want it!"

Melissa slapped her napkin on the table. Her nostrils flared with hurt and indignation.

"You don't know her," she seethed, her eyes creasing with anger, thinking of how Mark described her as a money-hungry vulture who would use anyone to get what she wanted.

"And you do?"

What was she doing? She took a shuddering breath, realizing that she was treading a very thin line and losing her cool. Her shoulders slumped in resignation, and she forced calm into her voice. "I have to get back to the office." She rose to leave. Clint clamped his hand down over hers, holding her in place.

"There's something bugging you, Mel." His dark eyes narrowed. "Ever since you took up with that Mark Andrews you've been a different person."

"Don't, Clint." She shook her auburn head vehemently. "Don't you question my personal life. You—" her voice cracked "—of all people."

Clint's grip tightened as he tried to control his mounting temper. His voice dropped to a low, threatening whisper. "When your personal life interferes with business, then that becomes *my* business."

She snatched her hand away, gave him one hard look and stormed off.

Clint watched her receding back with a mixture of disbelief and foreboding.

* * *

Terri checked her watch. She still had some time before Lisa stopped by to meet her for lunch. In the meantime she scanned her appointment book and compared it to the office scheduling for the next four weeks. Before she could make any plans to leave, she had to be sure that everything was covered. She certainly wouldn't feel comfortable leaving Stacy overloaded with work. Even if she did have a top-notch assistant. If everything turned out the way Clint had envisioned, they would be leaving the islands and heading straight for England for the holidays.

Pausing, she tapped the edge of the pen on her teeth. *England.* Just the thought of meeting Clint's daughter made her uneasy. If she could only believe Lisa and Clint. They seemed so positive that everything would work out. She only wished that she could feel the same way without reservation. Clint was the only reason she was putting her emotions on the line. If she didn't feel so deeply for him, the way she did, there was no way that she would be able to go through with it.

She looked at the phone and realized how much she needed to hear his voice, to let him reassure her. Even though they spent every free moment and nearly every night together, it never seemed to be enough. The mere thought of him made her feel warm and desirable. She reached for the phone to dial his number just as it rang.

"Terri Powers."

"Just wanted to let you know that the next time you need to get your point across, you don't have to send 'your boy' out with your messages."

"What? Alan? I don't know what you're talking about. I didn't send—"

"Sure you didn't. But believe me, baby, you won't have to worry about me anymore. I'm out of your life. For good.

Just the way you wanted it. Just remember, what goes around comes around." He slammed the phone down in the cradle.

Terri stared at the receiver as though it alone was responsible for the bizarre phone call. What in the world was Alan talking about? "My boy"? Paying him a visit? That was— Oh, no. She didn't want to believe it. It couldn't be. Not after her specific request to stay out of it.

It couldn't have been anyone else but Clint! But when? Her thoughts raced backward to their time together in L.A.: it had to be during the time he returned the car to the rental agency, she concluded. Her temper rose at an alarming rate. And if it was, he'd have a helluva lot of explaining to do. The nerve!

She pushed herself away from her desk, crossing and uncrossing her arms as she stalked across the floor. She nearly snatched the phone off the receiver when her intercom buzzed.

"Yes!"

"Sorry to disturb you, Ms. Powers, but Mr. Steele is here to see you."

The hairs on the back of her neck bristled. Terri let out a shaky breath. "I'm sorry, Andrea. I didn't mean to snap at you. Have Mr. Steele wait a moment, then send him in."

"Yes, Ms. Powers." Andrea looked across the small reception area and motioned to Clint. He rose from his seat and approached the desk. "Ms. Powers asked me to have you wait a moment. She'll be right with you."

"Oh, she did—did she?" He slipped out of his cashmere coat and draped it across his arm, while Andrea nearly swooned looking at him. He might not be too pleased to have to wait, she thought, but she was loving every minute of it.

Like a caged tiger he traced and retraced his steps in the narrow path he'd cut for himself on the beige carpet. This was the final insult of the day. Not only did he have to put up with Melissa—her attitude and disturbing behavior—now he was being put on hold by his woman. Just how much was a man supposed to take in one day? Then something hit him. He'd had just about enough. What he needed right now was to be in the comforting arms of the woman he loved. And he'd be damned if he'd wait a minute longer.

Before Andrea knew what had happened, Clint swept past her and into Terri's office.

Terri didn't have time to react before Clint pulled her into his arms and kissed her fully on the lips. "Hey, baby—" he breathed against her cheek "—I needed that." He raised his hand to stroke her hair, and she slapped it away.

"Don't touch me," she ordered.

"What? Don't touch you?"

"That's right, you heard me."

Clint took two steps back and looked at her as though she'd gone completely mad. "Is there something you want to tell me, Terri?" He looked ready to explode. "Or do I have to guess?"

She crossed her arms beneath her breasts and stared at him hard. "No, you don't have to guess, Clint, because I'm sure you already know what you've done."

"Done? Listen, now I'm getting pissed. I had a lousy morning, and the last thing I need—"

"I'll tell you what you need," she began, craning her neck back and forth, with both hands placed firmly on her hips as she spoke. "You *need* to stay out of my affairs. When I say something, I mean it, Clint. You *need* to stop thinking that you can walk into my life and take it over. You *need* to stop thinking that you can use scare tactics to settle your problems. That's what you *need!*"

Clint's mouth nearly fell open before he could find the words to lash back at her. He took a threatening step toward her.

"So Mr. Playboy called and told you that he'd been paid a visit." His voice rose. "And you're upset? I find that very interesting. First you didn't want me around when you knew you were going to be with him. Then when he tries to jump your bones, and I take matters into my own hands, you run to his defense! Maybe you *need* to rethink this relationship Terri," he taunted. "Maybe you *need* to run back down to L.A. and comfort your ex. Because it's obvious that you haven't gotten Alan Martin out of your system."

Without another word, he glared at her and slammed out of the office.

Terri stood in the pounding silence, shaking with anger. Not only did he think he could run her life, she thought, he honestly believed that she was still in love with Alan.

Well, let him, she fumed. She wasn't about to give him any explanations. Not after everything they'd been to each other over the past months. Hadn't she proven that she loved him? Couldn't he see that?

She turned away from the door just as Lisa bounced into the office, only to be stopped cold by the look of rage that fired Terri's eyes.

"If that's the kind of greeting I'm going to get, I'll leave now," she warned, stepping into the office and placing her purse on the desk. She cautiously approached Terri. "What in the devil is wrong with you? You should be on top of the world instead of looking like you're carrying it on your shoulders." Lisa took a seat and waited.

Terri spun toward Lisa, her red-and-gold dress fanning out around her. "He thinks I'm some sort of weak, incompetent female who can't take care of herself! I'm no damsel in distress that he has to come and rescue!" She threw her hands up in the air and stomped across the room.

Lisa's smooth face crinkled in confusion. "Honey, what are you talking about?" she asked softly.

"Clint! Who else?"

"Oh, of course. What exactly did he do?" Lisa hid her amusement behind her hand as she listened to Terri's tirade.

* * *

Terri huffed as she drew her story to and end. "Can you believe it? How dare he? You just wait until I—"

"Terri, hon." Lisa got up from her seat and stood next to Terri, placing a comforting arm around her shoulders. "I'm sure that Clint didn't intend to make you feel inadequate. You know how men are. He was only looking out for you. And I'm sure that his ego was bruised, too."

Terri pulled on her bottom lip. "Maybe you're right, but I can't have Clint going around running interference every time he thinks I can't handle something. He has to learn to wait for me to ask him. I've had someone manipulating my life for as long as I can remember. I'm not going to fall back into that trap. Not again."

Lisa cleared her throat. "Believe me, I understand how you feel. And on some points you're right. But, Terri, don't you think it's time that you had someone who cares enough about you to put *himself* on the line for a change? Don't you think you deserve that?"

Terri lowered her head. "Maybe," she mumbled. "But I just don't know if I'm ready to let go of everything and put my life, my emotions and my future into someone else's hands. You can understand that, can't you, Lis?"

"There's going to come a time, whether you want it to or not, when you won't have to ask yourself those questions. Everything will fall into place, and you'll wonder why life wasn't always that way."

Terri gave her a crooked smile. "That from someone who was in love with every male on the college campus," Terri teased. She hugged Lisa to her, then stepped back and held her at arm's length. "But in the meantime," she said, a mischievous grin lifting her lips, "I can't let him think that he can get away with it. Now can I?"

Lisa shook her head and said a silent prayer for Clint. The poor man didn't know what he had gotten himself into.

Chapter 21

Clint spent the rest of his afternoon at the health club trying to burn off the anger that had crept into his veins like a poison. He longed for the exhaustion that would make him so numb that he wouldn't dream, wouldn't think, of Terri.

But with each slam of the black ball against the wall, he thought of smashing the barriers that had been thrown between them. It seemed that from the beginning, they were doomed to have one obstacle after another erected in their paths. Everything from basic philosophies to old relationships haunted their happiness.

And right now, he thought, as he took his third lap around the track, he didn't know if he had the stamina to deal with them anymore.

Terri. He ran a little faster as the end of the lap approached. She was strong, opinionated, an extraordinary lover and a woman who could challenge him on every level. That's what he loved about her, he conceded, as he jogged over to the bench, collapsing on the wooden boards. He leaned his head back against the cool tiles and covered his sweat-drenched face with a cotton towel.

Couldn't she see, feel, tell, how much he loved her? Maybe he didn't say it often enough, he mused, as he angled his car into the underground garage of his apartment building. But he was not one for words of love. He never had been. He attempted to show how he felt. Unfortunately he usually chose the wrong way to show it. Or worse, not at all. His behavior, compounded with his inability to voice his feelings when a woman needed to be reassured, had contributed to destroying his marriage, and now it seemed to have caused him to lose Terri, as well.

Couldn't she understand that he'd taken action because of the way he felt about her? He thought he was showing her how much she mattered to him by setting Alan straight. Hindsight, he thought, the realization raw and painful.

He turned the key in his apartment door and switched on the lights. Empty. He'd grown tired of coming home to an empty apartment. He'd begun to look forward to the end of the workday with nothing but pleasure on the horizon. Terri had been the source of that change. Even his secretary, Pat, had noticed the change in him and commented on his continual sunny disposition. When he'd met Steve for after dinner drinks the previous week, he'd added his two cents.

"That woman has sure worked her magic on you," Steve had said, tossing down a Budweiser. "Looks like you finally got some sense into that thick head of yours and took my advice."

Clint thought about that now as he entered his empty apartment. He'd spent so many years burying himself in his work at the expense of everyone that was important. Being with Terri was like being reborn. It had taken getting a second chance to make him realize that there was more to life. He wanted Terri's voice, her laughter, her scent to fill all of the empty spaces in his life, not work. But what could he do when the woman he loved was in love with another man?

Clint's heavy sigh filled the room as he kicked off his sneakers and tossed his gym bag and coat on the couch. Through sheer force of habit, he went straight to his answering machine, secretly hoping that there would be a message from Terri. Instead it was an urgent message from Steve—about Mark Andrews.

Frustrated, Terri hung up the phone for the third time that evening. She was tired of listening to Clint's recorded voice and refused to leave a message. She wanted the real thing, especially when she was in the frame of mind to make a truce. She sucked her teeth in annoyance.

Where could he be? She checked the wall clock: 10 p.m. Humph! Obviously he had put their confrontation out of his mind, and the thought that he might be out enjoying himself while she was nursing her injured ego incensed her once again.

Perhaps she was right about him after all. But a small nagging voice inside her head told her that she was wrong. Just as she'd been wrong about him from the beginning. At the moment there was nothing she could do about it, she concluded, stretching out on the couch and taking a sip of fruit juice. Then suddenly she sprang up, nearly spilling the juice in the process. There was something that she could do. And she wasn't about to waste another minute.

Clint's anger had dissolved by degrees after listening to Steve's report. However, his anger was replaced by an unsettling concern that chilled him to the bone.

By rote, he made all of the appropriate turns en route to his destination, maneuvering through the stop-and-go traffic like the New York pro that he was.

He pulled up in front of the all-too-familiar apartment building. Just seeing the structure brought back vivid images of ecstasy. Now there was nothing but a dull ache in its place. But he'd face it down, just as he'd faced down all of the other challenges that had come his way.

Constructing an invisible wall of indifference around himself, he strode purposefully forward. He was determined to keep his feelings at bay. This was business. He had to remember that.

Resolved, he walked toward the entrance door just as the first sprinkles of snow began to fall. He pulled up his coat collar and hurried across the street.

Freshly showered and changed, Terri splashed on her favorite scent. She took a quick look in the mirror and was pleased with what she saw. The loose-fitting, lightweight wool-pants outfit in a soft emerald green did wonders for her spirits. Pleased, she slipped into her coat, grabbed her purse and headed for the door.

Once she'd made up her mind, there was no turning back. She had the shortcoming of reacting to situations without looking beyond the surface, especially when it applied to her private life. And it had always cost her. This time the stakes were too high for mistakes. She saw very clearly what she had to lose, and she didn't intend to. Not this time.

She stepped on the elevator and pressed the ground-floor button. She'd remain calm, she thought, knowing how easily her temper flared. She'd listen and try to understand even if she didn't agree. Mentally she ticked off her resolutions and made a silent promise to stick to them. Clint was worth every ounce of crow that she may have to swallow. But still, she thought naughtily, she couldn't let him off too easy.

Quickly she stepped from the elevator and hurried toward the lobby entrance, just as Clint pushed through the glass doors.

He'd come to her. Elation whipped through her. But the shock of seeing Clint coming through the door in no way prepared her for the shock of his chilling detachment.

She stood in front of him, her heart beating with expectation. She looked into his eyes, searching for the familiar warmth, and found nothing but a dark emptiness.

"Clint." She said his name hesitantly as though unsure if he would respond.

Clint swallowed hard, inhaling her heady scent, his pulse racing at her nearness. All he wanted to do was take her in his arms and kiss away the tremulous look that hovered around her mouth. But he wouldn't.

"I was just on my way to see you." She smiled up at him.

"Had I known, I could have saved myself a trip." He watched her recoil at his callousness, and a part of him withered inside. He shoved his hands into his coat pockets to keep from wiping away the stricken look on her face.

Her smile slowly evaporated. She cleared her throat, her back grew rigid and she jutted out her chin, looking him squarely in the eye.

"I see. Well, since you came all this way, you may as well tell me what this is all about."

"We need someplace to talk."

It would be so easy to tell him to come up to her apartment—to settle things between them—but she was just as determined as he to be difficult.

"What's wrong with right here?" she asked coyly. She saw his jaw tighten and knew she had hit the mark.

"Right here is pretty inappropriate, Terri," he uttered in a low rumble. He quickly scanned the lobby, then turned to her, his growing ire blazing in his eyes like hot coals. "Let's go to my car." It was more of an order than a suggestion. But she realized she had left herself no other choice. Then she thought, as she followed his rapid footsteps, the car was even more intimate than her apartment!

As they stepped out onto the sidewalk, they were met by a gust of wind full of bitter cold snow.

Terri opened her mouth to voice her surprise, but she was cut off by an icy blast that filled her lungs.

The swirling mass of white had built in dramatic intensity within a short span of time. Already visibility was limited to only a few feet.

Instinctively Clint grabbed Terri around the waist, pulling her next to him, in an effort to both protect her from the blasts of wind and to keep her from falling. He realized, as soon as their bodies made contact, that what he really wanted was an excuse to have her near him.

"This way," he shouted above the wind, ushering her across the snow-covered street.

With the heat turned on in the car, their chilled bodies quickly warmed, but the block of ice that sat between them remained intact.

Terri was the first to break the awkward silence.

"So, what did you want to talk with me about, Clint?"

He slowly turned his head in her direction. "The only way I can say this is the way it was put to me." He took a deep breath, then plunged ahead. "Terri, there is no such person as Mark Andrews. Before you met him, he didn't exist."

Chapter 22

Melissa stared up at the ceiling, unable to sleep. She angled her head toward her bedside clock. Midnight. She hadn't heard from Mark since he'd left her office. Maybe it was just as well. He was scaring her.

Clint had hit the nail on the head when he said she'd changed. She shut her eyes, recalling her outburst with Clint. She'd nearly blown everything. She shuddered. Mark would've been furious.

Mark...Clint...Mark.... Again the two men seemed to merge together. One appeared to slip further out of her reach with each passing day. And the other she had by default. A man who both thrilled and terrified her. But the thrill was slowly diminishing, and the fear was settling over her like a shroud.

Mark was dangerous. There was a dark side to his past that he merely alluded to. Somehow Terri Powers was at the core.

Melissa rolled onto her side determined to fall asleep

ıst as the shrill of her phone put that determination out of ːr head.

"Hello?"

"Hey, sugah, it's me." The excitement in his voice vibrated ːross the wires.

Melissa sat up in the bed, running nervous fingers through ːr hair. "How did everything go?"

Mark stretched across the queen-size bed, his smile match-ıg the easy movements of his body. "So far, so good. Has ːeele actually convinced Terri to do the PR?"

Melissa squeezed the phone between her fingers. "That's ːhat he told me today."

"Then we'll deal with it. Money talks, and thanks to Terri," ːe said, chuckling, "this time I have the capital to hold a ːry heavy conversation." He laughed uproariously at his own ːit.

Melissa waited until his deep rumble subsided before she ːsked the question that was burning on her tongue. "I don't ːnderstand something, Mark. I thought you wanted to hurt ːerri. What does pulling the rug out from under Clint have ː do with that?"

"Satisfaction, Mel." He closed his eyes and smiled smugly. ːThe satisfaction of seeing her suffer even at the expense of ːmeone else. When I get at Steele, I get at her. Simple. If ːe's part of the package, I get to pull the rug out from under ːoth of them."

"But how did you know that she and Clint would—?" Her ːuestion hung in midair.

Mark laughed. "I know Terri. And I saw the look that Clint ːad in his eyes the moment I started telling him about her. As ːuch as they may have tried to deny it, I could see they were ːttracted to each other. The rest was inevitable," he concluded, ːalice lacing his voice.

"You're in love with her, aren't you?" she accused, the ːords rushing out before she could stop them.

Mark laughed again, this time a cold malicious laugh th▸
cut through her like honed steel. "What's that song that Ti▸
Turner sings, 'What's Love Got to Do with It'?"

Chapter 23

It seemed an eternity before she could grasp the words that hung precariously in the cozy confines of the car. *Ridiculous* was the first word that leaped into her head. This time Clint had gone over the edge, she concluded.

But when she looked into his eyes and saw the sincerity, concern and conviction floating in their darkness, she knew that he was telling her the truth. And with that realization came a fear that sank to her marrow.

Her voice sounded choked when she tried to get the first words out. "I don't understand. How could he not exist?" A tremor sped up her spine. "Then...who is he?"

Clint thought about telling her just how long he'd been investigating Mark, and his reasons for doing so. But knowing Terri and her stalwart attitude—that she wanted no one and nothing to interfere in her life—he had second thoughts. Instead, he gave her his basic reason, but not the fact that his suspicions prompted him to continue in order to protect her. She'd have a fit if she knew. L.A. had taught him that.

"I always do a routine check on anyone I plan to do business with. And when our original deal fell through, I told Steve to call off the inquiry."

Terri's eyes held his, then briefly looked away. There was something that was missing from Clint's explanation. All she could do, however, for the time being, was play along.

"So, if you had Steve call off his investigation, are you telling me that you knew about Mark all along and never said anything to me?"

The question, bordering on accusation, caught him off guard. But he quickly recovered, noting the skepticism in her voice.

"Apparently Steve had other thoughts. He decided to pursue it on his own."

"You're saying that this is all routine?"

There was that tone again. "Exactly."

She nodded, seemingly mollified by the explanation. "Well, what *exactly* did Steve find out?"

Clint took a deep breath. "Mark's history goes as far back as a year prior to his employment with you. He has no previous address, bank accounts, school, or family information. Nothing. The trail went cold."

Terri tried to absorb the implications of Clint's story. She shook her head in disbelief. "Why didn't I check him out thoroughly?" she said almost to herself. She chuckled mirthlessly. "I know why," she continued, answering her own question. "I was so anxious to get some of the burden of the business off my shoulders and so overwhelmed by the circumstances of my private life, that I was negligent."

"Don't do this, Terri. We all make mistakes in business—"

"I'd been so impressed with him at the interview and with his résumé," she continued as if she hadn't heard him, "that I bypassed the usual follow-up. I guess I was wearing my wounds on my sleeve. He probably smelled my vulnerability from miles away," she added in a faraway voice.

"Was he recommended by someone?"

Terri frowned as she thought back. "No. I don't think so. I was running an ad as well as putting feelers out." She shook her head. "Things were just so crazy then." Briefly she shut her eyes against the enormity of what was happening. She had employed someone who had a very strong reason to keep his background a secret. Why? And why had he decided to use her and her business as a backdrop? Clint seemed to be reading her mind.

"He obviously had a reason for singling you out. Combine that with his under-the-table dealings, and you have all of the ingredients for serious trouble. What we need to find out is why he chose you."

"We?" She could feel her heart leap, both with fright and exhilaration.

"Yeah, we." He hesitated a moment, lowered his head, then twisted his body halfway in his seat toward her. "Listen, Terri—" he heaved a sigh "—no matter what you may think of me or the way I handle things, I care about you deeply. And I wouldn't sit back and let anything happen to you."

By this time the pulse was pounding so loudly in her ears, she could barely hear herself respond.

"Do you think I'm in some sort of danger?"

"No," he said a bit too quickly. Then he caught himself. "I'm sure it's nothing that serious. It's probably no more than financial manipulation. For some reason he felt that you were the perfect target."

Terri felt her heart begin to slow to normal at the sound of the reassuring words. Clint believed it was no more than pure greed. That reality was something she could deal with.

"If that's all you think it is, and I do, too," she added, "then why all of the concern? Mark is old news."

"Let's just say it never hurts to be careful. I'd feel a lot better if I knew what this guy's motive was."

Terri nodded. "So now what?"

"Steve is going to keep digging. But in the meantime I want you to keep your eyes and ears open, especially involving any new contracts."

"You think he may try something else?"

"I don't know. But I want you to be prepared if he should."

Terri took a deep breath, pulling her coat securely around her. "Thank you," she said softly. "I appreciate your concern." Self-consciously she turned her head toward the passenger window, locking her gaze on the swirling snow that had engulfed the city.

"I'd better be going," she said, making moves to leave. She turned toward him, then quickly reached for the door lock.

Clint's large hand clasped her shoulder, sending a shock wave of pleasure shooting down to her belly. She sat frozen, afraid to leave, afraid to stay.

Clint's voice was low and penetrating, unlocking her spine. "You'd said you were on your way to see me."

She turned in his direction, and his gaze held her in place. Terri blinked several times to rouse herself from the hypnotic pull of his eyes.

"I—" she swallowed, wishing that the dryness in her mouth would go away "—wanted to…"

"Yes?"

She inhaled and the words poured out in one breath. "I wanted to apologize for the way I acted, the things I said." She looked deeply into his eyes. "You didn't deserve that."

Clint's full lips curved unconsciously with a tentative smile. And Terri had the overwhelming desire to kiss them tasteless. "Are you saying that I'm not the monstrous, chauvinist pig that you thought I was?"

His caressing smile took the sting away from his words.

By degrees she felt the weight that had settled in her soul shift and ascend, leaving her feeling vibrant and alive again.

"I never thought that," she said meekly, a flicker of merriment dancing in her eyes.

"Maybe not in those exact words," he teased, "but pretty damned close."

They both laughed, letting their laughter wash over them, cleansing them, allowing them to enjoy the euphoric release of tension.

Clint's features softened as he soaked in the rhythm of her laughter. Instinctively he reached out to tuck a stray lock behind her ear, stroking her cheek in the process.

They both uttered each other's name in unison.

"You first," Clint offered, tracing her lips with his fingertip.

"So many things have stood in our path, Clint."

He sat straighter in his seat. "I feel the same way."

"And," she continued, "I'd begun to feel that there was no way we would ever be able to work things out."

"And?" His one-word question was full of hope.

"I know I've said this all before, Clint, and maybe you have no reason to believe me, but we can work things out between us. I want us to."

"Why?"

Briefly she looked away. She could feel her heart racing like mad in her chest. "Because I love you, Clint, more than I've been willing to admit to you or myself."

"Terri, I—"

"Please—" she held up her hand "—let me finish before I lose my nerve." She let out a shaky laugh. "I've been so wrapped up in being superwoman and shielding myself from getting involved, I wasn't truly ready to accept you, what you stood for, or the idea that someone actually cared enough about me to stick their neck out."

Her long thick lashes shielded the apprehension that hovered

in her eyes. She fumbled with the buttons on her coat to avoi
looking at him.

"You're worth it, Terri. You're worth all of that and mor
Give me half a chance, baby, and I'll put the world at you
feet."

He leaned forward and tilted up her chin, forcing her t
look at him. His breath caught in his throat when he saw th
shimmering fawn-colored pools that looked at him with suc
wistfulness.

"Don't you ever forget that. I love you, woman, and it's tim
that you began to accept just—" he planted a light kiss on he
cheek "—how—" then another on her lips "—much."

Her head began to spin, matching the speed and fury o
the raging snowstorm. Her body became infused with tha
old familiar heat that scorched her then turned her insides t
liquid fire.

Clint raked his fingers through her hair, letting its sensua
texture ripple through him. He groaned against her mouth
pulling her as close as the obtrusive stick shift would allow

"Come upstairs," she whispered.

The drapes were drawn back, allowing full view of th
storm that had swept the now silent city. A myriad of star
twinkled between the shimmering white flakes, giving th
heavens a mystical aura. But Clint and Terri were obliviou
to what stirred around them, immersed only in themselves.

Terri's eyes flickered lovingly across Clint's face as h
hovered inches above her. Her nude body glowed with th
fire that had been ignited within her by Clint's eager mouth
tempting tongue and maddening fingertips as he traile
languidly across her form.

She reached for him, stroking him in all the right places
awakening every nerve, every fiber, until his body screame
and he could no longer withstand the denial.

* * *

Hours later Terri lay nestled in Clint's arms comforted by
the steady beating of his heart. She'd make it work this time,
she silently vowed, snuggling closer. Even if it meant getting
over her fear of meeting his daughter. That day was drawing
closer, and as much as she tried to keep thoughts of Ashley
out of her mind, the more difficult it became. She eased out
of Clint's embrace. How would she act? Would Ashley like
her? She slipped out of the bed. What if she didn't?

Stifling a sigh, she eased into her robe and walked toward
the window.

She and Clint had been through so much in such a short
span of time. Furtively she looked over her shoulder at Clint's
sleeping form. Watching him lying there so peacefully, her
waves of apprehension waned.

She resumed her vigil at the window, allowing the purity
of the falling snow to embrace her and somehow rid her mind
of the unsettling thoughts. She and Clint had a bright future
ahead of them. That's what she had to concentrate on. That
and their impending trip to the Caribbean.

Just the thought of returning to her homeland filled her with
a sense of place and serenity. Those early days with Nana and
her brother, Malcolm, were some of the happiest days of her
life.

Yet with those feelings of happiness was a sense of melancholy. How different would her and her brother's lives have
been if Nana had lived to take care of them?

Thoughts of her brother sparked thoughts of Mark. How
different was she from him? Her own identity and sense of
being was constructed by her adopted parents. They tried to
take away everything that was sacred to her—her heritage,
her family, even her way of speaking. They said it was
uncultured.

Maybe if—

"What are you in such deep thought about?" Clint stood

behind her and wrapped his arms around her waist. He pulled her closer and pressed his face into her hair.

She sighed. "I was just thinking about our trip to the islands."

"Is that all? You were looking mighty serious to be thinking about something so pleasant."

She almost laughed at his uncanny ability to read right through her.

"Well, if you must know, I was thinking about my brother, my grandmother, and wondering how different my life would have been. And—" she turned around to look up into his eyes "—I was thinking how I'm not that much different from Mark."

Clint's brow immediately creased into a frown. "What in the devil are you talking about? There's no way you could compare yourself to him."

"Maybe, maybe not. But I'm not the person I appear to be, either. I'm a creation of my adopted parents." She smiled without humor. "Molded to their liking. Powers isn't even my birth name. Sometimes I feel like such a fraud."

He pulled her closer. "Oh, baby, no matter what their motives may have been, you turned out spectacular. Don't ever doubt yourself."

Her eyes sparkled. "You really think so?"

"Are you fishing for compliments, lady?"

"Maybe."

"In that case, yeah, I really think so." He bowed his head, sealing his statement with a warm kiss.

Feeling the warning signs of arousal, he reluctantly broke away. He rubbed her shoulders. "Since we're in the mood for revelations, don't you think I deserve to know the real name of the woman I'm getting ready to take back to bed?"

Terri giggled when he lifted her off the floor and headed for the bed. He tossed her unceremoniously on the cushiony mattress and struck a mock pose of seriousness.

"So are you going to tell me, young lady, or will I have to—" he curled his fingers "—tickle it out of you?"

"No! Please, don't," she squealed. "I'll tell. I swear."

"That's more like it." He eased down beside her and began stroking her hip.

"If you keep that up, you're gonna make me forget the question," she whispered.

"I don't think so, baby." He rolled on top of her. "'Cause I'm going to ask you again." He parted her thighs with his knee and slipped easily inside of her. She moaned softly as inch by inch he filled the walls.

Ever so slowly he moved within her, stunned again by the intensity that consumed him. His mouth covered hers, drinking in the sweetness of her lips. She played teasing games with her tongue, exploring all of the crevices of his mouth.

Forcing himself to pull away, he looked into her eyes. "Who is it that I'm going to pleasure until she can't take any more?"

Terri draped her hands around Clint's neck and rotated her hips, making him groan.

"My real name," she whispered, not missing a beat, "is Theresa Brathwaite. Terri for short."

Chapter 24

Terri scanned her closet, selecting the appropriate clothes and depositing them on her bed, while she balanced her portable phone between her ear and her shoulder.

"How have you been feeling these days, Lisa? I've been so busy lately, I've totally neglected you."

"Of course you've neglected me," she teased. "But seriously, don't be silly, I know things have been hectic for you lately. As for me, I think I'm handling the backaches, swollen feet and bizarre cravings like a pro."

"I envy you," Terri said wistfully, thinking once again of the child she'd lost.

"Envy me! Girl, you've got to be jokin'. You have it made, Terri. You have your own business, you travel around the world, you're intelligent *and* beautiful."

"Believe me, that's all superficial. What I want is a family of my own, a man who's crazy about me, and I want to know that I have that love and security every day."

Lisa was quiet for a moment, knowing that this was a

very touchy area for Terri. "Listen," she said softly, "all of those things will fall in place for you. You have Clint—whom I'm dying to meet. And from everything you've told me, he sounds as if he adores you. If that's true, can family be far behind?"

"Maybe," Terri admitted, not daring to hope.

"When are you heading out to Nassau?"

"The ship departs the day after tomorrow. I hope to be on it," she added, looking at the mess on her bed. "That is, if I ever get packed."

"The *ship* departs! Well, well, packing aside, girlfriend, Clint sure knows how to treat a sister, doesn't he?"

"He certainly does." Terri giggled wickedly. "He certainly does."

"Hey, I have an idea. Why don't you and Clint come by tomorrow night for dinner? Sort of a bon voyage. And of course it'll give me a chance to check out Mr. Wonderful up close and personal."

"Hmm. It's fine with me. I'll check with Clint, but I'm sure he'll go for it. The only thing I have on my agenda for tomorrow is dance class for my students before I leave. That's at five. Then just some last-minute details around here."

"Great. Check with Clint, and let me know in the morning."

"No problem. I need to see you anyway."

Lisa quickly picked up on the vibes. "We'll talk tomorrow."

"I'll give you a call before I try to teach my little protégés. We may not have a chance later."

"One of these days you're gonna turn out a star."

"I sure hope so. I deserve it!"

Both women laughed, recalling the torture that Terri went through to get her community program opened and then the grueling task of organizing an unorganized group of eight-year-olds.

"That's for sure. Well, I have to run. I have a doctor's appointment in about an hour."

"Okay. I'll call you tomorrow."

"Do try to make it. I have something that I'm dying to show you."

"What is it?" Terri's curiosity rose.

"If I told you, it wouldn't be a surprise."

"Come on, Lisa," she whined. "You know how I hate being in suspense."

"Yeah, almost as much as you hate me when I don't tell you my little secrets," she giggled. "'Bye."

"Lisa!" But all she heard was the dial tone. "Ya really irk me, girl," she mumbled, slipping into her native dialect. Terri replaced the receiver, then picked it right back up and punched in the numbers to her office. Andrea answered on the first ring.

"Hi, Andrea, it's me."

"Ms. Powers, good morning."

"Are there any messages?"

"No. Nothing urgent."

"Good. I'll be in later this morning. Let Stacy know so that she can be available around two o'clock."

"I'll tell her."

"Thanks. See you later." Terri replaced the receiver, then sucked on her bottom lip. With that out of the way, she could concentrate on her packing and about going home. The thoughts of home brought a smile to her face. Something deep inside told her that this trip was going to be a turning point in her life.

"This is Clinton Steele. I'd like to speak with Mr. Carpenter."

"One moment. I'll see if he's in."

Clint briefly shut his eyes and shook his head. If he had a dime for every practiced line a secretary uttered, he'd never have to work another day in his life. That's why he always made it a policy to tell his secretaries to be up front with people.

The gruff voice with the touch of a British accent cut into his thoughts.

"Clint, good day."

"Nat. I was calling to confirm our appointment for next Friday."

He cleared his throat. "Friday is fine. Contact my office when you arrive. I could have someone meet you if you wish."

"That might be helpful. I'll let you know. I'll also be bringing along Ms. Powers, the woman I spoke with you about."

"That's fine. I'm looking forward to meeting her. I've heard fantastic things."

Pride eased up Clint's throat and brought a smile to his full lips. "I'm sure you won't be disappointed."

"Are you still planning on taking the cruise to tour the islands first?"

"Yes. I feel it will give me a better handle on things before our meeting."

"You'll definitely enjoy the trip."

"I'm sure. We'll speak again Friday morning?"

"Yes. Good day, Clint."

"Goodbye."

Nat Carpenter pursed his thin lips. This whole deal was getting more interesting by the day. Brathwaite wanted in, in a big way. But he seriously doubted that Brathwaite could compete with Hightower Enterprises' capital. But Brathwaite seemed determined. Maybe he had a few surprises up his sleeve. However, for him, *money* was the operative word. He could give less than a damn about Steele or Brathwaite. He went with the winning team. The team with the cash.

Nat leaned back in his seat, stroking his mustache, and wondered which one of them it would be.

The aftermath of the previous night's snowstorm had brought the bustling city to a virtual crawl.

Terri dreaded the idea of having to navigate from her cozy apartment to her office. A cab was out of the question, and she detested the subway about as much as she detested liver. But if her staff could find a way to get in, so would she. Even if she was forced to creep belowground and take the subway. She visibly shuddered from the thought. It was inhuman.

She took a quick glance at the open suitcase full of outfits for the tropics, then reluctantly turned her sights to the white wonderland that greeted her outside her window.

"Yuk." She turned on her heel and walked toward her open closet.

She took a green-and-red-printed *galà* and wrapped it elaborately around her head. From a satin-covered hanger she removed a fire-engine-red knit dress that reached just below her knees. There was no way to get around wearing boots, she thought miserably, buttoning the tiny buttons that ran up the front of the dress.

Finished, she marched reluctantly toward the door and jammed her feet into her black, knee-high leather boots. She grabbed her cream-colored cashmere coat, her briefcase and keys, and headed out the door.

The subway was more crowded than Terri had anticipated. It seemed as though every body and soul in New York had opted for mass transportation. She took a deep breath and held on to the metal strap, swaying precariously as the train lurched and bucked along its dark underworld journey.

Just one more day, she daydreamed, bringing the sandy beaches, sunshine and crystal-blue water into sharp focus. She heard herself sigh heavily and quickly looked left, then right, to see if anyone was paying attention. Satisfied that no one could care less, she started to fantasize again when her gaze fell upon Mark Andrews, leaning against the train door.

Instantly she felt her pulse escalate, and something distant and familiar swept through her. Instinctively she knew that her feelings had nothing to do with Clint's investigation. It was something deeper. Something that she could vaguely touch. It was the same feeling she'd had when she first met Mark, and sporadically since then. But just as quickly as the sensation had taken hold of her, it disappeared, only to be replaced by cold anger.

They stared at each other above the sea of heads separating them. Mark's gaze was almost gleeful, she realized as a shudder enveloped her, as though he were privy to some secret. She wondered if he actually saw her or was only seeing through her.

Her question was quickly put to rest. The train doors opened and Mark squeezed his way out, but not before he nodded his head in her direction. She felt chilled and it had nothing to do with the weather.

It was several moments before she realized that her heart had slowed to normal. Reluctantly she inhaled deeply of the scents and smells and stepped off the subway at the next stop.

Ten minutes later Terri sat behind her desk, surrounded by all of her familiar things—the plants, artwork, handpicked vases, right down to the gold Cross pen that she kept encased in glass in memory of the first contract she'd signed.

Today everything seemed out of place, disjointed. She knew it had to do with her nerve-racking interlude with Mark. But she couldn't let that reality immobilize her. There was too much to get done before the end of the day, and thoughts of Mark could not interfere. With steadfast determination she went through the process of outlining her day and the days ahead during her absence.

But as the morning ran into afternoon, that nagging, unsettling sensation would not disappear. She reached for the phone and dialed Clint's office.

Mark returned to his apartment. Terri looked the same, he thought, as he tossed his coat onto the couch and took a seat. Mark pulled the sheaf of papers out of his breast pocket. He smiled. Melissa was very thorough. It was only a matter of time before he had Terri just where he wanted her. Destroyed, ruined, alone. Then when she begged for mercy, he'd tell her. He'd tell her everything.

Chapter 25

"Melissa, I've written detailed instructions about what to do with the cable station's stock transfers. I want to be sure that Mr. Anderson gets his rightful share. He gave me a great deal, and I intend to see to it that he's treated fairly. The members of the Board of Directors would love to see that he gets nothing. But I've already put a few bugs in several ears." He smiled. "There shouldn't be any problem."

Melissa sat quietly on the plush sofa, jotting down information that she knew she wouldn't need. She knew Clint's plans and ways of negotiation like the back of her hand. They both knew that she could handle the Board with her eyes closed, mouth taped and hands tied. However, she also knew it made him feel better if he thought she was writing everything down. Besides, it gave her a reason not to have to look at him and possibly reveal the turmoil that boiled beneath her serene exterior.

"…And," he continued, pacing the floor as he spoke, "tell Pat to give a call to my attorney in London and let him know

I'll be in town Christmas week and may need his services on very short notice."

"What about Jillianne and Ashley? Do you want me to have Pat purchase the customary gifts and have them sent?"

Clint heard the sarcasm in her voice but refused to rise to the bait. "No. As a matter of fact, I'll be doing my shopping when I arrive in London. I'm sure I can figure out what a four-year-old girl would like."

Melissa gave a silent sniff of indignation. "Certainly." She slowly rose from her seat. "Is that about it? I'm scheduled to meet with the new clients for the auto dealership in about fifteen minutes."

Clint absently waved his hand, his mind already on the days and nights ahead with Terri. "Sure. That's it for now. Let me know how the meeting turns out. I'd like to—" The ringing of his private line cut him off.

Instinctively Melissa hesitated.

"Hello?"

"Clint, it's me, Terri."

Clint's voice dropped two octaves as it reached across the phone lines to caress her. "Hey, baby. I was just thinking about you."

Melissa stiffened and wished once again that those words of endearment were directed at her. One day they would be, she vowed. If—no, not if—*when* Mark's plan was complete, she would leave Mark, and Clint would be hers. She cleared her throat to gain his attention.

Clint looked up, having completely forgotten that Melissa was still in the office. He covered the mouthpiece with his hand. "You can go ahead with your meeting, Mel. I'll check back with you later." He gave her an absent smile and went back to his conversation.

Melissa marched out in a huff, which was lost on Clint.

"You sound upset, babe. What's wrong?"

"Clint, I, uh, saw Mark today."

All of Clint's antennae shot up. "Where?"

"On the subway, of all places," she replied, trying unsuccessfully to make her voice sound light.

"And? Did he say anything, do anything?"

"No. He just…just…"

"Just what?"

"He just gave me a very uneasy feeling, Clint. I don't know how to explain it. It was almost as if I were seeing him for the first time, but in a way that was familiar. It's happened before."

"I'm not following you, Terri."

She exhaled an exasperated breath. "I know. I don't understand it myself."

"It's probably just a combination of everything that's happened lately and then seeing him unexpectedly."

"You're probably right," she conceded.

"Try to put it out of your head. We have a beautiful three weeks ahead of us, and I don't want anything to interfere with that."

Terri sighed in agreement. "Anyway," she said, trying to sound bright, "my friend Lisa has invited us to dinner tonight. Sort of a bon voyage. I told her we would probably make it."

"No problem. I'd like to meet her."

Terri chuckled. "That's the same thing she said about you."

"I wonder why?" he responded, his voice full of sarcasm. "What have you told her about me?"

"Only sweet, wonderful things."

He heard the laughter in her voice. "I bet. So what time is this shindig?"

"I figured that seven would be good. I have a class at five. It shouldn't last more than forty-five minutes."

"I'll pick you up at your apartment."

Her voice lowered. "I'll be waiting. 'Bye."

Clint felt the old familiar rush race through his veins at the sound of invitation in her voice. The next three weeks were going to be pure heaven.

Smiling, he held the phone in his hand for several long moments after Terri had hung up. The shuffling of papers brought him back to reality. His head snapped in the direction of Melissa, standing like a sentinel in the doorway.

Clint frowned, annoyed that she had stayed to listen to his conversation. He replaced the receiver. "I thought you had a meeting," he said in a tight voice.

Melissa straightened, holding her notes against her racing heart. "I came back. I wanted to be sure that there wasn't anything else."

Clint took a long look at Melissa, then took several steps in her direction. "Is something wrong, Mel? If I didn't know better, I'd think you were sick."

She emitted a nervous chuckle. "I'm fine. I was just thinking about everything that needs taking care of in the next few weeks. That's all."

Clint's eyes creased in concern. His voice held an inquisitive tone. "I have all the confidence in the world in you. I'm sure you'll handle everything the way you always have."

"I'd better be going. I'll see you before you leave, won't I?"

Her question sounded almost like a plea to Clint's ears. But that couldn't be possible, he concluded. "Sure, I'll stop by before I head out this evening."

Melissa nodded and walked out, leaving Clint with mixed feelings of empathy and apprehension.

"Come in. Come in." Lisa beamed. She gave Clint a swift once-over and winked her acceptance to Terri. "Clint, it's so good to finally meet you."

"Just please don't say you've heard so much about me." He chuckled as he shrugged out of his coat.

Lisa slipped a possessive arm around Clint's waist. "I promise," she said sweetly. "Now come on in. Brian is in the kitchen."

Lisa led the way into the living room, and Terri let out a startled expulsion of breath. "Lisa! Not again."

Clint looked at Terri skeptically, then at Lisa.

"Don't mind her," Lisa advised Clint in a stage whisper. "She gets a little spacey every time I redecorate."

"Believe me, sweetheart," Terri said to Clint, "if you had any idea how many times this woman redecorates her house, you would lose it, too."

"Are you just going to complain, or are you going to admire and cringe with jealousy?" Lisa hid her bubbling laughter behind her hand.

"She's determined to run me into the poorhouse," Brian stated as he stepped into the room. His eyes sparkled with love for his wife.

The trio turned in his direction. Lisa demurely approached her husband. She hooked her arm through his.

"Clint, this is my husband, Brian." They both walked toward Clint and Terri, with Lisa's blossoming belly leading the way.

Brian extended his hand, which Clint shook. "Good to finally meet you, Clint. I've—"

"Just don't say you've heard so much about him," Lisa cut in.

Brian looked at his wife curiously, while the other three erupted into infectious laughter. Brian shrugged his narrow shoulders, and unable to help himself joined in.

"Dinner was fabulous as usual, Brian," Terri enthused. "One of these days you should teach your wife to cook."

"We all have our strong points," Lisa said, trying to sound hurt. "Brian cooks and—"

"You remodel the house," her husband quickly interjected.

"Very funny. You're giving Clint the wrong idea."

"What idea is that?"

"Actually Lisa gets a great deal from a mutual friend of ours, Tempest Dailey," Terri advised. "We've all known each other for years. She decorated my offices also," she added.

"And you would think that my darling wife was trying to personally ensure Tempest's success." Brian chuckled.

"It's more of a bartering system," Lisa said. "She does the house, and I introduce her to a lot of potential clients through the foundation network."

"Interesting system. If she's half as good as these rooms indicate, I'd definitely like to meet her."

"And her husband, Braxton," Lisa offered. "He's the architect."

Clint's thick eyebrows arched. "Fantastic-sounding team. The next time you speak with them, ask them if they would be interested in a joint project in the Bahamas." Clint dug into his pocket and produced his business card, passing it to Lisa. "Ask one of them to give me a call." He looked at Terri. "Or Terri. She'll be as involved as I will. Besides," he added with a smirk, "maybe if we become chummy, they'll give me the same kind of deal you guys get!"

The table erupted into laughter.

"Speaking of the Bahamas, you two," Lisa asked, "what time are you leaving?" She rose to clear the table. Terri helped.

"We have to fly to Puerto Rico in the morning," Clint said, pushing his chair away from the table. "We have a seven a.m. flight. The ship sails from there."

"We're not taking the traditional tour," Terri added. "Since we need to get to Nassau by Friday, we're going to skip a couple of islands. Nassau is not on this route."

"But you will have time to go to Barbados?" Lisa asked, slowly making her way to the kitchen.

"Definitely." The two women entered the spacious kitchen. "I can't wait," she said wistfully. "I feel that something's awaiting me. Don't ask me what it is. But I feel certain that my life is going to somehow change."

Lisa gave Terri an encouraging hug. "Whatever it is, if it's out there for you, hon, you're sure to find it."

Terri smiled.

"And speaking of finding things. I think you've found yourself a winner this time, girlfriend."

Terri's eyes sparkled. "You really think so?"

"Of course." She nudged Terri in the side. "If I weren't so hooked on Brian, Clint would be just the kind of man I'd go after. Later for friendship! Me and you would just have to stop speakin'."

Terri broke out laughing until tears squeezed out of her eyes. "Belly and all, huh?"

"You got it!"

Terri bent over into another fit of laughter. "Girl, you are crazy."

"Crazy as a fox. So look out!"

Terri was finally able to straighten up. She wiped her eyes and took huge gulps of air, slowly regaining her composure.

"Seriously, Lis—do you think I'm making the right decision?"

"You mean about going to England and meeting his daughter?"

Terri nodded.

Lisa leaned to the side, resting her weight on her left foot, and placed her hand on the protruding hip. "From what I see and from what you've told me, you have a good man, Terri. And with the looks that he was giving you all night, I know he loves you. It's in his eyes. It's in his voice every time he

says your name. All you have to do is give it a chance. Give
his daughter a chance. Everybody deserves one."

Terri took a deep breath. "I know you're right. It's just that
I'm afraid that it'll all blow up in my face. After Alan and the
baby...I..."

Lisa placed a comforting hand on Terri's shoulder. "That's
the chance we all have to take if we're going to try for the
ultimate goal. Happiness. You have to decide how much you're
willing to sacrifice in order to have it."

Terri absorbed the full impact of Lisa's words. When she
looked up, Clint stood in the open doorway. At that moment
she knew that the illusive road ahead of them would be filled
with more than the simple challenges that relationships are
built on. Something much more awaited them in the days and
months ahead.

A slight shiver ran up her spine, and she silently prayed
that Clint would be able to keep the growing chill at bay.

Chapter 26

The apartment intercom buzzed.

"The cab is here," Terri called out to Clint. Within moments he emerged from the bedroom, a suitcase in each hand. He placed them by the door and helped Terri with her coat.

"We won't be needing these for long," Clint whispered against Terri's neck as he draped her scarf across the exposed flesh.

"Hmm. I can't wait," she purred, turning into his arms.

Clint planted a warm kiss on her lips. "Hot days and long sultry nights," he crooned against her warm mouth.

"And if we don't get out of here pronto, we'll be spending those nights looking at falling snow and slush."

"No way." Clint picked up the two large suitcases and a smaller one, while Terri draped the suit bag over her arm. With her free hand she carried the traveling bag that she and Clint would share.

She took a quick look around the apartment. "Do we have everything?"

"As far as I can tell. Do you have your notes?"

Terri nodded. "And you have the preliminary contracts for Mr. Carpenter?"

"Yep."

"Then, that's it. Let's go." Terri flicked off the light and stepped out into the hallway, walking stride for stride with Clint.

"As I said at our last meeting, Mr. Brathwaite, I can't make a firm commitment until I meet with Mr. Steele on Friday," Nat Carpenter intoned. He blew a puff of smoke into the stale office air.

Malcolm gripped the phone. "I understand. I was just calling to see if there had been any changes," he said in a controlled voice. "You know how to reach me. I'd be very interested in hearing what Steele has to offer."

"I'm sure. Well, I must be going. I have another call," he lied smoothly. "We'll talk soon."

"Of course." Malcolm hung up the phone, his jaw locked in irritation. He had to pull this off. If Steele came up with more money to finance the deal, he'd have to find a way to outbid him. He already knew he could outmaneuver Terri in terms of her ad campaign. Hadn't he been taught by the master? He was sure that he could easily make her proposal dismal in comparison to what he had in mind. But he needed more than a winning campaign, even though Steele would think that the campaign was the cause of him losing the account. Which was exactly what he wanted.

He had to put an immediate alternative strategy into motion. If Carpenter went for Steele's proposal, and Steele had the financial backing to pull it off, then he'd have to find another source of financing. And fast. Nothing could be left to chance.

Malcolm leaned back in his chair. Suddenly he sprang up as if hit with a jolt of electricity. A plan was rapidly forming in his mind. He reached for the phone, a malicious smile forming on his lips. Everyone had an Achilles' heel, and he'd just found the one he'd been looking for.

Terri felt her heart thump with excitement as she and Clint cut a path up the gangway and onto the *Christina II*. The magnificent ship was like something out of a Hollywood movie. Mirrored walls, lush greenery, ankle-deep carpet and crystal chandeliers were only the beginning. Winding staircases led to various levels of the ship, and the passengers were as stunning as the ship itself.

As much as she'd traveled over the years, she'd never been on a cruise. This was an experience she wouldn't soon forget.

Luxurious was the word that seemed to repeat itself over and again in her mind. She wanted to ooh and aah like an out-of-town tourist, but she fought to control the urge. Instead she squeezed closer to Clint, which he didn't mind one bit.

"I take it you like what you see?" he asked, looking down into her sparkling eyes.

"It's fabulous, Clint. I just can't imagine so much splendor being contained on a ship."

"You haven't seen anything yet. Wait until you see some of the salons and the entertainment rooms, not to mention—" he stopped, pulled her into his arms and looked deep into her eyes "—the suite that I selected for us."

The intimate timbre of his voice wrapped around her, and all thoughts of anything other than being with Clint flew from her head.

As Terri stepped from the steamy shower, wrapped from head to ankle in terry cloth, Clint slipped behind her, securing her snugly around the waist.

"Hmm," he breathed into her neck, pulling her closer as he

buried his face in the hollow of her shoulder. "Good enough to eat," he groaned, nibbling at her neck.

Bubbling giggles rushed up from her throat and filled the air. She turned fully into his embrace. "Is that a threat or a promise, Mr. Steele?" she taunted.

"Don't tempt me," he warned, deftly loosening the belt from her robe and sliding knowing hands along the silken curves beneath.

"We'll be late for dinner," she whispered against his bare chest.

Clint reluctantly stepped back and held her at arm's length. "Speaking of dinner, I have a surprise for you." His eyes darkened with mischief. "Stand right there. Don't move."

Moments later Clint returned from the bedroom carrying a large white box tied with a huge red-and-gold ribbon. His smile invited her to step closer. "I hope you like it." He grinned. "I had it sent directly to the ship," he added, seeing the questioning look on her face. He handed her the box.

Terri eased down on the champagne-colored sofa and gingerly untied the ribbon, periodically taking quick peeks at Clint for any sign of what might be inside.

Then in one swift motion, she tossed the cover aside and whipped open the gold tissue paper. Her quick intake of breath was Clint's first indication that he'd made the right choice.

Slowly he stepped forward as Terri's eyes widened in delight. Inch by inch she withdrew the black velvet that felt like butter beneath her fingertips.

"Clint," she breathed, "this is gorgeous." She stood up and held the floor-length gown in front of her.

"When I saw it, I knew you had to have it."

"How did you know what size to get?" she asked, holding the dress against her and knowing that it would be a perfect fit.

"I took a peek at the tags in your dresses. Then I double-checked with a call to Stacy. Try it on. I want you to wear it tonight when we have dinner at the captain's table."

"The captain's table?"

Clint grinned. "Of course. Did you expect anything less?"

"From you, you darling man, absolutely not." She planted a hot, wet kiss on his lips, hugged the dress to her and ran off to the bathroom.

Moments later she emerged. This time it was Clint who couldn't believe his eyes.

The gown fit Terri like a second skin, skimming and hugging all of her curves. The off-the-shoulder effect gave the viewer an appetizing look at silken brown shoulders that were encased in black satin with metallic-gold edging. All of which did little to hide the tempting valleys that fought for equal attention. The perfectly fitting gown embraced her body like a possessive lover, only giving way at the ankle where it widened into a fishtail—it, too, done in the same satin and gold.

"Baby," Clint whispered reverently, "maybe we should forget dinner." He stepped closer as Terri slowly spun around to give him the full effect of the devastating gown. He caught her in his arms and pressed his lips to her throat, making her whimper. "But then again, I want every man on board to see, and then know, that you're mine. Exclusively," he moaned in her ear.

Terri pressed her hands against his chest. "Always?"

"Definitely. I promise you, there's nothing and no one that could come between us." He covered her mouth with his and silently prayed that he could keep that promise.

Chapter 27

Dinner at the captain's table was an event straight off of network television, Terri thought as she savored the steamed mussels drenched in a hot butter-and-garlic sauce. Intermittently she had the hilarious notion of wanting to call the first mate "Gofer." However, no amount of television viewing could have prepared her for the opulence of life aboard a cruise ship.

The entertainment salons, game rooms and nightclub were more than enough to keep the passengers completely content. Not to mention the private saunas, exercise rooms, boutiques and hair salons.

But even with so much to keep the mind and body occupied, Terri could not contain her anticipation of returning home.

As she and Clint strolled along the deck, flashes of sandy beaches and tropical fruits danced along the fringes of her thoughts.

"Hmm." She sighed, looking out across the lapping

blue-and-white waves as they glistened beneath the brilliant full moon.

Clint slid his arm around Terri's narrow, velvet waist. "What are you thinking about?"

"Only that in a matter of days I'll be back home."

The childlike wistfulness of her voice touched him. He eased her closer and hoped that memories of her homeland lived up to her expectations.

"This is really important to you, isn't it?"

"If I could only explain how much." She stopped and turned toward him, her eyes willing him to understand. "It was the only time in my life when I was sure that I—" she hesitated "—existed—belonged somewhere—to someone."

A flash of anger rose. It felt as if all of the progress they'd made over the months had vanished. She *did* belong. She belonged to him. But with his next breath he understood that Terri would have to come to terms with that on her own, or it would never be real for her.

He needed to change the subject. "Tell me more about your brother, Malcolm."

Terri's coral-colored lips curved into a smile. "Malcolm. Malcolm was two years younger than me, but we were inseparable. He was always the prankster, and I was the one who was practical and wanted to stay out of trouble. I always felt... responsible for Malcolm."

She took a long pausing breath, and Clint began to think that she had come to the end of her story until she spoke again.

"Neither of us remembered our mother, and all we knew about our respective fathers was that neither of them were around." Her laugh was hollow.

"So you were sort of a big sister and a mother to Malcolm."

Terri nodded. "We had Nana, who we adored, but there was just something special about our brother-sister relationship.

The day we were separated, after Nana grew so ill…" her voice wavered "…I promised him that I would come back for him. That I'd find him." Tears of an unfulfilled promise stung her eyes. She quickly blinked them away. "I'll always remember that day. The way he looked at me…his eyes…" She felt a tremor scurry up her spine. "His eyes were like…"

Clint felt her shiver. "What is it? Like what?"

"They were just like—like Mark's eyes." She continued in a rush. "That day—on the subway." She turned and looked up at Clint, disbelief and something resembling fear hovering in the soft brown depths.

"Terri, come on. You couldn't possibly be thinking…"

She briefly shut her eyes against the impossible and shook her head. "It was just so weird. I mean, I know that Mark and Malcolm…" her voice trailed away "…couldn't possibly be the same person. "I would know." Her eyes trailed up to meet Clint's questioning stare. "Wouldn't I?"

Clint braced Terri's shoulders. "You're letting your imagination get the best of you. Now, listen—" he lowered his head and tilted hers upward with the tip of his finger "—your brother Malcolm is dead. You said so yourself. Mark is a whole separate issue. One that you need to put behind you."

"There was always something about Mark that I could never quite place but was still vaguely familiar," Terri went on, ignoring Clint's suggestion. She took a shaky breath. "His accent sounds pure New York. He claimed his roots were here. I never thought otherwise…but I guess you're right. Let's just forget it." Even as she forced a smile on her face, she remembered what Clint had discovered about Mark and his nonexistent past. So did Clint.

"That's better. Even though you could improve on that fake smile." He took her hand, and they walked in the direction of their suite. "Dedicate the next few hours to us," he whispered, "and I guarantee that I'll make you forget all about it."

But thoughts of Mark left a shadow over them both.

* * *

The next three days were a whirlwind of activities. The first stop was the magnificent island of Aruba, which seemed like two worlds rolled into one. The dramatic desert interior and spectacular blue-water beaches stood in sharp contrast to each other. Terri and Clint did the tour along Palm Beach and Eagle Beach, stopping off at all of the exclusive resorts with their renowned casinos along the way. The highlight of their stopover was the snorkeling that Terri insisted upon. Much to Clint's dismay.

"You look a little green around the gills," Terri teased as they returned to the hotel, laden with their equipment.

Clint tried unsuccessfully to pretend indifference. "I told you I wasn't too thrilled about going snorkeling. I had some paperwork…"

"Oh, mon, let's be for real." She chuckled, slipping into dialect. "You could have told me you couldn't swim, ya know." She covered her widening grin with her wet hand.

He turned a glowering look in her direction. "I'm happy you're so amused." He wiped his face with a mint-green towel.

Terri placed a reassuring hand on his bare shoulder. "I'm sorry, baby." She reached up on tiptoe and kissed his cheek. "I would have never guessed that you couldn't…"

"Don't say it, okay? There's always something that a person can't do. I just happen not to be able to…swim…very well. Is that so horrible?"

"Of course not." Terri fought down the chuckle that bubbled in her throat. "I mean…" she rolled her eyes up toward the air in thought "…I can't drive a stick shift. That should make you feel better, honey." With that last jab at his ego, Terri took off as fast as her feet would take her, barely escaping Clint's grasp.

"You're really asking for it," he yelled, taking off behind her. "You'll be sorry if I catch you!"

* * *

Mark walked out of the travel-agency office on Fifth Avenue. Swirling snow stung his eyes. He took no notice. A smug, satisfied smile eased across his cocoa-colored face. Wanting to reassure himself, he tapped the breast pocket of his black shearling coat. His ticket was in place. He wasn't taking any chances. He would be able to leave at a moment's notice. Now all he had to do was wait and see what happened on Friday.

He stood on the corner and hailed a cab. An evening with Melissa was just the thing to take the edge off, he mused. Soon he'd be rid of her, too. But in the meantime…

Chapter 28

After a day at sea, the cruise ship pulled into La Guaira, the port for the capital city of Caracus in Venezuela. The temperature at 8 a.m. was a sizzling ninety-eight degrees.

Undaunted by the stifling temperature, which continued to climb, Terri and Clint took the scenic half-hour tour ride inland that led to Caracus where Spanish antiquities were displayed at the *Colonial Art Museum*. Clint purchased several pottery pieces from local shops, and Terri selected a brilliant abstract painting for Lisa and Brian.

Before long the exhausted duo had to return to the ship. And it was on to Barbados.

As the ship rolled gently over the waves, Terri nestled in Clint's arm. He turned on his side, aligning his body with hers.

"I don't think I'll be able to sleep tonight," she whispered in the dark.

Clint placed a soft kiss on the back of her neck. "I know.

You've got me so worked up about it, I don't know if I'll be able to sleep, either."

Terri laughed softly. "Tomorrow," she said on a sigh. "It's only a few hours away, but it feels like an eternity."

"Before you know it, you'll be setting foot on solid ground." He stroked her hip. "Then I get to see this fabulous place you call home."

Terri was up with the sun and pulling Clint up behind her.

"We still have two hours before we dock, baby," he mumbled. With great effort he stretched and sat up in bed.

"I know, but—" she turned sparkling brown eyes on him "—I just want to be ready."

Clint shook his head in defeat. "At least let me order room service. I know you won't be able to sit still for a meal."

She continued putting clothes into the suitcases. "I couldn't eat a thing. But you go ahead."

Clint pulled himself out of bed and stood beside her. He picked up a freshly starched shirt and hung it in the carrying bag.

Terri turned and looked up into eyes that shone back with quiet understanding. No words were needed.

Two hours later Clint and Terri stood in the port capital of Bridgetown. The bustling town was brimming with activity. Small shops, restaurants and street merchants all vied for the tourist trade.

The streets were lined with mahogany and cabbage palm trees, providing a cool breeze in the balmy tropical paradise.

"I can't believe it, Clint. I'm finally here."

He hugged her next to him as they eased past a tour group. "Is it anything like what you remember?"

"Yes. Just bigger and more people."

Everywhere they turned, beautiful people in all shades of brown hurried about their activities.

"We'd better head on over to the hotel and get settled," Clint suggested.

"I want to take a ride over to my old neighborhood. I won't be able to rest until I do."

"Can't you at least put your things down first?"

"You go ahead. I'll meet you later. I shouldn't be long."

"Terri—"

"Clint, please try to understand. I know this may seem obsessive, but it's something I have to do." She stroked his arm. "And I need to do it alone."

He nodded. "If that's what you need. I'll see you at the hotel."

"Thank you." She reached up and kissed his lips, then turned to walk in the direction of Holetown, one of the three largest towns on the island. Within moments she was swallowed up in the ebb and flow of bodies, and Clint lost sight of her.

On the next corner, Terri hailed a taxi.

"Where to, lovely miss?" the affable driver asked. He turned and looked over his shoulder at Terri, exhibiting a bright gold front tooth when he grinned.

"Do you know where Codrington Hill is in Saint Michael?"

"Jon know where every'ting be on our lovely island. He know everybody and—" he grinned "—everybody's business, I been told. You name de place, I take you der." He flashed her another gold-tooth grin. "Jon Saint Hill at your service."

Terri laughed. He was the typical island cabbie. And she was quite sure that he was right about his assessment of himself. Maybe he'd even be of some help to her. "You're from Jamaica, aren't you?" Terri quizzed.

"Ah. You notice, eh? But I live 'ere for more years than I

can count. I be what you call an island hopper. One foot 'ere, one foot der. And you?"

"I was born here."

"You be raised up on de island?" he asked in disbelief. "You sound pure Yankee."

"True. It's been long, mon, since I been home."

Jon chuckled when he heard the lilting melody of the Bajan tongue. "Yeah, you true Bajan." He winked at her through the rearview mirror. "How long you been gone from home?"

"I moved to the States when I was about eight years old."

"You still have family 'ere?" he asked, taking a sharp right turn with ease.

"No," she answered so softly, Jon wasn't sure he'd heard her. He asked again.

Terri cleared her throat. "No. My family died a long time ago. My grandmother and my...my brother."

Jon was silent for a moment. "You come back to reclaim your roots, eh?"

"Something like that."

Jon stole a peek at her through the mirror. Her face held a faraway look, hopeful yet resigned. "What your family name?"

"Brathwaite."

Jon brightened. "For true? I know a Brathwaite. He come maybe once a year to visit. About this time, for true. Some year not at all. He grew up 'ere."

Terri felt her pulse begin to race. She leaned forward in the cab. "He?"

"Yeah. Maybe you two be related." He grinned. "Everybody on de island related one way or de other."

"So I've been told." She grinned at the old wives' tale that everybody with the same last name was somehow related. If it were true, then maybe she really did have some family left. The possibility excited her. "Do you know where this other

Brathwaite goes when he visits? Maybe I could track down some family members."

Jon frowned. "He go to a small house down dis next turn. He stand in front of de house and stare. Den he get back in de cab, and I take him to de cemetery outside Saint Michael. He bring a small bundle of flowers, drop dem on a grave site and leave. He be strange one."

"What do you mean?"

"Usually he talk a lot when he first get in me cab, tell me all about life in de States. But when he get back in, he a changed man. Almost evil." Jon gave a slight shudder. "Such a shame. I remember 'im as a boy."

Terri frowned. This Brathwaite didn't sound like anyone she wanted to know. But perhaps he was some distant relation who could shed some light on her family and provide the link that she so desperately sought. She'd have to put her misgivings aside.

"Have you seen him recently, Jon?"

"No. Can't say so, ya know. But, if ya let me know where ya be stayin', I make sure to tell ya, if I should see 'im."

Terri thought about it for a moment. Her first inclination was to deny Jon's request. Her years of living in New York had made her wary of strangers, especially friendly strangers. But this wasn't New York, and if she intended to get the help she needed, she was going to have to trust someone.

"All right," she said finally. She reached in her bag for a pen and paper, quickly jotting down her hotel name and room number.

Clint took a quick inventory of the suite. He was sure that Terri would love it. The sweeping balcony, just off the bedroom, overlooked the beach, which glistened beneath the dazzling island sun. Rows of palms swayed gently against the warm tropic breeze. The sunken living room, colored with muted corals, bronzes, soft copper and rich cream, whispered *comfort.* The adjacent bedroom echoed the same hues and was complemented further with blooming bouquets of island flora and a king-size canopy bed draped with sheer white netting. Every nuance of the luxurious bedroom invited intimacy.

Clint checked the kitchen. As he'd requested, he found the fridge and cabinets completely stocked.

"Perfect…" he smiled "…except for the lady of the house." He took a final look around the suite. Satisfied that everything was in order, he stretched out on the rattan couch and reached for the phone. It had been a while since he'd spoken with Jillianne and even longer since he'd heard his daughter Ashley's voice. He wanted to assure them both that everything was still on schedule, and that he'd be bringing a guest home for the holidays.

Chapter 29

"Ashley! Ashley, honey. Come down for lunch," Jillianne called. Her tall, toned body moved gracefully through the spacious rooms until she reached the kitchen, where her housekeeper and nanny, Mrs. Hally, was unloading bags of groceries.

"Oh, there you are, Mrs. Hally. Ashley will be down shortly. Please fix her a bowl of soup and a sandwich, would you?"

"Of course, Ms. Jill. Right off."

"Thank you."

Mrs. Hally was instantly caught in the magic of the breath-taking smile that had slowed the hearts of many, before Jill turned to make her way to the living room. She came to a stop in the center of the room, her jet-black curls glistening in the afternoon sun. With one hand on her slender hip and the tip of a finger pressed against full, pouty lips, she assessed the space.

Although her field was real estate, specifically selling mansions and large blocks of land which afforded her a lavish lifestyle, Jillianne always had a knack for decorating. She took every opportunity to practice her talent, with the living room and bedrooms being her favorite sites in the sprawling four-story town house. Very often she would offer decorating suggestions to prospective home owners, and in many cases her ideas helped to cinch the deals.

Today, however, her motivation for change was entirely personal. Clint was coming home, and she wanted everything to be perfect. More than perfect. Just the thought of seeing him, in only a few days, caused waves of desire to run havoc through her stomach. Maybe this time, she thought, he'd come home to her to stay.

Without conscious effort, his face danced before her eyes. Her long-lashed lids drifted closed. She envisioned the lips that she longed to claim, the hard muscular frame that promised total satisfaction. She trembled and wrapped her slender arms around her body as if to contain the fire within her. Clint represented everything that was wonderful in a man. He was handsome, sexy, warm and caring about everyone around him. Not to mention the charisma and power that he exuded in business, which to her was a natural aphrodisiac. What was most appealing about Clinton Steele was the mystery that coated him like a second skin. His elusiveness compelled women to seek him out and attempt to uncover the secrets beneath the picture-perfect exterior.

The ringing phone pulled her out of her romanticizing. Shaking her head, she reached for the phone. "Yes?"

"Hello. May I speak with Jillianne Davis?"

"This is Ms. Davis," Jill exhaled.

"You don't know me, but I'm a very close friend of your brother-in-law, Clint. My name is Mark Andrews."

"I'm sorry, sir, but that line is still busy," intoned the hotel operator. "I could ring your room back when the line is free."

Clint checked his watch. Terri should be back shortly, and they'd planned to do some shopping and then go to dinner.

"That's all right, operator. I'll try back later. Thank you."

How many times had he insisted that Jill get call waiting? Time and again she refused, stating that if the call was that important, they'd either call back or have the operator interrupt. There was nothing more annoying, she'd said, than to have a perfectly lovely conversation interrupted with another call.

He shrugged and made a mental note to call her later.

The cab eased up the dirt road that led to rows of two-story homes. Terri's heart quickened and filled with old memories. "It's just down the road, on the right," she whispered.

Jon's smooth caramel brow creased. "Dis be de place? Dis street?"

Terri nodded, swallowing the lump that sat in her throat. "Yes."

Jon shook his head and turned to look at her. "You *dat* Brathwaite?"

"What do you mean?"

"De family dat I speak of, der was a grandmother who took care of her two grandchildren, a little girl and de same Brathwaite fellow I told ya 'bout."

Terri's pulse quickened.

"What happened?"

"From what I be remembering, de grandmother got very sick and died. De authorities couldn't find no relatives to take care of de children—dey shipped off to foster homes. De boy stay 'ere on de island. No one know what happen to de girl."

"That's what happened to us," she whispered. "It has to be—"

"But you say your brother died. So it can't be. Dis man far from dead." Jon shook his head. "Maybe I be mistaken. It be so long ago."

Terri leaned forward in her seat. "The man that comes here, the little boy, I mean—has he ever told you his name?"

"Hmm." Jon thought for a moment. "He told me his name one time." Jon scratched his head while mumbling a string of names.

Terri held her breath.

Jon brightened. "Yes. I be remembering now. He say his name be Malcolm! Yes. Malcolm Brathwaite."

Chapter 30

"I don't recall Clint ever mentioning anyone named Mark Andrews," Jill responded, suspicion rising in her tone.

Mark chuckled. "That's Clint for you. You know how busy he is. He probably just forgot." His voice lowered two octaves. "But he's told me *all* about you."

Jillianne felt her heartbeat quicken. "Clint told you about me?" Her spirits soared.

Mark immediately heard the eagerness in her voice, and he pounced on it. "He certainly did. Wonderful things. I told him that you sounded almost too good to be true."

Jill laughed in pure joy.

He reeled her in a little more. "As a matter of fact, he's always telling me how much you mean to him. You're a very important person in his life, Jill."

She could hardly breathe. "What can I do for you, Mr. Andrews?"

"First of all, call me Mark."

"All right." She smiled.

"Well, I just called Clint's office and they told me that he would be away until after the New Year." He chuckled again. "I talked the secretary into telling me that he was coming to England for the holidays. Which is great because I plan to arrive tomorrow morning."

"Really? I'm sure Clint will be happy to see you."

"Yes. I'm sure." Jill mistook the cynicism in his tone for jest. "But I wanted to surprise him. We haven't seen each other in a while, and I was hoping that you could arrange something."

"Of course. I'd love to."

"Great. Why don't I give you a call when I arrive tomorrow? That should give you enough time to think of something."

"More than enough time. Where are you staying?"

"I have reservations at the Savoy."

"You're perfectly welcome to stay here, once Clint arrives," she amended. "I'm sure he would want you to."

"Thanks for the invitation. Let me think about it. But… how about if I take you to dinner tomorrow night? We could talk, get to know each other. I want to see if all of the fantastic stories that Clint told me about you are true."

Jill giggled. "That sounds wonderful, but let me think about it."

"I'll call you."

"That sounds fine. Have a safe flight."

"'Bye, Jill."

Jill replaced the receiver. A small smile dimpled her cheeks.

Mark merged with the crowd, moving with them toward the departure gate, and boarded the plane to England.

Chapter 31

Terri felt her throat constrict. She struggled to breathe as a surge of heat infused her body.

"*No.*" She wanted to scream the single word, but her voice was a mere whisper. Her hand trembled ever so slightly as she wiped away a bead of perspiration that slid slowly down her brow.

Jon glanced in his rearview mirror. "Be ya all right?" He pulled the cab to the side of the road. *Please don't let dis come-lately Bajan woman faint in me car. De wife she never believe another one.* "Can I get ya some'ting? Some water?"

Terri shook her head. Taking a deep breath, she blurted out the question that had been sitting on her tongue. "Can you take me to the grave site that the man goes to?"

His soft brown eyes held the unspoken question between them. What if she was that same little girl in the story? She was so lovely, with her silky mahogany skin and glistening locks. How could he deny those eyes that held such passion and sorrow?

Jon nodded and turned the cab in the direction of Saint Michael's cemetery.

It was nearly six o'clock. The evening sky was gray. Ominous. Melissa sighed. She'd be alone again tonight, just as she'd been alone every night since the last one spent with Mark. He hadn't called since then. She had no idea where he was or what he was doing. And she had no real desire to find out, not after the things he did to her when they were last together. Mark's lovemaking had taken on a dangerous tone. He was more aggressive, angry, as if he were trying to punish her. She shuddered. Mark was changing day by day, and it frightened her. An uneasy feeling had settled in her stomach days ago, and she couldn't seem to shake it. All she wanted to do was try to put Mark out of her mind. Slowly she rose from her desk, closed her appointment book and turned toward the window, wondering what Clint and Terri were doing on the sunny island of Barbados.

Her pulse drummed in her ears. Terri had everything! Everything! The resentment ignited in her hazel eyes, turning them almost black. Terri had a thriving business, beauty, brains and Clint. Melissa's smooth jaw clenched in frustration.

She crossed the room and snatched her coat from the closet. Through habit, she meticulously scanned the office, collected her purse and briefcase, and left.

She stood waiting for the elevator. Maybe she'd take herself to dinner. There was no reason to rush home, and cooking for one was depressing.

Melissa pushed through the revolving doors and was greeted by a blast of bitter-cold wind. She pulled her silver fox coat tightly around her slender body and slipped on a pair of dark shades to shield her eyes from the biting wind.

She stepped to the curb, intent on hailing a cab, when she heard her name whip across the windy street.

Turning in the direction of the sound, she caught sight of Steve's midnight-blue Lexus angling its way through the rush of pedestrians.

"Melissa!" he shouted again as he pulled to a stop on the opposite side of the street.

Momentarily she had a flash of their brief affair together as she watched him make a U turn and stop in front of her. Steve was a wonderful, caring, considerate man and a great lover. But he wasn't Clint, and she never gave him a chance to be anyone else. That compounded with his line of work led to the demise of their relationship. At times she still wondered what could have been. She inhaled the shudder of remembrance as she stepped toward the car.

"What brings you uptown? You know Clint is away?"

"Yeah. I know. I had some business up the street. I was on my way home."

"Oh." She smiled slightly and tugged on her coat.

"Want a lift?"

"No, thanks. I can take a cab."

"Come on, Mel. You have plans or something?"

"No."

"So...hop in. I'll take you home, and I promise I won't bite."

"I wasn't going home."

"Can I come?" A big grin overtook his features, and Melissa couldn't help laughing. Steve always had the ability to make her laugh, even when she didn't want to. The single memory warmed her ever so slightly.

"Why not?" she said finally. She rounded the car and slipped into the lush leather seat.

"That's better," Steve said. He gave her a private look which she tried to ignore as he maneuvered for a spot in the backed-up lane of traffic.

"How's everything been going?" Steve asked after several awkward moments of silence.

"Not bad."

"You don't sound too sure." He glanced in her direction.

"Let's just say that it's nothing worth talking about."

"Hmm. That good, huh?"

Melissa grinned. "You're rather nosey."

"That's my job. Remember?"

"Very well, actually."

They sat in silence for a few moments before Melissa spoke again. "Are you working on anything interesting?"

Steve thought about his answer, wondering if he should tell her that he'd been investigating Mark and her in the process. He decided against it.

"I was, but the trail, as we say in the business, ran cold."

"That doesn't sound like the Steve I know. You never left a stone unturned." She stared at his profile, reacquainting herself with the full lips, chiseled cheekbones, trim mustache, creamy brown complexion and the salt-and-pepper hair.

"Let's put it this way, my client decided not to pursue it any further. So..." He shrugged his shoulders in dismissal.

"You mean Clint?" She waited for a reaction.

"You'd make a pretty good P.I. yourself," he answered noncommittally.

"Clint told me about the check he'd run on Mark. I should have known he'd have you handle it. That's why you were at the office. Wasn't it?"

He tossed off her question.

"I guess he also told you that you could do better than Mark Andrews with buck teeth and a limp?"

Her head snapped in his direction. Her voice was clipped and precise. "I'll tell you just like I told Clint. My personal life is just that—personal! I don't need him or you telling me whom I should see!"

"All right! Calm down. We—he—I was only concerned

about you, Mel." His deep voice softened. "I've always been interested in your happiness. Whatever it was."

Melissa sighed and tugged on her bottom lip with her teeth. "I'm sorry," she said softly. "I didn't mean to snap at you."

"Sure you did," he said without malice. "And you're right. It is your business." He patted her shoulder.

"How about this?" he asked, cutting through two lanes of traffic. "Why don't I treat us to dinner? We can start over, pretend this conversation never happened. I'll even tell you detective stories." He grinned wickedly.

"Steve..."

"Mel...?" His thick eyebrows rose comically.

Melissa shook her head helplessly. "Where to?"

Clint lay sprawled out across the king-size bed. The barely audible sound of the local jazz station whispered in the background. Clint's eyes drifted closed.

Everything was finally coming together, he mused. He had Terri's love, he and his daughter would be together soon, and he was sure that now he could be the father that she deserved. Because of Terri his world had opened. Her revelations about her childhood helped him to see the importance of the parent-child relationship. She was right. Desi's death was not his fault, and in order to be all he could be for both Ashley and Terri, he had to finally let go of the guilt. Now that the doorway to his heart was opened, he was eager to have his daughter enter. He ached when he thought of all the time he'd wasted. But things would be different now. He was different now. He'd bring his daughter home where she belonged. They'd be a family.

To top everything off, he was on the verge of closing the greatest deal of his career. It seemed that since Terri'd entered his life, magic had happened. He felt alive again. He had a real purpose again. Most of all he had someone to share his joys.

A slow smile of contentment eased across his face. His eyes

fluttered open. Then, just as quickly as the smile had come, it disappeared when he looked up at the figure that stood above him.

Chapter 32

Like a catapult, Clint sprang up in the bed.

"Terri! For chrissake, you scared the hell outta me." It took him a moment to register the devastation on her face.

"What—" he got up, his eyes rapidly scanning her face, her body "—what is it? What happened?"

She seemed to deflate as she sat on the edge of the bed. Her voice was flat, devoid of the emotion that she felt. "My brother is alive, Clint."

"What are you talking about? You said your brother was dead."

"I know what I said! That's what I was told. That's the horrible, vicious lie I was told!"

He could see that she was on the verge of snapping. "Baby," he said gently, "please—start from the beginning. How do you know?"

Terri took a deep shuddering breath, then began her unbelievable story from the time she'd sat in Jon's cab until she'd stood in front of her grandmother's tombstone. The very same tombstone that Malcolm Brathwaite visited.

Clint shook his lowered head in a combination of disbelief and disgust. How anyone could have been so cruel to a little girl was unthinkable. He put his arm around her, pulling her close.

"What must Malcolm have thought all of these years?" Terri asked, the tear-filled voice registering her pain. "I should be happy that he's alive." She turned toward Clint, her large luminous eyes brimming with tears. "But instead I feel guilt."

"Guilt? Why would you feel guilty?"

"Maybe if I had come home, I—"

"Listen—" he squeezed her shoulder with the pads of his fingers "—there was no reason for you to disbelieve your parents, Terri. If you grew up believing that your brother was dead, why would you come back to look for him?"

She pulled away from his grasp and stood up. "I…always had a feeling, a sensation, I don't know what to call it—a gut feeling that he wasn't dead. I would imagine that I saw his face in the men I'd meet. But I never followed my instincts."

"Let's look at this rationally. Even if you had followed your instincts, you still might not have found him."

"But I could have tried! I never tried." The weight of her pent-up tears spilled over her lids, and her shoulders shuddered as the silent sobs shook her.

Clint wrapped her in his embrace, pressing her head against his chest.

"It'll be all right," he soothed into her cottony-soft hair. "We'll take care of everything when we get back from England."

Terri instantly tore away from him, nearly losing her balance in the process.

"I can't go to England. I won't go. I have to stay here—find out all that I can. I've got to find my brother!"

"Don't be ridiculous, Terri. You can't stay here. What do you think you can accomplish? We have business to take care of." His voice rose in unison with her mounting anxiety. "Your part of the proposal presentation is crucial to clinching this deal. You know that!"

"Deal? I don't give a damn about any deal! Not now. Not when I'm this close!"

"You'd let everything I've worked toward collapse on a whim?"

"A whim?" Her outrage at his insensitivity was complete. Her voice was low, icy cold. "Is that what you call this?"

"Yeah, dammit! A whim. What do you think you can do here? You have no contacts, no leads—you don't even have a picture."

She stared at him hard, a hundred thoughts tumbling through her head at once. The most troubling of which was that their relationship was coming to a devastating end.

"I'm not leaving." She was firm and unrelenting.

"I can't close this deal without you, Terri."

"You'll find a way," she answered coldly. "You always do."

For several moments he stared at her with unbelieving eyes. Then without another word he stormed out of the room. Moments later he returned with his suitcase.

"The room is paid for until the end of the week. After that it's up to you." He strode toward the door, then stopped. His hand clutched the doorknob. He looked at her over his shoulder. "You have our itinerary, if you change your mind." He opened the door.

"I won't." She tossed the two verbal daggers at his departing back.

The only sound in the tension-charged room was the pounding of her heart and the reverberation of the slamming door.

* * *

Clint tore along the winding road, barely missing the oncoming traffic. His thoughts were a collage of anger, hurt, disappointment and confusion. All of which fought for precedence over his emotions.

She was being a fool, he thought, as he made the hairpin turn toward the airport. It wasn't like Terri to think with her heart and not her head. She was always rational and clear in her thinking. He just couldn't understand her now.

His thoughts turned to the resort deal, and his anger flared anew. This was his dream—he wanted her to be a part of it. But she'd rather chase a fantasy instead.

He pulled into the driveway of Avis Car Rental, returned the car, then boarded the shuttle bus to the terminal.

As he stood in line waiting to have his flight changed, he saw her face float before him. He couldn't recall ever seeing anyone so hurt, so desperately wanting. And he'd left her alone at a time when she needed him more than ever. Visions of Desiree and their last night together collided with his vision of Terri. He'd lost Desiree because of his career; his wanting to have it all had been more important than anything else. His selfishness had cost him everything and Desiree her life.

"May I help you, sir?"

His eyes focused on the smiling reservationist behind the counter.

"May I help you?" she asked again.

Clint put his ticket on the counter. What was more important? The question rang through his brain like a thousand church bells, over and again.

The door chime tinkled softly through the sprawling town house.

Jill gave each room a satisfied glance as she passed through, en route to the door.

She pulled open the door and was pleasantly surprised by the handsome figure that stood before her.

"You must be Jill," the smooth voice greeted. "You're even more beautiful than your pictures. I'm Mark."

Chapter 33

"Mark, I wasn't expecting you until tomorrow. Please come in."

Mark walked past her into the corridor. He quickly scanned the open, inviting space. "Great place you have," he commented and turned toward her. "Did you have a hand in the design?"

Jill stepped through the foyer to stand next to him. "Decorating is a pet project of mine."

"You have excellent taste." He gave her an appraising look that made her fully aware of her femininity.

"Why, thank you. You can leave your bag here. May I offer you something?"

"No. I'm fine. But I would like to see more of the house. If you don't mind."

"Of course not." She smiled, reveling at every opportunity to display her handiwork, to the exclusion of propriety or safety. "Follow me."

"I'm sorry to show up unannounced," he said, following her

into the living room. "But I was able to get an earlier flight. I should have called. I know this is an imposition."

"Don't be ridiculous. It's fine. This gives us more time to work on a surprise for Clint. He should be here by the weekend. He'll be so surprised to see you."

Mark smiled.

"When I called his office, they said he was traveling with a *business associate*."

"Really? He didn't mention anything to me."

Mark saw an opening. "That's Clint for you. I would think he would have told you about her."

"Her?"

"Yes. Terri Powers. They're a real item."

Jill's spine clenched. "This is the living room," she said in a tight voice, trying to shake off the green monster that nipped hungrily at her heels.

The large room overlooked a magnificent garden and was decorated in a soft floral design. Strategically around the smooth mauve walls were portraits of Picasso, van Gogh and Rembrandt. Mark quickly assessed the value to be in the millions.

"Through the door on your right is the dining room." She walked in that direction. "Do you know Terri Powers?" she asked, trying to sound blasé and failing, much to Mark's pleasure.

"Very well. Her reputation as a gold digger precedes her," he said, adding salt to the festering wound.

"And you say Clint is involved with her?"

He duly noted the tension in her voice and the possessive way she said Clint's name.

"As involved as any man and woman can get. Beautiful room," he added, pretending to be unconcerned.

She inhaled her fury. "Upstairs are the bedrooms, guest room and baths," she breathed.

"I'm sure they're just as magnificent."

Her smile was wooden as she turned to face him.

"I can't understand why Clint would get himself involved with that type of woman. It doesn't sound like him." Her statement was more of an accusation than an observation.

Mark shook his head sadly, playing upon her blatant emotions like a master pianist. "Listen, since we're talking like this, I have to tell you, I feel the same way. I tried to talk to him about Terri, but he won't listen. He gets outraged if you say anything against her." He paused, watching her face tense.

"Personally," he continued, "I think it's the worst move Clint could have made. I'm really worried about him."

"There must be something that can be done."

Mark opened the door a bit farther. "Maybe there is. Why don't we go in the living room and talk. I was going to do this alone, but...if you're willing to help..."

Aimlessly Terri paced through the suite, trying to formulate some sort of plan. Maybe Clint was right. How did she think she could find her brother with no way of tracing him?

Jon was her only link, and he hadn't seen Malcolm in months. There had to be a way. Perhaps the foster-care agency that placed them could help her.

If she could only remember the name of the agency. She walked into the small reception area of the suite and took the phone book from the wall shelf.

Maybe if she saw the name of the agency, it would come back to her.

She flipped through the book until she found the section that she wanted. Quickly she scanned the names of the foster-care agencies with her index finger.

There it was! Little Hearts Foster Care. Her pulse quickened in a mixture of sadness and relief. It was a name that she had long since relegated to the recesses of her mind—one that she had fought hard to forget.

With shaky fingers she dialed the number and waited for what seemed like an eternity before a heavily accented woman answered the phone.

Jill thought long and hard about what Mark had proposed. The plan was dangerous. But if that's what it took to get Clint away from Terri and into her arms, she would do it willingly.

Sighing, she rose from the overstuffed sofa and slowly paced the hardwood floor. Finally she turned to him. "You're sure that no one will be hurt?"

"Of course not. Clint will believe it's all Terri's fault and see her for what she really is. Then she'll be out of his life."

He tugged on the noose that he had slipped around her neck. "I can tell you care a great deal about Clint."

Momentarily she looked stricken, but seeing the concern in Mark's eyes, she nodded in agreement.

His easy, open manner, his way of making her feel that he was in tune with her feelings, left her vulnerable. Without thinking, she opened herself up to him, revealing her deepest feelings.

"I've loved Clint for as long as I can remember," she said wistfully. "When he married my sister, Desiree, I was devastated. Then…when she died, I…"

"You thought he would turn to you," Mark said, finishing her sentence.

She smiled weakly, feeling for the first time that she'd found someone who truly understood. "Yes. But he never did. And now that he's finally coming back, I just knew he was coming for me."

Mark rose and stood next to her. Warily he put a comforting arm around her shoulder.

"I'm sure that Clint will finally see things as they truly are," he assured her. "How can he help but know how much you care about him? All he has to do is look in your eyes. He's the one who's been losing out all these years."

"Are you sure that this plan will work?"

"Absolutely. But timing is everything. Remember that. You keep me posted, and I'll walk you through it, step-by-step."

Jill nodded and prayed that she was doing the right thing.

She escorted Mark to the door. He opened his suitcase and pulled out a thick manila envelope and handed it to her.

"Hold on to these. I'll tell you what to do with them and when. But whatever you do, don't let either of them see it."

Her hand trembled slightly as she took the package and held it to her breasts.

"I'll call you," he said, turning for the door. "You know where to reach me." He stroked her cheek. "Don't look so upset. Everything is going to be fine."

"Why are you doing this?"

"Let's just say that I have a debt that's been owed to me for a long time by Ms. Powers. And—" his lips lightly brushed her cheek "—I love helping beautiful ladies. But…if you're having a change of heart…just tell me. I'll understand."

Jill's pent-up obsession with Clint blinded her and propelled her forward. "*No!* I…I mean no," she said with more calm. "I'll do whatever needs to be done."

Chapter 34

"Are you absolutely sure?" Terri insisted.

"Believe me, the records are sealed. There's no way I or anyone can give you that information, miss. I'm sorry."

"Thank you anyway." Terri reluctantly hung up the phone. Her one flicker of hope slowly diminished.

"Now what?" she said out loud just as the doorbell rang.

Frowning, she strode toward the door and pulled it open.

"Clint!"

"Is there room at the inn?" he asked humbly.

A soft smile lifted her full lips. "There's room next to me, if you don't mind sharing."

"Sounds perfect." He stepped across the threshold and pulled her into his hard embrace.

"I'm so sorry, baby," he crooned. "There's no way I could let you go through this alone. My ambition cost me my wife, and I'll be damned if I'll lose you, too."

She eased out of his arms and looked up into his eyes.

"Thank you," she whispered. "But you were right." She held his hand and walked to the couch.

"I contacted the foster-care agency that placed Malcolm and me."

"And…?"

"They told me the records were sealed."

Clint sat down. "There has to be a way to find him. There are agencies that help people find relatives. I'll make some calls. And I'll get Steve on it right away."

"Whatever you can do, Clint. I'd appreciate it. I know it's going to take a long time. Sometimes these searches can take years. But I just need to know something, for sure."

She slowly got up from the couch. "There's no real point in us staying here any longer. Your appointment in Nassau is tomorrow. I know how important that is to you."

He smiled at her. "Not as important as I thought. We'll do this together, Terri."

"I had a great time, Steve. Thanks," Melissa said.

"So did I." He paused. "I'd like to keep seeing you, Mel," Steve said.

"I think I'd like that, too," she admitted. The realization warmed her.

"I know that we could be good for each other," he rushed on. He searched her face and found acceptance in her eyes.

"Listen, Mel." He lowered his head then quickly looked into those eyes that he could never forget. "I know that things weren't the greatest between us…before."

She raised her hand to his chest. "Steve, you don't have to—"

"Yes, I do." He took her hand in his and squeezed it. "At least they weren't great for you. I know how you feel about Clint."

Melissa's eyes widened in surprise. She opened her mouth to refute his statement. Steve cut her off.

"I've always known, Mel. And I know that's the reason why you couldn't love me…the way that I love you." He exhaled heavily. "There, I've finally said it."

"Love me?" she whispered. Her brow creased in disbelief. "I didn't… I never knew."

"I know." He laughed a self-deprecating laugh and lifted her hand to his lips. "I can keep a secret when I have to. That's my business." He chuckled without humor.

Her eyes searched his face for any sign of deceit but found none. Had she wasted so many days, hours, months of her life wanting someone who would never love her when she had someone who truly did, only a phone call away? She wanted to scream at the injustice of it all. The things that she had done, what her resentment and obsession had driven her to do was frightening.

She shivered. Steve took it that she was cold and put his arm around her shoulders.

Before he could stop himself, his lips found hers and for the first time in longer than he cared to remember, he felt that he'd come home.

But even as she kissed him in return, she knew that revealing her role in Mark's plan could destroy the tiny thread of happiness that was weaving a path to her heart. She couldn't take that chance. Not now.

His mouth slowly released hers. He took a shaky breath and smiled.

"Tomorrow?"

"Tomorrow sounds fine."

"I'll call you." He lowered his head and brushed her lips one last time. "Sleep well."

Slowly Melissa closed her apartment door, amazed at how her predictable evening had turned around.

She'd put all of the negativity behind her, she decided. This was a chance for her to start over. She couldn't spend the rest of her life pining over Clint. Maybe in time she would come to truly love Steve the way that he deserved to be loved.

The future was finally looking brighter, and she had no intention of doing anything to jeopardize it.

With a lightness in her step, she kicked off her shoes and practically skipped into her bedroom.

She threw herself across the bed. A satisfied smile illuminated her face, until the ringing phone brought her crashing back to reality. She lifted the receiver.

"Mark!"

"Hey, Mel. Just calling to check on you."

Her heart thudded. "Why haven't I heard from you? Where are you?"

"Whoa. One question at a time. First, I've been busy, real busy. I wanted to see you before I left, but I didn't have time. Things were happening too fast. Now for your second question. I'm in merry ole England—and, baby, the plan is going even better than I expected." He laughed at his own cunning.

"I'm gonna have it all! And Terri Powers will be finished. Thanks to you."

Chapter 35

Jillianne returned to the living room and sat down heavily on the couch. She stared at the thick envelope. What could it possibly contain? Her curiosity burned her fingertips as she stroked the seal.

"Auntie! Auntie!" The sound of her niece's voice startled her, and she shoved the envelope between the cushions of the couch. She hadn't heard the school bus when it pulled up. Mrs. Hally must have let Ashley in.

"In here, Ashley." She put on her best smile as Ashley ran into the room.

"Hi, sweetie. Did you have a good day at school?" She gave Ashley a kiss on her cheek.

"We went to the park today," she said, her dark eyes, so much like her mother's, lighting up with excitement.

"That sounds like fun." Jillianne took Ashley's hand. "Why don't you run upstairs and wash up. I'll tell Mrs. Hally to fix you a snack."

Ashley raced off at her aunt's request, her thick plaited ponytail whipping behind her.

Just as Jill was about to retrieve the envelope, Mrs. Hally entered the room.

"Excuse me, Miss Jill, Mr. and Mrs. Rogers are here to see you. They said they have an appointment."

Jill pressed her palm against her head. She had completely forgotten that she was to show a house to the newlywed couple.

"I'll be right there."

"They do seem a bit anxious, Miss Jill."

Jill shot a glance in the direction of the couch and decided that the envelope would be safe until she returned. She went to meet her clients.

Nassau

"Do you have everything you need?" Terri asked while applying a stroke of coral-colored lipstick to her mouth.

"Yes!" Clint called from the front room. "Now would you please hurry? I hate being late for meetings. And this Carpenter guy is acting strange. I didn't like the vibrations I got the last time we spoke and I don't want to give him any reason to change his mind."

"I'm ready." Terri emerged from the bathroom, clad in an off-white linen shirtdress, cut in a low V in the front and trimmed with wide gold buttons. Her long locks were wrapped high atop her head, adding to the length of her slender neck, which was encircled with a thin braided chain of gold.

"Hmm, you look good enough to eat...again," he taunted, patting her on her round derriere.

"Not now," she purred seductively. "Later," she teased, pinching his cheek. The soft fragrance of her scent wafted through the air as she passed.

"I'm gonna hold you to that," he tossed back.

She collected her purse and portfolio, which contained the advertising presentation, and strutted toward the door, where she stepped into her shoes. Turning toward Clint, the light of love burned in her eyes.

"You were wonderful last night," she said softly, pulling him by his silk tie to stand in front of her.

"There's plenty more for you later," he answered in a low, intimate voice that tantalized her.

"I can't wait. Now let's go before we never get out of here."

Nat Carpenter reviewed the elaborate proposal that lay before him. The presentation by Terri had been inspiring to say the least, although it rang with familiarity.

He peered at the handsome duo over half-rim glasses. "Very impressive," he stated simply.

"Then we have a deal," Clint said.

Nat held up his hand and tilted his head slightly to the side.

"Not quite."

Clint felt the hairs on the back of his neck begin to tingle.

"What do you mean, not quite?"

"I've been approached by another prospective client. When you and I initially spoke, there were no other offers. However, things have changed."

Clint fought to control his mounting anger. "Exactly what are you saying?"

"What I'm saying is, one, you'll have to come up with a fresher advertising scheme. Second, I'll have to consider your offer under a sealed bid—with the contract, land and all the rights going to the highest bidder."

Slowly Clint rose from the leather-bound, high-back chair. Terri dared to look up at him and immediately saw the dark, dangerous lights flicker in his eyes. His jaw clenched.

"How much time do we have?" he asked with a calm that alarmed Terri.

"I'd say about five days. I'm expecting a call from your competitor later today. I'd like to close the deal before the holidays." He leaned back in his chair and linked his fingers across his rotund belly.

Clint leaned forward, pressing his palms down on the cherry wood desk.

"I don't know what you're trying to pull, Carpenter, but we had an arrangement. I've had this plan on the burner for months, and you know it!" he shouted.

"There's no point in getting irate, Mr. Steele. Business is business. You're a businessman, and you know how things operate. Get back to me with your best offer, and we'll take it from there."

Nat Carpenter stood up. His imposing presence filled the room. "If there's nothing further." He smiled. "I have another engagement."

Clint threw him one last parting look and snatched the documents from the desk. Terri had to double her step to catch up with him as he tore through the maze of offices to the exit.

"Clint! Clint! What in the world is wrong with you?" Terri cried as she tried to keep up with his blinding pace. But he wouldn't stop until he stood in front of their rented convertible in the parking lot. He briefly shut his eyes and slammed his fist down on the hood. He spun toward her.

"Didn't you hear what went on in there?"

"I did. But that's no reason for you to perform like some thug from the hood. It's not even like you."

He shook his head. His voice lowered. "Don't you see what's happening? My dream, my vision, is slipping way. No one, no one knew about this except you and me."

Terri's jaw tightened, hearing the light touch of doubt in Clint's voice.

He saw her look. "No. I don't think it was you," he assured. He looked away. "But who?"

By degrees she relaxed. "Did it occur to you that Carpenter is out to get as much as he can?"

"It's possible." He heaved a sigh. "Maybe. All I know is, I can't lose this. It's too important to me."

"You won't," she said softly. "I'll get to work on an alternative campaign as soon as we get to England."

He nodded. "I just have to figure how much I need to bid in order to go over the top." He put his arm around her waist and kissed the top of her head. "Thanks."

"Anytime." She stepped out of his embrace and looked up at him. "Now, let's go see your daughter."

Melissa sat behind her desk, reviewing the fiscal reports for the cable stations. This new acquisition was doing extremely well, she thought, pleased with the role she'd played in the negotiations. Clint was destined to be a very rich and powerful man. He had a way of making something out of nothing and turning it into dollars.

The irony was, he never cared about the money. He thrived on the hunt. That was the characteristic that had always appealed to her.

Enough of Clint. She closed the folder. She had to move on. But the memory of the phone call from Mark marred her new vision.

Mark was determined to hurt Terri for some inexplicable reason, at whatever cost, and she knew that it would ultimately hurt Clint as, well. Was that why she'd been more than willing to help Mark? What was he going to do with the information that she'd given him?

What she did know was that Mark, too, was a man who thrilled for the hunt. The one difference between him and Clint was that Clint salvaged his prey. Mark destroyed his.

She turned toward the window. Mark was in England now,

and Clint and Terri were on their way. A sinking feeling of
disaster swept over her. But what could she do to stop it if she
didn't know what it was?

Chapter 36

After a week of balmy tropical weather, arriving to the chill of England was a physical shock.

Terri snuggled closer to Clint's warmth as the cab sped down the open roadway toward his town house in Lancaster.

"What if she doesn't remember me?" Clint said, speaking more to himself than to Terri.

She turned to him. "How long has it been?"

"Over a year," he said heavily. "I just couldn't bring myself to go back after the last time."

"What happened?"

"Nightmares. Guilt. I couldn't find a way to get through them. Every time I looked at Ash, I saw Desi. So instead of being a loving father, I was a cold stranger, and Ashley felt it. I saw it in her eyes, the hurt, and I wanted to die. I wished that I could have reached out to her and explained, but I couldn't." He turned away from her, not daring to let her see the anguish that burned his eyes.

"Clint," she said gently, "we'll work through this. You have me now. You won't have to handle it alone."

But even as she uttered the reassuring words, she wasn't sure how she was going to deal with the reality of Clint's daughter, when the heartache of her own lost child was still so raw on her emotions. Her own loveless childhood had twisted her sensibilities, and she didn't know how she would overcome her fear of not being able to love a child that was not truly her own.

All she could be sure of was that Clint needed her. She would have to force her misgivings aside and be there for him. But how long would she be able to hide her real feelings?

Jillianne knelt down in front of her niece, and adjusted the wide collar on her blue velvet dress.

"You look beautiful, luv," Jill said with loving pride.

"Thank you, Auntie," Ashley beamed.

"Your daddy will be so happy to see you."

Instantly the smile faded. She crushed herself against her aunt's body, burying her face in Jillianne's neck.

"No, he won't!" she cried. "He hates me."

"Ashley, that's not true, sweetheart. Your daddy loves you very much." She pressed the tiny body against her own, wishing that she could absorb her hurt. Clint's inattention to his daughter was the one fault that Jillianne could not accept, even though she understood. She loved Ashley blindly, so much so that at times she believed the child to be her own.

She understood the difficulty Clint had in dealing with Desiree's death and the prospect of raising a young daughter alone. That's why she took over the rearing of Ashley in the hopes that one day Clint would see how much of a family she and Ashley were, and how much they both needed and loved him.

But Ashley's hurt over her father's indifference toward her

made Jillianne's job that much more difficult. And that Terri woman had complicated matters even further.

"If my daddy loves me, why does he stay away?" She looked at her aunt with large bright eyes filled with confusion.

Jill took a deep breath. "Sometimes adults do things that children don't always understand. Sometimes they don't know how to deal with their feelings, and they do strange things. Your daddy doesn't know how to be a daddy yet. That's why you and I have got to help him. Together."

"If we help him to be my daddy, will he stay here forever?"

"That's what we'll hope for. All right, luv?"

"Okay. You really think he'll like my dress?" she asked. Hope filled her voice.

"He'll love it. Just as he loves you. Now...give Auntie a big hug, and then you can have some ice cream."

"Yeah!" Ashley quickly threw herself into her aunt's arms and then tore off toward the kitchen in search of Mrs. Hally.

Jillianne smiled at the little figure, then turned her attention to the living room.

A magnificent seven-foot-tall Christmas tree stood majestically in the center of the room. She'd spent the entire previous evening decorating it with antique ornaments of gold and red. The only thing missing was the star on the top. She'd save that honor for Clint.

Satisfied with her handiwork, she walked toward the bar, intent on pouring herself a glass of wine, when she caught a glimpse of the brown envelope sticking out from between the couch cushions.

The doorbell rang.

"Miss Jill, Ashley, he's here," Mrs. Hally called.

Jillianne snatched the envelope from the cushion. Quickly she looked for a safe place to put it just as Clint walked through the archway. She slid the envelope into the small Queen Anne desk drawer.

When she looked up, she saw him. Her world seemed to stand still. She felt breathless and trembling with desire. She remained glued to the spot, afraid that if she moved this magnificent vision would vanish. Her heart beat wildly as she watched him close the distance between them.

"Jill!" He pulled her into his arms, and her head spun. How long had she waited for this moment? She inhaled his scent.

"It's good to see you. You look beautiful," he whispered in her ear.

Before she had a chance to recover, he stepped away. She hadn't even noticed Terri standing in the archway until Clint motioned to her, and the spell was broken.

"Jill, I'd like you to meet Terri Powers. Terri, this is my wonderful sister-in-law, Jillianne Davis."

Terri slipped out of her shoes and stepped fully into the room. Jill was immediately overcome by her regal presence. Even in bare feet, she was tall, statuesque with a crystal clear complexion of smooth mahogany. Her eyes were large, tilting slightly upward at the corners, giving her an exotic look that was both mystifying and intimidating.

As Terri slowly approached, Jillianne could almost visualize the voluptuous curves that defined the smooth-fitting suit of bronze silk.

Jill unconsciously patted her own silken, ebony hair when she looked at the luxurious shoulder-length locks that draped sensuously around the perfect face.

In an instant her jealousy of this woman ignited with a vengeance.

Terri stepped forward. An inviting smile of greeting illuminated her face. She extended her slender hand.

"I've heard so much about you," she said in a low voice edged with an island accent. "It's a pleasure to finally meet you."

Jill reluctantly took the outstretched hand. "I wish I could say the same about you. I mean," she added with a tight smile, "I wish Clint had informed me that he was bringing a guest." Her eyebrow arched as she gave Clint a look that he could not read.

But Terri read it very well, and the realization unnerved her.

Then, at the sound of footsteps, almost in unison the three turned toward the archway to see Ashley standing next to Mrs. Hally.

Clint looked briefly at Terri, and her smile reassured him. Slowly he knelt down.

"Hi, baby," he said softly.

Step-by-step she crossed the room until she stood in front of him. She kept her eyes riveted on her patent-leather shoes.

"Hi, Daddy," she mumbled.

"Can I get a hug? I missed you so much, Ash."

She looked up at him with such hope in her eyes, and his heart nearly broke. Gently he pulled her to him, and he wasn't sure whose heart was pounding the hardest.

"I missed you, baby," he whispered again. "I'm going to make it up to you. I promise. Things are going to be different from now on."

"Are you going to come here to live?"

Clint glanced up at Terri. "We'll talk about that later." He picked her up, holding her in one arm. "But first I want you to go out into the hallway and open the big box out there. It's a special pre-Christmas present."

Ashley ran into the hallway to see a large box decorated in brilliant Christmas colors. Her squeals of delight upon opening her gift rang throughout the large foyer.

"Let me carry it inside for you," Clint said. "It's almost bigger than you!" He brought the huge box into the living room and placed it under the tree, where Ashley immediately finished the job of demolishing the wrappings.

"It's a playhouse, Auntie! A real live playhouse."

"I see. It's beautiful, luv."

Terri stood on the sidelines, watching the picture-perfect scene unfold.

Clint was kneeling down next to Ashley with Jill close by his side. They had completely forgotten her.

As she watched, images of her own childhood emerged before her. How many Christmases had she sat on the side while her parents showered their own children with beautiful gifts? Even though she received her share of presents, it just wasn't the same. She always felt that she didn't belong, that she wasn't truly loved.

The old hurt and feelings of lonely isolation resurfaced. *She didn't belong here, either.*

Quietly, and unnoticed, she walked out of the room and into the foyer. She sat on the antique, pale peach chaise lounge and waited.

Several moments later Clint emerged and took a seat beside her.

"Baby, you were right about everything," he beamed. Even white teeth reflected against the dark skin. "It's going to work this time. I can feel it."

He's so happy, Terri realized.

She forced herself to smile. "I told you it would. You just had to give it a chance."

He hugged her to him and planted a solid kiss on her forehead. Then his expression changed. "Why are you out here?"

"Oh, I thought that, well, you know…family." She cleared her throat and smiled. "You need all the time you can get with your daughter."

"There you two are."

They both turned to see Jill standing in the archway.

"Mrs. Hally has your room ready, Clint. I'm sure you'll

want to get settled and freshen up." She gave Terri a cutting glance. "I'll have her get your room ready, Ms. Powers."

"That won't be necessary, Jill. Terri and I will stay together."

Jillianne pouted. "Now, Clint," she said in a stage whisper, "do you really think that would be appropriate? I mean…what will Ashley think?"

"You're absolutely right, Jill," Terri responded. "I wouldn't want Ashley's and my relationship to start off on the wrong foot, and please, call me Terri."

Jillianne inhaled and smiled triumphantly. "You see, Clint, Terri feels the same way."

Clint tossed up his hands in defeat. "I know when to quit." He pulled himself up from his seat. "Can I at least take Terri's bags to her room, or is that out of the question?" he taunted with a smile.

Jillianne giggled. "Of course. Don't be silly. As a matter of fact, I'll go up with you and help Terri get settled." She glanced at Terri, smiling sweetly. "That is, if you don't mind?"

"That's just what I need. Thanks." Terri struggled to hold back what she really wanted to say. Jill was being an unnecessary bitch, and it was obvious that she wanted to wedge herself between her and Clint. This trip was going to be even more difficult than she anticipated. Not only did she have a child to get adjusted to, she would have to deal with an overpossessive sister-in-law who was obviously in love with her man.

Clint collected the luggage and climbed the two flights to the bedrooms above. Jill remained close on his heels and Terri followed, keeping her temper in check with each step.

"You know where your room is, Clint," Jill said when they'd reached the landing. "And I think the guest room down the hall will be perfect for Terri." She turned to her. "I'm sure you'll love it."

"I'm sure I will." She smiled, realizing that her jaw was

beginning to ache from the plastic smile that she'd carved on her face since her arrival. She peeked over Jillianne's shoulder to see Clint grin and shrug his shoulders in helplessness. Terri wanted to scream.

Jill showed Terri to her room and busied herself fluffing pillows and checking windows.

"Everything seems to be in order. I'll have Mrs. Hally bring you up some fresh towels. Your bath is right through that door."

"Thank you," Terri mumbled.

"If there's anything you need, just ask."

I need you to give me some breathing room, she wanted to say, but instead, "I'm sure everything will be fine."

"Well, then, I'll check on dinner. It should be ready in about a half hour. Will that give you enough time to make yourself presentable?"

Terri's eyes flashed, much to Jill's pleasure.

"Excuse me?"

"I mean, will you have enough time to change? What did you think I meant?"

"It's more than enough time."

"Good. I'll see you at dinner." She turned to leave, then stopped and faced Terri. "By the way, how long have you known Clint?"

"A while. Why?"

"Oh, I was just curious. Clint never mentioned you, and we talk so often, of course." She shrugged her shoulder dismissively. "I could only assume that you relationship was short-term."

"You know the old saying about *assume*," Terri tossed back with a catty smile.

Jill's nostrils flared. She threw Terri a parting glance and left the room.

Terri sat down hard on the bed and silently prayed that she would be able to endure the next few days.

* * *

Dinner passed by relatively uneventful. Terri said very little during dinner, making comments only when necessary and smiling or laughing at the appropriate spots.

With each passing moment she felt more and more isolated. The pain of her youth seemed to overtake her, and she was again the small defenseless child trapped in a loveless home.

Clint focused all of his attention on Ashley, Jill hung on his every word and ignored her completely except to make an insinuating comment, and if she didn't know better she'd swear that Jill's behavior was wearing off on Ashley. Ashley barely said a word to her through the entire meal and responded to her questions about school and her friends in one-word answers. Apparently Clint didn't seem to notice a thing.

General talk about work, school and the weather dominated the conversation. Ashley said very little, but continually looked at her father as though he might disappear if she took her eyes off of him.

Mercifully dinner concluded. Clint attempted to take Terri's arm.

"When was the last time you tucked your daughter in?" Terri asked.

Clint looked at her curiously. "Why?"

"I think she'd like that a lot. Haven't you seen the way she's been staring at you all night?"

He glanced in Ashley's direction and saw the look of doubt in her eyes.

"Maybe you're right. But what will I say to her?"

Terri tiptoed and kissed his cheek. "You'll think of something." She said her good-nights and made a hasty escape to her room, while Clint took Ashley up to bed.

They spent the first few awkward moments in silence as they sat on the edge of the bed. Then Ashley spoke.

"Daddy, why did you bring that lady with you?"

"Terri?"

Ashley nodded.

"She's a very good friend of mine, and I wanted you to get to know her." He lifted the covers and placed Ashley beneath them.

"Why?" She snuggled down until the tip of the floral quilt reached her chin.

"Because I want you to know the people I know, and I want you to like them as much as I do."

"What if I don't like them?"

Clint was momentarily caught off guard. "Why wouldn't you like them?"

"Because."

"Because what, Ash?"

Ashley yawned. "I'm sleepy. Can we talk tomorrow?"

He leaned down and kissed her cheek. "Sure. Sweet dreams baby."

Slowly Clint rose from the bed and eased out of the door. Why had she asked that question? He shook his head as he walked down the hallway toward his room.

Terri aimlessly sifted through her dresser drawer and selected a nightgown of sea-green chiffon. She felt as if a heavy weight held down her spirit after she had struggled for so many years to free it from emotional bondage.

Slowly she walked toward the bathroom, turned on the tub full blast and filled the rushing waters with a mixture of African oils designed to soothe and relax the body and mind.

Within moments the steamy room was filled with the aromatic scent that rushed to her brain, and she sank into the calming waters.

Where was Clint? she wondered as she lay stretched beneath the cool sheets. The steamy bath had provided her with the relaxation she needed, and the twenty minutes of meditation had put on the final touches. She felt almost like her old self. If only Clint were here with her, everything would be perfect.

Her eyes drifted closed, so she had to be dreaming when she thought she saw Clint standing above her.

"Shh," he cautioned. He eased down beside her. "I don't want to wake Ashley, and I'm sure Jill is still awake. Mmm, you smell good." He nuzzled her neck, and she knew this was not a dream.

"Clint," she whispered, "I thought I was dreaming."

"Really? Does this feel like a dream?" His expert fingers caressed her breasts, making the chocolate peaks rise and harden at his command.

Her body moved rhythmically under his touch, her own hands rediscovering the hard muscular body.

"It feels like it's been forever," he groaned, pushing the sheer gown up above her hips. His hungry mouth sought and found hers, his velvet tongue exploring the warm cavern.

Her fingers, her mouth, stroked him, enflamed him until he was sure that he'd go crazy with longing.

"I love you," he moaned in her ear, pulling her to him, joining them.

She cried out with the pleasure of their union, and like a thief in the night, he took what lay open and waiting. And he took until they were both breathlessly satisfied.

"Clint," Terri whispered in the darkness.

"Hmm?" He buried his face deeper into her neck.

"Jillianne doesn't like me."

"Don't be silly," he said on a yawn. "Jill likes everybody."

"I'm not being silly." She snatched her leg from between his and turned on her back. "Didn't you see how she treated me?"

"Terri...come on. What did she do, help you unpack, show you to your room? What?"

She sighed in exasperation. "It's hard to explain. I can feel it. The way she looks at me."

"Jill can take some getting used to. But she's good people. You'll see when you get to know her better."

"Maybe. But Ashley acts the same way."

Clint sat up in the bed. "You're being paranoid. Ashley's just a child. Why wouldn't she like you?" But even as he asked the question, his bedside conversation with his daughter came back to him.

"Believe me, Clint, I know what I feel! I'm not imagining things. Did it ever occur to you that maybe they don't want me around because they want you to themselves?"

Clint shut his eyes. "It's probably my fault," he conceded. "I should have prepared them for your arrival."

He turned on his side and draped his arm across her waist. "But I know that once they get to know you, they'll love you just as much as I do."

Terri wasn't too sure about that, not with the looks that Jillianne gave her every chance she got. She was in love with Clint, and Terri posed a threat. And as the old saying went, *Hell hath no fury like a woman scorned*. What would Jill's fury be? The thought chilled her.

"Cold?" Clint pulled her closer and kissed her cheek. "Listen, why don't you and I take Ashley into London tomorrow and do some Christmas shopping? That will give the two of you a chance to get to know each other."

"I have to get busy on the ad campaign. Remember? And Christmas is not my holiday. I celebrate Kwanzaa."

"I know, I know. But this is more important. I want Ashley to get adjusted to the idea that you're in my life. Tell her about Kwanzaa and its importance. I'm sure she'll ask you a million questions. It'll give you two something to share."

Terri brightened. "If you think so." She took a breath. "I so want her to like me."

He pulled her into his embrace. "Oh, baby," he soothed. "I know it's hard. But I'm here for you, just like you're here for me. We can do this. You were the one who convinced me how important it was to establish a relationship with my daughter. I'm trying to do that. But I need your help and your support. It'll be all right, I promise."

"Yes, they arrived this afternoon," Jillianne whispered into the phone.

"Right on schedule," Mark said.

"Now what?"

"I'll let you know when to have the package delivered. The timing is important. Is everything else set?"

"Yes."

"So, how do you like Ms. Powers?"

Jill's pulse raced at the sound of her name. "She's everything you said she was," she said, trying to convince herself that her behavior was justified, even though deep inside she knew she'd seen nothing but goodness in Terri, and her genuine love for Clint.

Mark chuckled. "I'll call you tomorrow."

"Maybe it would be better if I called you. You never know when Clint might pick up the phone."

"You're right. Give me a call later in the day. I have to do some sightseeing tomorrow. Then everything will be in place."

"Fine. Good night."

Jill gently replaced the receiver. Was she doing the right thing? Methodically she paced the room, questioning her involvement in this scheme. But if she was to get Clint away from Terri permanently, she would do whatever needed to be done.

Quietly she eased out of her room with the intention of

going to the kitchen when she saw Clint slip out of Terri's bedroom. He turned down the corridor, never noticing her.

Jillianne's conviction was renewed.

Chapter 37

Clint met Jill in the den.

"There you are." He walked toward her and gave her a kiss on the cheek. "I was looking for you. After breakfast, Terri and I are going to take Ashley to London for some shopping."

"Oh, I was planning on us all spending the day together."

He held her shoulder and looked into her eyes. "Can we do that tomorrow? This is really important."

Her heart fluttered. "Of course. Enjoy yourselves. I have some clients to see anyway."

"Thanks." He turned to leave, then over his shoulder, "We'll be back in time for dinner."

"Great," she murmured. She crossed the room and sat on the love seat that overlooked the small pond that ran along the back of the property. She couldn't allow Terri to make any headway with Ashley. It would make things more difficult for her. She quickly ran upstairs to Ashley's room.

* * *

"I thought we'd go to Picadilly Square first and have lunch," Clint said to his silent riding companions. "Then we'll have enough strength to shop until it gets dark. How does that sound, Ashley?" He peered at her through the rearview mirror.

"Can I get whatever I want?" she asked in a soft voice.

"Of course. Today is your day."

Ashley took a quick look at Terri. "Then why does she have to go?"

"She? You mean Terri?"

Terri winced.

"Yes."

"Because I want to spend the day with my two favorite girls. And since you're so familiar with London, I thought that you would be the perfect guide for Terri."

"Oh." She sat up straighter in her seat, somewhat appeased.

This wasn't going to be as easy as he thought. He dared to look at Terri and instantly caught the pained look. He reached over and patted her hand. She smiled in response, but he knew her heart wasn't in it. What was he going to do if he couldn't win Ashley over and convince Terri that they could all live together as a family? Was he willing to give up one for the other?

Mark cruised down the back roads of Lancaster, intermittently checking the map he'd purchased at the hotel.

According to the map, the huge fork in the road indicated that a small town was off to the right and woods were to the left. He turned left.

He drove for about a mile down a dirt road shaded almost totally by enormous trees whose bare branches gave the deeply wooded area a sinister feel. If what Jillianne told him was true, he should be coming to his destination shortly. Then he saw it, directly in front of him. He brought the car to a stop. A slow smile crept across his face.

"Perfect."

He reached into his pocket and pulled out the worn, crumpled picture.

He stared at the tiny face, his irrational hatred burning his eyes.

"Soon."

"What do you want to do tonight, Mel?" Steve asked as he sipped his coffee.

"Let's rent a movie and relax. We've been out every night for the past week."

"Yeah, and it's been great!" He pulled her onto his lap and kissed her full on the mouth. "I'm glad you're back in my life, Mel. I didn't think it would ever happen."

She gently stroked his face. Steve had been a dream, a fantasy come true. She couldn't understand why she had forced him out of her life. He was good for her. Somehow she'd always known that, but tried to convince herself that if she waited around long enough Clint would...

Clint. Mark. Her conscience attacked her. She should tell Steve what was going on. But if she did, she'd have to also confess to her role. She wasn't ready to risk her first taste of real happiness. Clint was a big boy. He could take care of himself. And anyway, he had Terri to help him. She'd stay out of it.

Eagerly she returned Steve's kiss and pushed thoughts of Clint and Mark to the back of her mind.

Clint, Ashley and Terri exited the cozy café to be met by the chilly December air.

"Listen, you two," Clint said, "I'm going to take a quick peek in the jewelry store and see if I can find something for

Aunt Jill. Why don't you both head down to the toy store, and I'll meet you there."

Ashley looked up at Terri, and her warm smile convinced her. "Okay."

Terri took a deep breath and took Ashley's hand. Clint bent down and kissed Terri's lips. "Thanks, babe," he whispered. "I'll see you in about a half hour."

Terri nodded and took Ashley down the street.

"I have a friend with hair like yours," Ashley said in a timid voice.

"You do?" Terri smiled. "Is she as pretty as you are?"

Ashley giggled and nodded her head. "You have nice hands," Ashley commented, gripping Terri's hand tighter.

"And so do you," Terri replied.

"Do you like my daddy?"

"Yes, I do. Very much."

Ashley was quiet for a moment as if she had to digest the information. "My auntie likes him, too."

Terri avoided reading anything into her comment. "Your daddy is a very special man. A lot of people like him."

Everything her aunt had said came rushing out. "I love him. But he doesn't want me. Auntie was going to help Daddy love me—but…you want to take my daddy away from me." She was near to tears.

Terri stopped in her tracks and bent down in front of Ashley. Several pedestrians had to detour around them. Terri braced Ashley's shoulders and looked directly into her eyes. She spoke softly and firmly, praying that wisdom would come with every word.

"Ashley, your daddy loves you more than you could ever imagine. He told me. It's just that your daddy has been so busy, he thought it would be best if you stayed with your aunt. But he wants to be a part of your life. He just doesn't know how. It's going to take time. And I would never try to take your daddy away from you."

"Do you like me?"

The question startled her. When she looked at Ashley, the child's eyes were large with wonder and need.

"Yes, I do." And once she said the words, she realized that she really did. A sensation of warmth enveloped her, and she had the overwhelming desire to want to protect Ashley from the world. Instead she hugged her, and the hug she received in return almost brought tears to her eyes.

"Now—" Terri cleared her throat "—let's see how much shopping we can do before your dad finds us. Deal?"

"Deal."

As they exited the enormous toy store, Terri heard her name being called, and her spine stiffened. *It can't be.*

"It seems as if we keep running into each other."

Terri reluctantly turned around to see Alan Martin standing behind her. Her face hardened.

"What are you doing here, Alan?"

"I'm on a job." He glanced at Ashley. "Whose kid?"

"None of your business."

"No need to be nasty." He looked cautiously around. "No bodyguard? Or has Mr. Clinton Steele moved on to greener pastures?"

"That's my daddy," Ashley cried. "Do you know my daddy?"

Alan gave Ashley a lopsided grin. "Let's just say we've met."

Terri took Ashley's hand. "Come on, Ashley." She turned to go.

"Ashley, that's a pretty name."

Ashley grinned up at him. "Thank you."

"I'm sure we'll be seeing each other again, Terri."

"Not if I have anything to do with it."

Terri took off at a rapid pace, pulling Ashley behind her. Ashley had to run to keep up.

"What's wrong, Miss Terri? Is that a bad man? Is he a *stranger?*" She sounded almost excited.

"No, Ashley. Let's find your father." She pushed her way down the crowded street and ran smack into Clint.

"Whoa. What's the rush?"

"The crowd was beginning to get to me. I needed some air. And I think we have plenty of toys."

Clint looked at the two armloads of packages and relieved Terri of them.

"I'd say so." He looked down at Ashley. "There won't be anything left for Santa to bring." He grinned at Ashley. "Did you have a good time, sweetheart?"

Ashley nodded her head vigorously. "We met a stranger, Daddy," she chimed as they moved down the street toward the car.

"A stranger?"

"It was Alan," Terri said.

Clint caught Terri's look. "Alan! What does he have— radar? He didn't try anything, did he?" Visions of Alan and Terri, back in California, raced through his head.

Terri shook her head. "He was just obnoxious."

Clint put his arm around her. "Forget it. Alan isn't worth worrying about."

That's what she kept trying to tell herself.

Jillianne sat at the desk and opened the drawer. The manila envelope was still tucked safely inside. Mark told her that the next day she was to arrange to have the package delivered.

She turned the thick envelope over in her hands. What could it contain that could be so damaging to Terri?

"Auntie! We're back." Ashley raced into the living room just as Jill returned the envelope to its hiding place. Soon enough she would find out.

"Auntie, Miss Terri told me all about Kwanzaa. It's very

special," she said in her most serious voice. "And we get gifts for seven days!" she squealed. "I think I like Kwanzaa."

"That's very nice, dear," Jill replied, trying to hide her annoyance. She hadn't expected that Terri would have charmed her niece after all she'd told her.

"Why don't you find Mrs. Hally and get yourself a snack?" she told Ashley, who quickly ran off in the direction of the kitchen.

Clint, Terri, and Jill sat together in the living room, while Ashley rattled a nonstop conversation with Mrs. Halley.

"Can I get you something, Terri? Some wine, a drink?"

"No, thank you. I don't drink. But if you have some fruit juice, that would be fine."

Jill looked at her curiously. "I'll check with Mrs. Hally."

Clint eased closer to Terri on the couch. "See, Jill's not so bad."

"She's fine when she's around you, Clint. It's when we're alone that the daggers get thrown."

Jill returned several minutes later with a tall glass of cranberry juice. "This is all we have." She handed the glass to Terri.

"Thank you. This is fine."

"If you'll tell Mrs. Hally what you like, I'm sure she'll stock up." She turned to Clint. "Do you think you'll have some time for your dear sister-in-law this evening?"

"Sure. What did you have in mind?"

"Why don't you let me surprise you." Then to Terri, "You wouldn't mind if I borrowed Clint for a while, would you?"

"No." Terri stood up. "As a matter of fact, I have a ton of work to do." She turned to Clint with an "I told you so" look in her eyes. "I have plenty to keep me occupied. If you'll excuse me, I think I'll get started."

Clint gave Terri's hand a squeeze of reassurance as she passed by.

"I thought we could take a drive, like the old days, and just talk." Jill sat next to Clint, sitting as close as she dared. "How does that sound?"

Clint stretched back in the couch. "Sounds fine. When did you want to leave?"

"In about an hour."

"That'll give me time to get a quick nap. If I remember correctly, your 'drives' turn into major events."

Jill laughed at the memories and tapped Clint playfully on the thigh. "I'll meet you out front in an hour." Her spirit was light as she climbed the stairs. She'd finally have Clint to herself, and she was going to make the most of it.

The sound of laughter nudged Terri out of her sleep. Slowly she opened her eyes and tried to focus. She peered at the wall clock: 3 a.m. She shook her head to clear it and discovered that she'd fallen asleep at her desk, having worked on the ad campaign for hours.

The voices drew nearer. She instantly recognized Clint's deep timbre and Jill's sultry laughter. Had they been out all night? An irrational anger swept through her. Some ride, she fumed, rising from the padded seat. She stretched, trying to get rid of the knots that had formed in her back and neck.

Quietly she crossed the room. She definitely didn't want Clint to think she'd been waiting up for him. Soundlessly she opened her dresser drawer and extracted a nightgown. Moments later she was in bed…waiting.

The house grew quiet. Her anger switched to disappointment, then hurt. Clint hadn't even stopped in to say good-night! Were they together? Was Jill's obvious attraction to Clint mutual?

The unanswered questions tripped through her mind as she tossed and turned, finally falling into a fitful sleep full of images of Clint and Jill.

* * *

"Clint, good morning," Jill greeted upon finding him in the kitchen. "Where's Terri?"

"I guess she decided to sleep late," he mumbled, draining a glass of orange juice.

"I had a wonderful time last night," she practically purred.

Terri stood at the top of the stairs as Jill's suggestive voice floated upward. Her senses heightened while she waited for Clint's response.

"So did I. It's been a long time, Jill."

A long time. What did that mean?

"I know," Jill said softly. Her eyes caressed him. "Will you be here all day?"

"For the most part." He yawned. "Terri and I have some kinks to work out with a deal we're negotiating."

The sound of Terri's name broke the mood. Jill checked her watch. "And I have an appointment in about fifteen minutes. So I'll see you later. Mrs. Hally took Ashley to school. Today is her last day before the holidays."

"What time does she get home?"

"About noon."

"Good. I'd like to spend some time with her."

"She'd like that." She stepped closer. "I'd like it, too." She tiptoed and kissed his cheek.

Terri returned to her room, locked the door and sat by the window replaying the conversation over and over again in her head.

Had it been more than just a ride around town between them last night? The way Jill sounded, and from Clint's response, it appeared to be. She knew that Clint wouldn't betray her like that. Especially right under her nose. However, her feelings about Jill clouded her judgment. It was Jill that she didn't trust. Jill was not above doing whatever she could to get to Clint. Even though he seemed unaware of her intentions. Or was he?

Clint braced Jill's shoulders and looked squarely at her. He'd been trying to figure out the best time and the best way to tell her. There wasn't any.

"Jill, sit down. There's something I want to tell you."

Jill felt a sense of doom spreading through her as she blindly sat down in the kitchen chair.

"I don't know how to tell you this except straight out. I've been thinking about it for a long time, and now that Terri's in my life, I know it's the right time."

Her heart raced uncontrollably, and she suddenly felt faint.

"I plan to take Ashley back to the States with us after the holidays."

She was sure she couldn't have heard right. That was impossible. Ashley belonged to her. He belonged to her. Her insides twisted. "You can't do that."

Her voice was so soft and flat, Clint wasn't quite sure that she'd spoken. He reached for her hand, and she snatched it away.

"You can't do that," she repeated. Her voice rose and trembled as she spoke. "I raised Ashley. She's like a daughter to me. I did it for you! For you!" She leaped up from the chair. Tears streamed down her face. "How could you do this to me? How could you?"

She went for his face, but not before Clint grabbed her wrists.

"Jillianne—listen to me," he commanded.

She shook her head violently. "No. I won't. You can't do this. I won't let you." She snatched her hands away and raced from the room.

"Jill!" Clint took off after her. He reached her just as she stuck the key in her car door.

He grabbed her by the shoulder and spun her around, pinning her body between his and the car.

From her bedroom window Terri watched in agony as the obviously intimate scene unfolded before her. She turned away, not willing to allow herself to be hurt any further. Now everything that she'd overheard took on real meaning.

"Let go of me, Clint," Jillianne spat.

"We need to talk, Jill. I'm not taking her away from you. She's my daughter. And she needs to know that. You've got to be able to understand that." His voice softened, understanding her hurt and confusion. "I'd never do anything to hurt you, Jill."

"You already have." She tore away and faced him. "You already have."

Clint stepped back and watched her race out of the driveway. He breathed heavily. She'd have to come to terms with it, he thought. Somehow she'd have to learn to deal with it.

With a heavy heart he returned to the house. He needed to talk with Terri.

As Jill raced down the winding road, she contemplated what she was about to do. She never wanted to come back to this house. Not if she had to live in it without Ashley and Clint. Tear-filled eyes glanced at her purse that carried the package. It was worth it.

Chapter 38

The light knock at her door broke into her swirling thoughts. It could only be Clint. She wasn't ready to see him now. Her confusion mixed with anger did not bode well for any sort of congenial conversation between them. After what she'd heard and then seen, she didn't know what there was to talk about.

The knock came again. This time the doorknob turned as Clint called her name.

She stood still in the hopes that he would think she was still asleep. Moments later she heard his footsteps descending the stairs.

She couldn't avoid him forever. But at least now she'd have some time to think and sort things out before she confronted him. And confront him she would.

After a long shower, Clint decided to take a ride into the city. Driving always helped to clear his head. Maybe Terri would be up and around when he returned, and Jill would have calmed down enough so that they could have an intelligent conversation.

Anyway, he wanted to select a special gift for Terri for the holidays. Even if she didn't celebrate Christmas, he still wanted her to have something to open on Christmas morning. Something to seal their love and their lives together.

His thoughts warmed when she came to mind. She'd become everything he'd hoped for. He trusted her with his deepest thoughts and desires and truly loved her more than he thought he ever could. He smiled. He hoped the diamond brooch he'd ordered for Jill would help to ease her feelings of abandonment. Maybe he would ask Jill if she wanted to relocate to the States. He shook his head as he slipped on his coat. He didn't know what else to do. He wanted his daughter with him, and that was final. He, Terri and Ashley were going to be a family. Jill would have to decide if she wanted to be a part of it.

Clint put his hand on the doorknob just as the bell chimed. He opened the door and was surprised to see a young man from the local courier service.

"I have this package for—" he checked his log "—a Mr. Clinton Steele."

"I'm Clint Steele." Clint reached for the envelope and flipped it over. His brows creased in curiosity. There was no return address.

"Sign here, please."

Clint signed his name. Absently he reached into his pocket and tipped the courier.

He took the envelope and returned to the kitchen. When he began to review the contents, his head began to pound with disbelief. Page after page outlined his plans to buy the property in the Caribbean. Documents that no one had access to except him and Terri.

Every step of the plan, from concept to completion, was contained on the pages. And the most damning evidence of all were the notations of counteroffers and correspondence to Nat Carpenter from *Theresa Brathwaite*. His stomach lurched.

She'd set up a dummy company to run the project and compete with him for the deal. It was Terri all along!

A torrent of emotions ripped through him. How could she do this? Why would she do this? And all along she'd pretended to love him only to benefit herself in the long run. His thoughts swirled back to their initial meeting. Terri practically came out and told him that she disliked him and everything that he stood for. She lied to him when she feigned outrage at the things that had been written about him.

He knew she was ambitious. He knew that her business had been in trouble for a while. How far would she go to reach the top? He sat down heavily in the chair. Something like this he would have expected from someone like Mark Andrews, not Terri. Not Terri.

He'd told her everything about his plan. Everything! And she used that information against him.

His anger and sense of absolute betrayal rose to a point of explosion. Never before had he felt such a bottomless void, bereft of any emotion except to destroy.

He pounded his fist against the butcher-block table. If she thought she could get away with it, he'd show her who the real master of the game was.

He stuffed the incriminating contents back into the envelope. As he did he wondered briefly where the information had come from. *What did it matter?* He had it now. That's what was important. He'd find out the source soon enough. In the meantime he wanted her out of his house and out of his life.

Terri checked herself in the mirror. She refused to put off talking with Clint another minute. The anxiety and tension were eating away at her. She had to know, for sure, what was the extent of his relationship with Jill. Did anything happen between them? What were his feelings for Jill, and was he aware of her feelings for him? What was that scene in the courtyard really all about?

If she left the questions unanswered, there would always be a seed of doubt and lack of trust in their relationship.

With that determination made, she left her room in the hopes of finding Clint still at home.

Clint spun around at the sound of a presence behind him.

Terri involuntarily stepped back when she saw the look of pure rage and something bordering on pain hovering in the darkness of his eyes.

She opened her mouth to speak, but Clint quickly cut her off.

"How could you?" he seethed.

Terri's voice rose in bewilderment. "How could I what?"

"Don't play your innocence game with me. I know everything! I know what you've been doing."

"Clint, I don't know what you're talking about." She took a hesitant step toward him.

He instantly held up his hand. "Don't come near me." His voice escalated to a thundering roar, and for the first time, Terri actually felt afraid of the man who stood ominously in front of her.

"You were the one behind this whole competitor's scheme with Carpenter!"

For several unbelievable seconds, Terri couldn't absorb what she was hearing.

Clint equated her silence with guilt, and the bottom went out of his world.

"Have you totally lost your mind?" Terri cried. "I don't know what you think you've discovered, but I don't like the sound of it or what you're implying! If you have something to say, then say it!"

"Here." He tossed the envelope at her. She caught it as it landed against her stomach. "That says it all."

Terri's pulse raced. Her head began to pound as she scanned the pages of notes and correspondence. Her vision clouded over as her own anger spiraled to match his. *This* was the man who claimed to love her? How could he believe that she would do something like this? Yet everything looked authentic. Everything. To a point where she briefly began to think that she was losing her senses. If she didn't know better, she, too, would believe that these were documents she'd created, and all signed with her birth name. *Theresa Brathwaite*. The implication was unfathomable. Yet Clint believed it.

She looked up at him, pain-filled eyes meeting anguished ones. Maybe this was a sign, she thought, that things would never be right between them. Obstacle after obstacle erected themselves in their paths.

She dropped the documents on the floor. The line was drawn. She straightened her shoulders, drawing herself up to her full height. Her proud chin jutted forward defiantly.

"Think whatever you want, Clint. If you can believe this, then you'll believe anything about me. And that doesn't say very much about this relationship, which has now come to an end."

She spun away and walked purposefully out of the kitchen, willing herself not to crumple under the weight of her hurt.

Clint remained like a stone statue in the heavy silence that followed. Devastation swept through him. Could she be telling the truth? Had he allowed his anger to cloud his judgment and good sense? But when she saw the contents of the envelope, she never flinched. Not once.

He didn't know what to think.

Still, just looking at her left him with nagging doubts. If it wasn't Terri, then who was it? And more importantly, how did they get the information and know Terri's birth name?

Clint headed for the door. He was going to find the source

of the information. He took a fleeting look up the staircase as he opened the door. *No,* he decided. He wouldn't go to her now. He was sure she wouldn't listen, and she'd have every right. When he came back to her, he wanted to have the information and the name of the person who was out to destroy them.

Melissa sat across the table from Steve and thought about how happy she was. Yet her happiness was not complete. Her conscience gnawed at her. Was their budding relationship strong enough to withstand the secret that she held? Steve might eventually find out her role. Then what?

"You're deep in thought," Steve commented. He took a sip of hot chocolate. "Anything you want to talk about?"

She looked away. Her thoughts raced.

Steve reached across the table and covered her hand with his. "You can tell me, Mel. Whatever it is."

She looked into his warm brown eyes.

"Even if it may change the way you feel about me?"

He sat back in his seat, a look of concern darkening his eyes. Then he leaned forward. "Nothing could change the way I feel about you. What could be so terrible?" He smiled at her encouragingly.

Melissa took a deep breath. She couldn't look into his eyes as she slowly revealed her masochistic relationship with Mark and her involvement in his plan to hurt Terri and Clint in the process.

Hot tears burned her eyes while she mechanically threw her clothing into her suitcase. The door below slammed shut, and moments later she heard the roar of Clint's car tear out of the driveway.

The tears came hard and fast now, the emptiness and hurt almost more than she could stand. Who would do such a thing and why? More importantly, how could Clint believe it under any circumstances? Maybe she should have tried to defend herself, convince him that she didn't…wouldn't do anything like that.

It didn't matter, she concluded, slamming the suitcase shut. She and Clint were not meant to be together, and maybe this was for the best.

Terri closed her bedroom door and descended the stairs. She'd have to call a car service to take her to a hotel. At least until she could make arrangements to have her return flight to New York changed. Mrs. Hally should have a number.

Jillianne entered the lobby of the Savoy and approached the reception desk.

"Would you call Mr. Andrews's room, please?"

"Whom shall I say is here, madam?"

"Jillianne Davis."

"One moment."

Jill and Mark sat at a small table in the hotel's exquisite dining room.

"Why do you look so upset?" Mark asked as soon as the waitress was out of earshot. He leaned forward. "Did something go wrong?"

Jill shook her head. "I sent the package. He should have it by now."

"Great. So what's the problem?"

"He wants to take Ashley away."

Mark's jaw clenched. "What do you mean?"

Jill explained what Clint told her.

Mark thought about it for a moment, totally unmoved by Jill's plight. His main concern was the completion of his plan. This little twist only meant that everything would have to be moved up.

He patted her hand. "Don't worry about a thing. By the time

this is all over, he'll be so glad to be rid of Terri and have his daughter, he'll do anything you want. We move tonight."

"Tonight?"

"Yes. Now just remember what you have to do. I'll do the rest."

Steve felt as if his insides were being squeezed shut. He stared at Melissa in astonishment. He would have never imagined that Melissa could be capable of such duplicity. Had her obsession with Clint driven her to such lengths?

"Why, Mel?" he asked in a strained voice. "Why?"

Unable to face him, she looked away. "I was hurt. Confused. Obsessed." She looked at him. "Lonely. I thought if I could help Mark to get Terri out of the picture, I would have Clint. I even went so far as to let Mark be a replacement for Clint. But it never really worked." Her voice cracked. "Then Mark became more and more irrational, more demanding, frightening." Tears slowly fell from her eyes.

Steve rounded the table and knelt down beside her. He lifted her chin with the tip of his finger, forcing her to look at him.

"Whatever you've done can be undone. Now I want you to tell me everything you know."

Chapter 39

Clint arrived at the delivery offices of Quic Courier. With little difficulty he found a parking space and moments later stood in front of a very harried dispatcher.

"Yes? What can I do for you, sir?"

Clint started to speak but was cut off by the ringing phone.

"One moment, sir," he said to Clint. He then spat out instructions to the caller, while simultaneously answering another line and putting it on hold. He put his hand over the mouthpiece and spoke to Clint.

"I do apologize, sir. My assistant grew ill and had to leave. I'm the only one here at the moment. I'll be with you shortly." He returned to his conversation.

Clint paced as he watched the stout, middle-aged man move agilely around the small office, fielding phone calls and writing orders. The office of Quic Courier was small but neat. The reception area could hold a maximum of three people and then consider the place crowded. They prided themselves on personalized service, dealing mainly with the local residents and neighborhood businesses. If you wanted something delivered without a lot of hassle and high prices, Quic was the place to go. Clint couldn't remember a time when they weren't around.

Finally, the dispatcher was finished and turned his attention to Clint.

He exhaled deeply. "So sorry, sir. How can I be of service to you?"

Clint peeked at his name tag. "Mr. Willis, I received this package this morning." He put the envelope on the table. "It didn't have a return address. I want to know who sent it."

"Hmm." Mr. Willis slipped his Benjamin Franklin glasses onto his nose. He shook his head as he looked at the address. "I didn't send this out. Let me check the log."

Mr. Willis ambled down to the end of the long counter and pulled the log book out from the bottom shelf. Quickly he scanned the pages, then checked the office copy of receipts.

He returned to where Clint stood. "The client paid us in cash." He peered up at Clint. "There's no other information."

"Can I see that?" Clint reached for the receipt. "How can you accept something like this without a name?" He handed it back in disgust.

"As long as the delivery is paid for and the mailing address is clear..." He shrugged his shoulders.

"Would you at least remember what the person looked like?"

"As I said, I did not prepare this order. My assistant did. Perhaps she'd remember. If you'd care to pop in tomorrow, she may be able to help you."

Clint sighed heavily. "Thank you. Maybe I will." As his temper began to ebb, he had a strong sensation that he had been very wrong about everything. He turned to leave, wondering what his next move should be. He checked his watch. Ashley would be home shortly, and he wanted to select a gift for Terri. He owed Terri more than a gift, but at least it would pave the way for the groveling that he would have to do in order to get her to listen to the apology that she deserved.

He drove into the heart of London and found the most expensive jewelry shop in the city.

"You'll stay here in the hotel," Mark instructed Jill. "I can't take a chance that you'll cave in and ruin everything." He tossed the balance of his brandy down his throat.

"I can't stay here. They'll wonder where I am."

"That's even better. Clint will be so relieved to see you when you return, he'll be putty in your hands. Now let's go." He rose from his seat and took Jill by the elbow, leading her out of the dining room.

When he reached the door, he stopped short. "Wait," he urged. He pulled Jill back into the dining hall. "Over there." He pointed in the direction of the lobby. "That's Terri."

Jill saw her, too. "What is she doing here?"

"It looks like she's checking in."

They watched the bellhop take her bags onto the elevator.

"This changes things," Mark said. "We'll have to move quicker than planned. I can't afford to run into her in the hotel. And neither can you."

"Do you have Clint's phone number in England?" Steve asked Melissa.

"I have it at the office.

"Is anyone there?"

"Maybe one of the secretaries is still around. I'll call."

Melissa dialed the number to Hightower Enterprises. The phone rang for quite a while before it was finally answered.

"Hightower Enterprises. May I help you?"

Melissa readily recognized the voice of her assistant, Chris. "Hello, Chris. This is Melissa."

"Oh, hello, Ms. Taylor. Is something wrong?"

"I need a favor. Look in my office on my private Rolodex, and get me Mr. Steele's number in London."

"Sure. Hold on."

Melissa put her hand over the mouthpiece and spoke to Steve. "She's going to get it. I just hope that we're in time to stop whatever it is that Mark is planning."

Chris came back on the line. "Ms. Taylor. I have the number."

"Thanks, Chris." Melissa jotted down the number and hung up. She handed the slip of paper to Steve. He took her place at the phone and dialed.

The line was busy and remained busy every time they called for the next hour.

"Maybe there's trouble on the line," Steve concluded, hanging up the phone for the countless time.

"We can try again later," Melissa offered.

Steve nodded.

Clint returned home to find Terri gone. He quizzed Mrs. Hally until she was on the verge of tears, then found himself apologizing by giving her the night off.

He then spent the next hour on the phone trying to track down the cabdriver that had picked up Terri, only to find out that the cabbie was now gone for the day. He hadn't turned in his trip sheet and would not be back on duty for two days. The second hour was spent blasting the airline reservationist and anyone else who came on the line to tell him that they couldn't give out any information on passengers.

And where was Jillianne? he fumed. He paced the expanse of the living room until he finally flopped down on the couch in frustration. He'd really done it this time. He'd let his temper

blind him to the truth, and now he'd probably lost Terr
for good.

He had to find her. He had to tell her how wrong he wa:
and that together they would find out who was behind trying
to ruin them and their relationship.

Clint checked his watch. It was after two o'clock. He
frowned. *Where was Ashley?* He didn't even have the name
of the bus service that brought her back and forth. *Some father*
he was. And he'd been so busy apologizing to Mrs. Hally, h
hadn't thought to ask her. Now what?

Once again, he began to pace. His jaw clenched. Something
was wrong. He could feel the onset of trouble continue to brew
with each passing moment. Terri was gone. Ashley wasn't
home as expected, and Jill had torn out of the house in such
a state, he couldn't imagine where she might be. And where
was his daughter? That unanswered question disturbed him
most of all.

Mrs. Hally's phone number had to be around somewhere.
He went to the kitchen and checked the list of phone numbers
tacked to the corkboard. *Here it is.*

The phone rang endlessly. Annoyed, he placed the phone
back in the cradle. He felt completely impotent. There had to
be something he could do.

He'd go to the school. Maybe they had some extended
activity, and Jill had neglected to mention it. He headed toward
the door with one thought on his mind…Ashley.

Just as he reached the door, the phone rang. A temporary
feeling of relief loosened the frown that had hardened his
face.

He grabbed the phone.

"Yes?" he barked into the mouthpiece.

The voice was garbled, barely discernible, as if the voice
were electronic. Clint immediately concluded that it must be
some sort of crank call and started to hang up until he heard
the voice mention Ashley's name.

"What? What did you say about my daughter?"

"I suggest you listen carefully, Mr. Steele. And most importantly do not call the police. We have your daughter, and if you do as we say, nothing will happen to her."

"Who is this, dammit!" He gripped the receiver with such force that his knuckles began to hurt. "If anything happens to my daughter, I'll find you and I'll bury you!"

"No time for idle threats, Mr. Steele. Are you willing to listen, or should I hang up? The choice is yours."

Clint forced himself to breathe as millions of unspeakable atrocities whipped through his head. He pushed calm into his voice. "I'm listening."

"That's better. Now the first thing I want you to do is to contact Nat Carpenter and tell him that you're no longer interested in the resorts in the Caribbean."

"What? Are you out of your mind? What do the resorts have to do with my daughter?"

"You're asking too many questions again, Mr. Steele. I think I'll have to hang up."

The sound of the dial tone buzzed madly in his ear.

Clint slammed down the phone, throwing it to the floor. Blindly he stooped down and picked it up, staring at it as though the ivory instrument were at the root of this vicious joke.

Rage, fear and shock took over his body and his thoughts. He paced, unable to think clearly. His darkly handsome face was contorted into a mask of fury and pain. He pressed his large fist against his mouth to keep from screaming. Call, damn you!

Dear God, not Ashley. Not Ashley. He slammed his fist against the table. He'd never been a father to her—and now this. He had to make things right. No matter what it took. If those bastards wanted the resorts, they could have them and anything else they wanted. As long as he got Ashley back.

Call! He stared at the phone, willing it to ring. Moments later it did.

Clint snatched up the phone. "Yes?"

"Are you ready to listen now, Mr. Steele?"

He took a deep breath. "Go ahead."

"After you make that call to Mr. Carpenter, I want you to gather your liquid assets. I want two million. In cash. Out of sequence. By tomorrow morning."

Clint was momentarily stunned. "I can't get that kind of money by tomorrow!"

"If you want your daughter, you'll get the money and make the call. I'll call you in the morning and let you know where to drop off the money and pick up your daughter."

"Wait! How do I know you have Ashley? Let me talk to her."

"Why, of course. I thought you'd never ask. Ashley, your daddy wants to talk to you."

"Daddy? Daddy?"

"Ashley, sweetheart. It's me. I'm gonna get you home, baby. Are you all right?"

"I can't see. There's something over my eyes. Daddy, I—" The phone was snatched from her hand.

"That's quite enough. You have plenty to do to keep you busy, Mr. Steele. Expect to hear from me tomorrow."

The phone went dead.

Clint held the phone for countless minutes, trying to digest all that he'd heard. The money he could understand. But why the resorts? Obviously the kidnapper and his competitors were one in the same. Or at the very least his competition had paid someone to do this.

Finally he replaced the phone and went in search of Nat Carpenter's number in the Bahamas. A cruel and chilling thought seeped through his veins as he flipped the pages of his phone book. What if Terri did have something to do with this? But just as quickly he tossed it off. No. That's what they wanted him to think. Someone else was behind this, and they were determined to ruin them both. But why Terri? Who hated her so much that they would invent such an elaborate scheme to implicate her?

He didn't have time to dwell on that right now. He had to call Carpenter and get in touch with his accountant and his banker immediately. He had to find a way to get the money before tomorrow afternoon.

Chapter 40

"What are we going to do now?" Melissa asked Steve.

"We'll wait and try again later."

Melissa swallowed the knot of fear that had settled in her throat. Hesitantly she asked the question that had hovered in her head for hours. "And...what about us?"

Steve sighed heavily, stood up and walked to the other side of the bedroom. He turned and faced her. "I know how I feel about you, Mel. What you did was deplorable, but you still have a conscience. I think the reason you needed to tell me was because of how you're beginning to feel about me. Am I right?"

She nodded, and a flicker of hope lifted her heart.

"Then we can work everything else out. As long as we're honest with each other. Deal?"

Slowly she rose, then ran across the room and into his arms. "Deal," she whispered against his chest.

Steve took a step back and held her at arm's length. "Let's see if we can get Clint on the phone."

Melissa dialed the number again and was overjoyed to hear the familiar ringing sound.

"It's ringing," she said.

The phone was finally picked up.

"Hello?"

"Hello, this is Melissa Taylor."

"Ah, Ms. Taylor, how are you?" answered Mrs. Hally.

"I'm fine. Actually I need to speak to Mr. Steele. Right away."

"I'm sorry, he's not here. He told me I could have the night off, but when I finally arrived home I discovered I'd left my small purse with my house keys. I've just returned to pick them up and found the house empty."

"Do you have any idea where he could be?"

"No, I don't."

"Is Ms. Powers there?"

"Oh, no!" She shook her head vigorously and lowered her voice to a conspiratorial whisper. "She and Mr. Steele had a terrible tiff this morning. She packed her bags. I called a cabbie for her myself."

"What? Do you have any idea where she might be?"

"No, mum. She may be at one of the hotels, or she could have gone to the airport."

"All right. When Mr. Steele comes in, please tell him to call me. It's urgent that I speak with him as soon as possible."

"I certainly will. But you know our Mr. Steele, he does things in his own time."

"I know. Thank you, Mrs. Hally."

Melissa hung up and replayed the conversation to Steve.

"Damn! Everything's coming apart at once." He shook his head. "I'm sure I can track down Terri. I have a few connections in London. Maybe that's what we can do in the meantime. This affects her as much as Clint. I just wonder what the hell happened between them that would make Terri leave."

Melissa wondered, too.

* * *

Clint burst through the door, nearly knocking Mrs. Hally over with the sheer force of his entry.

He quickly clasped her shoulders to keep her from tumbling backward.

"Mrs. Hally," he breathed in relief. "Thank God you're here. Please sit down."

He quickly ushered her onto the chaise lounge in the foyer and told her about his conversation with the abductor.

Mrs. Hally made the sign of the cross three times and sent up silent prayers for Ashley's safe return as tears rolled down her cheeks.

Clint put his arm around her trembling shoulders. "We're going to get her back. I promise."

She nodded, putting all her faith in his words.

"I have to go out. But I'll be back as soon as I can. We're not to contact the police in any way. Or tell anyone. Do you understand?"

"Yes, sir." She sniffed.

"Fine. I need you to stay here to answer the phone."

"Of course, Mr. Steele. Anything."

He patted her back. "Thank you." He got up to leave when Mrs. Hally remembered the phone call from Melissa.

"There was a call while you were out." She blew her nose.

Clint's pulse raced. "Who?"

"Ms. Taylor from your office in New York."

His hopes slowly diminished. "Oh. I'll have to try to get back to her." He moved toward the door.

"She said it was very important."

Clint opened the door, then turned around. "Not as important as getting my daughter back safely."

Terri ordered room service but merely picked at the shrimp salad. She lay down the fork and tossed the linen napkin to the side. She pushed herself away from the table and walked toward the window. The city of London spread out beneath her view.

What an ideal place for the perfect romantic interlude, she thought, then laughed derisively. This trip had turned out to be anything but perfect.

She pulled the satin belt of her robe around her waist. How could things have gone so badly? She'd had misgivings about coming, but she never envisioned that the problem would be her and Clint.

Clint. Just the thought of his name made their painful parting resurface with a vengeance. How could he have thought such a thing about her? Did he have so little faith in their relationship that he would allow some vile lie to ruin what they had built?

She'd even begun to care about Ashley and believed that in time she would find it in her heart to truly love her. Their afternoon together had been the turning point. But now...

She turned away from the lights of the darkening city. Tomorrow she'd be back in New York. Once again she would have to reconstruct her life from the rubble of yet another failed liaison.

Sadly she lay across the canopied bed. Maybe happiness was not hers to have, she concluded, as she drifted off into a trouble-filled sleep.

There was a distant, persistent ringing. Slowly Terri floated up from sleep and tried to focus in on her surroundings. Where was she? She squeezed her eyes shut and quickly opened them again. *The hotel.* Then the reason for her being there came rushing back. The ringing continued, and she realized it was the phone.

Clumsily she reached for it as daybreak peeked through the drawn drapes.

"Hello?"

"Terri? Is that you?"

"Who is this?" She was fully alert and sat up in bed.

"It's me, Steve. Clint's friend."

Her heart began to race. *Something happened to Clint.*

"Steve? How did you get this number?"

"I find people for a living."

"Why did you have to find me? Has something happened to Clint?"

"No." He paused. "At least not yet. We've been trying to reach him since yesterday."

"Steve, you're scaring me. Get to the point. And who is *we?*"

"Melissa and I."

Terri frowned. "Are you going to tell me why you called me at six a.m., or are you going to make me guess?"

Steve exhaled. "This may sound crazy, but Mark Andrews is in England and he's out to get you, and Clint in the process…"

An hour later Terri sat on the edge of her bed, stunned by what she had been told. But after finally digesting the information that Melissa and Steve provided, everything began to make sense. The question now was, what was Mark's next move?

She had to get to Clint. There was no point in calling him and having him not take her call. She'd go to his house.

Why did Mark hate her so much? she wondered as she slipped into a pair of winter-white cashmere pants. What had she ever done to him, to anyone, to deserve such loathing? It had to go beyond just firing him. But what?

Maybe now she would finally get to the bottom of everything, she thought as she closed the door behind her. Hopefully whatever grudge Mark had against her would be settled once and for all.

Chapter 41

Clint hadn't slept the entire night. His eyes burned and felt as if sand had been tossed in them. But adrenaline pumped through his veins, giving him the stamina he needed to get through the next few hours.

He stood under the pulsing force of the shower, wishing he could miraculously wash away the nightmare that had become his life.

He hadn't even had a free moment to track down Terri. He needed her strength now more than ever. But she was probably in New York by now, he concluded. When this was over, he was going to get her back. No matter what.

He stood in front of the bedroom mirror and pressed the heels of his palms against his eyes. Ashley had to be all right. She just had to be.

He'd made arrangements the previous afternoon to have all of his holdings transferred into his London account. His banker had made special provisions to have the money delivered by courier yesterday evening. And he'd made the call to Carpenter. He'd done everything that he was told. Now the waiting began.

He stepped out into the hallway just as the phone rang. He ran down the hallway and answered the phone at the top of the stairs.

"Yes?"

"Mr. Steele?"

"It's me."

"Take down these instructions…"

Clint knocked on Mrs. Hally's door.

"Come in," she answered.

Clint peeked his head in the door. Mrs. Hally approached.

"Mrs. Hally, I'm leaving now. Did Jill come in last night?"

"No, sir."

He didn't have time to worry about Jill's temper tantrum at the moment. She'd come back when she cooled down.

"I'll need you to stay here until I get back. And when I do, I'll have Ashley."

She took his hand in hers. "She'll be fine, Mr. Steele," she said softly.

Clint's lips tightened and he nodded. "Please, you're not to tell anyone." He turned to leave and silently prayed that Mrs. Hally was right.

Terri stood in front of Clint's door. Several times she attempted to ring the bell, but her hand stopped in midair. She didn't want what she had to stay to sound like some sort of lame excuse to see him again.

She took a deep breath. This was too important for trivial ego-tripping. He'd just have to listen.

She rang the bell. Moments later the door was answered by a very distraught Mrs. Hally.

"Mrs. Hally, are you all right?" Terri looked beyond Mrs. Hally into the foyer for any sign of trouble, then focused back on the middle-aged woman.

Before she knew what she was doing, Mrs. Hally was in tears, blurting out to Terri everything that had transpired since Terri left, right up to Clint's departure.

"Oh, Ms. Powers," she cried, "if anything happens to our little girl…"

Terri hugged the plump body against her own. "Everything will be fine," she assured. Terri stepped back, and holding Mrs. Hally's shoulders, she looked down into her tear-filled eyes. "Where is Clint?"

Mrs. Hally gasped and covered her mouth with her hand. "Oh, heavens, I promised Mr. Steele that I wouldn't tell anyone. He'll be furious."

"That's not important now. I think I know who has Ashley. Where did he go? Did he tell you?"

She shook her head vigorously. "He got the phone call this morning and he left. He wouldn't tell me where."

Terri sighed. "I need to use the phone."

"You mustn't call the authorities. Mr. Steele promised that they wouldn't be contacted. Oh, Ms. Powers, please don't. For Ashley's sake."

"For Ashley's sake we have to tell the police, Mrs. Hally. Or her kidnapper will get away."

Terri walked past Mrs. Hally into the living room and dialed the police.

Clint pulled up to the enclosed wooded area as instructed. He waited five minutes, then left the car with the suitcase in hand. There was no one around and no sign of Ashley.

He placed the briefcase beneath a large stump at the foot of a small incline and returned to his car. He pulled off and drove directly to the service station two miles away and waited by the pay phone for the call.

* * *

"I'm telling you, officer, I know who has Clinton Steele's daughter."

"You have proof, Ms. Powers?" the skeptical constable asked.

"Not exactly. But we have every reason to believe that it's him. You can't ignore this information. Suppose you're wrong?"

Constable Langly looked scornfully at this woman who thought she could tell him how to do his job. How dare this Yankee dred come here and give orders? But good sense overrode his pride. She was right. If there was any validity in what she'd told him and he ignored it, he'd have hell to pay.

"All right, Ms. Powers. I'll have some of our men cover the airport, and bus and train stations. Do you have a picture of this bloke?"

Terri shook her head, then remembered the cover photo of the public-relations package that she used for her firm.

"One minute. I think I have something that you can use."

She returned shortly with a copy of the company brochure, complete with a close-up shot of Mark Andrews.

Constable Langly took the brochure, and Terri pointed out Mark. "This'll help."

Terri folded her arms, satisfied that she had done the right thing. She just hoped that she wasn't too late, and that Clint would understand her reasons for going against his wishes.

"We'll contact you as soon as any of this pans out, Ms. Powers. And tell Mr. Steele that we'll do everything we can to get his daughter..."

"You can tell me yourself," Clint stated, striding into the room. His eyes were two dark slits as he glowered at the assemblage of officers in his living room and Terri in the midst of them. He didn't know whether to be happy or furious at seeing her. "What the hell are you all doing here? I said o police!" He threw a murderous look at Mrs. Hally, who early collapsed under his unwavering gaze.

"This is not something you can handle alone, Mr. Steele," ffered Constable Langly. "We're trained for things like this." Clint opened his mouth to lash out but Terri hurried toward im, and for an instant his guard went down. She stepped into is outstretched arms and welcomed the power of his embrace. he swore she felt him tremble as if he held back the weight f the world. She looked up into his eyes.

"Clint. Oh, Clint, I'm so sorry about Ashley. I called the uthorities because I think I know who took her."

He grabbed her by her shoulders, the force of his grip urning into her flesh.

"Who? Who has my daughter?"

Terri quickly explained her conversation with Steve and Melissa.

Clint sank down onto the couch. He shook his head in disbelief. "Why? Why would Melissa do something like this o me?"

"Clint, Melissa is in love with you, or at least she thought he was. Her passing information to Mark was her way of getting back at you for ignoring her. She never imagined that t would come to this."

Clint braced his forehead on his palm. "Unbelievable."

"The person Mark is really after is me. He was the one behind the information you received. He's probably your competitor for the resort deal, as well."

"That would make sense. That's why the caller was so nsistent I tell Carpenter the deal was off." He raised his head and looked at her. "But what does all of this have to do with you?"

"Mark obviously believes that if he hurts you, he hurts me. If he could implicate me, that would turn you against me."

Clint swallowed. "It almost worked," he admitted. He took her hand in his. "You've got to forgive me, Terri. I was stupid

to ever think you would do something like that. I love you
You've got to believe me."

"I love you, too, Clint."

He pulled her into his arms, finding a momentary solac
in the warmth of her nearness. "We've got to find my baby
Terri," he groaned in her hair.

"We will. I gave the police a picture of Mark. They're goin
to be looking for him everywhere."

"Mr. Steele—" Constable Langly stood above him as h
sat "—what were your instructions?"

"I was told to drop off the money and then go to a phon
booth and wait for the call to tell me where to pick up Ashley
I waited for three hours. The call never came. It never came!"
He sprang up from the couch. His thundering voice rose to
the rafters of the house.

"When I get that little bastard, I'm going to kill him!"

Terri put a restraining hand on his arm. "Clint," she
cautioned.

"We'll get him, Mr. Steele. It's only a matter of time."

"A matter of *time?* My daughter is out there. Do you
understand? I don't want *in a matter of time.* I want *now!*"

Constable Langly nervously cleared his throat. "We'll do
the best we can, Mr. Steele." He turned to leave. "We'll cal
as soon as anything happens, and please try to keep the line
free," he said as he strode through the door, followed by three
other officers.

Terri tugged Clint's arm, forcing him to acknowledge her
"Clint," she urged, "they're not here to hurt, they're here to
help. And you practically threatening them is not going to
make them more cooperative."

Clint clenched his jaw. He jammed his hands in his pockets
"Now what?"

"Now we wait," Terri said.

They both took a seat on the couch, each caught in their

wn private thoughts. The sound of the front door opening
made them both look up.

Clint rose. "Jill."

Jillianne stepped into the living room, surprised to see
Terri standing next to Clint. Slowly she approached, and the
loser she got, the clearer Clint's face became.

She could see that he'd had little or no sleep. His beautiful
lack eyes were bloodshot. His usually smooth brow was
urrowed with worry. But most of all his spirit, his vibrancy,
vas missing. And she'd done that. To the man who meant
verything to her.

Clint came forward. Pain edged his voice. "Someone's
aken Ashley, Jill."

Jill stood stock-still.

"Actually we have a pretty good idea who it is," Terri
nterjected.

Jillianne's pulse began to gallop. She felt hot and cold at
nce. She couldn't speak. *Please.*

"Mark Andrews," Clint stated. "He used to work for Terri,
ntil she fired him for embezzlement."

This didn't make sense, she thought, confusion clouding her
mind. She looked from Clint to Terri and back again. Mark
vas Clint's friend. He said so. Jillianne began to sway back
nd forth. What had she done?

Clint hurried to her side and captured her around her waist.
'Are you all right?"

Weakly she nodded. "What does he want in exchange for
Ashley?"

"That's just it," Clint said. "I did everything he told me. To
he letter. But he didn't deliver Ashley."

Jill felt as if a great weight were pressing against her chest.
She couldn't breathe. *This wasn't the way it was supposed to
e.*

"The police have cut off the airports, bus and train stations,
nd boats. They're sure to find him," Terri said, trying to

reassure Jill, who looked as if she were going to faint an
minute.

If they found Mark, he was sure to tell them everythin
including her role in this whole sadistic scheme. And Mar
had broken his promise to bring Ashley back. Her bab
was out there, probably terrified. Her heart beat faster. Sl
couldn't let her stay there any longer. Maybe if she confesse
her participation before Clint was told by the police, he woul
find a way to forgive her.

Her voice was barely a whisper. "I know where Ashle
is."

"What?" Clint couldn't be sure that he'd heard correctl

"Clint—" she clutched his shirt "—please forgive me.
never thought he wouldn't bring her back. Oh, God!" sh
cried. Burning tears began to run down her cheeks.

Clint grabbed Jill and started to shake her viciously.

"Clint, don't," Terri cried. Clint ignored her.

"What are you talking about? Tell me. Now. Dammit. D
you hear me?"

Hysterical, Jill rattled on about the initial phone call fron
Mark, her agreeing to help him to get Terri out of the pictur
the delivering of the envelope and ultimately the plan to tak
Ashley in order to get the money he needed to cover the cost
of the resort deal.

Incredulity swam in his eyes. "How...how could you?"

"Clint, I love you. I've always loved you," she cried. "
waited for you all these years, waited for you to get ove
your loss of Desiree. I waited for you to come home to me
Finally to me. But when you did, you brought her." She threw
scornful glance at Terri. "And then you wanted to take Ashle
away." She shook her head, her body seeming to shrink. "
couldn't let you take her. She belongs here with me. I raise
her. I love her like my own. I took care of Ashley all these
years to show you how much I love you and how happy we
three could be together."

"You don't know the meaning of love." Clint pushed her away in disgust. She fell to the floor.

"Clint, please. You've got to understand. I did it for us. So that we could be together like we were meant to be. Terri doesn't deserve you."

Clint stepped forward menacingly. Jill recoiled. His nostrils flared. "She's more of a woman than you'll ever be, Jill. Now tell me where my daughter is before I hurt you!"

"She's in the old Wedgewood Cottage," she whimpered, cringing in the corner.

The irony of the location hit him like a kick in the gut. The cottage was where Desiree had conceived Ashley. Without another word, Clint sprinted toward the door.

"Call the police, Clint," Terri urged.

"No!"

She hurried to his side. "Then at least let me go with you."

Clint clasped Terri's chin in his hand. "I have to do this alone." He pressed his lips fleetingly against hers. "You, most of all, can understand that." He searched her eyes. Terri nodded her agreement. Her soft smile of comfort was the beacon he needed. He snatched his coat and scarf from the rack, then turned toward Jill. "Don't be anywhere in my eyesight when I return," he seethed.

Clint drove blindly along the darkened roads, which were slowly being covered with the first layer of snow. He took the route more from memory than from watching for signs, remembering the turns and inclines from traveling to the hideaway in his early years of marriage.

The cottage had been abandoned after Desiree's death, and he'd never had the heart to return. Imagining the condition it must be in and his daughter there alone incensed him, made his gut twist with hurt and rage.

His daughter. It was not until these past hours of mental and emotional torture that he finally realized just what fatherhood was all about. It was not sending a check once each month, or making a dutiful phone call. It was being there during the good and bad times. He loved his daughter, he realized with a powerful jolt. He truly loved her, and no matter what it took, he was going to be the father Ashley deserved.

The car's tires spat gravel as Clint sped up the lane that led to the house. The small cottage was enveloped in darkness. A single dull light illuminated the dust-encrusted window. The car ground to a halt. Clint jumped out and ran toward the door, only to discover it chained shut.

Quickly he searched for something to use as leverage to break the chain. Then better judgment took hold. He didn't want to add to Ashley's terror by breaking down the door.

He ran around to the side window. What he saw nearly tore him in two.

Ashley was huddled in the center of the bed, curled in a tiny ball. His throat constricted when he tried to call out to her. All that came from his throat was a grating, guttural cry, like a wounded animal. From deep inside he found the will to bang on the window. Ashley sat up in the bed and turned toward the noise, her eyes wide and glistening with fear.

"Ashley, baby. It's me, Daddy. I'm going to get you out, baby," he yelled. "It's all right."

There was no way he'd waste precious time searching for something to break the chain, when he heard Ashley scream his name over and over again… "Daddy, Daddy!"

He'd go in through the window. He tore the plaid scarf from his neck and wrapped it around his fist. Shielding his face with his free hand, he smashed the window. He tore away the rotting wooden frame with his gloved hands, hoisted himself up over the ledge and crawled through.

The few steps from the window to the bed were the longest and most painful he'd ever taken. He felt as if his feet were being sucked down in quicksand. He kept his eye glued on his daughter, who remained motionless, continuing to whimper his name as though unwilling to believe that she was moments away from freedom. Her eyes were red and swollen from hours of crying, and she hugged her stuffed dog to her like a lifeline. It was a picture that Clint would never forget.

Then all at once, he had her in his arms. He felt his own heart slam mercilessly in his chest. He stroked her, hugged her, kissed her, crooning her name over and again, trying to silence her sobs that now filled the dusty air.

She clung to him. Her tiny body shook with relief, relishing the comfort and security of her father's embrace.

Her lifted her in his arms and wrapped her in his coat. "Everything's going to be all right, Ashley," he whispered against her hair. "I'm never, ever going to let anything happen to you again. I swear I won't."

"Please don't leave me, Daddy. Please," she cried, clinging tighter to him.

"Never," he said in a strangled voice. "Never again. I've made a lot of mistakes, Ash. Because I was afraid." He hugged her tighter. "I'm not going to be afraid anymore. We're going to work things out. Together. You, me and Terri."

Cautiously she lifted her head from his chest. Bewilderment and fear mingled in her eyes. "You're going to leave me with Terri?"

"No, sweetheart. We're going to be a family. The three of us." He looked into her eyes. "A real family. And after the holidays we're going to New York to live. Start a brand-new life and put all of this behind us."

"Will you be in New York, too?"

His heart shuddered at the hope-filled question. When he looked at her, into the face that so reflected Desiree's, he knew without question that he owed it not only to Ashley, but to Desi, to make the life they'd envisioned for their daughter.

"Of course I'll be there," he assured. "That's what a family

is. People who love each other and want to be together. And
want to be with you, Ash, more than you'll ever know."

She buried her face against his chest. "I want to be with
you, too, Daddy, and Terri."

Clint cleared his throat. "Then let's get started by getting
you out of here."

"What about Auntie Jill?" Ashley asked as they approached
the window.

Clint's jaw clenched. "She has to go away," he said in a tight
voice. "But I'm sure she'll write to you." He swallowed the
knot in his throat and kissed her forehead. "Let's go home."

Chapter 42

Terri sat on the edge of Ashley's bed, gently stroking her face as she slept. She'd given her a warm bath, washed her hair and told her a silly story until she'd finally fallen asleep. As she watched Ashley, her heart filled with a wonderful feeling of warmth. She was so innocent and precious. So deserving of love and stability.

Over these past hours, Terri realized she'd discovered a part of herself that she hadn't thought existed, the part that could love this child as her own. Unquestionably.

The understanding was like being freed from the emotional quicksand that had suffocated her for so many years. Now she could truly look forward to the happiness she and Clint were destined to share together without reservation.

"What are you smiling about?"

Terri jumped at the sound of Clint's voice, nearly waking up Ashley in the process.

Gently she rose from the bed and tiptoed to the door.

"She's finally asleep," she whispered.

"Is that what the smile is for?" he teased. He gathered her in his arms and softly kissed her lips.

"No, silly. I'm finally free," she whispered.

He looked at her quizzically.

"Don't ask. I'll tell you some other time."

Arm in arm they left the room and went downstairs.

"You're great with her, Terri."

"You really think so?"

"You can see that she adores you. You were the one she asked to give her a bath. That has to mean something." He smiled.

Terri laughed. "I suppose it does."

They approached the kitchen and went in.

"Hungry?" Clint asked.

"A little."

"Let me see what we have." He opened the refrigerator.

"Is Jill gone?"

Clint breathed deeply. "Yes. She left about an hour ago," he added, with the slightest bit of pain in his voice. "I decided to take your advice and not press charges. She'll have her conscience to live with. That should be enough punishment."

Terri walked up behind him and wrapped her arms around his waist. "It's going to be all right," she said gently.

He nodded, unable to comment. This whole ordeal had affected him much more than he let on. Every time he thought about Jill being responsible for Ashley's upbringing, and her being so close to going over the edge, he shuddered. What else might Jill have done?

The phone rang.

Terri disengaged herself. "I'll find something," she offered.

Clint crossed the room and picked up the phone.

* * *

"…Fantastic! How long ago?" *They found Mark,* he mouthed to Terri. Then his whole relieved expression changed. "What…? Is he crazy…? Why the hell should she? All right, all right. I'll ask her, but I'm not promising anything. That son of a bitch doesn't deserve any consideration." He mumbled his good-byes and hung up.

"What is it?"

Clint turned to face her. "The constable said that Mark asked to see you. Alone."

Nervously Terri sat in the small dimly lit room, waiting for the guards to bring in Mark.

Maybe Clint was right. Maybe she shouldn't have come. What could Mark possibly have to say to her? But her curiosity and determination to have closure in her life propelled her to come.

She sucked on her bottom lip and paced the dingy gray floor, and nearly leaped out of her skin at the sound of the metal door opening.

A strapping guard ushered Mark in. Terri immediately noticed the handcuffs and felt a vague sense of relief.

The guard pushed Mark down in the chair and connected part of the cuff to a metal post at the corner of the table. "I'll be right outside this door if you need me, miss."

Terri nodded.

Mark stared at her with an emptiness that reached out and touched her heart in a way that was eerily familiar. The sensation overwhelmed her. Where had she seen that very same look before?

They sat facing each other for several minutes. Terri finally broke the uneasy silence.

"Why did you want to see me? What could you possibly say to me about what you've done?"

His voice was flat, vacant. "About what I've done? What about what you've done?"

"You're not making sense, Mark. I was always fair and decent to you from the very beginning."

His laugh was hollow. "You still don't know, do you?"

"Listen, if there's something you have to say, then say it. I'm tired of this cat-and-mouse game you're trying to play."

His voice remained without inflection as he slowly poured out the extraordinary story that was their lives.

"You talk about fair and decent. I don't know what that is. I was a little boy who depended on his older sister to keep her promise. I was the little boy who lived day by day, waiting at the window, on the corner, in my bed, for my sister to come for me like she promised," he spat, for the first time revealing the traces of his Caribbean accent.

Terri began to feel a tightness in her throat. Her head began to pound. *No. It's not possible.*

Mark looked off and seemed to return to the days of his childhood as he recounted the horrors of his youth. "They beat me," he said softly. "They told me how stupid I was, and that I'd never be anything. They gave me scraps to eat and clothes that never fit. But I knew my sister, whom I loved more than life, was going to come for me."

He looked at her, and the depth of his pain reached out from his eyes and engulfed her. "They told me that I was the bad one, and my sister was the good one. That's why she would always have the best of everything." His voice broke, and his eyes glistened. "But I was a good boy. I was."

He lowered his head and with difficulty reached into his pocket and extracted an old crumpled photograph. For several moments he stared at it.

"This was all I had. It was what kept me going. Until one day I finally understood that my sister wasn't coming back for me. And that I was doomed to a life of hell until I could find a way out. That day I promised myself that when I found her, I would make her pay for leaving me, for breaking her promise." He slid the worn picture across the wooden table.

Through tear-filled eyes Terri could make out the two little faces of the children they'd been so many years ago. She was looking directly into the camera, and her brother, Malcolm, was looking up at her with adoration. She remembered that day as clearly as if it were yesterday.

She looked across the table. "Malcolm..." How long had she wanted to be able to say her brother's name? "I didn't know." Her voice broke, and choking sobs overcame her. "My adopted parents told me you'd died. You have no idea what that did to me." Her body shook with the force of her crying.

He stared at her with disbelief. "They told you I was dead?" His question held the childlike tone of bewilderment.

Terri nodded.

"All the years I've followed you, waited for the perfect time, planned, obsessed—you never even knew I was alive."

Terri slowly got up from her chair to kneel beside him. Tenderly she stroked his face, his shoulders, his hand. "Life has played a vicious joke on us, Malcolm." She swallowed. "But it's not too late. You don't know how I longed for you, thought about you all these years. But I tried to force you to the back of my mind. Our parting was too painful for me to handle. I had my own nightmares to live with. You may have thought that I had a wonderful life, but I didn't. Those people," she choked out, "they never truly loved me. They were very civic-minded," she said, her voice filled with regret. "In their own way they thought they were doing some good deed for society by taking me in. They took a kind of pleasure in telling all of their friends how sorry they were for me and had adopted me. They gloried in the adulations that they received for doing such a humane thing. I blamed them for my unhappiness for years. I can't any longer. We were both victims, Malcolm. But we don't have to stay victims."

He looked at her, really looked at her, through eyes that

were no longer blinded by hate and resentment, and he knew she meant every word.

She leaned over and hugged him. Hugged him with all the love that had been buried, wishing she could erase some of the pain he'd endured.

Their falling tears mixed, blending into one cleansing stream, and they both knew that tomorrow would be brighter.

Epilogue

Terri lay nestled in Clint's arms. Their honeymoon cottage hideaway was right off the beach. Several miles away from where his first resort was to be constructed.

The full moon illuminated the cozy bedroom with iridescent, romantic light. Everything was just perfect, Terri thought.

Clint nuzzled her bare breasts. "So how does it feel to be Mrs. Clinton Steele?"

She moved seductively beneath him. "You mean Mrs. Theresa Powers-Steele?"

He kissed her neck. "This women's lib thing is getting to be too much."

Terri giggled and stretched out her left arm to look wonderingly at the flawless diamond that graced her ring finger. Clint had given it to her on Christmas morning, insisting that even though she didn't celebrate Christmas, she had to have something to open. She'd nearly collapsed with shock when she opened the box and saw the dazzling diamond winking at her with a million rays of light.

She sighed with contentment, reliving their beautiful wedding on New Year's Day. Everything was working out. Mrs. Hally had agreed to come with the new family to the States and was busy keeping up with Ashley in the couple's condominium in New York.

As for Malcolm, Clint had reluctantly agreed not to press charges against him, much to Terri's relief. And in a gesture that was so typical of Clint, he'd offered Malcolm a position with his company after he completed his psychological treatments. Malcolm had declined. He wanted a "new life," he'd said, "with no strings attached." He'd returned the ransom money to Clint. And he'd given back all of the money he'd taken from his sister's company, which Terri invested. Malcolm had said he wanted to try his hand at operating a radio station in New Orleans. The money would be there whenever he was ready, Terri'd decided. It was her way of trying to make things up to him.

It would be years before Malcolm would be truly well, but with her love, the support of his new family and the psychological help he was getting, she felt confident that one day he would be totally free from the demons that had possessed him.

Their budding relationship was slow but steady, and she looked forward to the visits and phone calls and finally getting to know each other.

Jill remained in England, still bitter and resentful of Terri. But she could live with that, Terri thought. She had Clint. Her deep love for her husband allowed her to be forgiving of others. It was she who persuaded Clint to agree that the barrage of letters Jill constantly wrote to Ashley would be given to her over time. Ashley was still unaware of Jill's participation in her abduction, and they wanted to maintain the memory that Ashley had of her aunt.

Melissa had submitted her resignation, but Clint had refused to accept it. He insisted he couldn't run his company without her. She'd decided to stay, and from the looks of things she and Steve were the next ones to jump the broom.

Lisa was getting as big as a house and happier than she'd ever been in her life. Brian was constantly redecorating to satisfy his wife's whims, and she'd recently heard that Alan was getting married. Poor woman. She should warn her.

"What are you thinking about, baby?"

"Oh…" she sighed "…just how happy I am. How happy you make me."

Softly he kissed her lips. "Not half as happy as you've made me." Slowly he parted her warm thighs. His strong, knowing hands stroked her hips. "You've given me so much, Terri." He took one nipple in his mouth and suckled, then released it. "You made me believe I could be a father to my child." He took the other nipple and released it. Terri moaned with yearning. "Through you I realized what love and trust really mean."

His tongue played teasing, tantalizing games with hers. "You showed me what true power is, baby," he breathed against her mouth. "The power to forgive. And I'm never going to give you the chance to regret one single moment of our life together."

In one long, slow motion, he joined them. As they became bound together in their love, riding the crest of their undeniable passion for each other, Terri knew that the happiness that had eluded her for so very long was only just beginning…

* * * * *

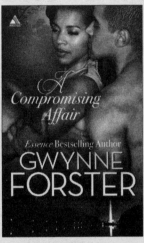

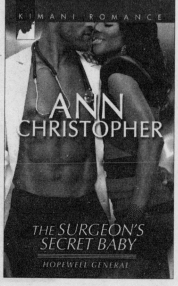